FIRE A

"I don't know w replied. "I don't kn you suspected me Dubratta's death an discover if I really was.

"Sought you out . . . is that what you think?"

"What other reason could there be?" she snapped and tried to pull away.

Josh bent closer to Caty's lips. He knew better. This was madness. Yet holding her in his arms, so close, so tempting, he could not resist. What else had he come here for, against all the arguments of his better judgment? What other reason . . .

He pulled her into his embrace, tightening his arms around her. His lips sought hers hungrily. Her mouth opened in surprise, sweet to his taste, her lips soft and cool. His hand slid up to cup her chin, seeking her lips even closer, his tongue outlined their lovely shape, until it could invade, searching out the depths within. He felt the firm curves and hollows of her body against his and he longed to slide his fingers inside her cloak.

Caty was conscious of the feel of his arms around her, the softness of his lips against her own. Instinctively she raised her hand to lay her palm against his cheek. She closed her eyes and let herself be enveloped by the rising warmth his insistent mouth worked on her. Her body began to tremble and she felt herself sliding, only to be caught in his tight hold.

Josh lifted his head and ran his fingers down her cheek, tracing the outline of her lips. "Is that reason enough?" he whispered.

PUT SOME PASSION INTO YOUR LIFE... WITH THIS STEAMY SELECTION OF ZEBRA *LOVEGRAMS!*

SEA FIRES (3899, $4.50/$5.50)
by Christine Dorsey
Spirited, impetuous Miranda Chadwick arrives in the untamed New World prepared for any peril. But when the notorious pirate Gentleman Jack Blackstone kidnaps her in order to fulfill his secret plans, she can't help but surrender—to the shameless desires and raging hunger that his bronzed, lean body and demanding caresses ignite within her!

TEXAS MAGIC (3898, $4.50/$5.50)
by Wanda Owen
After being ambushed by bandits and saved by a ranchhand, headstrong Texas belle Bianca Moreno hires her gorgeous rescuer as a protective escort. But Rick Larkin does more than guard her body—he kisses away her maidenly inhibitions, and teaches her the secrets of wild, reckless love!

SEDUCTIVE CARESS (3767, $4.50/$5.50)
by Carla Simpson
Determined to find her missing sister, brave beauty Jessamyn Forsythe disguises herself as a simple working girl and follows her only clues to Whitechapel's darkest alleys . . . and the disturbingly handsome Inspector Devlin Burke. Burke, on the trail of a killer, becomes intrigued with the ebon-haired lass and discovers the secrets of her silken lips and the hidden promise of her sweet flesh.

SILVER SURRENDER (3769, $4.50/$5.50)
by Vivian Vaughan
When Mexican beauty Aurelia Mazón saves a handsome stranger from death, she finds herself on the run from the Federales with the most dangerous man she's ever met. And when Texas Ranger Carson Jarrett steals her heart with his intimate kisses and seductive caresses, she yields to an all-consuming passion from which she hopes to never escape!

ENDLESS SEDUCTION (3793, $4.50/$5.50)
by Rosalyn Alsobrook
Caught in the middle of a dangerous shoot-out, lovely Leona Stegall falls unconscious and awakens to the gentle touch of a handsome doctor. When her rescuer's caresses turn passionate, Leona surrenders to his fiery embrace and savors a night of soaring ecstasy!

Available wherever paperbacks are sold, or order direct from the Publisher. Send cover price plus 50¢ per copy for mailing and handling to Zebra Books, Dept. 4363, 475 Park Avenue South, New York, N.Y. 10016. Residents of New York and Tennessee must include sales tax. DO NOT SEND CASH. For a free Zebra/Pinnacle catalog please write to the above address.

ASHLEY SNOW
SO WILD MY HEART

ZEBRA BOOKS
KENSINGTON PUBLISHING CORP.

ZEBRA BOOKS are published by

Kensington Publishing Corp.
475 Park Avenue South
New York, NY 10016

Copyright © 1993 by Ashley Snow

All rights reserved. No part of this book may by reproduced in any form or by any means without the prior written consent of the Publisher, excepting brief quotes used in reviews.

If you purchased this book without a cover, you should be aware that this book is stolen property. It was reported as "unsold and destroyed" to the Publisher and neither the Author nor the Publisher has received any payment for this "stripped book."

Zebra, the Z logo, and the Lovegram logo are trademarks of Kensington Publishing Corp.

First Printing: November, 1993

Printed in the United States of America

One

"Oh, madam, I've never heard anything like it in my life!"

Catherina Mandesi swept off the stage and into the wings where General Manager Cannio grabbed for her hand, planting kisses on each of her fingers. "Gloriosa! Stupenda!"

Catherina obliged him for a moment, murmuring modestly, "It was really nothing . . ." Behind her the applause from the auditorium swelled to earsplitting intensity, punctuated by shouts from the audience for her return.

"My public calls . . ." Reclaiming her hand, she swept back out on to the stage, the huge bouquet of roses spilling over in her arms. Flowers were every-where, raining down in a cascade of colors on the vast stage. She stood there alone, bowing deeply, one hand over her heart while, with the other, she struggled to hold on to the bouquet.

Backstage it was the same. The throbbing crowd pressed against her, fighting to touch her gown, while she pushed her way toward her dressing *room, trying not to be too abrupt with any of her fawning well-wishers, some of them still with tears in their adoring eyes.*

She swept into her dressing room where Mimi, her little French maid, fought to shut the door against the crowd that clamored for entrance. The room was awash in flowers. A pyramid of telegrams littered the table and she dabbled her hand through them before stopping briefly to admire herself in the long mirror. She did look uncommonly fetching in Marguerite's long, white shift with the blond hair of her wig falling to her waist.

"Oh, mademoiselle, you were wonderful tonight!" Mimi crowed, taking the cascade of roses from her arms. "I never heard such pure sounds, such gorgeous singing . . ."

"Yes, Faust *is one of my better roles," she answered modestly. "Mimi, are there any interesting telegrams?"*

"Just the usual, mademoiselle. Count Alexi begs you again to marry him and retire to his estates in Russia. There are three other offers of marriage as well, but none you would consider. One is even from a tenor!"

She arranged herself in front of the mirror and picked up a powder puff the size of a grapefruit. "Too boring . . ."

"And King Edward of England sends another wire begging you to meet him anywhere you choose . . ."

"That libertine? Never!"

"There are fifteen opera houses beseeching you

to sing with them. And Maestro Puccini begs you to allow him to write a new opera for you."

"Hmmm . . . Maestro Puccini? Well, he's not Verdi, but he'll do, I suppose."

"And Madam Collevetti, the world-famous teacher, asks if you would be so kind as to give her a few lessons."

She reached a languid hand for the face cream. "I'm so busy, but I might consider it. After all, she has such influence on young singers."

"And there is a diamond necklace from young Mister Astor. And the press is clamoring for interviews . . ."

"Lady! Will you please move your ar'se off the curb. You're holding up traffic!"

Cathleen McGowan looked around, stunned. The man behind her on the sidewalk, a big, red-faced fellow in a greatcoat, holding a huge parcel in front of him, reached out to shove her into the street.

"Go around me." Caty slapped his hand away. "There's plenty of room."

People swarmed on either side of her, taking advantage of a break in the traffic to rush into the wide street. The man gave a grimace and shoved ahead as she moved over just far enough to the side to let him by.

"You don't own the walk," he hissed as he passed. "And besides, the street's not for daydreamin'."

"Well, you don't own it either," Caty said as she watched him step into the street. "Odious pig!" she muttered to herself. "New Yorkers must be the rudest people in the world." Of course she *had* been daydreaming, she acknowledged before reaching the other side of the street. The truth was she didn't even remember how she reached the curb. When she started down Fifth Avenue she was just finishing the trio at the end of *Faust* and things simply took off from there. Now here she was at the corner of 39th and Fifth, and she had no memory of walking there. Oh well, it was always like that after she finished one of her lessons, even when Madam Della Russo was deeply dissatisfied with her, as she had been today. *Especially* when Madam Della Russo was deeply dissatisfied with her!

Caty inhaled the cool air, smiling to herself. She loved walking in this part of New York. She enjoyed watching the men in their blue serge suits, boiled collars and derby hats hurrying about their business. The ladies, too, in their huge hats and with their skirts trailing in the dust. Though ankles were still decently covered, skirt trains were not as long as they used to be, five years ago when the 1900s came in. In fact, they seemed to get a little shorter every year. It was one of those changes the new century brought with it.

There were others as well. One had only to look around at the congested streets, crowded with horse-drawn hansom cabs and fancy broughams, with wagons, drays and pushcarts. Change was especially evident in the long, shiny newfangled motor wagons—the Dureyas and the Pierce Arrows—that occasionally wound their way through the traffic. Even the noise was worse than ever—taxis clanging at every intersection, horns blaring, steel wheels and iron horseshoes of the carriages rumbling on the pavement, horses' whinnying, electric streetcars clunking along the crisscrossed tracks. Thank heaven, at least, the elevated trains had not been constructed along this section of town.

Yet it was the excitement of the city that she loved most—a vibrancy that reflected all the vitality and change of a new century. You could see it in the buildings thrusting ever higher upward, and the limits of the city pushing farther outward. You could feel it in the air.

A cold wind funneled gustily between the buildings, yet the sun seemed to be stronger than when she had left home for the ferry this morning. It promised to be a beautiful October day. Too bad she was going to have to spend most of it inside.

And yet she would not really choose to be any place else. So what if she was only a lowly member of the chorus or an occasional understudy? So what if "Catherina Mandesi" was not yet a famous prima donna? She was still in the opera house and singing professionally. Her day would come, she knew it in her heart. Besides, *Faust* was too high for her voice anyway.

"Fer God's sake, lady, watch where yer goin'!"

Caty dodged a cart laden with mounds of apples that a thin, pocked-faced young man was attempting to push across her path. She hadn't even seen him and this time she swallowed the snappy answer she started to make and shamefacedly moved back. She really must pay more attention to the traffic.

The cart pushed past and Caty, after carefully looking both ways, started across Sixth Avenue. The wide thoroughfare was crowded with hackneys, wagons and carts, and she had to backtrack twice when a cab careened in front of her. On the other side, a hackney stood at the curb, one of many waiting for potential passengers. She started in front of it, eager to reach the safety of the walkway, but the skittish horse bolted just as she crossed its path. Caty stood frozen for an instant while the horse reared in its traces, whinnying and flaying its hooves while the cab careened sideways into the street.

"Look out there!" the driver screamed as Caty leapt back out of the way, into the street where she was nearly run down by another passing cab. Without thinking, she reached out for the bridle on the frightened horse, pulling him down and struggling to hold him. The whites of his eyes flared with his fear and her heart, once its wild thumping calmed, went out to the poor animal.

"There, there, old boy." She leaned close to the animal's head and gently ran her hand down the velvet nose. "It's all right. Nothing to be feared of."

The horse seemed to calm a little under her quiet, gentle touch. She looked around to see a young boy standing beside the cab with a toy horn in his hand, looking up at them curiously. He lifted the horn and blew a loud blast. The horse's ears flattened against his head and he reared back while she struggled to hold him.

"Stop that!" Caty snapped at the child, who immediately put the toy horn behind his back. "You're frightening this animal. Poor fellow," she said, trying to calm the horse again. "All the noise in the street and this little horn sets you off. But there's no knowing what causes fear, is there now?"

"Damned old nag!" the driver of the cab yelled as he fastened the brake and tied the reins. Jumping down from the seat, he ran to the horse's head and grabbed the bridle from Caty's hand. "Stupid bag o' bones!"

Lifting a short whip, he slapped it against the horse's neck, biting into the flesh. The animal whinnyed in fright and moved back in the traces, wildly trying to avoid the whip.

"What are you doing? Stop it!" Caty grabbed at the bridle again, trying to still the animal while the driver flayed away at it. The horse careened crazily in its traces, and Caty had to jump back out of the way to keep from being trampled. Furious, she ran around to the driver and grabbed at his arm. "You're making him worse, you idiot," she yelled, trying to snatch the whip from the driver's hand.

"Here now, this is none o' your concern," he said angrily, grabbing at the whip. The two of them engaged in a tug of war over the whip while the skittish horse shuffled back and forth, his eyes flaring with fright.

All at once Caty's arm was grabbed and she looked up at a policeman in a blue coat who had stepped between her and the driver. "Let go of me," she snapped and yanked her arm away just as the driver's hand slipped on the whip. Grabbing it, she raised it to strike. "You see how it feels . . ." she cried before the policeman snatched her hand and wrestled the whip from her.

"Here now. What's goin' on? Disturbin' the peace . . ."

"She's interferin' in what's none of her business," the driver whined, seeing an adversary in the sudden appearance of the law. "This here animal belongs to me, and I can do what I please with the ornery thing."

"Cruelty to a dumb beast is my business . . ." Caty snapped as the policeman stepped between the two of them. The driver shook his fist around the policeman's shoulder into her face.

"If you'd of let him alone in the first place—"

"—and if you'd tried to gentle him instead of beating him—"

"—Now just a minute—"

"There are laws in this city regarding cruelty to animals. Officer, I demand that you arrest this . . . this villain!"

"Now, miss, that's a little hasty, ain't it? He's in his rights, you know."

"And this poor beast has no rights? Look at

him. He's skinny as a rail and probably never gets enough food or enough rest. And he's scared to death of the street. How long has he been out here?"

The driver shook his fist at her. "That's none of your business. Officer, I demand you arrest this woman for disturbin' the peace. She's probably one of them 'suffergettes' that goes around lookin' to cause trouble."

"I am not . . ."

"What's the matter, Johnson?"

A new voice. Caty was suddenly aware that a man was pushing his way through the small crowd that had gathered around them. She had an impression of tallness and broad shoulders beneath a brown plaid greatcoat. He was not wearing a policeman's uniform but he obviously knew the officer who was standing as a buffer between the driver and herself.

"Oh, Inspector Castleton. It's just a little misunderstanding here between the lady and this cabbie, sir. They both want me to arrest the other."

Castleton had a lean face with a wide mouth that struggled to suppress a smile. His face took on a serious mein while his gray eyes sparkled with mirth.

"The lady doesn't look as though she'd need arresting."

"It's just a little misunderstanding, sir."

Caty's ire rose as she watched the two officious men treating the whole thing as though it were a joke. As though *she* were a joke!

"This is not a 'little' misunderstanding. This man was mistreating a dumb animal. There are laws against that. The SPCA . . ."

"I was only handling what's my own, your honor," the driver said obsequiously to the man in the greatcoat. "It's my horse and my cab and this lady has got no right to interfere. She's a troublemaker. A disturber of the peace."

Castleton looked Caty up and down, obviously sizing her up. "He has a point, miss. Why don't you just go along peacefully and forget about all this?"

"I am Miss McGowan, thank you, and I will not go along peacefully. That horse nearly ran me down."

"Oh, he never did. If you had just gone around him instead of trying to take charge . . ."

Caty's voice rose with her fury. "And if you hadn't started flaying him . . ."

She wasn't sure of how it happened but the policeman had stepped away and now it was Castleton who was between her and the driver. He had one hand on her shoulder, pushing her back while the driver, as angry as she, leaned across him and continued to shake his fist at Caty.

"Nosy female . . ."

"Tyrant!"

She struck out at the fist that was so close to her nose but only succeeded in slapping the side of Castleton's head and knocking off his hat. He gasped in surprise and shoved the driver back with one hand while gripping her arm with the other. There was no mirth in his eyes now.

"Miss McGowan, either you move on peacefully and allow me to handle this matter or I will arrest you on the spot."

His voice was soft but his eyes had gone steely gray and Caty knew he meant every word. For a moment she was caught in the intensity of his glare, which seemed to pierce right through her to the depths of her soul. She felt an electrical pulse quiver through her body, an involuntary response to his magnetism. With an effort she forced herself to look away.

"You can't arrest me," she said lamely.

"Oh, but he can, miss," the policeman leaned forward to whisper in her ear. "He's a detective."

Caty tried to act unimpressed. "Arrest me and I'll lodge a complaint against you for it. I have rights!"

"Yes, you do. But so do others. And you are disturbing the peace," he added, glancing around at the watching crowd.

"The peace needs to be disturbed when a wrong has been committed."

"Yes, but you are hardly the judge of that."

"And I suppose you are, you insufferable, officious policeman. You didn't even see what happened."

Castleton pursed his lips, making an effort to curb his anger at this overbearing, aggressive creature. It was too bad her disposition was so strong, for he had seldom seen such a striking woman.

Her eyes were large for her oval face, the irises a deep green and crackling with life. Emerald eyes, of course, would go with that dark red hair, so thickly pulled into a large chignon at the nape of her long, shapely neck. The firm chin promised a dimple when she smiled, and the lips were pink and beautifully shaped. Her figure was stunning—tall, long legged as a colt beneath her ankle-length skirts, full bosomed, with a tiny, narrow waist and wonderfully flaring hips.

He struggled to get his thoughts back to the business at hand. "I shall take due note of what you saw and act on it," he said in his most brisk, businesslike voice. "In the meantime, why don't you go on about your shopping or whatever errand you're on?"

Shopping! Errand! Caty opened her mouth to inform him that she was a professional singer on her way to a rehearsal at one of the world's newest and best opera houses. But what was the use? She looked from the smirking driver's face to the horse who was standing between the traces, its head hanging, its flanks still trembling. "I want to lodge a complaint against this driver," she said more calmly. "For cruelty."

"I'm only trying to earn an honest livin', your honor," the driver whined.

"I'll handle the matter, thank you, miss."

"Oh yes, I'm sure you will," she said bitterly. She knew that she would no more than disappear around the corner before they would all have a good laugh and go back to their own concerns. And the poor animal would be no better off than before. Yet Castleton stood like stone beside her, blocking any effective action. And she was already late for rehearsal.

She straightened her shoulders and pulled her fur collar close around her throat, glaring at the detective. "I won't forget this," she snapped.

Castleton took the hat Johnson had retrieved for him and doffed it to her before setting it back on his head. "Have a nice day, miss."

With a last grimace at the detective and a vicious look thrown to the cabbie, Caty turned away and started down the street, trying not to think about the animal she was leaving to its bitter fate. She had tried to help and got nowhere. There was nothing else she could do. And Maestro Walters was going to be furious with her for being late again.

When she entered the rehearsal room, the chorus was already seated and the women were rehearsing the music to Cio-Cio-San's entrance in the first act of *Madama Butterfly*. Caty tried to make herself inconspicuous as she took her seat in the mezzo section at the end of the first row and opened her score, but she glanced up long enough to catch a murderous glance from the Chorus Master, Frederick Walters. She sank deeper into her chair and got through the rest of the rehearsal until Walters called for a break at the end of the first act.

"Ten minutes, people. And Miss McGowan. A word with you, please."

It was more of an order than a request. Caty knew what was coming and she got it: a long diatribe on the professional virtues of being punctual. "Tardy one more time, Miss McGowan, and I shall give your space to a more deserving singer."

"It couldn't be helped, sir," she said humbly, deciding that the better part of wisdom was to appear contrite. "Something happened on the street which delayed me. It was an accident. There was nothing I could do about it. I promise I won't be late again."

He pursed his thin lips and looked down his long nose at her. "You had better not. Now, having said that, it is my duty to inform you that you have been chosen to understudy Suzuki tomorrow night."

Her green eyes widened in surprise. "Madam Cabrini's understudy? How wonderful!"

"It wasn't my idea. I was forced into it by Manager Cannio. But I warn you, one more incident like this morning's and I will insist that you be replaced."

Caty gave him what she hoped was a properly submissive look and hurried away before she could say what she really felt. The rest of the chorus was strung along the hall in small clusters, or grouped around a table with a silver coffee urn at the far end. "Dictator!" Caty muttered under her breath. "Tyrant!" She headed straight for her friend Charlotte Conte, who sang with the sopranos.

"I'm to understudy Suzuki," she said, her eyes shining. "Of course it won't signify anything. Madam Cabrini never misses a performance. But still, it's something."

Charlotte gave her a quick hug. She was almost a head shorter than Caty, with a plump figure that supported her full voice. Her round, pink face was sprinkled with a cascade of freckles, and her eyes, a pale shade of plumbago blue, reflected her usually cheerful nature. She had been a member of the chorus longer than Caty and was one of the first people there to make her welcome in what was an essentially a very competitive company.

"Never fear, Caty," she said in her midwestern drawl. "Someday one of these singers will fall and break her leg and you'll get your big chance."

Caty sighed. "If I thought that were true I might arrange for a little accident myself."

"Speaking of accidents, have you seen the great Dubratta yet?"

"No. Has she arrived?"

"Oh, yes. She arrived early this morning." Charlotte leaned closer to Caty and lowered her voice. "She's a horror! So far she's managed to insult almost everyone in the opera house."

"She's probably self-conscious because everyone knows she's past her prime. What is this—her tenth farewell appearance?"

"She swears this one will be the last, but who knows? That voice! I heard her once when I was a child and she was good—I'll give her that. But now the voice is gone and she makes up for the lack of it by throwing tantrums. She has this mousy little maid who follows her around like an adoring dog, even though she treats her as badly as everyone else. Worse, in fact."

Caty giggled. "A typical prima donna."

"She refuses to sing with Jonas because he's shorter than she is."

"She refuses Jonas Creé? But he's a wonderful tenor."

"Maybe so, but she insists on someone else. Manager Cannio is so disgusted with her that he'll probably give her the worst singer he can find."

"That would have to be Morelli. Too bad the famous Carlo Gregorio hasn't arrived yet. He's probably the only tenor in the world Magda would consider worthy to sing with her."

"Yes, but he's not due for at least a while yet." Charlotte leaned her chin on her hand, looking pensive. "You know, there's something kind of sad about the Great Dubratta. She was a beauty in her youth, but time has taken its toll on her voice and her face."

The hall echoed with a tapping of the baton calling them back to rehearsal. "Oh well, it happens to all of us." Caty sighed. "I just hope I get my chance before it happens to me."

Later that afternoon, Caty had her first introduction to Madam Magda Dubratta when the famous European soprano made a brief appearance on stage as the entire company was practicing a walk-through of the first act of *Madama Butterfly*. She was a striking woman, unusually thin for a diva, of middle height, with a chiseled face, strong features, and arresting eyes with a riveting gaze. She had thick, black hair, beautifully coiffed, and wore a dress of burgundy watered silk that shimmered with every movement.

Yet Caty's admiration of Magda's appearance was quickly eclipsed by the singer's haughty manner and cutting tongue. She began by criticizing the chorus as the worst she had ever heard, a comment which—to Caty's delight—left Maestro Walters fuming. The stage was too vast for any kind of close rapport with the audience, the sets were ugly, the orchestra was of indifferent quality, and the hall would ruin the voice. The only person she did not get the better of was Madam Cabrini, who was singing the role of Suzuki. A consummate professional, Madam Cabrini had been around long enough not to be intimidated by the temperamental antics of an over-the-hill prima donna. When Dubratta tried to tell her not to stand too close, Cabrini looked her up and down and said haughtily:

"Basta! Cabrini, she-a sing in the first-time *Madama Butterfly* ever given. You don't-a need tell Elvira Cabrini where-a to stand!"

Magda's black eyes shot daggers but she tightened her lips and steered clear of the hefty mezzo from then on.

Caty spent the latter part of the afternoon brushing up on Suzuki's stage directions and reacquainting herself with the role. It was a little lower than was suitable for her voice and she wondered why she was given it in place of a true mezzo. But *Butterfly* was one of her favorite operas, and she wasn't about to turn down a chance to sing in it.

With time to spare before that evening's performance of *La Forza del Destino,* Caty and Charlotte went around the corner of 34th Street to a small restaurant to have supper.

Caty toyed nervously with her food. "I wish someone besides Manheim von Rankin was conducting tomorrow. He was once married to Magda Dubratta, you know. No telling what kind of conflicts that could raise."

"Maestro Manheim is too good a conductor to let his private feelings affect a performance," Charlotte answered between hearty mouthfuls.

"Dubratta must have been a real beauty in her youth. Do you think she . . . 'imbibes'?"

"I don't know. Why?"

"Oh, something about the way she moved at times this afternoon made me wonder. I hope her voice holds up for the entire performance."

Charlotte smiled, pointing her fork at Caty. "You'd better also hope that Mrs. Vanderbilt doesn't show up again wearing her enormous ruby. Madam Magda being what she is, she'll probably stop the opera and scold her for being late."

Caty giggled as she recalled the incident. "Were you there that night?"

"No, but I heard about it."

"Oh, it was something to see. She came galumping down the aisle, that huge ruby on its rope of pearls thrusting outward with every step. Of all the jewels in the place, that had to be the most spectacular. Every eye in the place swiveled around to look at her."

"Of course, that was just what she wanted."

"Naturally. These rich ladies come to the opera only to be seen. I doubt any of them really care for the music."

Charlotte reached up to fasten her hat with a four-inch-long hatpin. "Some do. I've heard that Mrs. Belcher is a big fan of Verdi. And Mrs. Delancey commissioned that production of *Faust* a few years back."

"Well, one can only hope that they don't clash jeweled horns with Magda tomorrow."

Charlotte smiled mischievously. "Oh, I don't know. It might be fun to watch."

The night's performance went off smoothly and by eleven o'clock Caty was out of her costume and makeup, and waiting backstage for her brother, Kyle McGowan, to arrive to escort her home to Staten Island on the ferry. Although it was not practical for her to live so far from Manhattan, the old, tall Victorian farmhouse overlooking New York harbor had always been a refuge for her, one she was unwilling to trade for a more sensible apartment near 39th Street. She was proud of the fact that her father, before his death, had run one of the more successful small farms on Staten Island. The farm had dwindled now to a few acres which her mother and brother valiantly kept going. Yet that fertile, dark soil was as dear to her as anything in her life, saving, perhaps, her music.

It was after midnight when Caty and Kyle finally walked up the hill to the front door, and a dim glow behind the fanlight told Caty that her mother was still up. As they walked into the front foyer, Sian McGowan came hurrying forward, a wide knitted fringed shawl wrapped around her robe and one long, graying braid trailing down her back.

"You know you don't need to do this, Mama," Caty said, as she removed her large veiled hat and laid it on the shelf in the closet.

"I know, luv, but I always want to make sure y'er both home safe. Come in the kitchen and have a little chocolate before you go to bed."

Caty, who secretly loved these quiet moments at the end of the day where she had a chance to tell her mother all about the day's events at the opera house, followed her diminutive mama into the big, spacious kitchen of their Rosebank home.

"I don't know why you think anyone would bother Kyle, as big and tough as he looks," she said, sitting at the table and taking the cup from her mother's hand.

"I know, darlin', but a mother always worries. And the city has gotten so bad. I declare, I never knew it to be so violent and ridden with crime when I was a girl. It makes me despair for the future . . ."

Sian McGowan went on reciting her description of New York as she had known it thirty years before, while Caty smiled, sipped her chocolate and waited patiently until it was her turn to talk. Her mother was small, pink-faced and charming, and Caty had often wished she was more like her rather than her big, quick-tempered father. Both she and Kyle had their father's large frame and red hair. She had probably inherited her voice from her father as well, for he had had a robust baritone with a sweet timbre. But it was her mother's dogged determination that had helped to make her a singer. From the time Caty first sang her little folk songs in a sweet childish soprano, her mother made up her mind she was going to be a famous diva someday. Over the years she had worked at every possible means to earn the extra money needed to make certain Caty studied with the best teachers. It was thanks to that excellent training that Caty won a place at the twenty-three year old Metropolitan Opera House. It wasn't quite the same as the old elegant Academy of Music, but it was a place to sing and that was all that mattered, both to Sian McGowan, and, by that time, to her daughter, Cathleen. Now, in Caty's mind, her career was almost as much her mother's as her own.

Yet when she began recounting her day to Sian, it wasn't the understudy role or even the antics of Magda Dubratta that she spoke of first. It was the poor horse she tried to help on her way to the opera house.

"You should have seen him, Mama. Frightened to death, skinny, trembling all over. It's not right that poor dumb animals should be worked like that."

"Oh, Caty, you were always one to side with God's creatures. It's the way of the world and you have to accept it. These hansom cab horses have to earn their keep just like the ones who pull the streetcars. Or, for that matter, any dray horse on a farm."

"Yes, but they shouldn't be abused in doing it. They're worked until they fall dead in the street and then left there to rot. I wish I could have harnessed that rude cabbie to those traces and let him pull that carriage around for an hour. Maybe he'd learn a little compassion. And the police were just as bad. You should have seen the plainclothes detective who forced me to move on. The most overbearing, officious, rude . . ."

Her mother sat opposite her and leaned across the table. "Caty, luv, what was it like at the opera house? Did Madam Dubratta arrive yet?"

"What? Oh, yes. She showed up for rehearsal. And I'm to understudy Suzuki tomorrow night."

Sian threw up her hands. "And you didn't tell me! Babbling on about a wretched cab horse with such news under your hat. I declare, child. Whatever am I going to do with you?"

All at once Caty realized how tired she was from the long, complicated day. She stood and stretched, wanting only to go to bed.

"You'll just have to put up with my quirks, like

any good mother of a prima donna. Good night, Mama, dear. I'll tell you all about the opera in the morning."

Two

There was always an air of excitement backstage at the opera house when a world-renowned singer was scheduled to perform. Caty noticed it the minute she entered the building the following morning. Today it was unusual, however, in that the excitement was tinged with an air of tension—brought on, no doubt, by the eccentricities of this particular singer.

"Has Magda been slicing off more heads?" she whispered to Charlotte, who had arrived in the rehearsal room ahead of her.

"No. She hasn't been around all morning and no one seems to know where she is. Besides, she left enough of them rolling yesterday to last for several weeks."

Caty sighed. "I suppose the disappearing act is all part of the trappings of a prima donna. She's probably sitting in a dark room somewhere, not raising her voice above a whisper."

The operas scheduled for the next two nights did not include a chorus, so Maestro Walters took the company briefly through those to be performed the following week and excused them early. Caty sang lightly and softly, just in case a miracle happened and she had to fill in for Madam Cabrini. She also attended another walk-through of *Butterfly* that afternoon. She wanted to feel prepared, even if it all turned out to be for nothing.

With Charlotte she went back to the same restaurant for the same light supper before returning to the opera house to begin putting on her Japanese costume. She had barely entered the hall leading to the dressing rooms before Jules Cannio, the general manager, came hurrying toward her.

"Catherina, thank God. I've been looking for you everywhere. Madam Cabrini has come down with a stomach ailment and you'll have to go on in her place."

Caty stood staring at the tall, thin manager, unable to speak. Beneath a shock of carefully coiffed white hair, his aristocratic features mirrored his growing impatience.

"Well, girl, don't just stand there. Come on— into your costume. Maestro Von Rankin wants to speak to you on stage before the curtain."

Charlotte grabbed at her arm. "Caty! It's your chance. I told you it would come someday."

A thrill of excitement caught at her chest. "Madam Cabrini is really ill? I don't believe it . . ."

Gregory Stillman, the stage manager, had stepped up to take Cannio's place as he hurried off to tend to the next of his myriad duties. Stillman firmly turned Caty toward the dressing room.

"For God's sake, go get dressed. I want to review the stage positions with you."

"But I went over them yesterday and today," she protested as he pushed along the hall.

"Yes, but there is a big difference between walking through a role just to become familiar with it, and knowing you're really going to sing the role. Hurry and get into your costume."

She was so excited she could barely sit still for Laura, the makeup woman, to transform her Irish face into something approximating a middle-aged Japanese maid. Madam Cabrini's costume had been proportioned to fit her considerably bulkier figure so Caty decided to go with her own from the chorus, even though it was not nearly as grand. A few touches helped to brighten it—a beautifully embroidered obi and several large, decorative pins in her wig. As the hour for the performance neared she felt the stirrings of stage fright, but she quickly shoved them down. This was the most exciting thing that had ever happened to her and she was determined to enjoy it. She was also determined to make a success of it since it might lead to other roles later.

"You look beautiful," Charlotte whispered as they emerged from the dressing room. Several of her other friends from the chorus gave her congratulatory comments and good luck kisses as she hurried on to the vast stage, already set up for the first act of *Butterfly*.

She stood looking around at the beautiful set—the paper-thin walls of Butterfly's house at one side, the low curving bridge over which the women would make their entrance near the center, the trailing trees and painted flowers of a garden—and her heart threatened to burst within her. This was what she had worked for and waited for most of her life. Tonight she would not be one of many women in the chorus, her beautiful voice hidden among the others. Tonight she would sing alone and act the part of an operatic role. Of course, she would not sing and act the really important part of Butterfly herself, but that did not matter. At least not now. That would come later, she was sure of it.

"You, Suzuki!"

Caty looked around to see Magda Dubratta standing in the wings dressed in her gorgeous Butterfly costume. Even in the shadows the gold threads of her embroidered robe glistened like fireflies. The heavy makeup she wore heightened what was left of her beauty and she made a striking figure as she swept out onto the stage.

"Oh, Madam Dubratta, I . . ."

"Listen to me. When I agree to come here they tell me I sing with the best. And now they throw this . . . this amateur on the stage to work with Dubratta, The *Great* Dubratta."

Caty had intended to tell her how honored she was to be singing with the *Great* Dubratta but she held back her words as Magda caught up the end of her robe in her hand and swept toward her.

"I tell you now, stay out from my way."

"I know the role, madam."

"You have sung it before, maybe."

"Well, no. But . . ."

She threw up her taloned hands. "Just as I thought. Some little nothing from the chorus, to play Suzuki to Dubratta's Butterfly. It is an outrage!"

Caty felt her temper swelling but she clamped her mouth shut. She was not going to let a tantrum spoil everything now. This was too important.

Magda paced back and forth in front of her until she came near to stumbling on a cable stretched across the stage. In the tirade of words that issued from her mouth, Caty suddenly realized her accent was fading. With a shock it came over her that this woman was not European at all. She was American. Somehow that took a little of the air from her sails in Caty's eyes.

"I won't have it. I told Cannio so, but I was overruled! Me, the greatest voice of the times! Well, you had better listen, you little nothing from the chorus." She waved a blood-red finger in Caty's face. "You follow the stage directions to the inch, you understand? Don't you once get between me and the audience. You stay in the background, sing your lines and fade away. Is that clear?"

"But madam, Suzuki is Butterfly's friend and comforter. How can I be that if I have to stay in the background?"

"Don't contradict me, you little nothing! This is Butterfly's opera and I don't need anyone else to make it Butterfly's. You heed my words or, so help me, I will see that you never sing on this stage again, not even in the chorus."

Caty's anger was rapidly turning to amusement as she watched the singer's grotesque, contorted face. What in the world, she wondered, was there about a successful career that could turn an ordinary human being into a petty tyrant? Magda was almost funny in her grandiose haughtiness—not the effect she obviously wanted to produce. Caty lowered her head to fuss with her robe, trying to hide the smile that she knew would only set the soprano off again.

"Is that clear!" Magda hissed, bending into Caty's face.

She pursed her lips to keep from laughing and nodded meekly.

"Good. See you do as I speak," she added, lapsing again into her version of accented English. Caty glanced up and was relieved to see Gregory Stillman coming on to the stage to walk her through her role.

"What did the great Magda have to say?" he asked as he guided her toward the Japanese house.

"She's not happy that I'm taking over Suzuki's part."

"She only pretends that. In truth, she's probably delighted because Cabrini would never put up with her shenanigans. Nor would she allow herself to be upstaged."

Caty smiled. "Hmm. Perhaps I won't either."

"Now, now. None of that. Suzuki is a minor

role in this opera. You just do the best you can and let Magda go her own way."

As Caty took her place on the porch of the Japanese house, all at once she was swept with the reality that soon she would be standing on this vast stage singing to thousands of people. A sudden wave of fright, like nausea, rose in her throat. "Oh, Mister Stillman," she cried. "Do you think I can do justice to Cabrini?"

The little man gave her shoulder a squeeze. "Caty, you have a beautiful voice and I'm certain you will have a successful career. This is a good start for you—important, but not too important. As an understudy you learned this role inside out—something not all singers bother to do. Don't even think about Dubratta, just concentrate on singing the best you can. Do that and you'll be better than Cabrini."

Caty knew it was unusual for the temperamental stage director to be so supportive, for she'd seen him tear into too many singers in the past for not following his directions to the letter. In fact, it was something of a joke among the chorus that Stillman's short physique, balding head, and portly figure gave a "fatherly" appearance to what was in reality an extremely high-strung, artistic personality. Yet right now she felt only gratitude for his encouraging words.

"Thank you, Mister Stillman. I'll remember what you've said."

"Good. Now let's get to work."

"What do you think you're doing!"

Dubratta again. Caty turned, half expecting to see the angry soprano sailing down on her once more. Instead, she saw that this time it was a hapless scene shifter who had set off this latest tantrum. He had been moving the Japanese screen from the last act and caught the end of her robe on a nail, causing the diva another near stumble. There was a minute tear in the fabric but it was enough to make Dubratta raise her voice to a shrill scream, something not even Caty had managed to do.

"I'm sorry, ma'am . . ."

"You're sorry! You're sorry! You stupid oaf, do you know what this costume cost?"

"I didn't mean it. It was a nail there . . . see . . ."

Dubratta swung back her arm and slapped the man across the face. "Idiot!"

Gregory went hurrying over to separate Magda from the burly stagehand whose eyes flashed anger at the singer. From where Caty stood she could see him clench his fist, though he didn't dare to raise it. She recognized Boris Borinsky, a mechanic who had come to work at the Met several months before. He was a big, beefy creature with amazing muscular strength and limited mental ability—a combination that made him the butt of many a practical joke with the rest of the crew, and which exacerbated his naturally surly, sullen personality. Still, he did not deserve such a harangue from a soprano who ought to have recognized an accident when she saw one.

It was rather pleasant, though, to see someone else receiving the brunt of Magda's terrible tongue, Caty thought, as she tried to turn away and concentrate on remembering where she was to stand and when she was to move.

"I want this clumsy oaf fired!" Magda exclaimed angrily. "He does not deserve to work around artists!"

"Now, Madam Dubratta . . ." Stillman went on in his level voice, trying to maintain a sense of proportion. From across the stage Caty could see the sudden panic in Boris's eyes at Magda's threat. The fellow probably had few friends to come to his defense. Even Stillman was less interested in saving the man's position than in calming the singer's overwrought nerves.

He managed to ease Magda offstage and back to her dressing room, then sent Boris off to bring up a prop. By that time the conductor for the evening, Manheim von Rankin, had joined Caty on stage to give her a few last-minute instructions. Soon she forgot Magda's temper tantrums and began to concentrate on her imminent debut, fighting her trepidations and concentrating on the thrilling excitement that consumed her. She found a quiet corner and ran through a few vocal exercises, thinking to herself that her voice really did sound in fine form. Now, if she could only manage not to let her excitement get in the way . . .

Suzuki had a brief scene at the beginning of the opera, which helped Caty since it got her moving right away. Yet once she left the stage that terrible mixture of thrill and fright almost got the better of her again as she waited backstage for her entrance with the women of the chorus. Magda did not come up to join them until almost the last moment, accompanied by her mousy little maid who fussed over her, arranging her train, putting a last-minute touch to the pins in her black wig.

Magda shoved the woman's hand away. "Leave me alone, Lulu! Always fussing and buzzing about. You're worse than a nagging wasp."

The little woman cowered away and went back to arranging Magda's train.

"And that tear had better not show," Magda snapped, looking around at her.

Lulu knelt to lift the end of the embroidered fabric. "You can never even tell it was there, madam. Look, I mended it perfectly."

"Hand me my fan."

Immediately Lulu was by her side, spreading the big colorful paper fan. She handed it to Dubratta, who promptly dropped it. "Sing beautifully, my lady," Lulu said, scrambling to retrieve the prop. She looked up at Magda adoringly as the music for the entrance swelled.

Magda lifted her head and threw back her shoulders, spreading the fan across the front of her gorgeous kimono. "I always sing beautifully!"

As Caty moved to take her place behind Magda, Charlotte reached out and squeezed her hand. "Great start. Good luck with the rest."

Caty smiled her thanks and added a silent prayer as the women began their offstage singing. She joined with them as Magda's voice rose above the others and they all started over the bridge.

There was not a lot for Suzuki to do in the first act of *Butterfly,* so Caty was able to mince around in her part and still observe Magda as she sailed into her role. The aged diva was a true professional, projecting the character of the timid, shy, little Japanese heroine in spite of the fact that she was years older and her personality was completely opposite. But it was the voice that startled Caty the most. In the beginning of the act there was enough of the resonance and beauty of Magda's lyric soprano as to lead one to forgive her for all her tantrums. Her notes were ringing or exquisitely pianissimo and all were gorgeous in their tone and clarity. Caty was beginning to think she and the others had made a mistake in underrating this artist.

But by the time the beautiful love duet commenced near the end of the act, she stood in the wings listening to Magda's voice as it began to fade. There was still enough of the dramatic presence to almost override the increasingly distressed vocal tones but Caty knew there were still two acts to go and both of them belonged mostly to Butterfly.

Nevertheless, Magda received a thundering ovation during her curtain call at the end of act one. Her adoring fans, known in the press as a claque, were out in force. They applauded politely for the rest of the cast but they brought down the house for Magda, especially when she appeared alone. It was a little discouraging for Signor Morelli whose serviceable tenor had no adoring claque, but Magda clearly reveled in it and stayed out on the stage far longer than was seemly.

"I hope they're still applauding by the end of act three," Caty whispered to Charlotte as they stood in the wings and watched the soprano kneeling to the crowd.

"I suspect that she could stand out there and recite the omnibus schedule and they would still go crazy. Adoring fans will forgive almost anything."

"Perhaps, but I think by the end of this opera there will be a lot to forgive. Oh well, at least Mrs. Vanderbilt didn't clump down the aisle with her ruby."

"It could still happen. Her seat is empty."

Caty turned to go back to the dressing room to try to relax during the intermission. "Well, all I can say is she had better not distract everyone while I'm singing."

Act two proved to be a real trial, but not in the way that Caty anticipated. Mrs. Vanderbilt did not make an entrance—she had decided to forego the opera that evening. All of Caty's problems were on the stage and they all centered around Butterfly.

As Caty had feared, Magda's voice was fading fast. Her big aria, "Un bel dì vedremo" was a disaster. When she began to go flat on her top notes it became obvious that it was going to be a long evening. Yet Caty could have forgiven her even that, if only her onstage behavior had been a little less overbearing.

The trouble was that as Magda worked harder, Caty's rich, clear, beautiful mezzo grew stronger and more assured. At the beginning of the act her fright caused her to hold back. But that soon was overcome as she became joyfully lost in the role and the music. She was having the time of her life when she realized that Magda was not-so-subtly upstaging her. Beneath the soprano's excellent acting Caty could sense a growing outrage directed at her. Soon Magda was positioning herself to block Caty from the audience, was throwing herself so violently into her dramatic role that all attention was focused on her. Worst of all, when they were singing together she either held a note too long or cut if off too quickly, which made Caty look unprepared. Even the beautiful "Flower duet" became almost a solo for Magda, and the notes which were to harmonize so beautifully sounded discordant because the soprano was flat. By the time the act closed with the lovely soft humming chorus offstage, Caty was near tears and convinced her debut had turned into a disaster.

Nor was she expecting the tirade Magda turned on her once the curtain closed, accusing her of singing off-key and trying to upstage her.

"I never . . ." Caty tried to say but the soprano railed on, ignoring her.

"No one takes the stage from Dubratta . . . No one! And certainly not a little nobody from the chorus! I refuse to go on with this . . . this *ama-*

teur who is trying to win recognition at my expense."

Caty began to fume. "That is a lie! If anyone is upstaging, it's you!"

"Ladies, ladies," Gregory Stillman cried as he hurried on to the stage. "Please calm down. We have another act to get through and these difficulties will only harm your voices."

"I won't sing!" Magda snapped. "I refuse to finish the opera with this Suzuki."

Gregory laid a comforting arm around the diva's shoulder and gave Caty a quiet wink as he led her off. "Now, now, you just need to relax before the last act. This has been a strenuous performance for you, Madam Dubratta, but you have handled it beautifully. And such ovations! Your fans are out in force tonight."

Dubratta threw Caty a spiteful glance and leaned heavily on Stillman, allowing herself to be calmed down. "Yes, I sing beautifully, that is true."

"And after all, it is the opera that matters. We must see Butterfly to her tragic end, mustn't we?"

Magda turned, throwing Caty one last, long, dark glance. "Yes, that is true. Butterfly must die. It is the opera."

Caty fumed to herself as she watched Stillman's diplomatic performance. "The old hag. She's not worthy of such treatment," she muttered under her breath as she sought a quiet corner where she could get her own temper under control. Though she would gladly have strangled Magda Dubratta she knew Stillman was right. It was the opera that mattered and this tragic story was not yet finished. She must concentrate on that.

Since she had no costume change, Caty waited impatiently in the wings for the last act to begin. Restlessly she wandered on stage, running her fingers over some of the props, and positioning herself where Suzuki would have spent the long night. She stopped thinking about Magda's antics and concentrated on feeling the simple, sad emotions which would have consumed the Japanese woman at that moment.

Her concentration helped, for when the act finally began she was able to sing and act her role as Butterfly's heartbroken servant to the absolute best of her ability. Her voice was better than ever and she used it like an instrument. Meanwhile, Magda threw herself into her role with a new level of histrionics which might have been more appropriate in Milan than the more subdued American stage of the Met. She wept and sobbed, and staggered back and forth across the sets so wildly that Caty began to wonder if she had perhaps had a few drinks during intermission. She clutched at Suzuki so hard and so often that she left the marks of her talons on Caty's arms. She came close to mauling the child who represented her son, "Trouble." By the time she retired behind the paper screen on the left side of the stage to commit hari-kari, Caty was almost wishing she could wield the knife herself.

With three crashing chords the opera ended. For a moment Caty could not move from the floor where she sat holding the child actor while the tenor, Pinkerton, bent over the lifeless body of Butterfly where she had crawled halfway from behind the screen. The music was so tragic and so beautiful, and, Caty had to admit, even though Magda's acting was overwrought and her singing poor, the soprano had touched a depth of feeling which left Caty overwhelmed with emotion. She sat there with her head bowed, listening to the roar of applause on the other side of the curtain, unaware of the swarm of stagehands who poured over the set, waiting for her emotions to subside. Part of it, she knew, was sadness that the wonderful experience of creating and singing a real character was over and now she must return to the chorus. Part of it was the tragedy of a woman's misdirected life, so beautifully and powerfully represented in music that touched the soul. And part of it was pity for Magda, whose great career was ending in this pitiful blend of forced singing and grandstand tantrums.

Yet Magda would certainly revel in the applause coming from the house, which even now was chanting her name over and over. As the child wiggled out of Caty's arms she felt a hand lifting her and looked up into Stillman's smiling face.

"You did very well," he whispered, in what Caty knew was high praise coming from him. "Go take your bows."

Caty began to feel the joy of a triumph realized. She straightened her kimona and hurried to the outer curtain, which was being pulled back for the curtain calls, glancing briefly back at the darkened stage. Magda was so overcome with emotion that she still lay on the floor where she had crawled at the end of the opera.

Or else she wants to wait until she can have the stage to herself, Caty thought, as she was pulled out in front of the curtain by the tenor, Mario Morelli. She felt a surging thrill as applause rained down on her, even though the shouts for "Magda, Magda" grew in intensity. When the singers moved back behind the curtain Caty noticed a group of people clustered at the back of the set where Magda still lay on the stage.

"What . . . ?" she started to ask before being pushed back out for a solo bow. She heard the level of applause increase, a tribute to her excellent job in a secondary role and for a moment the cries for Magda were nonexistent. She knelt in recognition, feeling a joy more intoxicating that any she had ever imagined in her dreams. But it was Butterfly's opera and she carefully did not stay out there too long soaking up the applause.

When she stepped back behind the curtain she could sense that something terrible had happened. The group huddled around Magda was larger now, and there was an air of subdued horror about them. Caty started over to see what was going on but Stillman, his face white and drawn, grabbed her arm.

"No, go back out . . . all of you . . . Sharpless, Pinkerton . . . everyone who sang a note, go back out there and take your bows."

"But what has happened? Madam Dubratta . . ."

"Never mind. Just go . . ."

Holding the hands of the other characters in the opera, she went back to bow twice again, but it did little good. By now the stomping of feet and the cries for Magda had swelled to earsplitting proportions, and no amount of appearances by the other characters could satisfy that audience. As she hurried back behind the curtain once again Caty heard a scream, horrible and agonizing, that carried even over the roar of the house. She glimpsed Lulu, Magda's maid, bending over the soprano, then flinging herself down on top of her mistress.

"My God, Gregory, what is it?" Caty cried as Stillman tried to push her onstage for another solo bow. "I won't go back out there again until you tell me what's happened to Madam Dubratta."

Stillman's eyes darted to the back of the stage where the sobbing maid cradled Magda's head in her arms. "Something terrible. Not possible! I can hardly believe it."

"Did she get hurt throwing herself around so wildly at the end of the act?"

"Worse than that," Stillman said, still gripping Caty's arm. "She's dead. She's been stabbed with Butterfly's knife!"

Three

Caty sat as far as possible from Magda Dubratta's body, on a part of the set that was under a tree whose vines trailed nearly to the floor. People were milling about. The stage crew, who had been ordered not to break down the sets, stood aimlessly glancing over at the floor of the Japanese house where Magda lay. The principal singers, members of the chorus—some of them dressed in street clothes now—the prompter, stage manager, and even the makeup crew—all wandered out on to the stage to stare at that dreadful form lying on the floor of Butterfly's home. Caty could hear General Manager Cannio speaking to the house on the other side of the heavy gold curtain, trying to placate them with the suggestion that Madam Dubratta had suddenly become ill and could not take her bows. A groan went up, a collective wail of disappointment and concern from Magda's fans, and Caty dropped her head into her hands.

She could not believe it yet. Only a few moments ago she had been acting and singing with this woman. Her heart had been moved by the tragic emotion, the dramatic power Magda Dubratta evoked onstage. What on earth had happened? And how?

"It's fortunate that you were in the audience. She's over here."

Caty looked up to see Manager Cannio hurrying on to the stage, followed by three men, all of them in white tie and tails. The tall one looked familiar but it took her a moment to recognize Detective Castleton with whom she had locked horns over the abused hansom horse the day before.

"Oh, no, not him," she groaned, but she continued to watch as he bent to lift one corner of the white cloth someone had spread over Magda's body. He pulled it back to inspect the wound, then he stood and spoke to Cannio in low words Caty could not catch.

Cannio turned to the people on the stage. "This gentleman is a policeman and he would like to talk to everyone who was on the stage when this dreadful accident happened. All the rest of you must move to the rooms backstage."

"Don't leave the building, though, any of you," Josh Castleton broke in. "I'll want to get all your names and addresses, and I'll need to speak with some of you tonight."

Cannio began ushering all the unnecessary personnel off the stage while Caty moved to the center along with the baritone who had sung Sharpless, Mario Morelli, who sang Pinkerton, conductor von Rankin, the prompter, and the small child who had played the part of Trouble.

"We won't need the child," Castleton said as his mother quickly grabbed him up and hurried away. "But the rest of you, please just stay here. I won't keep you long."

"Thank heaven," Caty muttered. She was extremely uncomfortable at being forced nearer Magda's body.

She saw Castleton give her a quick, quizzical glance. So he didn't recognize her. That was not too surprising since she was still in her Oriental makeup and black wig.

"If you could all just stand over here a moment," the detective said, motioning them nearer Butterfly's house.

Caty glanced toward the form on the floor. "Couldn't we do this somewhere else?"

Castleton gave her another studied, questioning look and Caty smiled to herself. Obviously he recognized her voice if not her face.

"Yes, I realize this is uncomfortable and I will talk to each of you later in one of the rooms. I just have a few quick questions while you're still close enough to the end of the opera to remember."

"As if I could ever forget," Caty murmured.

"You, er . . . Suzuki. You were the one who was closest to Madam Dubratta when this happened. Did you see anything to make you suspect she was going to take her life?"

"If you mean this was suicide, no, I didn't. In

fact, I would have thought Magda Dubratta was the last person to kill herself. She was entirely engrossed in her role. Except for . . ."

Castleton waited. "For what?"

Caty shrugged. "It doesn't matter. The point is she was completely caught up in singing her role."

"Could she have been so caught up in it as to actually kill herself as Butterfly was supposed to do?"

"Of course not. That's ridiculous."

The baritone who had sung Sharpless grumbled, "She would not have chosen to miss those curtain calls for anything. Magda reveled in applause."

"I wasn't onstage when this happened," Signor Morelli said, all but wringing his hands. "I entered afterward."

"Just afterward," Castleton said.

"Yes, but she was all bent over and I thought she was still acting the part. I didn't even realize she was . . . was *morta* until . . ."

"All right. I know this has been a strain for all of you. Just one more thing. Was there any way Madam Dubratta could be seen from backstage when she used that knife?"

"Why don't you ask Gregory Stillman? He's the stage manager." Caty's voice sounded testy even without her trying. It must be the residue from this boor's behavior the day before, added to the horror of Magda's death. "Please, can I get out of this costume? This wig is very heavy."

A battalion of policemen were streaming over the set. Caty gripped her hands and thought if she did not leave this place soon she would go into screaming tantrums.

"Yes, of course. Go ahead and dress but please don't leave the opera house until I've had a chance to talk to you. Each of you."

Still in shock, the singers left for their dressing rooms. Caty wondered how she would find Kyle and tell him she would be late tonight—very late. She only hoped her mother would not sit up worrying about the two of them.

Fortunately, she was one of the first people ushered into the greenroom where Detective Castleton and another policeman had set up several chairs and a table. She knew the instant he saw her that he finally remembered where they had met.

"Miss . . . McGowan, wasn't it? I knew there was something familiar about you."

"It must have been the voice," Caty replied haughtily, taking her seat.

"The voice, yes. You sang very beautifully tonight."

"Thank you. I'm very tired. Could we please get on with this?"

"Of course," Castleton answered, resuming his seat and ignoring the curious glances of the other policeman. He began asking her questions while the other man wrote down her answers in a red ledger.

Caty answered them absently. She had changed to her high collared shirtwaist and long skirt, and carried her coat over her arm. Once she was free to go she intended to leave this ugly yellow brick building as quickly as possible.

Castleton had a program open in front of him. "I've looked over this list of singers several times but I don't remember seeing a Miss McGowan among them."

Caty ran her finger down the names of the chorus members. "Right there," she said. " 'Catherina Mandesi'. That's me."

Castleton glanced up at her, trying to suppress a grin. "A good Irish name."

"I thought an Italian name would help my career. Opera lovers want their singers to be Italian."

"What nonsense. Magda Dubratta was not Italian."

"No, but she built her career in Europe. In America if you want to be successful, you've got to sound like you came from Italy. I only filled in for Madam Cabrini tonight as an understudy. Cannio announced it at the beginning of the opera."

Castleton looked away. "Yes. Well, unfortunately, I didn't quite make the beginning of the opera."

No, you wouldn't have, Caty thought to herself, noting the very formal white tie. All the wealthy patrons came late in order to be seen arriving. But somehow she could not figure out why a New York detective would be among them and dressed to the nines as Castleton was. He must have come as a guest of one of the rich subscribers who rented the boxes.

"Please, can I go now?" She was so weary that

the lamplight in the room seemed to waver, casting deep shadows on the walls.

"Just one thing more. You seemed to be very sure that Madam Dubratta would not have used that knife on herself."

"As I said before, she was the last person I would expect to kill herself."

"But then, that would mean that someone else must have killed her. Do you think that was possible, given the circumstances?"

"You mean . . . murder? Right there on the stage in front of all those people? Certainly not. It's unthinkable. Ludicrous!"

Castleton leaned his chin on his hand, his brooding gray eyes boring into her, seeing, she felt, past the surface and deep within to her innermost thoughts. She stirred uncomfortably in her chair.

"And yet Madam Dubratta is certainly dead. What other explanation is there?"

He has beautiful hands, Caty thought. Long tapered fingers, strong yet graceful, with carefully manicured nails. He was smiling at her, a kind of mocking, gentle smile that emphasized the delicious curve of his broad mouth.

She shook herself mentally. "How do I know? It's your job to answer that." Her eyes flashed, and she realized she was overreacting. "I wasn't paying her any mind, you see," she said, more levelly. "I was very engrossed in Suzuki's part. At the time Butterfly goes behind the screen, Suzuki holds the child and cries until Pinkerton comes rushing on."

"And when Madam Dubratta came crawling out from the screen?"

"I kept my place. The dramatic action at that moment is completely on Butterfly and I wouldn't for a moment think of drawing attention away from her."

"Oh? Why is that? Was Madam Dubratta sensitive about such things?"

"Sensitive! More like hysterical. She had already made very sure I wasn't going to take any of the glory away from her."

The smile had broadened and Caty realized she was allowing her anger at Dubratta to show perhaps a little too much for a murder investigation—if, in fact, that was what this turned out to be.

Castleton shifted position and drummed his fingers softly on the table. He was having a difficult time concentrating on the proper questions instead of on the attractive woman who sat before him. A professional singer! And he had told her to get on with her "shopping" yesterday on the street. Now, she was not only part of a murder investigation, she was a very real suspect. She had motive, and, though she could not have thrust the knife into Dubratta herself, she had easy access to the weapon. She might have rigged it so that an unsuspecting actress . . .

No. It was not the problem of the murder that bothered him. It was that he was finding it so hard to separate his investigation from his interest in this particular suspect. This had never happened to him in all the years he had been on the force and he wasn't at all certain he liked it.

He went on in his best businesslike manner. "As a matter of fact, her behavior was very noticeable during the second act when the two of you were on stage together. Did she perhaps say anything to you before the opera about not getting in her way?"

Caty hesitated. He must know that already or he would not have used Magda's very words. Well, that was not too surprising. Any number of people could have heard Dubratta's tirade onstage.

"Yes, she did. And not in very pleasant terms, either." She lifted her chin and met the challenge in his eyes directly. "And yes, I was angry enough to want to take that knife to her myself. But since I have several thousand witnesses that I was nowhere near her at the time . . ."

He gave a low chuckle. "Everyone is a suspect, Miss McGowan . . . or Madam Mandesi. Which is it you prefer?"

"Miss McGowan will do nicely," Caty snapped.

"Yes, well, you can now go to your well-deserved rest."

But not to her after-the-opera party, Caty thought bitterly. That moment of triumph would not happen tonight since it was already far too late and the company far too sober for festivities. She threw her coat over her shoulders and started for the door.

"By the way," Castleton called. "I may want to question you again tomorrow. Will you be here?"

"I don't know what more I can tell you, but yes, I'll be here."

"Good. Good night, Miss McGowan."

She fumed all the way home, listening to Kyle who could talk of nothing except how Madam Dubratta had died just like Butterfly. At one point she interrupted him with a direct question as to how he thought she had done in her debut.

"Oh yes, you were good. But just imagine, while you were sitting there so close she was stabbing herself with that knife!"

As Caty feared, her mother was still up and close to wringing her hands. They had barely got through the door before Kyle was spilling out all the details of Magda's death.

Sian McGowan laid her arm around Caty's shoulders. "How terrible for you, luv. Were you backstage at the time?"

"No, I was right there, not ten feet away."

Sian's round face was a mask of confusion. "You mean she stabbed herself right there in front of the chorus? With all those people around?"

"No, Mama." Caty sighed, pulling off her coat. "The chorus had finished. I was still on stage because I filled in for Madam Cabrini in the role of Suzuki."

Sian stopped dead, staring after her daughter as she started up the stairs to her room. "You sang a role! All by yourself! At the Metropolitan!"

Caty turned back. "Good grief, I forgot, you

didn't know. Yes, for once they actually needed me to sing the role I understudied. I sang it, Mama, and I sang it very well. And then it was so overshadowed by Madam Dubratta's death that I didn't even remember to tell you about it." Her eyes rolled heavenward. "If that isn't Magda's final revenge, I don't know what is!"

Josh Castleton was back at the opera house early the next morning. He went in through the back door where Arthur, the old man who kept watch at the stage door, ushered him down a long hall that led toward the newfangled elevator to the offices above.

"I'd like to take a look at the stage first," Josh said on a sudden impulse.

"Kind of bare and dark in there right now, sir."

"All the same, I think I'd like a look at it before going up to Mister Cannio's office."

Arthur shrugged and collared a stagehand who had just come into the building, asking him to show Officer Castleton to the stage. Josh followed the man, a tall, heavyset, chunky fellow who motioned him down a dark hall without saying a word.

Josh searched his memory of the people he had questioned the night before. "You're Boris, aren't you?"

The man nodded. "That's right."

"I'll be needing to talk with you again, Boris, later this morning."

"Why? I ain't done nothin'."

"No one is saying that you have. I'm going to need to talk to everyone again this morning."

"Oh." The man shrugged again and started up a low flight of stairs that brought Castleton backstage. "Can you find the elevator?" he asked.

"Yes. You don't have to stay."

Josh watched him lumber off. A man of few words, he thought, and, judging from appearance, fewer brains. Putting Boris out of his mind, he walked out onto the dark, vast stage, his footsteps echoing in the great empty interior. He walked to the edge of the proscenium and looked out at the darkened house, dimly lit by filtered daylight.

The horseshoe tiers of boxes with their burgundy seats were familiar to him from out there, but he had never seen them from the stage. He knew this opera house well. His mother had brought him often since he was a young child and now, as an adult, he came frequently enough to know his way around. It had never been a well-designed structure. From where he stood nearly half the seats had only a partial view of the stage. But then it had been built in 1882 simply because a handful of rich men, for all their wealth, could not purchase boxes at the old Academy of Music and, in true Yankee fashion, built their own opera house instead. They wanted it to be "grand" opera in every sense of the word and they hired Josiah Cleveland Cady, a prominent architect, to do the job. Unfortunately Cady had never designed an opera house and although he made the interior as huge and opulent as his patrons wanted, his design left many a frustrated opera lover in the upper circles with only a view of half the stage. However, what was wanted was a fashionable place to be seen, and that his rich patrons now had.

Josh smiled to himself when he remembered how Cady had put up a building whose exterior was so bleak and ugly that New Yorkers called it the "yellow brick brewery."

He turned his back to the house and began examining the stage where the sets for *Butterfly* were still in place. That had caused some screaming from the stage director the night before, since the sections of the sets for the next opera were sitting on the sidewalk at the back of the building. However, Josh was not sure there was going to be another opera this evening, and he needed time to leisurely examine the place where Magda died as well as the area surrounding it.

Half an hour later, he was seated in the general manager's office, trying to calm that nervous, distraught gentleman.

"You can strike the sets now, if that's any consolation," Josh said, settling into the plush armchair that faced a long arched window.

"But how can we go on as though nothing happened? What will people think? We ought to shut down out of courtesy to Madam Dubratta if for no other reason."

Clearly Cannio was thinking of what one night's darkened house would do to his budget.

"Isn't that a decision the board should make?" Josh asked.

"Yes, and they're convening this morning at eleven. But I should make some recommendation to them, and I confess, Mister Castleton, I don't know what to say."

Josh tapped the ends of his fingers together and studied the manager over them. "Well, I can't tell you what to do, but as far as the police go, the sets are not needed any longer and all the individuals who were in the area will be questioned at length today."

He had a quick mental image of "Catherina Mandesi"—or Miss McGowan, with her rich, flaming hair, striking emerald eyes, and statuesque figure. Her pale cheek, creamy as the inside of a shell, the small dimple in her chin, the beautifully shaped lips . . .

Resolutely he pushed the image away. "We've impounded the *Butterfly* sets but there's no reason why another opera can't replace them. You'll just have to reschedule *Madama Butterfly.*"

Cannio ran his fingers over his thick mane of white hair. "That should not be a problem. We only had one more performance and we can change that to a benefit. I have one coming, you know."

Josh stared at his fingertips and thought, how convenient. At least Cannio would benefit from Dubratta's death. These "managerial" benefits usually meant several thousand dollars to go directly into the pockets of the general manager.

"But what about the press?" Cannio went on. "We announced that Dubratta was ill last evening. What do we say now? That she died of the illness? Oh, this is just terrible!" he cried, looking wildly around the room as if help might materialize out of the corners. "What general manager ever had such a trial? Her fans will crucify us when they learn the truth!"

Josh answered in a level voice, hoping it would calm the man. "I think you have to announce that she's dead, but I wouldn't say how yet."

"What do you mean? She was a suicide. She emulated Butterfly's death right there onstage. The whole thing is just too, too dramatic and the newspapers will have a field day with it." He pulled out a handkerchief from his vest pocket and dabbed at his face. "It's too much. That terrible woman! She was simply trying to get even with me, I know it."

"Oh? And why do you think that?"

"What else would she be doing? She was an evil, vindictive, egotistical harridan who would go to any lengths to pay back a grudge."

"Committing suicide on stage is rather like cutting off your nose to spite your face, isn't it? Besides, what possible grudge could she have against you?"

It was asked so quietly and easily that Cannio almost didn't realize how incriminating his answer could be. His long face suddenly shut down into a mask. "Oh, well, it was really nothing. Some little minor disagreement years ago in Vienna, when I was director of the opera house there. She probably did not even remember it."

Josh tucked this comment away for the moment and made up his mind to do some inquiring about those years at the Vienna Opera. "I'm afraid your problem with the press is going to be more complicated than you thought. I don't think Madam Dubratta committed suicide."

Cannio's head shot up. His normally pale complexion faded to near white. "What do you mean?" he asked breathily.

"Just what I said. Do you recall the dagger Butterfly is supposed to use to kill herself?"

Cannio slipped into his chair. "Of course. It's the usual stage dagger. The blade slips into the hilt when it's pressed against the body."

"Yes. Well, someone tampered with this one making it impossible for the blade to be pushed back. When Madam Dubratta stabbed herself with that knife there was no way it could deflect from her body."

"But that's absurd! She was behind a screen, remember? She didn't even have to use the knife. She could have simply let it clatter to the floor and then crawled out from behind the screen."

"Exactly. But remember, she was found with the blade buried deeply in her heart. Nor was it your usual dull, blunted stage dagger. This was a stiletto, as sharp as broken glass."

The general manager dropped his head into his hands, trying to blot out the memory of Magda's crumpled body on his beloved stage. His thin body gave a shudder. "You can't mean . . ." he said, looking up at Josh, who was taking in every detail of the man's reaction.

"Yes. I think someone was either waiting there or slipped in unseen and drove that dagger into Dubratta's body. It's the only explanation I can see since suicide doesn't make any sense at all. Granted, she was a vindictive woman, but that's going a little far just to get even."

"But Inspector! In front of four thousand people!"

"No. That little space behind the screen could not be seen, either from the stage or the wings. I checked so as to make very sure of that. And, of course, no one was expecting anything like this. Who would even be watching?"

Cannio all but wrung his hands. "It's impossible. Ridiculous. What will I ever tell the press?"

Josh pulled himself to his feet. "If you can come up with a simpler explanation, Mister Cannio, I will be happy to listen. In the meantime, I have a long day ahead questioning these people and trying to determine what really happened behind that screen that left Magda Dubratta bleeding to death. Please let me know what the board decides later this morning." He pulled out his round gold watch from the fob pocket of his vest. Miss McGowan should have arrived in the house by now. "Good morning, Mister Cannio," he added as he walked to the door.

The general manager did not answer as he dropped his head down on the desk.

***

Josh took a chair beside the table which had been set up in the greenroom the night before. To his right, Sergeant O'Leary sat with an ink pot and a pen in front of him, poised to begin writing again.

Castleton settled himself for a long morning, a little disappointed he had not seen Miss McGowan waiting among the group of people outside. Oh well, he thought. She would simply be interviewed later rather than earlier.

"Who goes first this mornin', sir?" O'Leary said in his thick Irish brogue.

Castleton ran his eyes down the list. "The maid, I think. She looked as though she was ready to fall apart out there in the hall. We might as well take her first and let her get out of here."

O'Leary stepped to the door to call out, "Miss Lulu Donnegan," then hurried back to the table. Castleton rose politely as the little woman shuffled in, a wet handkerchief clasped to her face.

"Please, sit here, Miss Donnegan. We won't keep you long."

Lulu looked up at him with the most haunted eyes he had ever seen. As a policeman he had encountered grief and its aftereffects in many guises, but he had never seen it so starkly painful as etched on this woman's narrow face.

"Madam Dubratta's death has affected you deeply, I can see," he said sympathetically. His kind words brought on a torrent of tears and both men had to wait until the woman got herself under control. Josh was surprised at the depth of feeling in a lady whose appearance suggested passivity and subservience. She was not as old as her stooped figure suggested. Her hair was moderately speckled with gray, but it was pulled back in a severe knot which made her look older. Her face was unlined and so pale as to be almost gray. Her brows were dark and thick over faded blue eyes glistening with tears.

"I loved her so . . ." Lulu said between sobs. "She was . . . she was the greatest singer who ever lived. It was an honor to serve her."

"Forgive me, Miss Donnegan, but it has been reported to us that Madam Dubratta treated you in a way that should not have inspired so much devotion."

The blue eyes flashed fury for an instant. "Idiots! What would they know about being close to a great diva like Magda Dubratta. It was only right that she grew impatient with me now and then. I am nothing and she was . . . she was everything! She gave her voice to the world, and the world adored her."

"I see. But did you never, ever have a little tinge of anger toward her, great artist that she was? I mean, most people would object now and then to being insulted and ordered around in spite of the fact that they give good service."

"She was not 'most people'," Lulu said contemptuously. "Besides, her words meant nothing. She loved me. I served her for twenty years, since her career first began to grow internationally. I was her friend and confidante, as well as her servant."

I'll bet, Josh thought. He had seen this before, but it still amazed him how some people could build a web of fantasy around their lives and cling to it so tenaciously. "Since you knew her so well, tell me, was she the kind of woman who would kill herself?"

"Never!" Lulu cried amid a new burst of sobs. "The Great Dubratta! Why would she do such a thing? She had everything to live for."

Josh waited until the woman calmed. "Can you think of anyone, then, who might have wanted to harm Madam Dubratta?"

Another flash of pale blue fury. "Of course not. Everyone loved her. Everyone!"

Josh ran his finger along the edge of the table. He could see they were getting nowhere with this woman. Either she had lost touch with reality completely or she knew what Magda was like and refused to accept it. Either way, it would be better to talk to her when she was more rational and not so close to Magda's death.

"Just one more thing, Miss Donnegan. Did anyone speak to Madam Dubratta in her dressing room last night? Was there, for example, any threat or confrontation?"

"Of course not. The madam kept completely to herself before a performance, getting herself ready in her mind to sing the part."

"No visitors at all?"

Lulu dabbed at her eyes. "I don't know. There may have been one or two who stopped by to wish her well. I never paid them any mind."

"Thank you, Miss Donnegan. You can go now."

Lulu rose and dragged herself to the door. Her servant's black dress made her look as though she was robed in grief. Bowed, crying into her handkerchief, she seemed as though the weight of the world was pushing her down.

O'Leary closed the door after her and waited for Josh to tell him who to call next. The inspector sat thoughtfully looking at his hands.

"What do you think, Sergeant?" Josh said.

"I'd say that her grief was genuine. I never saw anyone so broken up. She'd have to be Sarah Bernhardt to put on that kind of a show."

"What about an accent?"

"I didn't hear any. She's American I'd say."

"Yes. So would I. As was Magda Dubratta, though that's not generally known. I wonder how the two of them got together. Look into that, Sergeant. I want to know as much about Dubratta's past as I can. Lulu's, too."

"Right, sir. Who's next?"

Josh thought for a moment, wondering if Miss McGowan had arrived yet but not wanting to ask. "The stage director, I think." He glanced at the ledger. "Gregory Stillman."

Four

Caty was deliberately late leaving for the opera house that morning. She stood by the rail of the ferry as it plowed through the choppy, gray waters of the bay, and examined her reasons. One of them, she knew, was the lingering horror of the night before. Magda Dubratta's death had transformed the glittering magic of the opera house into something foreboding and dark. She had never expected to feel this way. Since the first time she stepped through the stage door of the Metropolitan, everything in her had responded with joy and excitement. Here was a place where beautiful music mingled with high drama, and not even the drab, ordinary workings behind the scenes could diminish the thrill it gave her to be a part of it.

Until last night.

A flock of squawking gulls executed a series of balletic swoops along the trail of foam left by the boat. Caty watched them absently, wishing she had remembered to bring along some bread crumbs from breakfast to throw out for them. There had been little room in her mind for such mundane things. The image of Butterfly's sprawled, blood-smeared body on the stage of the Met had driven away all else. Not even the appearance of that obnoxious policeman could dispel that terrible sight.

He was the second reason she was reluctant to go in this morning. It was too bad, really, that with all the detectives in the city, Josh Castleton had to be the one who attended the opera last evening.

Of course, he was nice looking. In fact, she had not recognized him at first, dressed in his white tie and tails. She would be willing to bet the stickpin on his shirtfront was a real diamond. How could a working policeman afford such luxuries? Unless he was open to a bribe now and then from the wealthy nabobs who controlled most of the money in New York.

She stared down at the water, thinking how much it resembled the color of Castleton's eyes. Gray, steely, hiding mysterious depths, maybe just a little bit dangerous . . .

What nonsense! He was an overbearing, officious bully who gloried in using his authority to lord it over other people. She could not even think why he would want to talk further with her, since it was obvious she could have had nothing to do with Magda's death. He was using it as just another excuse to get even with her for daring to cause a ruckus on the street that morning.

A blast from the bass horn brought her out of her reverie. The ferry pulled into the slip and Caty hurried to join the crowd streaming off the boat and on to the battery. She had to walk two blocks north before she was able to catch the cable car and then the streets were so jammed with traffic that she did not arrive at the "yellow brick brewery" until close to noon. She shrugged off any lingering guilt over arriving so late. Perhaps Castleton had finished talking with his suspects by now, and had returned to the station. It would be a relief not to have to face him again.

Sergeant O'Leary carefully laid his pen alongside the ledger, then closed the book, smoothing the cover. "Well, that's the lot, sir."

Josh glanced over at his sergeant, absently rubbing a long finger along the bridge of his nose. Miss McGowan had still not arrived in the house and he had just about questioned everyone else who had been there the night before.

"What do you think, O'Leary? Was our murderer sitting here this morning?"

O'Leary swelled with importance. The inspector did not often ask his opinion about anything, much less about a murder suspect.

"Well, sir, it seems to me it has to be one of them. The person with the best opportunity is that slow-witted Boris. The one with the best motive could be her former enemy, Manager Cannio. And the one who might appear the least likely and therefore the most suspicious, is that withered maid of hers.

Josh smiled. "That narrows the field."

O'Leary sat back in his chair and pulled down the tabs of his blue jacket. "However, our friend Boris doesn't strike me as having the wits to kill Madam Dubratta in the middle of a performance. He'd be more likely to bash her over the head in a darkened hall with nobody about."

"Yes, her death was intentionally dramatic. No getting away from that."

"And as for the general manager, would he risk his career to repay an old grudge? After all, he'd be putting a very successful job on the line. Seems to me he'd want to find some place less associated with himself. And then there's that maid. Well, sir, if I ever saw genuine grief, that was it. It's hard to believe she'd jab a dagger into a woman she cared so much about and had served so long."

Josh pushed back his chair and rose to his feet. "Congratulations, Sergeant. You've identified all the obvious suspects and then eliminated each one of them."

O'Leary jumped to his feet. "Sorry, sir, but you did ask my opinion."

"Oh, it's quite all right. Everything you've mentioned has occurred to me as well. Which leaves us precisely where we were before. Well, come on then. Let's take time to have lunch and then we'll come back and go over the scene once again."

Grabbing up his ledger and pen, the sergeant followed Josh to the door and into the hall. A woman was walking toward them, a handsome woman in her high shirtwaist with lace molding her slim throat, close-fitting gray jacket, long dark gray skirt, and wide hat with a brim crowned with folds of pink gauze. It took O'Leary a moment to recognize the singer from the night before without her heavy makeup.

Josh knew her at once and quickly suppressed the smile that threatened the corners of his lips.

"Miss McGowan. I had about given you up," he said diffidently.

"Sorry, Inspector. I got off to a late start this morning." Caty realized she was looking everywhere but into those steely gray eyes. "Do you still want to talk to me?"

"Yes. We were just taking a break for lunch, however. You'll be here this afternoon?"

"Yes, I will." Caty wanted to continue on down the hall but the inspector's broad body was directly in front of her. She waited for him to move.

"I'll just go along then, sir," Sergeant O'Leary said, hurrying around her.

"Yes, go ahead. I'll meet you here again in an hour."

The sergeant disappeared down the hall while Caty waited for the inspector to move out of her way. He did not seem inclined to do so.

"If you'll excuse me . . ." Caty murmured and tried to slip past him, but he stepped in front of her again.

"Well, as a matter of fact, I was just thinking that if you would have lunch with me, it would offer us a chance to talk in more pleasant surroundings. You do take lunch, don't you?"

Caty looked up in surprise. "Yes, but . . ." She

glanced at the sergeant's retreating back. "Don't you need him to record anything I might say?"

"Ordinarily, yes. But in this case, well, there are a few things I'd like to go over with you and I'd prefer to do it in a more relaxed atmosphere."

Caty felt her cheeks growing warm under the intensity of his eyes. "Is this usual police procedure—to take a witness to lunch?"

Reaching out, he took her arm and pulled it through his. "No, it isn't. And if you complain to my captain I shall be in a small deal of trouble. However, I think on reflection, you will agree with me that it is better to discuss some things privately. After all, you were the person who was nearest to Magda when she died. It is possible that you might have seen something without realizing that you did. Besides, I know this little place around the corner that serves the most delicious oyster stew in New York. You don't mind joining me, do you?"

Caty found herself being pulled back down the hall. "Would it matter if I did?" she asked testily, conscious of the feel of his arm beneath her hand.

"Of course it would."

Yet as he moved steadily toward the stage door, she felt sure that it would not. This insufferable man was quite accustomed to making people do his bidding, as she well knew from bitter experience. And something about his invitation worried her. She felt certain he was not taking her to lunch merely for the pleasure of her company or to discuss any details she may have seen during that fatal third act.

Once they reached the street, she deliberately pulled her hand from his arm and walked alongside him with a very formal, detached air.

"Delaney's is just over there, you know," she said in a cool voice as they reached the corner. "It serves a very fine lunch."

"All the opera people are regulars at Delaney's. I think I'd prefer a place where we won't be so acutely observed. Besides, I feel in the mood for oyster stew."

Oh, of course, and that is all that matters, she fumed silently.

Traffic in the congested streets was heavier than usual. Hansom cabs and their complacent horses vied with gravy boat-shaped broughams and an occasional shiny metal Daimler. Vendors with pushcarts hawked everything from live crabs to fresh strawberries, newly arrived from the farms of Staten Island. Had either Josh or Caty wished to make small talk it would have been impossible in the cacophony of ear-splitting noises on the street. The cries of the vendors mingled with the steel wheels of the horse-drawn carriages, the shouts of the drivers and the clanging of the Daimler's gong to form a wall of noise in which one had to shout to be heard.

But small talk was the last thing on Caty's mind as she walked alongside Josh. She was torn between resentment that she had been given no choice, and a deep-down, barely acknowledged delight that this attractive man wanted to take her to lunch. But, of course, that was nonsense. Josh Castleton might be handsome and personable, but he was also overbearing, bossy, and a policeman. The idea that she would be attracted to such a man was ridiculous.

He led her down 39th Street to Sixth Avenue where he turned north. Across the street the park, formerly the old reservoir, was cluttered with the paraphernalia of the construction used in building the new library. Only the outside was completed as yet and its massive shadow loomed on the other side of the park. Caty was so busy looking at it that Josh caught her by surprise when he stopped by a handsome wooden door and pushed it open for her to enter.

She stepped inside another world. She had an impression of soft, dark gloom and blessed quiet. It was a homey place. The one window facing the street was filled with stained-glass designs whose jeweled colors reflected on a long, wide mahogany bar with a gleaming brass rail along its edge. There was sawdust on the floor, heavy round wooden tables scattered opposite the bar, and delicious odors of fresh bread permeating the narrow room. Josh gave a brief hello to the bartender who recognized him at once, and took Caty's elbow to lead her toward the rear where a smaller room was filled with tables and booths. He chose one of the booths, upholstered in burgundy leather. Two menus nearly two feet high lay on the table but Josh pushed them aside.

"You don't need these. Oyster stew and Andre's fresh rolls make the best lunch in New York."

Caty laid her reticule on the table. "So I don't get to choose here, either?" She picked up the menu and opened it.

"Well, if you'd prefer something else, I suppose that can be arranged. Though I don't understand why you would want it when I can vouch for the stew."

Caty ran her eyes down the list and deliberately chose crab cakes, though they were not her favorite food. Josh gave their order to a waiter in shirtsleeves and a long white apron, then sat back, eyeing her across the table. He noticed that she kept her eyes everywhere but on him, and with her chin in the air, and that faint look of distaste on her face, he was almost tempted to forget the whole thing and walk out.

And yet . . .

She was a handsome woman, no getting around that. He had noticed the looks she received from the men on the street during their walk to the restaurant. Tall and graceful, her thick hair, red as a flawless ruby, and caught in a bun at the back of her neck, those eyes, gleaming like fine emeralds, her shoulders thrust back and her curvaceous bosom thrust forward . . . she was a woman to raise the warmth in a man all right. Her clothes were well done, too. The fabric was not rich and had none of the heavy ornamental stitching of fine dressmakers, yet it fitted her to perfection and the blending of colors showed a natural fashion instinct.

She was also arrogant, had a terrible temper, and, at the moment, was not inclined to be very pleasant. He wondered if he had been wise to bring her here instead of questioning her in the drab room at the opera house. He wished he could be certain she was only what she appeared to be—a damn fine-looking woman whom he found much too attractive for his own good.

"You know," he said casually, "it won't be much longer before oysters will not be available anymore in New York."

It was the last thing she had expected him to say. "Oh . . . really?"

"Yes. It's too bad because during the last century they were a mainstay for the poor and rich alike. I suppose people thought the rich beds would never give out."

"I had no idea they were so popular. Personally, I don't care for them."

"I remember my father telling me that back in seventy-four, at a Convention of the Episcopal Church, over eighty thousand oysters were consumed by the guests. It's almost more than the mind can conceive, isn't it?"

"It is a high number."

Josh studied her silently for a moment. "Come now, Miss McGowan, can't we call a truce here? Are you still so angry with me about that incident with the cab horse that you can't bear to make casual conversation?"

For the first time Caty looked directly at him. "You were overbearing and insensitive," she snapped. "That animal was suffering."

"I realize that, but it is a policeman's job to prevent public brawls in the street. Sometimes they lead to innocent people being hurt."

"So one should just look the other way when one sees an injustice?"

"No. One should seek the proper channels and lodge a complaint. We do try to follow up on them, you know. Would it make you less annoyed to know that the horse in question was taken off the street that day and the driver was given a summons? I heard later that he lost his job. Most responsible cab companies don't want drivers who intentionally abuse their animals. After all, without healthy horses there is no business."

Caty's eyes widened in surprise. "It was? He did?"

"Yes. You would have learned that, had you made a complaint."

She looked down at her hands in her lap. "I owe you an apology, Mister Castleton. I just assumed nothing was done. Just that morning, on my way to the opera house, the streetcar passed two horses dead on the side of the street and I suppose that added to my sense of injustice."

"That is a problem we have yet to solve satisfactorily. A dead horse means a dead weight of several thousand pounds and they are not easy to remove. However, we try to have the SPCA cart them away before they become a sanitary hazard.

It would help if the dray owners would do something to prevent it, but most of them are content to drive the animals until they drop, then walk away and let the city deal with the problem."

"That's what I mean. So many of those owners are insensitive."

Josh hesitated. "You must be very fond of horses."

For the first time a softness touched her luminous eyes. "Yes, I am. We have always had one or two and I find them gentle, amiable, and obedient. They respond to good treatment."

Josh wanted to remind her that she never depended on one for a living, but he hesitated to put a wrinkle in the tentatively pleasant mood that was growing between them. At that moment the waiter arrived with their steaming plates and for the next ten minutes both of them concentrated on their food. Caty found the crab cakes delicious, but the tempting aroma from Josh's bowl of stew almost made her wish she had not been so eager to make her own choice.

Not until Josh laid down his spoon did he raise the subject he was there to discuss.

"I'm hoping you may have seen something last night, Miss McGowan, something you may not even think was important at the time but which might help us. You were probably nearer to Magda than anyone during the time she died. Did you notice anything at all which might seem out of place or unusual?"

Caty looked away. "I haven't really wanted to

think about it," she said quietly. "The thought that . . . of what was happening to Magda while I was right there . . ."

Josh sat back in the booth and folded his arms across his chest, studying her with darkened eyes. "Can you think of anything even slightly out of place, anyone who shouldn't be where they were, anything you noticed?"

Caty shook her head. "No, I can't. I was concentrating so on my role and on the music. I don't even remember glancing offstage at all."

"When you did glance offstage, perhaps earlier, whom did you see?"

"The stage director, of course. The other singers waiting for their entrances, the lighting technician, oh, and the chorus master. And, of course, the prompter was always visible at the front of the stage."

"There is no chorus in the third act of *Butterfly*, is there?"

"As a matter of fact, no. But I can't swear that I saw Mister Walters during the third act. It might have been earlier. They do sing offstage at the end of act two."

Josh signaled for the waiter to bring them two coffees. "What about the knife that Butterfly was supposed to use? Did you see that before the act began?"

"Yes. It's merely a stage prop."

"Where was it?"

"It was lying on the low table behind the

screen, along with the scarf she wraps around her throat."

"Did you notice anything different about it?"

"No. I got to the set a little early and I was simply walking around, trying to get my mind properly ready for the drama."

Josh lifted the cup which the waiter placed in front of him. A thin spiral of smoke rose gently from its surface. He took a sip, then carefully set it down. "And did you touch the knife?"

Caty looked at him blankly. "I . . . I don't think so. I don't really remember. I was concentrating on the opera. Why?" she asked, suddenly suspicious.

"Someone saw you pick it up and handle it. Naturally we have to check that out."

"Who saw me? Wait a moment . . . I know, it was that Boris, that surly stagehand. I do recall seeing him just before I went out on the stage. It was him, wasn't it?"

"Who it was is not the issue. I am more interested right now in what you remember about your movements at that time."

Caty angrily pushed her cup away. "But why? Are you saying I am a suspect? I was right there in front of the audience when Magda was killed."

"I'm not accusing you, Miss McGowan. It is important for me to know everything I can about what went on behind that curtain in order to get at the truth. The stage prop knife had been reworked into a dangerous stiletto, yet right now we cannot be sure if Miss Dubratta accidentally used the tampered knife on herself or if someone stepped in to plunge it into her body."

A think lump rose in her throat. "Oh, thank you, Inspector. You certainly know how to make pleasant conversation over a meal."

"Sorry, but you did ask. What about Magda Dubratta? Did you know her well?"

"I hardly knew her at all except by reputation. Six years ago, near the end of the last century, she was one of the most famous singers in Europe. She had a magnificent voice and a dramatic presence onstage. Offstage she was known to be . . . well, 'difficult' is an understatement."

"Did you find her so?"

"Oh yes. She insulted everyone, from General Manager Cannio on down. She was especially incensed that I was taking over the part of Suzuki. She felt I was an experienced nobody and she deserved better. She warned me I had better not get between her and the audience. That was not a problem as it turned out. She upstaged me so badly I never had the chance."

Josh smiled at her. "If it is any consolation, you outsang her by a mile. Everyone in the audience was aware of it."

Caty felt her cheeks grow warm. "Thank you. I felt I did well. Unfortunately what happened afterward rather diminished my accomplishment."

"Yes, you might say it was the ultimate 'upstage'."

Caty glanced quickly at him, realizing by his

mischievous smile that he was making a small joke. She laughed, for the first time. "I suppose it was, though I'm sure she never intended to go to such lengths."

"You're very pretty when you laugh."

Her cheeks grew warmer. "I thought we were here to discuss Magda's murder," she said, a little too brusquely.

Josh coughed. "Well, that's true. We are. Did you feel any resentment against Dubratta for her treatment of you?"

The small pleasantness of a moment before vanished. "Do you mean, was I angry enough at her to murder her? No. I hardly knew the woman."

"It seems so, but I have to tell you, Miss McGowan, the more we learn about Magda Dubratta, the more we find people at that performance who had all kinds of ties to her in previous years. It has made it difficult to sort out what really happened. And getting at the truth, after all, is my primary purpose. I hope you can understand that."

He seemed so sincere that for a moment Caty was almost willing to forgive him for accusing her. She found her eyes lingering on his strong jaw and beautifully curved upper lip, on the long lashes that fringed his eyes, on the slight crease down his cheek that dimpled into a line when he smiled. The sudden warmth that flared in her chest made her drop her eyes and turn her head away to hide her burning cheeks. She forced herself to remember he had brought her here under the pretense of a pleasant meal when all he really wanted was to "check her out."

"Inspector, I might have picked up that dagger. If I did, it was done absently-minded, as part of getting into my role. That's all I can tell you."

"And you're certain you don't remember anything at all that was different during that third act?" Josh went on. "Anything that should be there which wasn't, or was there that shouldn't be?"

"No. I wish I could help you but, as I told you before, I was concentrating on my character. Surely there must be others who could be of more help to you? The backstage people, I mean."

"That's part of the problem. There are so many of them. Stagehands, directors, technicians, even a few of the chorus. Like you, most of them were busy with their own concerns and paid little attention to what was happening onstage. Well, if you should happen to recall something . . . anything, no matter how small, please tell me, even if you think it is too insignificant to mention."

"Yes, Inspector. I'll be sure to do so. And thank you for the lunch," she added coolly. "It was delicious."

"Yes, this is quite a nice place, and not so well known as some others in this neighborhood."

Caty reached for her purse. It was not difficult to see why Andre's was not as heavily patronized as the other restaurants in the area. Everything about it screamed money and elegance, from the burgundy upholstery, rich mahogany furnishings, and ornate stained-glass window in the front, to the excellent food served. Most of the struggling musicians at the Met would not be able to afford lunch in such a place. It still surprised her that a policeman could—unless he was one of those well-known officers who accepted bribes from Tammany. Somehow, Josh Castleton did not seem like a man who would sell out for money, but that could be because he was playing a clever part for her benefit. After all, hadn't he even been putting on an act when he brought her here?

Josh paid the bill and, once outside, drew Caty's arm through his own again. He was pleased that this time she left it there. Perhaps, he mused, it was an indication that their meal together had brought them a little closer. And, after all, that had been one reason for bringing her here. That, and the fact that he was compelled to ask her about Butterfly's knife. It was impossible for him to imagine that this lovely woman would have fashioned a stage prop into a dangerous weapon, yet he had been a policeman long enough to know that you could never rule out any suspect, no matter how much you might like to.

He was still not sure why he wanted to know her better. Opera singers were an egotistical lot as a rule, and this budding professional promised to be up there with the best of them. She was going to be successful, he was certain of that. Her voice had an exceptional beauty which she combined with excellent technique and quite good stage presence. Like a rough diamond, she was not fully polished yet, but the brilliance was there and someday its glitter was going to bring the world to her feet.

So why should he bother with a girl whose life promised to be so different from his own? A girl whose part in a dramatic, detestable murder might be a lot deeper than she claimed?

He mulled over her curious discrepancies as he walked back with Caty to the opera house, very conscious of the light touch of her hand on his arm. She was very pretty in a striking kind of way. Her manner appeared to be unspoiled and a little self-effacing—he especially liked that. And any opera singer who would go to battle for a tired old hackney horse had to be an interesting person.

Once inside the stage door and away from the street noises, he gave her a small bow and thanked her for sharing lunch with him.

"Perhaps we can do it again sometime."

Consumed with a sudden awkwardness, Caty found herself avoiding his smiling gray eyes. "Perhaps," she mumbled. "If you'll excuse me, I must get to rehearsal."

"Of course." Josh was watching her disappear down the narrow hall when he heard Sergeant O'Leary call his name. The sergeant ducked around Caty and came hurrying toward him.

"Glad you're back, sir. I've picked up a bit of information I thought you'd like to hear."

"Oh? It sounds as though you had a busy lunch."

"That's right, sir." O'Leary said, falling in beside Josh as they started back to the interrogation room. "I dropped in at Delaney's—not a place I'd usually go, but I figured one of them opera people might have a loose tongue. Well, sir, I was right. I was invited to sit with a group of them and they was talking about nothing but the murder and Magda herself.

"Seems most of them agreed if any singer deserved murderin', it was Dubratta. Not one of them had a good word to say about the woman, saving, maybe, that she was a good singer once."

Josh opened the door to the greenroom, then closed it after they were inside. "We know that already, Sergeant. That's all we've heard from the people we've already interviewed."

"Yes, sir. I'm aware of that." O'Leary leaned closer and lowered his voice, though there was no one in the room but the two of them. "But it seems one of these fellows sang in the chorus someplace in Europe years ago before Magda became so famous. He was trying to impress the others with his knowledge, so he says, real secretive like, that he knew the musician she was married to when she was just starting out."

Josh forced down his growing impatience. "She had several former husbands. One of them was the conductor of the opera last evening. But like Miss McGowan, he was in full view of the audience the whole time."

"No, sir, this was one of the husbands we didn't know about—nobody knew nothing about, except that gentleman from the chorus, and he only because he was around when it happened. It didn't last long. Once the great Magda began to be famous she dropped him faster than Patty's off-ox. Her star rose and he went nowhere."

Josh felt a prickle on the back of his neck, something that had happened only a few times before when casual information promised to be a bit more. "And what was this gentleman's name?"

With a pompous slowness, O'Leary pulled out a small notebook and began leafing through the pages. Josh bit his tongue and waited, knowing the sergeant could have told him without verifying it.

"Here it is," O'Leary said, thumbing the pages. "Warring. Herman Warring. Violinist."

"Herman Warring?" Josh glanced down where a program from last night's opera lay casually tossed on the desk. "Isn't that one of the names . . . ?"

"That's right, sir. He was the last stand, last chair in the violin section of the orchestra. And he was here last night."

Sergeant O'Leary's round face beamed with success.

"Good work, Sergeant. I'd like to talk with this Herman Warring right away. See if you can find him."

"I already have, sir." O'Leary pulled a large round gold watch from the top pocket of his jacket and held it out at arm's length. "He ought to be arriving at the house in about ten minutes and I've told Arthur to bring him here first thing."

Five

"You were once married to Magda Dubratta?"

Josh hoped his astonishment wasn't too obvious. From all he had heard of the fiery, temperamental soprano, from the strikingly handsome woman in her photographs, even from the power of her dramatic performance in *Butterfly* the night before—he could barely imagine such a woman linked to the little man sitting on the other side of the table.

Herman Warring was a short man, nearly bald, with tiny eyes in a moon-shaped face and thick, perpetually moist lips. His stooped, slight figure was redeemed only by his hands. He had the long tapering fingers of an artist even though it was difficult to appreciate them, they trembled so. The fringe of hair around the back of his head dropped in greasy strands over his coat collar, a coat which, like the rest of his cheap suit, was in great need of pressing. Josh wondered how such a man had made it into the orchestra of a great house like the Met, even if it was only to the last row of the violin section.

"Yes, that's correct," Warring mumbled, pushing his round glasses up on his nose. "I don't know how you heard of it. It isn't generally known."

"We know a great deal about Madam Dubratta's life. How long were you married?"

The little man shrugged. "A few months. And we were not together much of that time. Our careers kept us apart."

He had a slight accent Josh strained to place. Viennese, he decided. "And where did you meet?"

Warring looked up at him over the rim of his glasses. His reluctance to speak about Magda was obvious, yet he also seemed to feel that the police already knew so much it was useless to try to put them off. He studied his hands for a moment, then sighed.

"We met in Frankfurt. She was just starting out at the opera house there and I . . . I was giving concerts and teaching at the conservatory. I have not always played fourth violin, Inspector. My career was going very well then and I think . . . well, she perhaps thought I could help her get the roles she wanted."

"This was a calculated marriage?"

Warring's lips turned up into a wry smile. "If you mean were we madly in love, no, we were not. There was, perhaps, some feeling there, at first, but it did not last long. Once Magda's considerable talents began to be discovered, she no longer needed to be married to a violinist. We parted amicably."

Josh drummed his fingers on the table. "If you

parted friends, why then did she never mention the marriage? She had several others which are well documented. What happened to yours?"

"Perhaps she felt it was too short and too insignificant to matter. I don't know. As her star ascended, mine fell, and I soon had more to worry about than a failed marriage."

"Come now, Mister Warring. Are you telling me that you never had the least resentment over the way she left you? That you never felt any bitterness over the fact that she was a huge success and you were not?"

Warring pushed up his glasses with a long finger. "You may believe me or not, as you wish, Inspector, but the truth is, I quickly stopped thinking about Magda Dubratta. I may have had an occasional twinge of jealousy but that is not uncommon in musical circles. Most of the time I was happy for her."

Josh and O'Leary exchanged a glance that said they both felt that if they had ever heard a lie, this was one. Either this little man was deluding himself or he was trying to delude them. Josh was fairly certain which it was.

"And last night? You were playing in the orchestra the whole time?"

"Where else would I be?"

"Where indeed. Only one more thing, Mister Warring. Had you seen Magda at any time during the intervening years, before she arrived in New York for this performance?"

"No. We've had no contact since those early

years. I passed her in the hall after she arrived, and she looked right through me. Of course, I've changed somewhat since that time."

"Are you saying she did not recognize you?"

"I am saying that she chose not to recognize me."

"And you let that go by without any comment at all? You did not try to speak to her, or arrange a private conversation?"

Warring shook his head. "It seemed better to let the past remain buried. I never thought anyone here in New York would even know about our marriage. She obviously did not wish it to be known."

"Thank you, Mister Warring. Please give your address to Sergeant O'Leary. We may want to talk to you again."

Warring rose to his feet. "I have nothing more to tell you."

"I know. It's just a formality."

The violinist told O'Leary his address, then shuffled out of the room, leaving the two men to stare at each other in astonishment.

"Something's wrong there, sir," the sergeant muttered as he slipped his notebook into his coat pocket.

"You mean that a woman like Dubratta could have ever married that wizened little man?"

"Yes, sir, that, of course. But fancy her walking right past him without so much as a nod. Why, any self-respecting man would have grabbed her arm, turned her around and demanded at least a decent hello."

"I think any self-respecting man might have done even more than that."

"Well, sir, if ever a woman needed a comeuppance, that lady did."

"And she got one, too. A rather severe comeuppance. Remember, Sergeant, that's what we're here to solve. I don't think our violinist friend was telling us the whole story by a mile. My guess is he did see Magda, or at least, tried to, before that performance. I want you to talk to her maid again. See if she remembers Warring coming around at all."

"Very well, sir."

"And find out if Lulu knew anything about Warring's early marriage. Magda may not have mentioned it to her, either." Josh drummed his fingers along the table. "Damn!"

"Sir?"

"Warring is a prime suspect with an excellent motive. The trouble is, like Miss McGowan and Maestro Von Rankin, he was in full view of the house at the time Magda was killed."

Much against her will, Caty found herself unable to forget that enjoyable lunch with Detective Castleton. It lingered at the back of her mind like a pleasant sensation, impinging on her consciousness, not just at leisurely moments such as when she stood at the rail of the ferry watching the gray waters of the bay, but even at times when she least wanted to remember, like in the middle of a rehearsal or during a singing lesson. She soon became quite annoyed with her recalcitrant mind, yet trying to force the memory down never seemed to drive it away completely. Finally, she had to face the fact the she found Castleton attractive and pleasant, even if he was a detective, and even though he probably considered her a suspect.

The opera house was in full gear, but that did not help Caty forget her lingering delight. When, two weeks after Magda's death, the sets for *Butterfly* were released and the opera was put on the schedule for one more performance, she thought that perhaps she might be allowed to sing Suzuki again since she had done so well before. But it turned out that Madam Cabrini was under contract for it and did not intend to have to bow out a second time. Caty resigned herself to the chorus and simply hoped she could get through the opera without being too obsessed by her memories—both good and bad.

The fact that someone had seen her pick up Magda's knife and had reported it to the police festered like a small sore in her mind. She was certain it had to be that surly, unpleasant scene shifter, Boris Borinsky. He was always sulking about, watching everyone with those hooded eyes and downturned mouth. She half suspected him of killing Magda himself—after all, the diva had threatened to have him fired earlier that day. He probably told Castleton that he had seen Caty pick up the knife, just to throw suspicion away from himself.

She made up her mind to speak to him about it, but a busy series of operatic performances pushed it from her mind. Until one night nearly a week later.

The curtain had fallen to the heavenly choral hosannas that closed *Faust* when Caty headed back to the dressing room to remove her medieval costume. Her brother, Kyle, was standing in the hall waiting for her, so she hurriedly put on her street clothes and pinned her hat atop her piled hair. She was about to join him to head for the stage door when she remembered she had left her music backstage. After asking him to wait for her, she ran down the narrow halls to the huge, cavernous stage area. Most of the sets were already down though a few workmen were still milling about. The dark area was lit by scattered gas lamps that threw ghostly circles of light that only served to make the areas outside them seem even blacker. Caty found her folio, tucked it under her arm and started back toward the hall when a sudden thick shadow loomed in front of her. With a gasp, she took a quick step back as the man stepped into the light and she recognized Boris.

"Shades of Saint Peter, you gave me a fright!" she exclaimed. "You might have warned me you were here."

He glowered at her, thrusting his big head forward. "You got me in trouble," he muttered.

"I got *you* in trouble! What are you talking about?"

"Why'd you tell them policemen about that woman saying she was going to get me sent away? You didn't have to do that. Now they think I stuck that knife in her."

"Why did you tell them you saw me pick up the knife? You were trying to accuse me, weren't you?"

He looked at her blankly. "You're daft. Just like the other one."

He thrust his head closer, and Caty shrank away. The light from the gas lamp threw dark crevices on his thick features and slanted eyes, giving them a satanic cast. She was seized with an unreasoning fear which she quickly thrust down. It was probably just the residue of having been so involved in that medieval opera in which the devil himself played a prominent role.

"Look," she snapped. "I'm telling you to stay away from me. And don't make up stories about me just to draw suspicion away from yourself. It won't do you any good."

His eyes narrowed. "You did pick up that knife. I saw you do it, and put it back down."

"Then you also saw that I did not do anything to it. I don't even remember picking it up. You had more reason to kill Magda Dubratta than I."

"She was a bitch. Thought she was better than everybody else just because she was famous and had a lot of money. She deserved to die." He saw

Caty take a quick intake of breath and added, "Whoever killed her did a good thing."

There was such a crazy glint in his sunken eyes that Caty began to feel her skin crawl. "I have to go," she said firmly. "Please let me pass."

"You don't talk about me to them, you hear?"

"Are you threatening me?"

"You just listen to what I say."

He half raised his arm, his big hand clutched in a fist. Caty sensed a violence so barely contained and bridled that fear caught at her breath again. She fought against letting it show.

"Your threats won't stop me from telling the truth. If you don't like that, then that's just too bad."

Boris slowly raised his fist higher, glaring at her. She glanced over to see two of the workmen still moving about the stage. Their presence seemed to be all that held him back.

"Get out of my way!"

To her great relief, he slid just far enough to the side that she could get around him. Without looking back, she half ran down the darkened halls to where Kyle was waiting for her. Her brother's big frame and jovial round face had never looked so welcome.

"You're out of breath," he said, falling in step with her. "You didn't need to hurry. We've got plenty of time before the last ferry."

"I know. I just wanted to get out of this building. It's not the same place it was before Magda died."

* * *

Caty did not have to be back at the opera house for two days. She spent them relaxing at home on Staten Island, sitting for a fitting for the dresses her mother sewed for her, putting in her daily round of vocal practice, and riding her old mare, Sally, out beyond the cluster of houses in Rosebank to the dirt roads that meandered among the small farms and forested hills farther inland.

It was with great reluctance that she set out early on the morning of the third day to return to Manhattan, to the house that had once been such a happy place for her. The loss of that joy and delight was almost worse than the feeling of foreboding that dogged her steps all the way to 39th and Broadway.

She had just turned the corner to head toward the stage door when she heard someone calling her name. Looking up, she saw Josh Castleton dodging the traffic, hurrying toward her.

"I was just coming to look for you," he said, brushing the dust from a passing hansom off his coat sleeve.

"I'm not sure if I should be pleased or apprehensive," Caty answered, stepping back from the crowded street.

"Not apprehensive," Josh said, taking her elbow and moving away from the traffic. "I'm not here in my 'official' capacity this morning." He started leisurely down the sidewalk.

"I'm pleased to hear it. You know they're bringing in another soprano to sing Butterfly again next week?"

"Yes. In fact, I recommended we release the sets. Are you singing Suzuki?"

"No, unfortunately. Madam Cabrini was under contract and anxious to make up for having had to bow out the last time. So I shall just be another member of the chorus."

They had reached the low steps to the stage door when Josh stopped, obviously not anxious to go inside. Caty waited, wondering if she should take her leave of him.

"Look," he said abruptly. "I know this is short notice and terribly bad form, but will you go to a party with me tonight?"

It was the last thing she expected him to say. "A party?"

"Well, dinner, actually, with a little dancing afterward. It's come up on the spur of the moment and I had planned to make my apologies and then I thought that, well, there will be some people there whom you should meet. They might be helpful to you someday, in your career."

He cursed himself for making such a botch of this invitation. Not the way to do things at all, yet the idea of escorting her was too tempting to pass up. And it really *could* be helpful to her.

"Tonight? But . . ." She looked down at her serviceable morning suit. "I don't have anything to wear. If I had known I could have brought an evening dress but now . . ."

"Borrow one. From the costume department.

I've been through it, and they have more dresses than they can ever use. Surely one of them would fit you."

"But I don't have the proper jewelry."

"There must be some paste diamonds around backstage."

"I can't wear paste to a formal dinner!"

"Why not? Of course, they'll all recognize that they are paste, but then you are in the entertainment business and they'll expect them to be. Please say you'll come."

Caty's cheeks flared with color. "The entertainment business! The Metropolitan opera house is hardly a burlesque palace. These singers are artists. *I* am an artist!"

Josh silently cursed himself. "Of course you are. I apologize if I sounded as though I was suggesting anything else. I only mean that no one is going to fault you for not wearing a lot of rich jewelry. No one is even going to care. And I will be honored if you would accept."

Caty only hesitated a minute. This invitation sounded too good to pass up even if she had to go in her shirtwaist and skirt. To a singer trying to get ahead, *it will help your career*, were magic words. The thought of being escorted by the handsome Detective Castleton was an added incentive, though, now that she considered it, this might be just another attempt to trap her into revealing herself as a murderess.

But no, she would not worry about that. She did not get this kind of an invitation that often.

"All right," she said, giving him her best smile. "I'll ask Josie in wardrobe to help me get properly turned out. What time shall I meet you?"

Josh pulled out a very large round gold watch. "Let's see. The opera tonight is *Traviata,* isn't it? Not much for you to do after the third act. Could your transformation be complete by the time the curtain falls?"

"I think that can be arranged."

"Good. I'll meet you then, here by the stage door."

Just like a suitor, Caty thought warmly, then gave herself a good shake. "That sounds perfect, Detective," she said, tripping up the steps to the door.

Josh smiled up at her. "I think since we are going to be attending this together, you might at least call me Mister Castleton. Josh would be even better."

Caty pushed open the door. "I'll see you tonight, Mister Castleton."

She spent the latter half of the afternoon going through costumes with Josie, a short, round little Irishwoman who had the costume department since the house was opened in 1883. Josie thought it a great lark that Caty needed outfitting for a party, and she threw herself into fitting her out with as much delight as if she were the one going to the affair.

It was Josie who found the black satin evening

dress tucked far back in the racks of clothes designed for the ball scene of *Die Fledermaus*. It looked as though it had been worn only once or twice, and needed just a few tucks in the waspish waist to fit Caty like a glove. It had a low sweeping neckline, a slimming waist that flared out framing the hips, and a train that swept behind by nearly four feet. The skirt was ornamented with tiers of tiny black sequins and beads. They rummaged among the jewelry until they found a black jet-beaded choker, five inches wide that framed Caty's slim neck to perfection.

"I'd rather wear the jet beads than those fluppery rhinestones," Caty said, holding the choker up against her throat.

"I don't know, miss. Them rhinestones glitter right pretty from the stage."

"Yes, but up close, everyone will know what they are. Someday I'll have a real diamond necklace, but until then, I refuse to pretend. This will do fine."

Later, when she stood in front of the mirror in her dressing room and turned first to one side, then to the other, admiring her outfit, she was sure she had made the right choice. She swept her hair in rolls and waves that flared out like a turban, than fastened a long black feather that curled up the side and over the top and was held in place by a silver pin. The dress and the choker looked just right. Josie had even found her a long velvet cloak to match the dress. It was terribly dramatic, but that was all right. After all, she was a singer.

"You look smashing," Charlotte said from the doorway. "I'm glad I waited to see you."

Caty pirouetted around. "Do you really think I'll do?"

Charlotte fastened the pin in her hat. She'd been ready to leave for home half an hour before, but was determined to see Caty off. "You'll be the envy of every woman there. I don't know how you manage to keep such a small waist."

"Don't tell anyone but it's the corset. I can barely breathe." She pulled up the sweeping décolletage of her dress. "It's not too revealing, is it?"

"Of course not. We women might have to wear out shirtwaists up around our noses during the day but in the evening we're supposed to show a lot of bosom. Yours ought to drive thoughts of detecting right out of that policeman's mind."

"That's not why I'm going," Caty said with a frown. "He told me I would meet some people who could help my career and that is all that matters."

"Oh, and the handsome detective has nothing to do with it?" Charlotte said, smiling at her. "Where is this party, anyway?"

"I don't know. He didn't say."

"Probably Delmonico's or the Waldorf-Astoria. That's where they usually have these things, I'm told."

"Oh, dear. Are you sure I'll look all right?"

"You look fine. Really fine," she said, pulling on her coat. "Enjoy yourself. I want to hear all about it tomorrow." She paused beside the door. "What did Kyle say about leaving you in the hands of the handsome Detective Castleton?"

"He didn't like it much but I talked him into it. He's probably halfway home by now."

"Good. See you tomorrow, then."

As the door closed behind her friend, Caty found herself wishing Charlotte was going to this party, too. It would give her moral support. She gave herself one last glance in the mirror, then picked up her cloak. There was nothing left to do but go out and wait for Josh Castleton.

He was there already, waiting for her near the stage door, with several other younger men in formal attire, some of them holding bouquets, all of them with expectant smiles on their faces. Josh presented her with a single perfect rose, and told her how nice she looked as he wrapped her cloak around her shoulders. They stepped outside into a coolish wind off the river that threatened to pluck the feather from her hair before she could be ushered inside a waiting coach. It was cozy and warm inside with a pleasant smell of leather. Josh crawled in beside her, thumped the roof with his cane, and they rolled away.

Their conversation was a little awkward at first, until Josh raised the subject of the evening's opera, particularly the French soprano who had sung Violetta.

"She has a spectacular voice, but she's a little heavy for a woman who is dying of consumption," Josh stated.

"They've been saying things like that about this opera since the first time it was performed. It's the singing that matters in opera. The music, the voice! Everything else is secondary," Caty said.

"Oh, I disagree. Opera is a unique blend of music and drama and both are needed if the audience is going to suspend reality and become lost in the performance. After all, singing speech is not really a natural thing."

"Are you saying the drama is all that matters?"

"Of course not. I'm saying both are needed. If my heart is going to bleed for Violetta, my eyes must at least see a woman who looks like she is wasting away. This Violetta looked as though she could push the scenery around by herself."

Caty suppressed a laugh. "But the music tells the tragedy so beautifully that it doesn't matter how she looks. Besides, opera singers must have the breath and power to be heard above the orchestra. I doubt that a singer who actually had consumption could be heard by the prompter."

"I didn't mean that she should actually have consumption . . . oh, here we are."

Josh was rather glad that their arrival had interrupted the conversation before it went any further. He had been tempted to point out that Caty, with her tiny waist and glorious voice, was a living refutation of her own argument, but it was just as well he hadn't. She would probably have taken it in the wrong way, as she seemed to do everything he said.

He spoke to the driver, then turned back to

where Caty stood on the sidewalk staring up at the huge pile of yellow stone that loomed in front of them. "This is a house . . ." she murmured.

"Yes, didn't I mention it? It's a private party."

Caty looked up the wide street. It had to be Fifth Avenue. Though she had never been inside any of the mansions that lined the road, she had driven down the street enough times to recognize them. "But this is the Vanderbilt home, isn't it?" she said, still rooted to the sidewalk.

Josh put his hand under her elbow and steered her toward a large double doorway. "It's Mister and Mrs. Fields' mansion, actually. She's a Vanderbilt and her parents live just next door. The houses are sometimes called 'the twins', though inside they're quite different."

He certainly seemed right at home, she thought, as she followed him up a low tier of marble stairs that led to the actual door of the house. It stood open, a footman waiting to welcome them, silhouetted against a blaze of lights beyond. The entranceway was huge and all of marble. At the end of the long hall Caty could see a large group of people moving leisurely through open double doors into a room beyond. Josh slipped Caty's arm through his and made his way sedately toward them, smiling and speaking briefly to the other guests, most of whom seemed to know him.

"We're right on time," he leaned over to whisper into Caty's ear. "They're just going in to supper."

The dining room was very large, probably the width of the entire house, Caty mused. It had dark curtains, towering stained-glass windows and a long oblong table burdened with massive candelabra, huge mounds of flowers in silver bowls, gold-rimmed dishes and silvery cutlery. The gas jets along the wall and the hundred candles on the long table lit up the room like day.

Yet even that light paled beside the glitter of the jewelry worn by the women present. Caty had to force the astonishment she felt from her face, and tear her eyes from the endless array of diamond necklaces, chokers, earrings, brooches, pendants and rings, the ropes of gleaming pearls, and the bright glint of sapphires, rubies and gold. She felt as though she had walked into Aladdin's treasure cave and she was very thankful she had settled for jet beads in place of rhinestones.

She was suddenly conscious of Josh's hand on her arm and his warm breath as he leaned close to her cheek.

"Not too overwhelming, is it?" he asked lightly.

She gave him a brilliant smile. "On the contrary. I think I'm going to enjoy this very much."

Six

Caty found herself concentrating on the guests so completely that she barely tasted the food. She vaguely realized it was delicious, and the service was exceptional; a server filled her glass after every sip, and silverware no more than touched the plate before the formally attired waiter behind her chair removed it. But her real interest focused on the people around her, their conversation, their gorgeous clothes, and eye-popping jewelry, and the way they casually took for granted all the opulence which surrounded them.

The table was too wide and too cluttered to allow for conversation with the people across from her, so she concentrated on those on either side. The young man on her left introduced himself as Charles Poore, an incongruous name if she had ever heard one. He had come with the young lady who was sitting on his left, but most of his conversation was directed to Caty. Handsome in a studied kind of way, tall, not very broad, a little stooped, he wore a pencil-thin mustache that was perfectly shaped and clipped, and long, fashionable sideburns.

Caty was taken aback for a moment when she realized the elderly gentleman on her right served on the board of the Metropolitan, until he so charmed her with his pleasant manner and interesting anecdotes about the first twenty years of the opera house that she soon ceased to be overawed. She had almost forgotten about Josh, who sat two places down, until she finished the meal and he appeared at her elbow to escort her up the wide marble stairs to the ballroom above.

"You seem to be enjoying yourself," he whispered, as they made their way up the stairs. "I feared all this might be a little overwhelming but I see I should not have worried."

"It is overwhelming, but I find I like it. Mister Belmont was delightful and I even enjoyed flirting with Mister Poore."

"Humph. Watch out for that fellow. He's a 'Stage-Door Johnny' if ever there was one."

"I'll remember."

The ballroom turned out to be another revelation—a yawning expanse of marble with a dais at one end for an orchestra, and huge urns filled with massed flowers along the walls between tall floor-length windows. Opposite them gilt chairs were spaced at intervals between the urns. Caty headed for one of the chairs but the music started up and Josh took her hand to lead her onto the floor.

"You do waltz?" he asked, smiling mischievously.

"Of course." No need to tell him she didn't waltz very well—he'd find out soon enough.

Josh Castleton turned out to be such a good partner that she appeared to dance far better than she actually did, and she soon began to relax and enjoy the music. To her surprise, she found herself enjoying even more the feel of his arm around her waist and the strong grasp of his hand holding hers. He was so close to her that she found herself concentrating on tantalizing things about him—the smooth darkness of his cheeks, the firm line of his brows above those captivating gray eyes, so alive with mischief, the curve of his upper lip when he smiled, the breadth of his shoulders . . .

This would never do! Caty mentally shook off the delicious warmth swelling through her body. Then the music came to a stop and they paused near a window to catch their breath.

Caty opened her fan and smiled up at him over it. "You know, you really amaze me, Detective."

"Oh? Why is that?"

"You're an expert dancer, you know all these fashionable people, and you seem right at home around all this wealth. That's not exactly what I would expect of a New York City policeman."

"We're not all of us just off the boat from Ireland, you know."

Her chin went up. "I don't take kindly to remarks about the Irish."

Josh laughed. "I meant no offense. You know most of the policemen on the force are Irish. Besides, aren't you trying to be more Italian than Irish? For professional reasons?"

"I might have to take an Italian stage name but I shall never renounce my good Irish background," she answered testily. Not until he took her arm to lead her toward a small group of people nearby did she realize he had turned her question from himself without really answering it. Before she could say so he interrupted her thoughts.

"Miss McGowan, I'd like you to meet Mister and Mrs. DeLancey Schyler and their aunt, Miss Matilda DeLancey. Caty McGowan, also known as 'Catherina Mandesi', of the Met."

Mrs. Schyler lifted a gloved hand circled with a glittering diamond bracelet. "I'm so pleased to meet you, my dear."

Caty took her hand and gave the politely proper response. Mrs. Schyler was a stunning woman. Though nearing fifty she had the classic features that must have made her a beauty in her youth. Her dress of shimmering pale green silk fell around her chair like the waves of the sea. Her husband, portly and dignified with a thick white mustache, bowed formally to Caty, then kissed her hand. Behind him, the aunt, an elderly lady in a midnight blue velvet dress and a wide choker of gleaming pearls, murmured a shy hello.

Josh turned to Caty. "Mrs. Schyler is one of the people I wanted you to meet."

Caty caught back her surprise. She had assumed Mister Belmont was the person at this party who could assist her career. Before she could find an answer Frances Schyler broke in.

"I heard you sing Suzuki at that ill-fated performance of *Madama Butterfly* and I wanted you to know that I believe you have a great future. You have a beautiful voice, my dear, and a good stage presence. I think you'll go far."

Caty beamed, her creamy cheeks deepening with pleasure. "How kind of you. Thank you so much."

"Come and sit here beside me and tell me about yourself," Mrs. Schyler said, patting the empty chair next to her. "I told Josh that evening that I wanted to get to know you better. So many of our young singers come from Europe that I feel it is extremely important to nurture American talent when we find it. You've heard of Geraldine Farrar, of course?"

Caty took her seat and arranged her skirts. "Oh, yes. A beautiful woman and a fine artist."

"Her career is just beginning and I am sure it is going to be a spectacular one. I have followed it closely since I first heard her sing. Tell me, with whom do you study?"

The next hour flew quickly by as Frances Schyler encouraged Caty to reveal more of her private life and past experiences than she had ever expected to in such company. Easy to talk to, the society matron drew information from Caty with a deft hand. Josh quietly left them for a while to take part in two other dances and by the time he returned to draw Caty away, she felt almost reluctant to leave. Not until later, when they were seated in the coach for the long drive to the Battery, did she realize she had been talking to one of the patrons of the opera as though she was an old friend.

"I can't believe it," she said, still enjoying the fairy-tale quality of it all. "She's so . . . so nice. Just like a real person."

"She is a real person. What else would she be?"

"You know what I mean. She's rich and she has all that power, yet she's so friendly."

Josh shook his head. "You have an exaggerated idea of wealth. Those people are no different from anyone else except that they have more money."

"A *lot* more money! And more breeding."

"Not necessarily. Though I concede Frances Schyler has both dignity and good breeding and little of the artifice that sometimes comes with wealth. In that, she is remarkable."

Caty settled back against the seat. "I liked her. Wait until I tell Mama that I had supper with Mister Belmont and Mrs. Schyler. She'll burst, she'll be so proud."

Her head was still so filled with the glitter of the party that she did not realize until they reached the ferry terminal that Josh intended to see her across the bay. The lateness of the hour meant there were only a few people about. They caught one of the first ferries of the day and watched the first faint rays of dawn break across the water as they crossed. A hansom carried them to the big farmhouse in Rosebank, where Josh stopped beside the door.

"It's nearly morning. Do you have to go back to the opera house today?"

"Yes. But not until this afternoon. I don't mind. It was worth it."

He smiled down at her. "I'm glad you enjoyed it."

There was an awkward silence. Caty knew she should go inside, yet she also felt she should somehow show her gratitude for an exceptional evening. "What about you? Are you . . . on duty?"

"Later." He looked down at her, admiring the way the soft light accentuated her features, the curve of her lashes on her cheeks, the slightly sleepy look in her eyes. "Thank you for going with me," he said, taking her hand and lifting it briefly to his lips.

Caty felt a slight shiver course through her body at his touch. "Thank you for taking me."

"Good night, then. Or rather, good morning."

"Good morning."

She smiled and slipped inside the door, leaning against it. The house was very quiet, though from the barn, she could hear her mother's cow announcing it was time to be milked. Her mother would be down soon.

"Good morning, Detective Castleton," she said, smiling to herself.

Josh Castleton stepped out of the doorway of his apartment house and looked up at the clear, brightly washed sky over Central Park. It had rained during the night, giving a numbing chill to the November air. Yet the city sparkled as cleanly as if it had been laundered. All colors appeared deeper and richer—the dun stones of the apartment house, the lingering green of the trees across the avenue, the bronze shine of the horse's coats, and the glimmering sheen of black leather of the hansom cabs. He took a deep breath of cold air, felt it all the way down, and decided impulsively to walk to the station.

It took an hour and by the time he reached the ugly, stone building with the huge arched windows along the front, the city did not seem so clean or inviting. His long overcoat had been splattered with mud, twice from speeding cabs and once from a passing Pierce Arrow that had to be traveling at the unlawful speed of eleven miles an hour. He had noted its color and make and intended to file a complaint. Big, shiny, custom-made automobiles were still a rarity in the city so it should not be too difficult to trace its owner.

He had no more than entered the dark foyer than he was stopped by one of the policemen on his way out. Josh recognized him—Patty Mahoney, all decked out in his heavy blue overcoat with the brass buttons polished to so high a gloss Josh could see his reflection in them.

"Captain's asking for you," Mahoney said, as he adjusted his hard helmet on his balding head.

"Oh?"

"Aye. He passed the word you should go up the minute you arrived."

"Thanks, Mahoney. I'll see him right away."

"Don't mention it, Inspector," the policeman

said, touching his helmet. He went out the door smiling with satisfaction over being the first one to tell Josh his superior was calling him on the carpet.

Josh took his time reaching the captain's office, stopping to remove his coat and hat, check his desk and pick up a cup of hot coffee from a table in the hall. He knocked briefly on the closed door, waited for the muffled "enter," then pushed it open.

Captain Neil Sheldon glanced up from a stack of papers on his desk. He was in his shirtsleeves and vest, the arms caught tight in black bands just above the elbow. He had a face shaped somewhat like a triangle with the wide end near his chin, made all the broader by two bulging walrus mustaches and a wide underlip that turned down in a pink crescent beneath them. On first impression one might think he had a benign look but Josh, who knew him better, was keenly aware of how deceived one would be.

"You wanted to see me?"

"Yes. Come in." Sheldon went on rummaging through the papers, appearing to be searching for something but Josh knew it was a ruse to kill a little time for effect. He settled in a chair opposite the chief, crossed his legs and sipped his coffee as though he had all the time in the world.

Sheldon, like most of the men who ran the police department, and unlike most of the cops on the beat, was not Irish. Though he knew Josh Castleton was an excellent policeman, he felt certain he had got where he was more through knowing the right people than through working his way up. As chief, he was accustomed to having people enter his office in a trembling, uncertain state, and it never failed to rile him that Josh was so casual and complacent.

He pushed the papers aside, lowered his chin and looked up at Josh from under hooded lids. "I want to know how this thing is going at the opera house."

Josh took another sip of his coffee. Two could play this game. "About as well as expected, which is to say, not very well at all. It's an unusual case."

"Nonsense. A woman is stabbed with a knife, either she did it or somebody else did it. Make up your mind which and find out who it was. What's so complicated about that?"

"If someone else did it, it's difficult to see how. If she did it herself, it's almost impossible to understand why."

"There must be some suspects. Who are they? How many have you eliminated? Who is the prime one now?"

"There are almost too many suspects. Magda Dubratta was an egotistical, unpleasant person and it seems that a number of people she stepped on just happened to be at the opera house that evening. A stagehand she threatened to fire; a general manager who had a long feud with her, stretching back to an incident in Europe; not one, but two ex-husbands, one of whom she ignored for years."

"And that singer—what about her?"

Josh carefully laid down his cup. The chief had already read through the reports and he knew all this. Why go through this empty ritual? "You mean the woman who sang second lead that evening. It was her debut and Magda systematically tried to shove her into the background, even threatened to prevent her from ever again singing another role if she got in her way."

"That sounds like enough motive to me."

"Come now, chief. I simply can't see this woman committing murder to save her career. She's not the type."

"There's a type? You know better than that, Castleton. Look, I know you've been seeing this woman. I know about the lunches and the party at the Field mansion and I think you're letting your personal feelings get in the way of your judgment. She was seen handling the knife just before the murder, wasn't she?"

Josh pursed his lips to keep from asking why, if the chief knew all this, he had to go through it again. Sheldon seemed to read his mind.

"You've got to get on with this, Castleton," he said, leaning back in his chair. "It's taking too much time. The nabobs at the Met want it finished and over with, the curtain rung down. They want to put it behind them before the house gets a reputation. You, of all people, ought to know that."

Josh recognized a veiled reference to his background. "I do know it, and I'm trying to discover some answers. But I don't intend to accuse anyone until I have reasonable proof. That would be disastrous."

"Then say so to some of your high-uppity-up friends over there on Thirty-ninth street." He leaned over the desk, his massive jaw thrust forward in a bulldog stance. "I'm getting pressure from above, Castleton. I don't like it. This thing is in your hands and I expect you to find a solution. Do I make myself clear?"

Josh deliberately paused before answering. "You do indeed."

"Then finish it. And don't let that red hair and those big, green eyes put you off the scent. If that singer is responsible for murder, I want her charged. Remember that!"

For the first time Josh felt a real twinge of anger. "I think you know that I would charge anyone I had reason to think actually murdered Magda Dubratta, whether or not I knew them socially."

Sheldon waved a thick hand. "Oh, I'm sure you would. But you might overlook something if you are too busy staring at that lady's impressive figure. It might be better to stay away from her until this thing is solved."

Josh stood up to leave, determined not to let Sheldon see he had got to him. "I shall be circumspect. You can depend on that."

"You had better be."

Josh closed the door and took a moment to get hold of himself. Sheldon had a knack for finding his Achilles' heel and locking his big teeth on it. It was probably that talent that brought him this far in the department. Yet he seldom managed to get under Josh's skin and it bothered him that he had done so this morning. He made his way back to his cubicle, deep in thought.

It was because he cared about Caty McGowan that Sheldon had got to him. That was an inescapable fact and a very unwise situation. Perhaps it really had been a mistake to get to know her better. And yet . . .

He simply could not believe she had anything to do with Magda's murder. She was too honest, too decent. Or, at least she seemed to be. He stood at the clouded, dingy window looking down at the street where the traffic appeared to be moving sluggishly through a fog. He smiled as he remembered how Caty had handled herself at that dinner at the Field mansion. The elegant simplicity of her black dress and jet beads were such a striking contrast to the overblown opulence and studied display of wealth shown by most of the guests. It could have seemed a pitiful contrast of the poor versus the rich except that she had carried if off with such flair and assurance that she might have been one of the Astors effecting simplicity. If she was the least bit awed by that crowd, no one would have known it, and he admired her for that.

He more than admired her. He wanted her. He wanted to unpin that thick hair and let it cascade around her face, then lay his palms on either cheek and draw the sweetness of those luscious lips to his. He wanted to slowly, carefully, remove all those confining female garments until she stood naked before him, revealing all the long graceful beauty of her body. He wanted to span his hands around that slim waist and lift one of those round, enticing breasts to his lips. . . .

Josh shook himself to ward off the rising warmth in his lower regions. "This is crazy," he muttered and moved back to his desk. Even though he could not believe that Caty McGowan was involved in Magda's death, the chief had a point. He was in danger of losing his objectivity and that would never do. Perhaps it would be just as well to stay away from her for the time being.

As the time drew closer for the next performance of *Madama Butterfly,* Caty began to feel increasingly filled with an unreasoning anxiety. She told herself she was being silly. Magda's death had been a single event, unlikely ever to be repeated. Nothing could be more ridiculous than to let that one dark experience ruin a gloriously beautiful opera.

All the same, she felt relieved not to be singing Suzuki again. As a member of the chorus she was only onstage during the first act, and singing offstage in the second. She might even be able to leave for her house in Staten Island before the third act ended.

Yet she knew she wouldn't. Then she discovered that some of the other singers felt the same nagging sense of dread.

"I don't know why they didn't take it permanently off the roster," Charlotte complained as they were having lunch two days before the performance. "It's unlucky, that's what it is."

"Nonsense. It's a beautiful opera and it's only been in production a little over a year. It would be a terrible loss to remove it because of one bad experience."

"Well, all I know is I wouldn't want to be singing Butterfly. I think Madam Ferinzi has a lot of courage."

Caty pushed her fork around her plate wishing she had more appetite. "She has a wonderful voice and she'll make it a great success. She's also sung it several times before in Italy."

"She'd better check that knife before the third act."

"Oh, Charlotte. You know the police will do that. I've heard they're going to be all over the place, though I don't know what good it will do. They haven't even been able to find out what happened the first time."

Charlotte looked up as she caught an edge in Caty's voice. "Speaking of the police, whatever happened to that handsome detective Castleton who seemed to take such an interest in you?"

Caty shrugged and looked away. "I suppose he's busy detecting."

"Hasn't he invited you to any more fancy parties? Taken you in for questioning? Forced you to have lunch with him again?"

Caty carefully made her voice sound casual.

"You know he hasn't. Perhaps he no longer considers me a suspect."

"Oh, come on! Would he have invited you to dinner at the Vanderbilt mansion if he thought you had committed a murder?"

"I wouldn't put it past him. It might have been his way of observing me, or trying to see if I would say something that might reveal my guilt. That's what policemen do, isn't it?"

Charlotte smiled. "They don't usually go to quite such lengths." The tightness in Caty's jaw told her that it might be better to drop the subject of Detective Castleton. For Caty he was obviously an unpleasant memory.

Caty herself, thinking back about the conversation later, hoped she hadn't let her irritation with Josh Castleton be too obvious. That lovely evening at the Field mansion began to seem more and more like Cinderella's ball, and now she was back at the hearth wondering if it had really happened or if she had dreamed it. She had expected that night to be a door opening on all kinds of new possibilities. Instead she had only been granted a single glimpse of light before the door closed. Since that evening she rarely saw Josh Castleton, and on two of those occasions he had been so formally polite and distant, she wondered if she had offended him in some way she was not aware of. She had not had a glimpse of Mrs. Schyler or any of the other patrons whom she met at the party, though she knew they had attended the opera several times since then. Her hopes of receiving their encouragement for her career grew dimmer every day.

More and more she began to be convinced that Josh took her to that party to try to trap her in some way. He was so cold toward her now that there did not seem to be any other explanation.

There was an extra edge to the excitement backstage two days later as last-minute preparations for *Butterfly* were put into place. Caty took her time getting dressed, not really anxious to make her way backstage. Her flowered kimona and black wig got so much careful attention that finally Charlotte had to come back and drag her out of the dressing room.

It was a madhouse backstage. The chorus member in their bright costumes merged with the technicians, directors, and stagehands, all trying to put final touches to the scene outside Cio-Cio-San's house. In front of the great gold curtain the squawking of the instruments tuning up mingled with the sounds of the singers doing scales backstage as they warmed up their voices. Caty pushed her way though a knot of chorus members in the wings so she could peer at the set, and ran straight into Josh Castleton.

"Good evening," Josh said, taking a quick step backward and trying to mask the pleasure he felt at seeing her again.

Caty saw only that he moved away from her as she gave him a tight smile and a murmured, "Hello." He was wearing street clothes tonight and she could not help recalling that first time he came backstage decked out in full white tie regalia. "Are you watching from the wings tonight?"

"No. Just thought I'd be on hand. Not that I expect anything to happen." He recognized right away that the distance he had put between them had hurt her, but then what did he expect? It would be useless to explain that his work required it, that he did not really want it this way.

Her usually expressive face might have been carved from stone. "I promise you I won't touch Butterfly's knife, if that makes your job any easier."

She turned on her heel, switching the train of her kimona behind her. Josh watched her disappear into the chorus, feeling more disturbed than he wanted, both at seeing her again and at knowing he had hurt her. He turned his back to look out at the set. It could not be helped.

By the time Caty took her place among the women waiting for their entrance she had forced herself to be more calm. After all, there were more important things to be concerned about right now. The magic world of the opera was beginning to unfold.

The chorus did not appear until well into the first act. Caty watched without envy as Madam Cabrini slipped into position to make her entrance as Suzuki. Tonight she was just grateful to be a member of the chorus. If anything did happen—and of course, it would not—it couldn't possibly involve her.

The music carried the drama forward to the moment when Butterfly first appears, accompanied by her friends, for her marriage to the American naval officer, B.F. Pinkerton. Most of the men of the company were already on stage watching the Japanese heroine as she made her way over a small curving bridge to one side of the Japanese paper house, followed by the ladies of the chorus—all to some of the most divine music in opera. The beauty of the sets, the glorious music, and the special beauty of Butterfly's ringing soprano gave Caty a lift of her heart as she joined the procession making its way onstage. Among the first singers to follow Butterfly over the bridge, she walked with the mincing steps of a Japanese woman, her paper umbrella balanced on her shoulder. Singing her heart out, totally engrossed in the music, she had just stepped onto the stage itself when there was a loud, tearing crash behind her.

Her mouth opened but no sound came out. She turned quickly, just in time to see the bridge waver and collapse inward, carrying the women who were still strewn across it downward in a falling tangle of debris. The harmonic sounds became a cacophony of screams, shrill, and dissonant. Caty stared, frozen in place with horror, as the women in the chorus collapsed among the broken timbers of the bridge. She caught a brief glimpse of Charlotte's white face before she disappeared beneath the bodies of two other women. Only then did she realize the loudest of the screams came from her own throat.

Seven

She stood frozen with shock while noise and confusion erupted around her. Dimly she became aware that the orchestra had stopped playing and someone was shouting from the wings to lower the great gold curtain. Then she felt a firm hand on her shoulder and turned her head.

"Are you all right?" Josh asked.

She nodded her head briefly. "Yes."

He went past her toward the collapsed bridge. Huge sections of wood lay tangled among the gaily colored costumes of the women who were struggling to climb out of the debris. Several had already got to their feet while two or three others remained on the floor of the stage, moaning and crying. A rush of people—stagehands, the stage director, the principal singers—swarmed around the mangled bridge. Caty shook off her numbing shock and ran to push her way through them, trying to reach Josh.

"Charlotte . . . my friend. She was still standing on it . . ." she cried, trying to see over the heads of the people bending over the broken bridge.

"I think she's hurt," Josh called back. "Is there a doctor anywhere?"

Caty heard Gregory Stillman's frantic voice behind her. When she saw him hurrying in from the wings she grabbed at his arm.

"We need a doctor. Can you ask out front if there's one here?"

Gregory glanced at the pile of debris at the back of the stage, then reluctantly turned back to the wings. "I'll take care of it," he said and disappeared.

Caty wanted to run away from the stage as fast as her legs would take her, but first she had to know if Charlotte was all right. It was beginning to be obvious that while most of the singers had got back on their feet, there were still several who were half buried beneath the debris and several of them appeared injured. She forced herself back to the bridge area and stood to the side, waiting.

Stillman reappeared with not one, but two men who had the no-nonsense air of the medical profession. They were ushered close in to the knot of people around the broken bridge, where they knelt beside the victims. When Caty was certain no one was seriously hurt, she left the stage to walk into the wings. No one seemed to be taking charge and though she doubted that the performance would continue, still she hesitated to return to the dressing room until she knew for sure. She found a darkened corner where a barrel sat upended and headed for it. Her knees began to tremble so strongly she knew she would fall if she did not sit down.

She sank on to the barrel, thankful for a perch of any kind. Only then did she spot Boris Borinsky standing behind her, nearly indistinct in the shadows and staring at the activity on the stage.

Caty gave a quick gasp of surprise, then said angrily, "Why aren't you out there? They need help."

His dark eyes flickered briefly on her face. "Nothin' I can do. They got plenty of people workin' there."

"Well, they need more. People are injured."

The features on his dark face might have been carved in stone, they were so impassive. "Not you, though," he said, his tiny eyes boring into her. "You didn't get hurt."

"By the grace of God. I had just stepped off the thing."

His big shoulders sagged in what she supposed was a shrug. "Ain't you the lucky one."

"Go on. Get out there where you're needed," she snapped. For a minute she thought he was going to ignore her, then he moved slowly away, carefully circumventing her perch, and out on to the stage.

"Creepy man," she muttered. "It wouldn't surprise me if he was responsible for this."

She did not know how long she sat there, staring at the stage as the crowd milled around the scene of the accident, like some stark tableau. The doctors had not been there five minutes before men arrived from the nearest hospital, bearing stretchers. Not until Caty recognized the skirt of Charlotte's kimona trailing from one of them did she return to the stage again. She bent over her friend, taking her hand.

"Oh, Charlotte," she said, stricken at her friend's white face. "Are you badly hurt?"

Charlotte gave her a thin smile. "It's my leg. They think it's broken. It hurts something fierce. But . . . the voice is all right. That's all that matters."

Caty squeezed her hand. "It should have been me . . ."

The stretcher bearers pushed on, bearing Charlotte off the stage and, presumably, to the waiting ambulance wagon. Three other singers followed in quick succession while Caty stood watching numb with shock.

It should have been me. Why had she said that? Why shouldn't she consider herself fortunate that she had stepped off the bridge just in time to avoid its collapse? Instead she was consumed with a senseless guilt, as though it was somehow her fault. She had not been involved in Magda's death—why should anyone think she was involved in this?

Because he suspected you of the other. He'll suspect you of this, too.

Caty gave herself a shake, trying to rid her mind of these foolish ideas. God knows it was a terrible thing to have happened. She wondered if the house would ever want to put on *Madama Butterfly* again. But it had nothing to do with her.

"Perhaps you had better return to your dressing room," a voice said at her shoulder. She looked up into Josh Castleton's worried face, half expecting him to point a finger at her. Instead she saw only concern in his cloudy gray eyes.

"The opera . . ."

"Madam Ferinzi is too shaken to go on, so they've decided not to continue. You can go on home if you want."

He laid a hand lightly on her shoulder, giving her a gentle push toward the wings.

Caty did not move. "What happened? Why did that bridge collapse?"

"We're not certain yet, but it appears to be an accident. We won't be sure until we can clear it away and look more closely. You're very pale. I really think you should leave this place now."

"But, won't you want to ask questions? Talk to everyone?"

Josh smiled. "This is not another murder, Miss McGowan. If we need to get information we'll interview all of you who observed the accident in the morning. Meantime, get some rest. You look as though you need it."

He laid his arm around her shoulder and led her to the wings. This time she moved, though reluctantly. Josh was glad to see her go. Something in her eyes worried him, as though she was waiting for another dreaded axe to fall. He watched for a moment as Caty made her way down the stairs to the long hall, then went back to look closer at the pile of mangled wood that had been the bridge to Butterfly's house. He knelt there, inspecting one of the wooden frames, then glanced up at the stagehands who were pulling away the large pieces on the edge. One of them raised a section of the frame and started off the stage with it.

"Hold on," Josh cried. "Don't remove any of this debris."

The man turned and he recognized the stagehand, Boris, who had nearly been fired by Magda Dubratta.

"It's trash," the man muttered, still holding the section of the wood.

Josh stood. "No, it isn't. We'll need to examine every part of this thing to figure out what made it collapse. Just lay all the pieces out on the front of the stage."

One of the other hands moved to take the piece out of Boris's hands. "He told you to put it over there, you numbskull. Don't you ever listen to nobody? Do what the copper says."

Boris gripped the frame tighter, glaring at the stagehand and Josh. Reluctantly he let it go. "Waste of time," he muttered and turned away, thrusting his hands in his pockets and stalking off the stage.

"Hey! Come on and give us a hand here," the other workman called. Boris turned to glare at him again, then stalked back toward the ruined bridge and grabbed up one of the larger, crescent-shaped sections, lifting it as easily as if it were made of paste.

With his surly attitude, Josh wondered why the management kept him on. Boris certainly had the brawn needed to move these large sets around but his sullen and uncooperative attitude made it surprising he hadn't been fired long before Magda came on the scene. He would bear watching, Josh thought. He also wondered if there had been anything in Boris's hands when he shoved them into his pockets. If there was anything missing here, he would know where to look for it first.

The opera house remained closed for two days and Caty was grateful for the breathing space those days gave her. She went into Manhattan early on both mornings for her singing lessons but returned on the ferry immediately afterward to spend the rest of the day relaxing at home. She studied scores, practiced her exercises, worked on memorizing the chorus sections of a new opera, and took time to read, to ride her gentle, elderly mare, and to walk to the few stores that lined the main road half a mile away from her mother's house.

By the second day, she was beginning to put the unpleasantness of the accident behind her. She convinced herself it had nothing to do with her and she was being foolish to worry that it had.

And then Josh Castleton appeared on her doorstep.

She had been helping her mother in the kitchen when the bell at the front door rang. Though her mother employed a woman to assist with the chores, she was not what would be considered a house maid and Caty laid down her peeling knife at once to answer the bell. When she opened the door and recognized the tall policeman standing there, she gaped in astonishment.

"Good afternoon, Miss McGowan," Josh said, removing his hat. "I hope I'm not inconveniencing you by dropping in like this."

Caty glanced down self-consciously at the apron covering most of her skirt. Her sleeves were folded halfway up her arms and her hair was caught loosely in a chenille net. She felt as though she looked like a milkmaid.

"Mister Castleton! I . . . how . . ."

Josh turned the felt brim of his hat in his hands. "You'll remember I brought you home once, the night after the party. I knew where you lived and I needed to ask you a few questions about the accident, so I just took the ferry and came over. I hope it's not a bad time?"

"Why, no . . . no. Come in, please."

She hoped her voice did not betray her dismay. With a brisk, "Thank you," Josh stepped inside the sunny hallway of the old house just as Mrs. McGowan came in from the other end, wiping her hands on a towel.

"Who is it, Caty? Oh, my goodness . . ."

"Mama, this is Detective Castleton. You remember I told you about him. He's looking into the trouble at the opera house."

Sian McGowan's pink face broke into a wreath of smiles. "Why, yes. I do remember. You're the gentleman who invited my girl to that fine party. How do you do, Detective."

Josh took her hand and bent over it. "Very well, thank you, Mrs. McGowan. You've a lovely little farm here. I was much impressed as I drove up."

"Why, thank you. It was much finer when Caty's father lived but since he passed on, well, my son and I do our best. We're small compared to most of the farms on the Island. Just do enough to sustain ourselves with a little left over for . . ."

"Mama, Detective Castleton wants to talk to me about the accident. Why don't we just sit in the parlor, Mister Castleton? I'll only be a moment, Mama."

Sian was having none of her daughter's formality. She had decided on an instant that this tall, striking man was not going to be fobbed off so easily. "Nonsense. I think perhaps Mister Castleton might like to see the place, small as it is. Would you, Mister Castleton? I'll be happy to show you around."

Caty broke in hurriedly. "I'm sure the detective is too busy . . ."

"I'd love to, Mrs. McGowan," Josh exclaimed. "Would you believe I've worked in Manhattan all these years and only been across the bay to Staten Island three times in my entire life. I'd love to see more of it."

"Wonderful. Come along, I'll show you the barns. Caty, you can come if you want, or you can finish those vegetables if you'd rather."

Caty watched speechless as her mother drew Josh Castleton's arm through hers and led him down the hall toward the kitchen and the rear door. He turned just long enough to throw her a mischievous wink and meekly followed, leaving her staring behind them.

"I think I'll finish the vegetables," Caty called after them, but they were too busy talking to hear her.

They were gone over half an hour. Caty had long since finished peeling the carrots and potatoes but she refused to go searching for her mother and her guest. Instead, she brewed up some tea, then sat at the kitchen table, stewing about the whole situation until she heard her mother's laughter as she approached the house. When they came through the door, they both seemed in such good humor that it irritated her more.

"You have a delightful place here, Miss McGowan," Josh said, stomping the muddy leaves off his shoes as he entered the kitchen. "And your mother has a wealth of good Irish stories. She's kept me laughing the whole time."

"How nice," Caty said in clipped tones.

"Oh, you've made the tea," Sian exclaimed. "Lovely. You must have a cup, Mister Castleton, after that brisk air. Just you sit here at the table."

"Mama, you can't serve Detective Castleton in the kitchen," Caty said in a loud whisper. "Please go into the parlor, Mister Castleton, and I'll bring the tea,"

"I have a better idea. I really did come here to talk to you, Miss McGowan, and before I remove this heavy coat, I'd rather go back outside and try one of those paths that overlook the bay. Your mother told me they are one of your favorite walks. Will you join me?"

"But . . ."

"Oh, go on, Caty," Sian spoke up. "I'll get your cloak with the hood. It's a bit brisk out."

She returned with the cloak before Caty could think of a reason to object. Josh took it and draped it around her shoulders, then held the door for her. Caty yanked the hood over her hair and stalked out of the kitchen, her manner as cool as the outside air.

Neither action seemed to affect Josh's good humor. He followed her along the path that narrowed between rows of deciduous trees, skeletonlike now in the November afternoon, interspersed with tall, thin pines still flaunting their greenery. They walked over a path thick with old leaves that crackled underfoot, littered with huge rocks and winding up toward the higher ground. Once on the ridge, the vista opened up, revealing a wide expanse of water dotted by sails and reflecting a cloudless sky as blue and gleaming as a lapis brooch.

"How lovely," Josh exclaimed. "No wonder you like to walk here."

Caty pulled her cloak tight around her. "I sometimes sit on that boulder there in good weather. It's too cold for that now."

Josh stepped up beside her and took her arm. "You're right. We'd best keep moving. Besides, duty compels me to ask you about that incident the other night."

Caty threw him a searing glance. "What did I see? Where was I standing? Why wasn't I hurt? Listen Inspector, I had just stepped off the bridge before it fell. I don't know why it didn't collapse while I was still on it. I was busy concentrating on my singing and watching the choral director offstage and I didn't even notice the bridge until I heard it crack."

Josh stared down at her in surprise. "You're angry. Have I offended you by coming out to your home to ask you about this?"

"Well, I don't see the need for it. I had nothing to do with that accident, Mister Castleton. I wasn't anywhere near that bridge before the opera began!"

Josh stopped, whirling her around to face him, his hands gripping her arms. "What are you talking about? Did you think I came here to accuse you? What kind of a man do you think I am?"

He looked down at her blazing eyes, her pursed lips. When she glanced away suddenly, her face so close he could see the crescent shadows of her lashes on her cheeks, his hands tightened on her arms.

"I don't know what kind of a man you are," Caty replied. "I don't know anything about you except that you suspected me of being involved in Magda Dubratta's death and have sought me out trying to discover if I really was."

"Sought you out. . . . Is that what you think?"

"What other reason could there be?" she snapped and tried to pull away. His fingers were hurting her arms.

Josh bent closer to her lips. He knew better. This was madness. Yet holding her in his arms, so close, so tempting, he could not resist. What else had he come here for, against all the arguments of his better judgment? What other reason . . .

He pulled her into his embrace, tightening his arms around her. His lips sought hers hungrily. Her mouth opened in surprise, sweet to his taste, her lips soft and cool. His hand slid up to cup her chin, seeking her lips even closer, his tongue outlined their lovely shape, until it could invade, searching out the depths within. Her body was rigid with shock, then gradually she seemed to slacken, to melt into his arms. He felt the firm curves and hollows of her body against his and he longed to slide his fingers inside her cloak and stroke her breasts.

Caty was conscious of the feel of his arms around her, the softness of his lips against her own. Instinctively she raised her hand to lay her palm against his cheek, feeling the brittle edges where he had shaved. She closed her eyes and let herself be enveloped by the rising warmth his insistent mouth worked on her. Her body began to tremble and she felt herself sliding only to be caught in his tight hold.

Josh lifted his head and ran his fingers down her cheek, tracing the outline of her lips. "Is that reason enough?" he whispered.

Slowly Caty regained control of herself, stunned as much by the warmth of his kiss, as she was astonished by the fact that he had kissed her at all. Her own reaction astonished her even more. In just a few moments, he had unleashed a torrent of feelings deep inside her that created as much havoc as pleasure. She forced herself to step back, fighting to make sense of all her confusing emotions.

"But why? When you didn't see me again . . . after the party . . ."

"I apologize for that," Josh said, struggling to regain his own control. "I thought that since I was in charge of the investigation and you were a suspect that I might be violating my work ethics by seeing you. I told myself to stay away, to let you alone. I even pretended to myself today that I came out here to talk to you because the opera is closed and you were not in the city. The truth is, I wanted to see you again. And I've wanted to kiss you like that since the first time we met."

"Forgive me, but I got the impression the first time we met that you wanted to arrest me."

"That, too. We do seem to be at odds rather frequently."

Caty turned to look out over the bay. Her hood had slipped off and the cold wind bit against her face. She pulled it back over her head and tightened her grip on her cloak.

Damn this man, anyway! He always upset her somehow. Why couldn't he just do his job and leave her alone? She had a career to think about and she wanted to be happy with her place at the Metropolitan. First a murder, then this accident, and now this! What was she to make of it all?

Abruptly she turned to face him. "Mister Castleton . . ."

"Josh."

"Mister Castleton, did that bridge collapse accidentally?"

"We think it did. I've been over it several times and it appears to be a simple matter of a flimsy piece of equipment not holding up."

"But you're not sure?

"No. Two of the metal braces are missing. It's possible that someone deliberately set it up improperly."

"Are you going to tell me now that somebody saw me fingering those metal devices before the opera?"

"Of course not. This isn't the kind of thing a woman would contrive."

"Oh? I forgot that you know so much about women and crime."

Confused by her anger, Josh could only imagine that he had been too forward by kissing her as he did. Some women insisted on the proprieties. Yet he would have sworn Caty McGowan was more hotblooded than that. And singers were not known to be overly puritanical.

"If I offended you, Caty . . ."

"It's Miss McGowan, please. I think you'd better go, Inspector. There is nothing more I can tell you about that dreadful accident. I'll make your apologies to my mother."

She turned on her heel and started back down the path. Josh looked after her, thinking she had to be the most stubborn, pigheaded, infuriating female he had ever met. How insulting to have kissed her with all the warmth in his heart, only to have her send him away. Blast the woman, anyway!

He yanked his coat close around his collar. He wished he could have at least had that cup of tea.

Eight

The following morning, an emergency meeting was called between General Manager Cannio and the three most influential members of the Metropolitan Opera Board of Managers. The four men grouped themselves around one end of the thick mahogany table which gleamed like bronze in the dim light from the arched window. There had been none of the usual niceties about this meeting—no silver coffeepot and bone china cups, no Irish linen napkins or delicate pastry puffs on Limoges platters. The three board members—Belmont, Morgan, and Stevens—had been summoned from the heady world of finance to this hurriedly arranged, impromptu meeting and all three appeared anxious to get through it and back to the real world.

Cannio ran his long fingers through his shock of white hair, betraying his extreme nervousness. He was under a terrible strain and had more to deal with than he had ever bargained for when he took on the running of this noble house. No manager should have to handle such matters as dead sopranos and collapsing sets. It was unfair to expect him to know what to do or how to proceed, and it was time these patrons took some of the burden off his shoulders.

He did not quite have the courage to put all this in words, however. Instead, he fingered the leatherbound folder in front of him and coughed nervously.

"So good of you to come, gentlemen. I would have spared you if I could but . . ."

"Yes, yes," Morgan interrupted impatiently." Get on with it. What exactly do you want us to decide?"

"Well, you know, this latest accident has got the whole place in an uproar. Just when things were settling down again and I believed the worst was behind us."

"What is being said about this latest 'unpleasantness'?" Belmont asked. "Has it been determined yet?"

"They're saying it's probably just an accident. Detective Castleton . . ."

"Josh Castleton?"

"Yes. He's handling the investigation since he was on the scene at the first . . . unfortunate incident."

Morgan ran a plump finger along his mustache. "Hmm. Well, I suppose since the police are involved, it's better that we have one of our own."

"Exactly," Cannio said hurriedly. "He has been

very careful. No heavy-handed business, you'd hardly know an investigation was going on."

Stevens lounged back in his chair. "That's good. We don't want any more bad publicity for the opera house than is necessary. Bad for business, you know."

"So far it has only served to draw more interest, as far as I can see," Belmont offered. "Sold-out houses, I understand, Cannio, since Dubratta's death?"

"Nearly so. The upper tiers seldom have an empty seat."

Morgan leaned his tall frame over the table, jutting his big head forward. "Yes, but the boxes. Have they fallen off? That's where the money is."

Cannio coughed again. "They aren't any emptier than usual. I do not think the proceeds have suffered because of all this. On the contrary, once or twice, they have even improved."

"Well, you know the common man loves a scandal. They'll flock to the house if they think they are going to see a disaster."

"Yes, but my good Belmont, the common man is not the real support of this house. It's the subscriptions that pay our bills. We can't have that damaged."

"Mister Morgan is correct," Cannio said cautiously. "We were counting on Signor Gregorio's debut to boost attendance all round. Now, if we have to keep the house closed . . ."

"But why should we keep it closed?" Stevens

broke in. "If that incident last Tuesday was simply an accident, why not go on and put it behind us?"

Morgan drummed his fingers on the table. "We can't lose Gregorio. It's taken two years to get him here. He's the finest tenor in Europe and half the city is waiting to hear him."

"Yes, but I fear he may not wish to appear here unless we can put these appalling accidents behind us. Singers are notoriously superstitious, you know. If Signor Gregorio gets it into his head that we are . . . 'unlucky' . . . nothing on earth will convince him to sing with us."

"But we have a contract," Belmont said in an injured voice. "I brought back the copy myself from Milan last August. He must sing."

"I agree," Morgan said. "He has to fulfill his contract. Besides, all this will blow over soon. I admit that accident with the set didn't help matters but it should not be allowed to ruin our season. I vote that we continue as usual."

Cannio looked around at the three men in their exquisitely tailored suits, their manicured mustaches, their diamond stickpins in their silk cravats, and his heart failed. They understood money, he knew, but he wondered how much they really understood the ways of the music world. Opera was not just a business, it was a calling, an emotion, a way of life. A lot rested on the delicate vocal chords of this great Italian tenor and right now it was not resting very solidly.

Robert Stevens caught some of the general manager's anxiety. "Where is Signor Gregorio now?" he asked.

Cannio glanced up at him across the table. "He's on a liner crossing the Atlantic. He is due to arrive in New York next week."

"Well, then," Morgan boomed, "if he's on a ship, he probably doesn't know anything about all this commotion. I, for one, think we should not mention it to him."

"For God's sake, Henry," Belmont said. "You know there's probably a wireless aboard. Even a newspaper. You of all people should know one doesn't drop off the world when one crosses the Atlantic."

"All the same, I think we should make light of this. Open the opera and go on about our business as though the incident was not important enough to matter. Attitude is half the battle, you know."

"I agree," Stevens added. "The less said, the better. In all likelihood this will end the matter and once the police make a decision about Dubratta, we can put it all behind us."

"It might not hurt to have a welcoming committee for Signor Gregorio, however," Belmont said. "The three of us, perhaps, and Manager Cannio, of course. Perhaps we should get Mister Vanderbilt down there, too. Make the little Italian feel he's important."

"That would be very wise," Cannio said with relief. "Singers have delicate egos, as you all know."

"Only too well," Morgan muttered. He had little

patience with the artistic vagaries of musicians, famous or not.

Cannio gathered up his leather folder. "Gentlemen, I thank you. We shall reopen tomorrow and carry on as usual."

The three men pushed back their chairs. Morgan headed round the table toward Cannio, while Stevens stepped up to Belmont.

"You've heard this tenor, August. Is he really as good as he is reported to be?"

"He is undoubtedly the best I've ever heard. Great power, pure tones, dramatic presence. He is going to be a sensation, I'm sure of it."

Morgan leaned toward Cannio and lowered his voice. "No word yet from Castleton on what really happened to Dubratta?"

"Not yet. In the house, we think it was a suicide but Detective Castleton seems convinced it was murder."

"What about that girl who made her debut that night? Mandesi, I think her name was?"

"She is still in the chorus, but she hasn't yet taken another role."

"Might be better if she didn't, at least until something is settled about that night and we can put it behind us. We don't want to bring it back to memory, so to speak."

"Should I let her go? She has a fine voice and good potential but if that is what you want . . ."

Morgan picked up his velvety felt hat and ran his finger around the brim, his brows creased with thought. "No, no need for that. Let her remain in the chorus and not call attention to herself for the time being. Who knows, perhaps Signor Gregorio will be so spectacular that people will forget about Magda Dubratta and all that unpleasantness."

Caty read about Signor Gregorio's arrival in the paper the following week. The picture showed the diminutive tenor, with chin thrust upward and outward under the jaunty angle of his hat, flanked by the three most prominent members of the opera board and General Manager Cannio, the 51st Street Cunard pier in the background. She was not surprised that the Met would go all out to welcome the singer since his reputation preceded him. He was easily the most eagerly awaited European artist of the season, completely overshadowing Magda's farewell appearance and the Swedish Wagnerian soprano who was expected to perform the Ring cycle in the spring.

"He looks like a pouter pigeon," Kyle said, bending over her shoulder to stare at the photograph. "But with that chest and that broad face, I'll wager he'll have no problem being heard over the orchestra."

"Perhaps he'll make people forget all about Dubratta's Butterfly," Caty commented. "If he can do that, it won't matter how he looks."

When she arrived at the opera house later that day she found that the excitement over Gregorio's debut had indeed almost chased away the shadows of the previous unhappy incidents. There was a thrill in the air, a stirring of anticipation that Caty found exhilarating—until she remembered that the very same feelings had been there when Magda Dubratta arrived. She decided to put such gloomy thoughts from her mind and enjoy the anticipation as the other chorus members were doing. Then she turned a corner on her way to rehearsal and came face to face with Josh Castleton.

"Whoa!" Josh said, gripping her arms and smiling good-naturedly. "Why such a hurry?"

"Excuse me," Caty answered in clipped tones. "I'm late for rehearsal."

She tried to step around him, but he shifted position just enough to block her way.

"I haven't seen you in these halls lately. How have you been?"

His voice was formal and polite; his smile was warm. Caty forced herself not to look directly at him, hoping it would reinforce the lack of interest she wanted to project. She resolutely fought down the tiny thrill the touch of his hands around her arms had given her.

"I've been around. The opera was closed for a short time. Why are you here? I should have thought that by now you would have sorted out all that police business."

Her frigid manner was too much for Josh to fight. He had been delighted to see her, hoping that when they ran into each other again, she would have put the incident of that kiss on the bluff behind her. Obviously she had not.

"It's not quite completed but should be soon.

When are you singing again? I'd like to come and hear."

Caty felt her cheeks grow warm. "I'm not. At least, they haven't spoken to me about it. I still understudy, but no one's fallen ill."

"About the other day . . ."

"Please excuse me. Maestro Walters gets quite annoyed when we're late for rehearsal."

"Oh. Of course. Sorry." Josh stepped aside and she pushed around him, brushing slightly against him. He watched her hurry down the hall, unable to tear his eyes away. He wished he could talk with her leisurely, tell her that he was hanging around the house because he was half convinced that Boris Borinsky had deliberately arranged that accident with the bridge, and that once he could prove it, he would link the man to Magda Dubratta's murder. He wished he could talk to her about anything. The longing to know her better, to hold her in his arms again, was a dull ache in his chest.

Yet it was better this way, he thought with a sigh. At least until he got things sorted out.

Josh was unaware that his casual question about the next time she would sing touched a very sore spot with Caty. She had wondered for days now why the management hadn't given her a chance to sing a leading role again, especially when every comment about her Suzuki had been so complimentary. She had just about given up expecting to be handed another role simply because she had done so well with the first one. By now she was back to hoping, vainly, that some lead singer might fall ill and she would be called to step in again as an understudy.

Nor did seeing Josh Castleton again help to raise her spirits. The strong attraction she felt for him, even the searing memory of his kiss, raised all kinds of conflicting emotions. She wanted to keep her distance, to concentrate on her career, to never allow herself to care enough to be hurt. She wanted to be outraged that he took such liberties. Instead, she found herself trying vainly to push down the desire to be close to him, the longing to have him kiss her again. She was discouraged over her future with the opera and she was tormented by her feelings for this man. By the time she joined the chorus in the rehearsal room, she was thoroughly disgusted with herself.

After practicing in the rehearsal room, the chorus moved on to the huge stage to review their positions for next week's production of *Nabucco*. They had only been there a short time, suffering a harangue from Stillman for their slowness in following directions, when Cannio came bustling on to the stage to interrupt.

"I would like a word with the members of the chorus," he announced to the irritated stage manager. "It will only take a moment."

Stillman reluctantly stepped to the side while the chorus, which had been straggling across the vast stage, gathered in a small semicircle around the manager.

"My people . . .". Cannio began pompously

while Caty raised her hand to her lips to hide a smile. Beside her one of her friends, an American baritone, John Coleman, leaned over to whisper, "I refuse to be 'one of his people' while I'm only earning two dollars and seventeen cents an opera!"

Caty did not bother to answer since she knew John was one of those ringleaders in the chorus threatening to form a union in order to make their salary more equitable. She also hoped to hear something of importance from the general manager, but in that she was disappointed. Cannio proceeded to deliver a long, flowery speech about how the board in their wisdom had decided to continue with the schedule, and he hoped everyone would rally around the management and do their bit for the house, etc. The only excitement occurred when Cannio neared the end of his talk and a commotion erupted in the wings as three men swept on to the stage.

Two of them had that sleek, well-fed look of members of the board and nabobs of the city. The third one—short, full-faced, wearing a long cashmere overcoat and a jaunty felt hat with a small feather in the band—was instantly recognized by everyone there, even though they had only seen him before in photographs. A spontaneous wave of applause broke out around him.

Signor Carlo Gregorio lifted his hat and beamed all around at the group, smiling broadly.

Hiding his irritation, Cannio politely introduced the famous tenor, then added, "I was just encouraging everyone to carry on and help us make this our best season ever, in spite of all that has happened."

Gregorio barely waited for the manager to finish before sweeping his arm around and booming at the chorus, "Si, I uner'stand, you-a 'ave *molto dolore, mio amico*. No matter. Now Gregorio, he is-a here, an' all will-a be well. Stupendo! You see!"

The chorus broke into a loud round of applause, sprinkled with good-natured laughing.

"You know what he'll be earning per performance," John said, leaning closer to Caty's ear. "Fifteen hundred dollars. Compared to our two dollars and seventeen cents. It isn't fair."

Signor Gregorio's good humor was too infectious to be dampened by Coleman, no matter how right he might be. "You can hardly compare the two," she hissed. "He's a great artist and he carries the lead."

"All the same . . ."

Gregorio gave them a few more heavily accented comments, then swept regally from the stage leaving Stillman to move quickly in to begin ordering people back to their places. Caty was about to move when she heard Cannio calling her name.

"May I have a word with you, Miss McGowan?"

Caty looked back at Stillman, who was already working himself up into a red-faced fury over what he perceived to be the slowness of their response.

"But . . ."

"It's all right. Maestro Stillman is aware that I needed to call you away."

A faint glimmer of hope thrilled to life in her chest. Perhaps this was it—the call she had been waiting and longing for so long. She followed the tall, slim manager off the stage and into the wings. To her surprise he continued on until they stood in the narrow hall leading back to the dressing rooms. Cannio looked around to make certain there was no one else around, then coughed nervously.

"How are you, then, Caty? You were not injured in that unfortunate accident, were you?"

"No, sir. I had just stepped off the bridge before it fell."

"Hmm. That was a bit of luck. We won't be doing *Butterfly* for a while again. However, Maestro von Rankin informed me this morning that he intended to ask you to understudy Santuzza for *Cavalleria Rusticana* next month."

Caty caught her breath. Santuzza was a great dramatic part and a leading role for her voice. It would be the closest she had come to singing a lead. She pushed down her swelling joy and fought to control the wide smile that threatened her lips.

"I told him . . . that is, I had to dissuade him from that. I'm terribly sorry about it, so sorry, in fact, that I felt I should inform you myself."

Her hopes plunged as quickly as they had soared. She felt as it a pail of cold water had been thrown over her. "Sir!"

"I know it seems unkind. But, you see, until

that business about Magda Dubratta is cleared up . . ."

"But, Maestro Cannio, I had nothing to do with that."

"Well, we don't officially know that yet."

Her green eyes sparked to deep emerald with sudden fury. "I know I had nothing to do with it! It is not fair to condemn me for something that did not involve me at all."

"But it did involve you. You were on stage when it happened and you are now identified with it."

"I sang very well that night."

"Yes, you did. It was a fine performance. Unfortunately . . ."

Caty fought down the tears that sprang to her eyes. She would not break down in front of this posturing, pompous man. "What are you trying to tell me? That I'm to be let go?"

Cannio waved a manicured hand. "No, no, no. Nothing like that. It's just that now that Signor Gregorio has arrived and we are all looking forward to his first night here, I felt, that is, the board felt, this was a good time to put all the unpleasantness that has happened behind us. The less the audience or the press is reminded of it, the better. I'm sure you can understand."

Caty turned away, pursing her lips. *No, I don't understand*, she wanted to cry. *If I am good enough to sing well once, then I ought to be allowed to sing again*. Yet she held back from arguing with the manager of the house. Her place in the chorus might not be all she wanted but it was all she had and it was too important to risk losing.

"I see you are upset. Would you like to take the rest of the day off?"

"No. I prefer to work." She added bitterly to herself that, surely, lost among the faceless crowd of the chorus the house would be safe from any horrible emanations she might give off.

Cannio laid a sympathetic hand on her shoulder. "Actually, it would not be a bad idea for you to take some time off. A week, perhaps, just to rest and put this all behind you. Then when you return, we can reconsider Santuzza for a later date. The spring, perhaps."

She glanced up at him from under slanted lids. She suddenly realized he didn't want her there when Carlo Gregorio made his debut and this was his way of getting rid of her. Damn him! In the superstitious world of professional musicians, she was in danger of becoming a pariah!

"I'd prefer to work," she said again, in clipped tones.

Cannio was uncomfortable. He knew he was not being fair to this girl, who, given better circumstances, ought to be singing roles by now. Yet nothing, nothing must risk Gregorio's first night. One more "accident" like that bridge and he might be forced to resign as general manager. "Well," he hedged, "let us think about it. Why don't you finish the week since there are only three more performances, then we will talk again."

"Yes, sir," Caty snapped and turned on her heel

to walk briskly back to the stage. Yet she paused in the shadows of the wings to fight down the churning emotions that threatened to overwhelm her. She wanted to cry, to scream, to kick something or punch somebody. She wanted to yell to everyone that she was being treated unfairly, that she hated the idea of enforced idleness, that behind it lay the fear that even after she returned to the chorus, she would never again be given the chance to prove herself.

She forced down her feelings and walked back out on the stage.

Hell's Kitchen. That was what the "goys" called the West Side of the city. It would have been more appropriate, Boris thought, for the Lower East Side, with its dirty streets and crowded, stinking tenements.

He looked briefly around the small, dingy room where he lived with four other people—at the one bed with its sagging springs, the pallets on the floor, the newspapers spread on the boards between, the one, small clouded window, at the rectangular table at which he sat trying to choke down a breakfast of cold potato soup—and he was filled with an urgency to escape. That was the most important thing his job gave him, the chance to get away from this teeming, dark, rat-infested cluster of tenements and escape into another world. It was even more important than the money he earned, which only went to his miserable father, anyway. Yet he did not even mind that, as long as he had the opportunity to travel uptown to that other world of light and air and order.

And Manny. Manny, who had made it all possible, who had got him his job at the opera house, who had brought love and warmth into his life, who had given his life a direction and purpose. He cared nothing for the music—most of the time it sounded like caterwauling. The people there were arrogant and snooty, flaunting their wealth like the nobility in the old country, but without any of the reasons. Opera was silly, people singing when they could just as easily speak. He would never understand it or care for it like Manny did.

But what did that matter? It was a job and they were hard to get in this part of town. How many people did he know, from the peddlers crying the streets behind their pushcarts to the prostitutes working up and down Allen Street, who would sell their soul for a steady job? And he had Manny to thank for it, and for so much more.

He heard the springs creak behind him as his father shifted on the bed. The old bastard was waking up. All the more reason to get out of here. He threw down the spoon and grabbed up his jacket, slipping his arms into the sleeves. He nearly made it to the door when the old man saw him and let out a string of epithets.

"Get me my breakfast, you worthless son of a bitch," the old man spewed in Yiddish still tinged with a Russian accent. "I see you trying to leave."

"Get it yourself, old man," Boris snapped. Though his hand rested on the doorknob, he couldn't turn it. The old ways, the old deference to a parent, even a terrible parent, made him pause. A shoe flew by his head, just missing his ear. It slammed into the door and clattered to the ground.

"Goddamn you, you know I can't," the old man yelled. Boris turned to glare at the shriveled, yellow face of his father. It was too bad the accident that crushed his legs didn't hurt his arms as well, he thought. Instead his immobility in one part of his body had served to make the other even stronger. He bent to pick up the shoe, its sole half hanging away from the upper part. Flinging it at the bed, he stalked to the table, lifted his half-eaten bowl of soup and a roll and carried them to the bed, resisting the urge to fling them into the old man's face.

"Here." He thrust them into his father's hands and turned to go.

"Ungrateful bastard! How am I supposed to use the pot if you go off uptown? Who's going to help me?"

The whining note in a voice that was usually heavy with belligerence only made Boris hate him the more. "Get one of the boarders to help you. They pay three dollars a week. Let them earn it for something besides sleeping on the floor."

"How do I know when they'll be back? You come here!"

Boris yanked open the door. "That's your problem."

He stalked down the dark hall, ignoring the old man's screams behind him. Let him fend for himself. What had his father ever done for him beside beat him when he was too small to fight back? The old man had left his mother and him to take care of themselves for years. Then when his mother died, worn out from poverty and work, he'd taken over their one room and immediately rented space to three other people. Until he was hurt, he had never needed a son. Let him get along without one now.

He pushed open the front door of the tenement and stepped out on to the low brick steps that led to the walk, picking his way through the garbage. At the curb, a group of children played king of the hill on a dead horse. A familiar urgency to escape this place took over and he hurried at a brisk pace down the street, barely missing the contents of a chamber pot tossed from an overhead window.

His celluloid collar was tight and uncomfortable, but he wore it anyway. It was his badge as a working man with a job uptown, away from this stinking hole. He would get out, too. Manny would help him. He owed everything to Manny.

Yet it bothered him that his friend had lately been a little aloof, probably because of all that bad business at the opera. He would get over it, of course, once he realized that everything had been done for him, only for him. That nasty woman—

she deserved to die. And that bridge . . . nothing must be allowed to hurt Manny. He would see that it didn't.

A peddler with a long, mottled gray beard shoved a pushcart toward him, nearly blocking the walk.

"Eh, Boris. You wanna buy a *bulbeh*? Or maybe a schmaltz herring? Only a penny, six cents for both."

Boris grabbed the cart and shoved it aside, nearly tipping it over. "Get away, *dummkopf*. I don't want nothin' from you."

He continued on down the street, ignoring the peddler's string of Yiddish invective behind him, his thoughts already focused on the opera house.

Caty suffered through the long trip home to Staten Island without even attempting conversation with Kyle. She was grateful that her weary brother slept most of the way, since she was too absorbed in her own thoughts to be sociable.

All day she had fought against the depression brought on by her conversation with Cannio. It was not just the idea of never leaving the chorus, or even taking a week off, that bothered her, though both were depressing to contemplate. Even worse was the thought that all this meant the beginning of the end of her career. It implied that she would never have much of a future with the Metropolitan. Either she must give up her dreams of becoming a great diva and settle for mediocrity, or she must take a long hard look at her life and start in a totally new direction. The first was too horrible to think about, and the second too frightening. Especially since her family did not have the funds to send her off to Europe to build her career there.

Of course there was Mr. Hammerstein's new opera house, the Manhattan, which would be opening very soon. Perhaps she could audition for him, though considering the rivalry between the two, she had better not let the management of the Met know about it.

Shortly after midnight Caty and Kyle reached the bluff where the farmhouse sat overlooking the bay. It must be the hour, Caty thought, and the fact that she had been stewing all day over her future that made her so very tired and discouraged. By the time she walked into the hall and slipped off her coat she was ready to give it all up, all her dreams and hopes. What did it matter anyway?

Her mother met her with an offer of a cup of cocoa which Caty declined, deciding instead to go straight to bed. She was halfway up the stairs when out of the corner of her eye, she saw a large white embossed envelope lying on the hall table. "What's that?" she asked, pausing.

"Oh, goodness me, it's so late, I nearly forgot." Sian wrapped her heavy shawl around her nightdress and handed the envelope up to her daughter. "This came for you today, not by the mail but delivered by hand. It looks ever so imposing."

Intrigued, Caty turned the heavy paper over in

her hand, carefully examining the gold-stamped monogram in the corner and her address written in a flourish of curlicues. She opened it carefully and stepped back to the hall to hold it up under the gas wall lamp. The signature at the bottom was unmistakable for all its fancy script.

"It's from Frances Schyler. Imagine! I thought she'd forgotten me."

With a leap of the heart she leaned closer to the paper, reading aloud. "Dear Miss McGowan. I am having a few houseguests visit at my country estate week after next and I would be so pleased if you would join us."

Caty paused as she heard her mother give a short yelp. "It will be quite informal," she continued reading, "except that we will dress for dinner. Otherwise, simplicity is the keynote. There may be riding but do not worry about a habit as I'm sure we will be able to outfit you."

"A riding habit . . ." Sian breathed.

"Please do say you'll come. Let me know on which train you'll be arriving and I will have Fred meet you with the Duryea motor."

Caty turned to her mother, her eyes round with wonder. "She wants me to visit her country estate!"

"Oh, Caty. Just imagine. You'll go, of course."

"I don't know . . . do I have the clothes? Everyone there will look gorgeous."

"Now don't worry about that. I've a week to get you ready and I can do it if I drop everything else. You want to go, don't you? You're not afraid of holding your own around all those fancy people?"

"Of course not. I'm sure she'll want me to sing and that is all that matters. Oh, Mama. I had just about given up hope. This could not have come at a better time."

"Given up hope . . . what nonsense. You're going to be famous someday. This is just the first step. I always knew something like this would happen."

Caty gave her mother a fierce hug. "Yes, you did. And I am going to enjoy every minute of it—for both of us!"

Nine

The railroad car was nearly empty so Caty chose a seat on the left side where she could look out the window at the river as the train chugged northward. Although it was not her first train ride, it was the first time she had been up the Hudson and she stared in fascination at the beauty of the tall hills and the sweeping, silver river.

It was pleasant to sit back and let the train carry her away from New York. This last week had been so full that she was still unable to take it all in. This trip seemed like a fairy tale—Cinderella off to another ball. But it was all too real and, aside from occasional trepidations that she would not be properly dressed or know how to act—she was determined to enjoy it. Her luggage was crammed with dresses that her mother had slaved over, plus a few ready-mades. She might not look as elegantly turned out as the wealthy ladies of the group but she would look stylish and fashionable. And though she had never been to an elegant country party, she was pretty certain she could hold her own there. She would watch and listen and be herself and, when asked to sing, dazzle them all.

She had asked Cannio for a week off without informing him of the reason. It was none of his business what she did with her leisure time. He was so happy she would not be there for Signor Gregorio's debut that he had not given it another thought.

A flock of seagulls soaring off the surface of the river caught her attention. The Hudson River valley was spectacular. It was amazing to realize that such beauty lay just outside the city with its reams of dirty red brick tenements and cobbled and tarred streets. Staten Island was still rural yet it did not have the soaring loveliness of the river valley which reminded her of pictures of the Rhine in Germany. Who would have thought all this beauty could be so close to the city!

The trip took over an hour and by the time she arrived at the small station with its peaked roof, she was growing too nervous to even admire the scenery. This was like making a debut all over again, with the difference that when she had actually made her debut she hadn't had so much time to think about it beforehand.

She barely stepped on to the platform before she saw a heavyset gentleman approaching. He wore a burgundy coat with shiny gold buttons, a chauffeur's cap with a leather visor, and tall, gleaming black boots. With a graceful motion he removed the hat and snapped it under his arm.

"Miss McGowan?"

"Yes."

"I'm Fred, Mrs. Schyler's driver. The car is right over there, miss. I'll get your luggage."

Caty's eyes widened at the sight of the long, silver automobile drawn up beside the platform. It would be her first ride ever in a car! Fred hurried to the door and pulled it open.

"It's not enclosed, ma'am, but the house is only a short distance. I've a duster for you if you'd like."

"No, that's quite all right," Caty replied, easing herself down on the gleaming burgundy seat. "I'll be fine."

While the chauffeur threw her luggage in the boot, she gave an extra twist to her hat pin just in case. But she needn't have feared. The car never went more than seven miles an hour even as it climbed the hill from the tracks. Once at the top it turned to follow a narrow road a short distance before turning onto a brick path that paralleled the river. It chugged along this road to a house at the end where it pulled up in a circular driveway before the door.

It was a beautiful house, Georgian in style and formed of rose-tinted bricks with spotless white columns along the portico. On either side huge stone urns overflowed with cheerful bright yellow mums, all of which seemed to say, "welcome." Caty stood on the graveled walk taking in the beauty of the place while Fred hurried over to take out her luggage. The door opened and a young girl in maid's white cap came bustling out.

"Miss McGowan, is it? Welcome, miss. I'm Mollie. Mrs. Schyler says I'm to show you to your room."

"Oh. Thank you, Mollie."

Caty followed her up the low steps and into a circular hall that for sheer grace and beauty took her breath away. She paused to admire it and saw Mrs. Schyler coming down the stairs.

Frances Schyler's gray hair lay in manicured waves around her classic face. "Caty, dear," she said, extending her hand. "I'm so happy you could join us this week. Welcome to Beechwood, my dear."

"It was kind of you to ask me, Mrs. Schyler."

Mrs. Schyler gently turned Caty toward the stairs. "Nonsense. I've wanted to get to know you better since that party at the Fields' and this seemed the first opportunity. I have to warn you, however, you may be asked to sing. Will that be all right?"

"I was hoping you would," Caty answered with a smile. If this gracious woman only knew how glad she had been to receive this invitation, she would realize she could ask Caty to do anything and she would be happy to do it.

"Good. Now as for the rest, you are to completely relax and enjoy yourself. No need to take part in anything you don't wish to. Mollie will take you up and then, after you freshen up and if you feel like it, why don't you join us in the drawing room for coffee?"

"Thank you. I'd love to."

As Mrs. Schyler swept off, Caty followed Mollie upstairs to a long hall connecting two wings on either side of the house. Her room was at one end of the hall with a huge double window overlooking the river. Large, airy and elegantly furnished, Caty had to force herself not to stand in the middle and gawk. She removed her hat and laid it down on the dresser, then watched Mollie lay out her things as though she had done this all her life. Not until the maid had left the room did she pivot around with her arms outstretched, giggling to herself. Then she made a careful tour of the room and the adjoining bath, admiring the fancy appointments and mentally making notes. The room contained a big bed covered in a satin spread and piled with pillows edged in blond lace, heavy and intricate. There was a dressing table lined with an ecru silk skirt, an ornate mirror, a divine chaise lounge in robin's egg blue, a round table with a blue silk skirt and several lamps with elaborately painted glass globes. The rug was Oriental and so thick she longed to take off her shoes and walk barefoot across it. There were two large landscapes on the wall along with several smaller prints of French fashions of the 1850s. The window was covered with a filmy lace curtain and draped with dark blue satin hanging, gracefully pulled back and fastened with saucer-shaped brass knobs. In one corner, a small marble cherub stood watch near a round table which held a vase of freshly cut flowers.

It might have been Mrs. Schyler's room rather than just another one for a guest, Caty thought. Imagine a house where all the bedrooms were laid out as gorgeously as this. Imagine having that much money! She made up her mind there and then that when she became rich and famous she would have a bedroom just like it. And her mother, too!

She took a few minutes to freshen up from the train ride, then went back down the stairs. Mollie appeared as if by magic at the foot to direct her to the drawing room, a spacious room in understated elegance at the back of the hall. Several people were grouped at one end near the long French windows and Caty moved to join them.

"Miss McGowan, please come join us."

Frances, sitting in a wing chair before a table piled with an ornate silver service and several china cups and saucers, waved her over. "Let me introduce you . . ." she began but was interrupted when one of the other guests stood up and took Caty's hand.

"We've already met," the young man said, lifting her fingers to his lips. Caty looked at him blankly.

"Charlie Poore, don't you remember? From the Fields' supper? I only live a small way down the road, but when Frances told me you were coming I invited myself to join the party. I've been hoping we'd meet again."

She had a vague recollection of a vapid young

man from that magical evening. "Oh yes, Mister Poore. It's nice to see you again." It was coming back, the slim, slightly stooped gentleman with the thin mustache and wicked smile whom Josh Castleton had warned her about. *A Stage-Door Johnny, if ever there was one*. Caty carefully removed her hand from his grasp and concentrated on the other people in the room. The two women were almost carbon copies of Frances Schyler, matrons in silk dresses and draped with pearls. There was also one young girl of about fifteen in a ruffled dress with hair falling to her waist, and an elderly English gentleman in a pince-nez. Their polite welcome had an air of coolness as they made room for her on the satin loveseat next to Belinda, the young girl.

They were too well bred to ask Caty many questions about herself, other than commenting in a vague way about the opera house. She drank her coffee but was too excited to try any of the small, luscious-looking pastries. After half an hour's strained conversation, when they disbanded until luncheon, Charlie offered to show her something of the grounds. Caty's longing to see more of Beechwood overcame her reluctance to encourage a "Stage-Door Johnny" and she quickly agreed.

At the door, Mollie appeared with her coat and hat as though she had overheard the conversation, and Caty accepted them as if she was accustomed to a maid waiting on her every day. However, once outside, they found the wind off the river was too strong for comfort and so ventured no farther than an arched arbor to one side of the house, looking rather bare now in the late autumn. Caty caught a glimpse of gardens with enticing walks and, beyond them, open fields flanked by outbuildings, one of which had to be a stable. Though Charlie Poore took her arm through his for most of the walk, she was relieved that his manner toward her remained respectful and gentlemanly. By the time they returned she began to think Josh Castleton maligned him, probably from some sort of policeman's warped view.

Though she had spent the rest of the day indoors, it passed quickly. Every comfort and every kind of entertainment was available to her. She had only to seek it out. Mrs. Schyler did not organize activities, she allowed her guests the free use of her gracious home and Caty soon found this the most entertaining activity of all.

She was a little worried about dinner which was "formal" but soon found her fears were groundless. The emphasis was on the excellent food and stimulating conversation more than on how one dressed or what amount of jewels they wore. At the end of the first day, Caty fell into her comfortable bed more relaxed at "at home" than she ever expected to be.

Rain swept in the following day, keeping everyone indoors. By this time she really longed to go out and see something of the surrounding area but reluctantly put it off. She spent the afternoon going through some of the music Frances Schyler had on hand, preparing to sing at the following afternoon's tea.

"I'm having a larger group in for supper tomorrow—just a few of my neighbors—but I wanted you to sing for us first. There's no need to make a production out of it, after all. Will that be acceptable?"

"Mrs. Schyler, I will be happy to perform before whomever you wish. You need only say the word. I love to sing but it is always more satisfying to sing for others. And I don't wish to get 'rusty' with all this relaxing."

"No, of course. You must feel free to come into the music room and practice any time you wish." Frances leafed through some music, glancing up at Caty. "I suppose you should know that I am aware you missed Signor Gregorio's debut by coming up here this week. I hope you did not mind."

"Not at all." Her throat tightened as she remembered Cannio's concern over getting rid of her. Had Frances Schyler known that? Was that why she invited her here? "Actually," she went on, "I prefer to hear him later after he settles down and is accustomed to the house. It is usually difficult for a famous artist to perform that first night when his or her reputation has led people to expect so much from them."

Frances nodded and went back to concentrating on the music. "What do you think about this Schubert . . ."

***

Friday dawned blustery and dark, with dismal, gray clouds blowing in from across the river. Caty stood at her window and watched the wind whipping branches across the sweep of the back lawn. A fire burned in the grate but the room was still drafty, and she pulled her housecoat closer around her shoulders against the cold. She was to perform that afternoon and this was not the time to catch a sore throat. Though Frances Schyler assured her she would only be entertaining a few close friends of the family, still she felt she must make a good impression if she was to keep Mrs. Schyler interested in her career.

Once she stood at the grand piano that afternoon, all concerns faded except the sheer delight of singing. Charlie Poore, who, it turned out, was a fair accompanist, played for her while she sang two Schubert lieders, a Brahms composition, and an aria from *Samson and Delilah*. They were all beautiful and she was soon so enthralled with the music that she forgot about the audience. She finished up accompanying herself for two of her favorite Irish songs, the hauntingly beautiful, "My Lagan Love" and "Red Is the Rose." She felt the program included some nice contrasts—the reverent Schubert, the exuberant Brahms, the sensuous Delilah, and the folk magic of the Irish tunes. One of her gifts was the ability to project all these emotions through the music and she felt the audience had sensed this. She left them chatting among themselves and went upstairs to dress for dinner feeling very satisfied.

***

Caty picked her nicest new frock for the dinner since there would be some new people there—more of Mrs. Schyler's neighbors. Made from a deep, emerald green satin, it had a daringly low neckline, a tiny waist, and a flaring skirt that ended in a small train, trimmed with beaded patterns. Mollie brushed out her hair, then helped her pile it up in rolls and curls with one long tendril across her shoulders and down the front. A pin holding one circular feather provided the only decoration. She slipped on her long, white gloves, picked up her fan and went downstairs, hoping she would be able to eat with her tight stays.

At the foot of the stairs, Mrs. Schyler met her and asked her to step into the music room for a moment. She saw at a glance that the room was empty, and as Mrs. Schyler closed the ornate double doors, she was overcome with a sudden dread that her hostess was unhappy with this afternoon's performance. She perched on the edge of a gilt chair and clutched her fan while her hostess opposite her.

"My dear, I'm afraid I have a confession to make," the lady began.

"Oh?"

"Yes. I had a motive in asking you here beyond my wish to get to know you better. And this afternoon, I was not simply anxious to have you entertain my friends."

"Oh?" Caty took a deep breath, wondering if perhaps she had committed some social *faux paux*.

What other reason could Frances Schyler have for this private conversation?

"No," Mrs. Schyler said, her eyes dancing in the dim light. "You see, I have for some time been thinking of sponsoring a new production at the opera house but I could never decide which opera to chose. My cousin and my sister are going to be silent partners in this production, and I wanted them to hear you and then help me make up my mind. Now we have decided."

"Oh? You have?"

"Yes." Frances reached out and grabbed both of Caty's hands, squeezing them. "We have decided to sponsor a new production of *Carmen* and we want you to sing the lead!"

Her mouth opened but no words came out. She knew she was staring like an idiot yet she could barely take it in. "*Carmen?*" she stammered when she found her voice. "Me? But . . ."

"Oh yes, I know. There are already at least two other famous Carmens at the Met. But that doesn't matter. The staging is tired and old and needs a new look. And my sister and cousin agree with me that you have the perfect voice for it and should be given a chance. We don't intend to sponsor the new production unless you sing the lead."

Caty's hand went to her throat. "Oh, Mrs. Schyler!" Carmen! One of the most exciting roles in all opera. Fiery, strong, individualistic, passionate—who would not want to sing the part? And in an entirely new production! "I hardly know what to say," she stammered. "It's . . . it's so exciting. I feel so honored . . . that you would believe in me . . ."

"Yes, well, there may be some who say that you are not ready for such a role yet."

"I am ready. I know I am."

"We believe that you are. In fact, I think you will be a great success and I'm counting on it to launch you into a successful career."

Caty rose because she was unable to sit still. She walked briskly across the room and back, fighting to keep her excitement under control. She wanted to leap and dance and jump about but instead she took Mrs. Schyler's hands in her own and said, "How can I ever thank you?"

Frances gave her a motherly pat. "By working as hard as you can and doing the best job of it that's possible."

"I will, I promise you that."

"I think you will, too. Now, let's be practical. A new production takes a long time and there is much to be decided before the singers even begin practicing. Set design, sets and costumes produced, staging worked out . . . . I have some firm ideas about this opera which I intend to bring in over our autocratic Maestro Cannio's head, though he doesn't know it yet. I would suggest that you begin now studying the libretto and the score until you know them completely. Look for every nuance that gives you some insight into this woman, Carmen. I want this production—and you—to set the city on its ear."

She laid an arm around Caty's shoulders and began steering her toward the door. "Oh, and by the way, I think perhaps you should drop that Italianized version of your name. You don't need it, and besides, Americans should know they have one of their own singing for them. What do you think?"

Caty smiled at her, remembering Josh's comments. "I was thinking of doing it anyway. It doesn't seem nearly as important as it once did."

"Good. Now I think we should go out and greet our newly arrived guests for supper, don't you?"

"I suppose so," Caty added, "though I feel so excited I don't know how I can eat a bite!"

She followed Frances through the double doors to the drawing room, already crowded with people standing in small groups sipping cocktails. Caty gave a swift glance around and realized about half of them were total strangers, yet her spirits were soaring so high that a roomful of people she had never met before was not the least daunting. She sailed in beside Frances Schyler with such aplomb she might have been the hostess herself.

Mrs. Schyler took her arm and began introducing her to her other guests. She was halfway around the room when a small group opened up and she found herself staring into Josh Castleton's gray eyes.

Caty gave a small gasp of surprise as Frances commented, "Oh, of course, you two already know each other. How could I have forgotten?"

"Yes, we do," Josh said easily, his eyes full of

mischievous humor. "How nice to see you again, Miss McGowan."

Caty did not miss the emphasis on her last name. "And you, too, Detective."

Frances swept her off to meet the rest of the group but Caty hardly heard their names or their polite comments, her chest thumped so hard. Josh Castleton was the last person she expected to see in this company, though when she thought about it, it should not have surprised her. He knew these people—he was the one who had introduced her to Mrs. Schyler in the first place. Yet somehow she had not linked him with this elegant world and his presence here seemed too much a reminder of the unhappiness in New York, which she thought she had left behind, temporarily anyway.

Be honest, she thought to herself as she tried to get her mind back on some question one of Frances's neighbors just asked. She murmured a reply and found herself confessing that the thrill of seeing the handsome detective had been a little too strong and too sudden for comfort. That kiss on the bluff and all it evoked were all at once very real in her mind, and she felt her knees give way slightly. She quickly took a cocktail off a tray which a waiter was passing and moved to the nearest empty chair. She had barely arranged the folds of her emerald skirt before Josh took the one beside her.

"You look very lovely tonight," he said quietly, sitting back and crossing his legs, right at home in the elegant drawing room.

"Thank you. Forgive my surprise. I didn't expect to see you here."

"No, I suppose you wouldn't. I'm not following you around in case you're wondering. The truth is my family home is just up the hill from Beechwood and I've known the Schylers for years. I was invited here as a neighbor, not as a policeman, and I hope you will think of me that way, too."

Caty turned to stare at him. "You live here? In this . . . this neighborhood?"

Josh laughed. "Yes. I told you once that not all New York policemen are just off the boat from Ireland. My family has lived in Westchester for several generations."

"But how . . . ?"

"Did I get on the force? Well, you may not believe this, but I truly like the work. It is challenging and it is real. On the other hand, it would be very easy living out here to think the whole world was like"—he waved a hand around—"all this. I knew early on that it wasn't. I wanted to do something to serve society. If my religion were stronger, I might have become a parson. Instead, being the cynical soul that I am, I chose police work. So far, I've never regretted it."

Caty shook her head. "Somehow it just doesn't fit."

Josh set down his drink and leaned toward her, resting his arms on his knees. "I'd like to show you that it does. You will be here for a few days longer. Why not spend some of it with me? I can show you something of the area and at the same time prove to you that not every person who comes from this gilded world has to be a Wall Street nabob. What do you say?"

Caty hesitated, catching her full underlip in her teeth and battling her inclination to refuse his invitation outright. She studied his face, earnestly watching her. She noticed for the first time how his eyes were framed with long lashes for a man, that his chin was broad and had a tiny cleft in the center, that his mouth had a lovely curve to its contour, the way his hair fell over his high forehead. He laced his fingers together and she saw they were long and slim but strongly formed. The spotless white cuffs of his shirt, a tiny edge below his jacket sleeve, barely concealed soft golden hairs that grew on his arms. She felt a shiver along her back and forced herself not to reveal it.

"All right, Detective. Why not?"

Josh gave her a broad smile. He had half convinced himself she was never going to unbend for him.

"Wonderful. I'll call for you about eleven tomorrow. But since we are going to spend the day together, do you think you could bring yourself to call me 'Josh'?"

Caty smiled back at him, creasing the dimple in her cheek. "Well, it still doesn't sound right, but all right. Josh it is."

"This calls for a celebration. Your glass is empty—let me bring you some more champagne?"

His good humor was infectious. "I'd love it."

"Stay here and I'll get it for you," he said, rising

from his chair next to a huge brass urn spilling over with green fronds.

Caty watched him walk away, intrigued at the turn their relationship had taken. He really is attractive, she thought, and yet . . .

Her thoughts were interrupted when she heard a woman's voice on the other side of the urn speaking Josh's name. Although she knew it was impolite to listen, she was helpless to move. When she heard her name mentioned as well, she leaned closer to the big, green elephant-ear leaves and strained to catch the softly spoken conversation.

"I wonder if Lavinia knows Josh is giving 'Madam Mandesi' so much attention?"

"Probably not, but I intend to tell her. It's only right."

"Of course, Charlie is just as bad."

"Yes, but Charlie chases every light-skirt he meets. I always expected better things of Josh Castleton."

"Admit it, Gloria. You're still smarting because he didn't court your daughter when you expected him to."

"He hasn't courted anyone's daughter! He's never shown the slightest interest in girls from his own set. But what can you expect of a man who spends his life around beggars and criminals? Still—a professional singer!"

"Well, the opera house is better than a music hall after all. And she does have a beautiful voice."

"Yes, Frances always recognizes talent. However,

I do wish she would not make a houseguest out of a professional singer. It tends to blur the social edges, don't you think?"

Caty saw Josh bearing down on her, two glasses of champagne in his hand. She quickly eased out of the chair and down the side of the room, drawing him with her as far away from the two women as she could get.

She only half listened to Josh's comments on the music and the dancing. All the happiness of her visit here, not to mention the prospect of appearing in a new *Carmen*, seemed at first to be shattered by the careless comments of the two women she had overheard. Then, getting a grip on herself, she shook off her growing distress. She would not let this visit be ruined by the snobbery of Mrs. Schyler's friends. She would put on her most gracious, professional persona and face them all down. They might be society, but she was going to be an opera star!

"Would you like to dance?" Josh asked, setting down her glass.

She gave him an exuberant smile. "I'd love to."

But who, she wondered, as he led her out on to the floor, was Lavinia?

Ten

"Josh"

She still could not get used to calling him that. Somehow it didn't mesh with "Detective Castleton"—the stern, nosy, suspicious policeman who looked at everyone with the idea that behind their facade of normalcy lurked a mad killer. The nagging thought that he was only trying to lure her into revealing that she was some kind of criminal still lurked at the back of her mind. She could not entirely rule it out, not even though her heart gave a flutter at the thought of spending the day with him.

Yet when, shortly before noon, she found herself sitting alongside Josh Castleton in a serviceable chaise rolling along the clay roads of Westchester, the beauty of the countryside and the pristine clarity of the day almost drove such unworthy suspicions away for good. The bad weather cleared the way for a clear, crisp morning where the world seemed as new as Eden. The last lingering stains of yellow and magenta sprayed a dull but colorful cast on the hills above them. In the distance, the river glittered as though it had been scattered with sequins and where it was broken by the splash of fish or a diving bird, a spray of diamonds spread out in a circle across its blue surface.

Josh looked very handsome in his tweed overcoat and round felt hat. Not like a policeman at all. And she admired the way he handled the reins with a casual competence, as though he had driven these lanes all his life. Perhaps he had.

Caty adjusted the veil on her hat, hoping she looked as elegant as she felt. She had dressed very carefully in a pale blue walking suit with a blouse of blond Irish linen, edged with tiny ruchings and fine lace, beautifully stitched by her mother. The jacket and skirt had pipings of a darker blue in velvet which gave it an understated elegance. She wore her treasured leather kid gloves and her one good piece of jewelry, a string of creamy pearls. She felt pleased by the obvious glint of admiration that flashed in Josh's eyes when she met him at the foot of the stairs.

"Where are we going?" she asked as the carriage turned away from the river and toward the rising inland hills.

"I thought I would show you something of our area. It's interesting and attractive, especially to a New Yorker."

"More interesting and attractive than Staten Island?"

Josh smile down at her. "Infinitely."

She had a mental picture of staring at millionaire's homes all day. And how like Detective Castleton—"Josh"—to take her where he wanted to go rather than asking what her interests might be. Thus she was surprised when they made another turn on to a narrow lane shadowed by overhanging oaks and evergreens, and when Caty called out as they passed an old cemetery, he obligingly pulled up and asked if she'd like to look around it.

"Very much," Caty said. It was very old and still choked with its summer quota of thickets and weeds. The red stone markers, rising up from them, were so worn with age and the weather as to be almost unreadable. Still Caty enjoyed wandering among them, trying to decipher the names and dates, and the interesting verses carved on them. Josh proudly pointed out a famous neighborhood landmark—a brick wall still showing the damage caused by a cannon fired from the river during the American Revolution.

Not until they were back in the carriage and continuing along the lane did he comment, "I didn't know you were interested in antiquity."

"Is that something you don't expect of a singer? I am Irish, you know. To the Irish the past is as real as the present."

"Well, you've come to the right place. Westchester is full of history."

"Now that surprises me. I thought it was only a place where the rich built their country homes."

"Oh, we have the usual number of robber barons. But long before the millionaires came this was a thriving area, as far back as the seventeenth century. And during the Revolution, it was fought over repeatedly by both the British and the Colonials. If you know where to look, you can still find many indications of it."

Caty settled back on the leather seat and thought that this was going to be a more interesting day than she had expected. She was not disappointed. They first explored a small village not far from the cemetery, tucked between two rolling hills and within sight of the river. It was market day and they found many interesting stalls to browse among, as well as enticing homemade foods for sale. Many of the stalls displayed farm produce or shellfish, but some offered cottage crafts and artifacts from the area. Though she had grown up on a farm, Caty now spent so much of her time in the city that she found this display of rural bounty fascinating.

They left the village and headed for the hills behind it, going at an easy pace to allow for the climb. The view was stunning from the heights, a broad sweep of the narrowing river framed on the horizon by the smoky foothills of the Catskills. Josh told her that the early settlers believed the rolls of thunder along the mountains were actually made by elves bowling nine-pins.

"I've read Washington Irving, too," Caty quipped. Yet there *was* such a sense of magic about the area and it was easy to see how these fanciful stories came to be attached to it.

They were halfway down the hill when Josh surprised her by pulling up in front of a white clapboard house standing on a long slope of emerald grass. The four columns along the porch supported a classical pediment. Low steps from the porch gave out onto the wide lawn, cropped by a small group of sheep, and banked by rows of rhododendron which had obviously once been landscaped but were now overgrown and ragged. A graveled drive circled the house. Josh pulled up in front of the porch and fastened the reins before turning to her.

"I'm afraid I am guilty of a slight deception. I thought you might be hungry by this time and would welcome a pleasant place for tea."

She looked at him in confusion. "Is this an inn? It's a lovely old house. I'll wager it's one of those 'historic' places you were talking about. And the view is spectacular."

He jumped down, waiting for a young boy who came running around the side of the house to cradle the horse's nose in his arms.

"Afternoon, Mister Josh," the boy said. "You want me to stable Druid?"

"Good afternoon, Teddy. No, we'll be going back out again in an hour. Just take care of him for me until then."

"For sure, Mister Josh."

Josh walked around to hand Caty out of the carriage so the boy could pull it on down the path. She stood looking up at the facade of the house, a growing suspicion darkening her eyes. "This isn't an inn, is it?"

"No, I'm afraid it isn't, and though it is old, it was built after the Revolution."

"Don't tell me it is where you live."

He smiled mischievously. "You're almost right. Actually I don't live here anymore—at least, not all the time. I have a place in town. But this is my family home and I did grow up here."

Caty looked in awe at the sweeping front of the big white colonial. She tried to hide the amazement she was feeling while at the same time she tried to assimilate all this into the picture she had formed of Josh Castleton. He really was "one of them." Far from pushing his way into the world of the Schylers and the Fields through graft or Tammany bribes, he had been born into this silver-spooned elite. But why on earth then was he working, much less as a policeman. . . .

Josh took her arm and led her up the steps to the porch. "I tried to tell you last night," he murmured, bending toward her, "and I promise I'll explain it all later. But right now I think we should have some tea."

A Negro man in a neat dark suit and smiling broadly opened the door for them. "Mister Josh," he said, taking Josh's coat and hat. "Mrs. Castleton says to tell you she is waitin' for you in the family parlor."

"Thank you, George." He looked up to catch Caty's questioning glance as she handed her outer coat to the servant. "My mother," he said, with a wink. "She keeps the old-fashioned custom of high tea and I told her today we would join her."

Caty stopped dead. "Your mother! And you didn't warn me?"

"There is no need for concern. Actually, the Castletons were once up there with the Schylers but they've long since fallen on hard times. Now we are as ordinary as the rest of the world except that we work hard to keep up appearances."

She bit back a caustic laugh. It all made sense now. Josh's family might no longer be rich, but Josh was every bit as much a social aristocrat as anyone in the Schylers' "set."

Caty followed him down the hall which ran the length of the house to a closed door at the far end. As he reached out to open it she had a sudden thought and grabbed his arm.

"What is your mother's given name?"

"Her given name? Lavinia."

"Oh God!"

She almost turned on her heel to run back outside but he gripped her hand and pulled her toward him. "It'll be fine," he said, smiling down at her. "You'll like her. And I know she'll love you."

Josh propelled her firmly into the small, warm room that was the family parlor—to distinguish it, no doubt, from the more fancy visitor's parlor. It was a comfortable, homey room with none of the grand showiness of the Schyler house. A woman was sitting on a sofa at the far end near a long window. She smiled as Josh moved to kiss her cheek but the warmth there faded to politeness as she extended her hand to Caty.

"I'm pleased to meet you, my dear. I heard you sing once and I was very impressed."

Caty thanked her and took a chair opposite the sofa, studying Josh's mother while he talked about their ride. Mrs. Castleton must have been a very lovely woman in her youth, Caty decided. She still had a flawless complexion, vivid blue eyes, and silver hair pulled severely back from her face and caught in a thick chignon at the base of her graceful neck. She wore a dark blue silk dress, subtly decorated with narrow lace at the neck and a string of pearls so long that one end lay crumpled in her lap. Everything about her screamed "aristocrat."

The door opened on George bearing a large silver tray loaded with a china teapot, cups, saucers and small plates and several trays of sandwiches, small tarts and delicious-looking cakes. Though she was hungry enough to dive into them, Caty ate sparingly. It soon became obvious that Mrs. Castleton, though pleased that her son had taken an interest in a ladyfriend, was not entirely comfortable with Caty. She carefully avoided any mention of the theater.

"Josh spends so much time at his work, I'm afraid his social life suffers," Lavinia Castleton said, ignoring her son's withering looks. "I can hardly get him out here anymore for an afternoon's visit, much less a whole weekend. I was never more amazed than when he told me he was coming."

"Have another cucumber sandwich, Miss McGowan," Josh said, resisting the urge to signal his mother to change the tenor of her conversation. "I know you must be famished."

"Yes, I am, thank you," Caty replied, trying to hide her discomfort. The enticing thought simmered at the edge of her mind that perhaps Josh Castleton had decided to visit his home when he learned she was going to be a guest of the Schylers. And yet, that was unlikely. It was probably just a coincidence that he decided to visit his mother this weekend.

"I confess I was a little surprised to see him at Beechwood yesterday, but only because I thought that dreadful business with Magda Dubratta would keep him in the city."

"It's all but solved, at least from the department's point of view. They want it declared a suicide. I'm the only one holding out because I'm still not satisfied that it was. I think it was murder and I'm pretty confident of who did it, though I don't have enough proof to arrest him."

Caty gave him a sideways glance. "Him?"

"Yes, 'him'."

She sipped her tea. So that was why he was being so nice to her—he no longer considered her a suspect. Well, thank heaven for that!

Mrs. Castleton waved her hand, frowning. "I don't want any talk of murders. I can't tell you, Miss McGowan, how it distresses me that my son involved himself in this dreadful profession. I did my best to talk him out of it to no avail. He is as stubborn as a mule once he makes up his mind about something and he will doggedly pursue it, no matter how it affects anyone else. It is a trait he inherited from his father."

"Yes, I've noticed," Caty said, smiling wickedly at Josh over the rim of her cup. "But being a policeman does not always involve murder and mayhem. In fact, I've been told a great deal of the time it is slow, boring work."

Josh sat back, crossing his legs. "That's true. We get involved in all kinds of frivolous things, from defending abused hansom horses to dragging hysterical citizens off the street."

Caty felt her cheeks warming. "May I have some more tea?" she said quickly. Mrs. Castleton obliged by lifting the pot and asking her about her visit with the Schylers, a subject Caty was glad to move on to. The food was delicious even though the conversation remained a little awkward. Caty did not notice how the afternoon had darkened outside the window until George came in to build up the fire. "Good heavens," she exclaimed, thankful to have an excuse to leave. "I had better get back to Beechwood. Mrs. Schyler will think I've got lost."

"It's my fault," Josh said, rising from the sofa. "I forgot how early darkness comes on, now that winter is nearly here. George, will you please have Teddy bring the carriage around."

Mrs. Castleton accompanied them to the door, chatting amiably and inviting Caty to come back again, though Caty felt pretty certain she was just being polite. This was a lady who would make all the correct, polite comments, no matter how she really felt inside.

They were soon bundled into the carriage with a woolen lap robe over their knees, rumbling down the hill toward the river. "Your mother is very tactful," Caty said. "She mentioned right off that she had heard me sing but never once said anything about that dreadful accident on the same night. I appreciated that. Most of the time when someone compliments me on my debut, they move right on to Magda's death."

"My mother prefers to ignore what I do for a living but I'm sure she was also trying to be kind to you. It's her way."

The wind had picked up and they were riding straight into it. Caty moved closer to Josh, reveling in the warmth from his body. Encouraged, he inched closer to her as well, though not from a need for warmth. He was acutely conscious of the fact that the closer she got, the more his body heat rose.

"Was she there that night, then?"

"Yes. We came together, as we often do. When I was called backstage she went home with friends." He paused. "I hope you will ignore those pointed comments about my social life. Bear in mind that when I'm in the city my life is my own and I don't share it with her."

Caty laughed. "In other words, she doesn't know what a secret roué you really are."

Josh looked down at her, twirling an imaginary mustache. "Of course."

"I didn't pay it any mind," she added, becoming more serious. "Actually, though she could not have been more polite, I had the feeling she really did not like the idea of her son squiring around a singer or any other kind of professional entertainer. It only slipped out once or twice but I'm rather sensitive to that kind of thing."

Josh did not deny it. "You have to remember she is of another generation when entertainer usually meant 'loose' woman. She tries not to let it influence her but sometimes it slips out anyway. She would like to see me marry some impeccable society belle who would keep a good house and produce a respectable number of grandchildren for her to coddle."

"And is that what you want?" Caty said archly.

Josh did not answer immediately. "I suppose it is. I was raised to think that way. However, that's all in the future. Right now, I'm far too busy to worry about such things."

Caty fussed with rearranging the rug on her lap. Where did that leave her? she wondered. Was Detective Castleton simply indulging in a flirtation on the hope that he would make a mistress of a fledgling opera singer? Was his interest in her based more on lust than friendship or even, possibly someday, love? She felt her hackles rising and forced her resentment down. It was foolish to think such things when she barely knew this man. Better to not expect anything and see where the relationship went.

They had barely turned on to the drive that led

to the brick house when Josh pulled up the reins. He turned to her, taking her hands.

"I've enjoyed this day so much. But there is one more thing I want to show you."

"Oh?"

"Yes. You cannot really appreciate this area unless you see it from the river. Will you go sailing with me tomorrow?"

"Sailing! In November? Is that wise?"

"I grew up here, remember? I've sailed in all kinds of weather. But we'll only go tomorrow if the weather is as fine as it was today, and we'll get back early, before it begins to get darker and colder. Please say you'll come."

She did not even hesitate. "I've only been sailing a few times, but I loved it. Of course I'll come."

He raised her fingers to his lips and smiled down at her, leaning close, his eyes boring into her face. "That's wonderful. Be ready early. I'll come by for you about seven o'clock."

For a moment, she thought he was going to kiss her. Then, remembering their conversation, she pulled her hand from his and inched a little away from him. "I'll be ready."

A flash of disappointment crossed Josh's face, then quickly vanished. He turned to slap the reins on Druid's broad back and they went rolling up to the portico.

Sunday morning dawned even more clear and pristine than the day before had been. Caty was relieved that Josh's invitation had allowed her to miss the house party's excursion to the local parish church which she certainly would have had to take part in otherwise. The thought of sailing on the river, to say nothing of spending the day with Josh Castleton, was as intoxicating as fine wine.

She had tried to temper her excitement with the thought that Josh would probably invite several friends along and make a party of it. Instead, when they arrived at the bay where the boat was moored, it soon became obvious that this trip was to be for the two of them alone. The little craft turned out to be just the right size for two and would never have been roomy enough for more than four at the most.

"I'm counting on you to crew," Josh said, as he readied the boat. "You can work a tiller, can't you."

"I think I can manage that, but you'll have to be in charge of the sails. I haven't done that much sailing."

"Of course. I'll be the captain," he said, smiling at her mischievously.

"Well, someone has to be in charge on a boat and I don't think I'm qualified."

Josh pushed off and soon they were gliding smoothly over the water, heading for the wider section of the river. Though it was early, there were already several colorful sails dotting its silvered surface. Caty sat in the stern with her hand on the tiller while Josh maneuvered the lines to raise the sail, and marveled at the peaceful veil that settled over them as they moved out onto the water. It was as if all the worries and concerns of their lives fell away, left behind on the shore while they glided into a world suspended, quiet, and utterly restful.

Caty lifted her face to the breeze and drank in the cool, sweet air. "It makes me want to break out in song," she said, laughing. "'Ode to Joy' or 'The Spacious Firmament.' It's beautiful!"

"Go ahead. I've often felt that way but since I cannot carry a tune, I refrained from offending the gulls."

They headed toward the widest part of the river, tacking against the tide. The ground rose away from the shore into rusty green hills dotted with houses visible from the boat, some of them imposing enough to impress even from that distance. Josh pointed out landmarks to her or the homes of people he knew. They sailed for more than two hours before dropping anchor and breaking out a lunch basket he had brought along. He settled on one of the seats opposite her, stretched out his long legs and poured them both a glass of wine.

"To our getting to know each other," he said, raising his glass.

Caty didn't reply but she touched his glass and sipped the wine. "Is that what this is all about?"

"Of course." Josh studied her quietly. She had pulled her hair back into a netted bun at the nape of her neck. The brim of her hat cast a shadow across her large eyes but the glint of green was still evident. The sun had given her skin a rosy cast which might easily become a burn if she stayed in it too long and he resolved that he would not let it happen. She wore a sailor's blouse that strained against her full breasts, a sash tight at the waist and a skirt of navy blue. Very appropriate, he thought, and was certain Mrs. Schyler's deft hand had been involved. As he watched her more closely while the boat bobbed gently on the water, he felt a need for her spreading through him. How he longer to touch that fair skin, to kiss those laughing lips. The longing for her was like a wave of electricity emanating from him and sweeping her up in its force.

Caty felt it, too. Her laugh died as her eyes fastened on his direct, challenging gaze. His eyes were the color of the water, gray-green today, though she remembered seeing them dark and smoky. His tanned skin radiated health and vitality. He had folded up the sleeves of his jacket, revealing strong arms lined with tufts of golden hair. His shapely lips invited her, drew her like a magnet and she felt a shudder course through her body at the thought of pressing her own to them.

She turned away, shaking off the mesmerizing attraction that held them both. "Where are we going now?" she asked in a matter-of-fact voice.

Josh began busying himself putting things back into the basket. "Well, I thought we might go downriver a little farther, then take the tide back. I had hoped to go north but it's easier returning with the tide. Perhaps next time I'll show you the northern reaches."

Caty ignored the pleasure that his "next time" gave her. "I'd like that." She looked around at the wooded, rocky shore not far from where they had anchored. "You must have enjoyed growing up here. It's so beautiful and so rustic that it's hard to imagine we're as close to the city as we are."

"I did enjoy it. I thought the whole world was like this but I've learned since how lucky I was. When I see the children in the tenements with their pale faces and only the streets to play in, I thank the Lord for my good fortune."

They set off again, catching a breeze, which had picked up rather suddenly. Josh told her about his boyhood and some of the escapades he had enjoyed living near the magnificent waterway and Caty was so engrossed that she barely noticed the bright day began to darken. Only when Josh looked around, cursing himself for being so neglectful as to forget to watch the sky, did she begin to worry.

"A storm? That's impossible. It's been so sunny and clear."

"You don't know this river. A storm can come up very quickly from behind these mountains. We're too far downriver to make it back to our dock but we'll turn anyway and try."

For the first time she felt a twinge of concern. "But what if we can't?"

"Don't worry. There are one or two small bays where we can wait it out. How annoying that it should spoil what had been a perfect day," he said, frowning at the banks of dark clouds on the horizon.

"It won't spoil it. I like storms and besides, if you want me to see the river, I should see it in all its aspects. What should I do?"

Josh was busy reefing the sail. "Just keep a strong hand on the tiller. See that cove over there? We'll head for that."

It did not look like much of a shelter, Caty thought, but she did as he told her, steering the boat in that direction. She had never seen a storm blow up so quickly. Before they were halfway there, the dark clouds moved in over them, bringing a light mist at first that quickly turned into a downpour. There was none of the dangerous lightning of a summer storm, yet the rain and wind, now in November, dropped the temperature so severely that by the time they reached the choppy waters of the cove she was soaked though and shivering uncontrollably, even beneath the oilcloth slicker Josh gave her. Josh headed for a dock that extended out into the roiling water, where he fastened the boat. The bay was shallow, which made the boat rock all the more and for a moment Caty thought she might face the indignity of being sick in front of him. She was grateful when, after he had tied up the boat, he took her hand and helped her on to the dock. The rain was coming down now in silver sheets and she could see nothing through it.

"Where are we going?" she yelled through the noise of a rolling cannon of thunder.

Without answering he took her hand and began running down the dock toward the shore.

Eleven

A small house loomed up out of the rain. Josh threw open the door and pulled her inside, but not before she noticed it was made of logs, like the kind of beach house one would expect to find at the seashore. Caty stood in the middle of a tiny room with a massive stone fireplace at one end and reveled in being out of the stinging rain. Rivulets of water ran down her face to her skirt and on to a straw mat on the floor. Long strands of her hair were plastered to her cheeks and her shoes were squishy with water. She had no idea what had happened to her hat.

"I think I can get a fire going," Josh said, throwing off his wet slicker. He bent to the hearth and began inspecting the debris among the pile of ashes. "You'd better take off the worst of those wet clothes before you get completely chilled."

"I already am," Caty murmured as she pulled off the soaked oilcloth. "What is this place?"

"It belongs to a friend of mine. I've used it before for emergencies such as this. That's why he keeps it. When I get this fire going I'll see if there are any dry clothes you can use."

The room had a low ceiling, which was drumming with the rain. One door at the rear led off into a hall, which Caty presumed gave off to a kitchen and perhaps a small bedroom. It was so dark and chilly she inched closer to where Josh was blowing a flame to life. On the stones near the hearth a basket lay holding dry wood. Caty picked up a log and handed it to him.

"Your friend thinks of everything."

He smiled up at her. "He's very resourceful."

The fire sputtered into a growing flame and Caty bent her hands to its warming glow. She began shivering so strongly she could not hold them still.

Standing Josh put an arm around her shoulder. "You really must get some dry clothes on or Frances Schyler will have my head for giving you pneumonia. Here, stay close to this flame while I search for something."

Caty did not argue with him. Her heavy skirt, weighed down with the dampness, and her wet blouse were both so uncomfortable that all she wanted was to get out of them. From the corner of her eye she saw Josh digging through a cedar chest against the wall until he came up with something that looked like a robe and a long shirt.

"Not very fashionable but they'll have to do," he said, handing them to her.

"What about you?"

"I'm used to being soaked to the skin," he said,

pulling off his wet jacket. "I'm more concerned about you."

The fire was beginning to put out a little warmth which felt heavenly to Caty. She bent close to it until the shivering in her body subsided a little, then stood up and reached behind her to try and unfasten the tiny buttons on her blouse. The cloth was so damp and her fingers so chilled that she could barely manage them. Josh had disappeared into the kitchen where she heard him rummaging about, opening doors and clanging pans. She twisted around to try to get at the buttons but only succeeded in pulling a muscle in her arm.

"Here, I'll help you," he said, walking in from the kitchen in time to see her struggling. He stepped up behind her and began working at the buttons. "You women. I think you design these things just to make your lives difficult."

"It's not so hard when you have a maid to get you in and out," Caty quipped. His fingers through the wet cloth tickled against her back and a shudder went through her, which she hoped he would think was from the cold. One side of the opening on the blouse began to fall away, leaving the air cold against her neck. He had worked his way down to her waist now but the blouse and her chemise beneath it were so wet they lay contoured against her skin.

A subtle change began to take place in the matter-of-fact way he was undoing her. He slowed, taking his time, carefully slipping out the buttons on her cummerbund and lifting it from her waist. Beneath it her skirt was fastened with hooks, which he undid, one by one. A shudder went through her body as his hands slid up beneath the edges of her blouse, pulling them away from her back, a shudder which Josh knew this time was not from the cold. His body warmed and he leaned closer to her, expecting any moment for her to step away in indignation.

But indignation was the last thing on Caty's mind. The warmth which flowed in waves through her as his hands slipped beneath her blouse was welcome and exciting. The rain on the roof, the flickering light from the hearth making a single bright nimbus against the dark of the room, created a kind of warm cocoon in which the rest of the world was suspended. She felt Josh's hands, rough yet tender in their touch, slide along her back, gently lifting away the damp cloth. He moved against her and she felt his body press against hers.

Josh slid his hands up to her shoulders and pushed the blouse off and down her arms. Her skin was damp and cold to his touch and he gently kneaded her flesh, feeling the tiny raised gooseflesh there. He wanted to say something but he was afraid to break the spell that seemed to settle around them both. He slid his hands down her back and around her waist to press her back against him. Then, slowly, teasingly, he moved up to cup her breasts in his palms.

"You don't know how long I've wanted to do

this," he whispered as he bent to kiss the nape of her neck. Her breasts were firm and round and filled his hands with their wonderful sweetness. His lips coursed her neck, tasting the soft dew there, then slid up to kiss the lobe of her ear.

Caty lifted her head, baring her long, graceful neck to him. The growing warmth that filled her as his hands moved sinuously beneath her breasts was like an intoxicating wine. When he lifted his thumbs to gently tease her hard nipples she thought her knees would give way.

Josh felt her response. He turned her around to face him and laid his palms alongside her face, lifting her lips to his and drinking in the sweetness of her mouth. When he lifted his head, he saw that her eyes were closed and her face filled with longing and ecstasy. He reached behind to unpin her hair, then pulled the damp tendrils over her shoulder and down over her breast.

Her eyes were open now and they met his frankly and honestly. There was hunger in them, he felt sure, the same hunger that consumed him.

Caty looked beyond that need and into his eyes and saw the question there. She knew this was the moment she could step back, halting all the excitement between them. She knew, too, that if she did not step back, if she allowed this intimacy to proceed, it meant they would be crossing a threshold which would change forever the casual attraction they felt for each other. She knew it and she did not care.

His shirt was open at the throat, revealing the

light golden hair on his chest. She laid her hands on his shoulders and leaned to kiss his inviting, tempting mouth. His arms went around her, crushing her to him and his tongue darted against her lips until they parted just enough to allow him entry to the secret places of her mouth. It was a long kiss where lips moved against lips, seeking, drawing, tasting.

When he tore his lips from hers it was to course her cheek and down her neck. His hands pulled away her blouse and then gently pushed down the edges of her chemise to bare her breasts. With a gasp he lifted them to kiss first one, then the other, holding them in his hands as he might a flower.

Caty reached behind her to pull the waist of her skirt open and allow it to fall around her feet. Josh slipped to his knees, winding his arms around her hips, kissing her waist and gently working her petticoats down and away from her body. He pulled her against him, his hands grasping and gently holding her hips. He was on fire, engorged and ready for her, yet he held back. With an agonizing sigh, he pulled away from her to stand and begin removing his own clothes. Caty watched in admiration as the firelight danced on the long, lean lines of his body. Grabbing up the blanket she had discarded, he spread it on the floor before the hearth, then reached to pull her down beside him.

A tremor of fear went through her body, quickly exorcised by the warm touch of Josh's hands. Spreading her knees, he knelt in front of her, bending to lift one breast to his lips. Her back arched as his tongue began its magic, circling, licking, teasing until the nipple was erect and hard beneath his lips. With one arm he cradled her, gently laying her down on the blanket until he could suckle, first one taut breast, then the other. Her body began to sing as waves of warmth coursed through her. She sighed with sheer delight and let her fingers explore his thick hair until he had her too excited to think of anything else.

"Oh . . ." she cried as Josh lifted his head, leaving her limp in his arms. "I didn't know . . ."

He wondered at her inexperience, yet he did not comment on it for fear of breaking the spell. Instead he deliberately slowed, taking his time to lightly touch her breasts, her waist, her hips. Gently he explored her inner thigh, and only when he knew she was oblivious to everything else did he work his way up, tickling and thrusting inside her. She opened her thighs to welcome him and he began massaging the electrifying nub that would bring her to her peak. His own body was ready, hard and longing, yet he forced himself to wait, delighting her with the skill of his fingers. Her sighs became more urgent, more instinctive, as she rose on waves of pleasure, beyond thought to that plateau of pure sensation she had never known before.

Josh allowed his lips to course up her body to her face where he claimed her mouth in a wild, open kiss. His tongue sought the deepest places of her mouth and, to his surprise, she also sought his, exploring his tongue, his teeth, the roof of his mouth. She was consumed with a flame every bit as strong as his and he felt a sudden surge of desire for her inspired by the strength of her passion. Yet still he tormented her with his fingers inside her until she hardly knew what she was doing. Giddily she broke away, arching away from him and lifting her breast to his mouth again to be suckled, not tenderly this time, but wildly, urgently. Her body writhed beneath his insistent lips and fingers. Her hips moved in concert with his; she was like an instrument in the hands of a great musician and he played her for all he was worth.

"Oh, oh . . ." she cried, as he rolled over to cover her with his body, thrusting deep inside her, gently but demanding as his own passion swelled into a torrent of desire.

Her arms went around him, clasping him against her. Her hips arched to meet him. She felt the sweet fullness of him, the hard thrusting against her until the wall gave way and he sought the lovely depths of her. The mild pain she felt was eclipsed by the soaring waves of sheer delight that carried her along with him. She was barely conscious that he, too, was soaring with her, lost in the starry infinity of love. She only vaguely heard her own cry as she was swept away with him.

They lay there together for a long time, clasped in each other's arms. The rain was still drumming on the roof, not quite as hard as before but still strong. A shutter on the window rattled in the wind. A log on the fire fell in a shower of sparks and a sudden glare of light. Outside the small circle of its glow the room was clothed in a darkness that seemed deeper and more mysterious than before.

Caty nestled her head in the hollow of Josh's neck and waited for her pounding heart to ease. She was filled with such a sense of comfort and satisfaction that she wanted to dance around the room, yet, at the same time she wanted to meld into his warm, intoxicating body. And what a wonderful body it was. She ran her fingers lightly across his chest and down his waist to his flat stomach and felt the shiver that went through him.

"I've never seen a naked man before, you know," she whispered against his neck. "Except for statues and such."

Josh smoothed the long strands of her hair from her face. "I hope I measure up to Michelangelo."

She lifted her head to look into his smiling eyes. "Better. You're so . . . soft . . . and so . . . warm . . . ."

"I'm certainly warm," he replied, kissing the tip of her nose. "But that's your doing."

"You have a wonderful body," she murmured, and went back to exploring with the ends of her fingers. She outlined the strong shoulder and the long stretch of chest, along the middle of his stomach and down the curve of hip, inward to the thigh and then, lightly, delicately, along the hills and hollows and length of his well-endowed masculinity.

Josh resisted the urge to tell her that hers was

the magnificent body and simply lay back enjoying the tickling sensation of her fingertips.

"Oh, my dear," he said, sighing. "Keep that up and you'll find out just how wonderful this body can be."

"I already have," Caty said. She turned to lie on her back, breaking off the tantalizing tease of her fingertips. Josh pulled up one end of the blanket and rolled it around them both. Resting on one elbow he looked down at her.

"What are you thinking?"

"Oh, just how unreal all this is. Everything seems far away now, the opera, my career, even Mrs. Schyler's house party. I wonder how I'm going to feel when I get back?"

"Are you thinking you might regret what's happened between us?"

She smiled into his eyes. "No. Not regret. It was too good for that. I've spent a lot of years wondering what the great mystery was between men and women and now I know. I was ready to know."

Josh rolled over on his back with his hands beneath his head. "And I came along. How convenient."

"You know I didn't mean that. I wanted you every bit as much as you wanted me. Only . . ."

"Only, now what?"

"Yes. What happens when we get back to New York and you go back to being a policeman again? Do we forget about this? Will I be sorry? A woman wonders about those things."

Josh reached out and pulled her into his arms, his lips against her hair. "Now listen to me, my lovely. I did not simply take advantage of you because circumstances put us where it could happen. Though I tried to think of you as just another suspect in a murder, I gave that up long ago. I've wanted to know you better, to hold you in my arms since almost the first time I saw you. Somehow I knew even then that we were meant to be important to each other."

Important to each other. Caty let the words roll about in her mind, wondering just what they meant. Though she could not express it in words, she did not know what this kind of an experience led to. Did the two of them simply go on about their lives as though it had never happened? Did they move on to a clandestine affair in which she became the mistress and he the man who keeps her? That was certainly not going to happen. Yet somehow she knew it would be unwise of her to start thinking that they had entered into some kind of commitment because of making love together. She was not ready for that and she was certain Josh wasn't. Besides, from everything she had heard, nothing turned a man off quicker than a woman demanding fidelity to her alone.

Josh studied her face in the flickering shadows of the fire. "Of course, you could marry me."

Her eyes flew open. "What?"

"Well, it is a solution, just in case you feel like a fallen woman or something. I mean, I wouldn't mind. I'd be honored, in fact."

Caty sat up, pulling the blanket around her shoulders. "Josh Castleton, sometimes you say the most ridiculous things. I do not feel like a fallen woman. And even if I did I would certainly not want you to marry me merely to save my reputation. That's going a little far."

He reached for her, pulling her back down beside him. "It was merely a suggestion, though I won't promise not to ask you again sometime. Would I make such a bad husband?"

"Of course not, for a young lady of 'impeccable lineage', as you put it. But I'm a singer determined to have a career. Marriage is just not something I can face for a long time. I'm also the daughter of an Irish farmer and his seamstress wife. I wouldn't fit in with your mother and her society friends at all."

"Nonsense. I've met your mother and she's charming. The more I think about it the more right it seems. Yes, it's a fine idea."

"It's a crazy idea! Come now, be serious. Did you know that Mrs. Schyler is going to fund a new production of *Carmen* and she wants me to sing the lead? It's my first chance to become famous."

"Yes, I know about it and I promise I won't stand in your way."

She tried to read his eyes, to see if the merriment in them was an indication he was teasing her, but he was facing away from the fire and it was too dark. His voice sounded serious enough and Caty began to feel a sense of being cornered.

"And I promise not to stand in the way of your being a policeman! Don't you see? You have your career and I have mine and they are as different as night and day."

"But you'd sing your Carmen. You'd have your great moment."

"And then what? You would expect me to make a home for you, wouldn't you? To keep house while you're out catching criminals and have supper waiting when you get back."

Josh hesitated. "Well, isn't that what wives usually do? I don't see anything wrong with it."

Caty clucked her tongue. "Oh, you don't? Well, what do you think of this scenario? When you come home from catching criminals you can read my letter from Milan all about how my latest Delilah went so well at La Scala. Or perhaps it was Cavalleria at the Paris Opera, or . . ."

"All right," he interrupted, laughing. "I concede the point." Lifting her chin he drew her face close to his, looking down into her luminous eyes. "I simply want you to know that this is not something frivolous to me. I don't go around taking advantage of beautiful young virgins, then walk away whistling." His voice softened. "I really do care for you, Caty. I think I could care a lot more."

Caty caught her breath at the sincerity on his face. "Oh, Josh. I care for you, too. More than I ever dreamed I would." Her arms went about his neck and she lifted her lips to his. She did not want to think about impossible things like marriage. She did not want to think about the future at all. All she wanted was the feel of his lips on hers, the warm, soft touch of them and the delight they awoke in her body.

Josh put his arms around her and pulled her down across him so that she was lying over him. She liked that, being above him. Instinctively, she broke off the kiss and rubbed against him, feeling him harden against her. He lifted his hands to frame her face.

"You're so beautiful," he breathed, drinking in the shadows of the fire against the planes of her cheeks, the hollow of her throat, the long fall of her hair. He worked his fingers into her long tresses, lifting her head to kiss the shadowed hollow of her throat.

Caty murmured in delight. She moved above him, shifting her weight to allow her breast to drop on his mouth, teasing him. He grabbed for it eagerly, suckling the nipple of first one, then the other.

She moaned as the flame rose within her once again, flaring into life by the insistent working of his mouth. He slipped his hands along her hips, cupping them, kneading them until she thought she could bear it no longer. She spread her knees on either side of him and rose to allow him to enter, gently, easing upward.

It was so delicious. She arched her back to his hands on her breasts and groaned with the sheer pleasure of it. Because her weight was on her knees, Josh was able to ease himself up into a sitting position, bringing her with him until she was cradled in his lap, impaled on his hard thrusting shaft. He clasped his arms around her and buried his face in the warm comfort of her breasts.

"How did you do that?" she whispered between gasps of pleasure.

He did not answer, being so intent on the enjoyment of her. Before she knew how it happened he pressed her down on her back and was above her, pulling out and scouring her waist with his lips, then coursing down to her moist, welcoming femininity.

Caty closed her eyes and lay back, lost in the surge of delight he evoked in her. Then delight flared to ecstasy, waves of longing and need.

She heard herself cry out for him, begging for him. Yet still he teased her, driving her to the brink of a desire so strong she could not bear it.

"Come to me . . . come . . ." she heard herself pleading. She knew he was as excited as she. His ragged gasps told of his need yet still he went on tormenting her.

"Do you want me?" he said, his voice husky. "Say that you want me."

"Yes . . . yes . . . I want you!"

Quickly he rose to thrust inside her waiting void, driving into her, mingling his own cries with hers. The room had been dark but now it was alive with light, shrieking and streaming across the heavens. They cried out together as they were swept into the void and over the threshold of a sensation so strong it seemed to meld them together into one being.

The thunder of that exalted peak slowly quieted until there was no sound in the darkened room but their ragged breathing. With his arms still wrapped tightly around her, Josh buried his face in her throat and waited for the familiar exhaustion that followed release. When he could move he kissed the hollow of her neck briefly, then rolled over on his back beside her, giving himself up completely to the weary but fulfilled contentment that possessed him.

"You did that on purpose," Caty said with a giggle.

"Did what?"

"Got me so worked up, then made me beg. That wasn't playing fair."

"Of course it was. You didn't see me walk away, did you?"

Caty laughed and nestled against him, completely satisfied and content. Still, she made up her mind that when she knew a little more about this thing called making love, someday she was going to make him beg for her! His body felt so firm against hers. It gave her great pleasure to know that he had shared it with her, melded with hers. His lashes were long on his cheek and his breathing grew slower and deeper as though he was falling asleep. She nestled closer, closed her eyes, and allowed her happiness to envelop her like a warm comforter.

She had no idea how long they lay there quietly

resting. At length, in the sudden silence she realized for the first time that the rain had slackened to a soft flutter on the roof. Caty sat up and reached for her chemise which Josh had spread over the back of a chair before the fire. Though it was still damp, it was wearable and she slipped it on, reaching behind to try to fasten the tiny buttons.

"Allow me," Josh said, reaching up.

"I thought you were asleep."

"Almost, but not quite."

"I'm not sure it's safe to let you touch me," she said, laughing. "Not because of you, but because of me."

"Don't tell me I've discovered a wanton? I promise not to let you take advantage of me again. Besides, we probably should be getting back before Frances Schyler sends out a search party."

"I'll wager she knows you better than that."

Josh ran his fingers along her back, then bent to kiss her between her shoulder blades. "Contrary to what you may have heard, I am not in the habit of bringing luscious young damsels to this cabin to wait out a storm in such delight. In fact, I've spent many an hour in misery here, wondering if I'd ever be able to get back on the river before nightfall. I'll never see the old place in the same way again."

"Do you really think I'm 'luscious'?"

He slipped his arms around her and ran his tongue along the nape of her neck. "Good enough to eat!"

Caty giggled with pleasure but forced herself to pull away and begin dressing. Her skirt was still damp and heavy but her petticoats and blouse were nearly dry. As she fastened them on she glanced now and then at Josh, who reluctantly began pulling on his clothes. Somehow he still managed to finish dressing before she did and took over the job of buttoning her up. The fire had died down to a few embers and the cabin was beginning to grow cold again.

Josh twisted the last button, then turned her to face him, slipping his arms around her. "This has been the most marvelous afternoon," he sighed, pressing her against him and entwining his fingers in her hair.

Caty slipped her arms around his neck and sought out his lips. She was filled with a terrible sadness that their magical time was ending, that the real world beckoned, and that she hadn't the least idea what would happen between them once they were back at Beechwood.

"It was marvelous for me, too," she whispered when he broke the kiss. "I'll never forget it."

"I won't let you," Josh said, tipping her chin to raise her lips to his again. "But we'd better go or I'll be stripping those clothes off you all over again and I don't think I could face those buttons one more time."

He doused the fire, then led her outside. The storm had brought on an early darkness but Caty was surprised to realize how long they had been inside the little house, lost in the lovely world of exploring each other's bodies. The river was very choppy but Josh thought he could manage it, especially since the wind was with them. It turned out to be a sold and uncomfortable sail but with the strong wind they made it back to the dock in less than an hour. Caty gave silent thanks that Beechwood lay so close to the river, for the carriage that Josh had stabled there when they left that morning proved to be almost as drafty and cold as the boat had been. The temperature had dropped at least ten degrees and the wind was blustery, blowing the last of the summer's growth around them. By the time they rolled up to the portico she was chilled through, her teeth refused to stop chattering and her throat was beginning to ache. She was barely aware of Mollie hurrying out the door to meet them as Josh jumped to hand her down, then laid his arm around her shoulders and rushed her inside the house.

The hall was brightly lit and blessedly warm. Caty dragged off her wet oilcloth to hand it to Mollie as Mrs. Schyler came bustling down the hall, fussing over them and at them at the same time. Two other figures followed but Caty barely noticed them.

"I declare, I was worried sick," Frances went on. "I told Mister Schyler we ought to send out a party to find you, but he said Josh was a good sailor and could take care of himself. All the same . . ."

"It was all right," Josh broke her off. "We waited out the worst of the storm in Piedmont."

"Yes, but look at poor Caty," Frances went on. "She's chilled through and it wouldn't surprise me if she came down with some terrible sickness from all this. Really, Josh, you should have turned back when you first saw that the weather was changing."

"It's all right," Caty cried. "It came up so quickly and before that, it was a beautiful day. I'll be all right."

She glanced up to see Josh staring over her shoulder at the man who had come down the hall behind Frances. Looking around Caty saw a tall, beefy figure in a dark blue overcoat with shiny brass buttons, his helmet under his arm.

"Sergeant O'Leary," Josh said in astonishment. "What are you doing here?"

"Sorry to have surprised you like this, Detective, but the captain sent me up to fetch you back to the city as soon as you can get away. Your mother told me you'd probably come here first so I came along to wait."

"Back to New York? Why?"

O'Leary glanced quickly at Caty, then away again. A faint tinge of color rose in his round face at the obvious conclusion he was drawing about where the two of them had been.

"You remember Miss McGowan," Josh said. "Officer O'Leary."

O'Leary bobbed his head briefly at Caty, then focused on Josh. "It's something important, Inspector. There's been another murder at the opera house."

Twelve

It was like being underwater. Josh stared through the clouded window at the street scene below, straining to make out the shapes of horses, cabs, and milling pedestrians through the layers of city grit that had built up on the glass. A young boy hawking apples darted in front of a brougham, creating a mild traffic logjam and he watched bemused as the shouting, gesturing drivers and passersby went at each other. The slush in the street did not help. Yesterday's storm had been the herald of winter coming in for good, and since then, a light dusting of snow had drifted in from an overhang of thick, dark, ominous clouds. It perfectly matched his mood.

"It's all there in the report," his chief said, shoving a folder of paper across his desk. "Too bad it had to cut short your holiday but these things don't happen to fit our schedules."

"I planned to be back tomorrow anyway," Josh muttered, trying to force memories of yesterday afternoon from his mind. It would have been nice to stay that extra day—nice to have more time to see Caty, to hold her in his arms again, to kiss her warm lips, and possess that passionate body. . . .

"Doctor says he was strangled, though it's difficult to tell if that killed him or if it was the fall. Seven stories straight down is enough to do the job."

Josh turned back to the desk and picked up the folder, forcing himself to concentrate on its contents. "Did he fall off the roof or was he shoved?"

"Now how was the doc to know that? It's pretty obvious, though, that a man doesn't go walking on the roof of a building for a constitutional. Of course he was pushed."

"It might have been suicide."

"Not that again! And I suppose he tried to strangle himself first. I won't have this straightforward murder messed up by trying to call it suicide. Somebody wanted to kill him, first by throttling him and then by shoving him off the building. You find out who, Castleton, and this time, no pussyfooting around."

Josh calmly pulled up a chair and sat down, not the least perturbed by his chief's anger, a fact that served to irritate Sheldon even more.

"Don't you think it's suspicious, a murder following an accident, following a very public suicide, and all of them at the same opera house. I believe they are all related somehow but the problem is, there has not yet been any factor that links all three. It's there somewhere and I'll find it if you will just give me time."

"Yes, well, time is not always there to give. Especially where the richest men in the city who run the place are screaming at me to solve this thing before it ruins their little play toy. Did you know the victim?"

"Yes. His name was Herman Warring and I interrogated him after Dubratta's death. He was married to her once, long ago, in Europe. I even thought he might be a suspect in her death since he had some reason to carry a grudge against her, but I could never find any evidence to substantiate it."

"Hmm. Maybe I'd better rethink this suicide thing. It could have been remorse over her murder. . . ."

"I don't think so," Josh said with a withering look which the chief did not miss.

"And what do you think?"

"I believe there is a connection between the two deaths and I think I know the person involved. But I'll need some kind of proof before I can bring him in. Perháps I'd better get over to the Met and begin asking questions again. If I can put this fellow at the scene, it will be enough to bring him here for some serious interrogation."

"Yes, well, perhaps you had. Just remember—I want this thing solved, and soon!"

The chief's words echoed in his mind all the way to the Metropolitan. As if he, Josh Castleton, wasn't anxious to wrap this mess up! At the rate they were going, before long Morgan and Belmont would be calling for somebody else to handle the

The Publishers of Zebra Books Make This Special Offer to Zebra Romance Readers...

AFTER YOU HAVE READ THIS BOOK WE'D LIKE TO SEND YOU 4 MORE FOR *FREE* AN $18.00 VALUE

No Obligation!

ONLY ZEBRA HISTORICAL ROMANCES "BURN WITH THE FIRE OF HISTORY" (SEE INSIDE FOR MONEY SAVING DETAILS.)

MORE PASSION AND ADVENTURE AWAIT... YOUR TRIP TO A BIG ADVENTUROUS WORLD BEGINS WHEN YOU ACCEPT YOUR FIRST 4 NOVELS ABSOLUTELY *FREE* (AN $18.00 VALUE)

Accept your Free gift and start to experience more of the passion and adventure you like in a historical romance novel. Each Zebra novel is filled with proud men, spirited women and tempestuous love that you'll remember long after you turn the last page.

Zebra Historical Romances are the finest novels of their kind. They are written by authors who really know how to weave tales of romance and adventure in the historical settings you love. You'll feel like you've actually gone back in time with the thrilling stories that each Zebra novel offers.

GET YOUR FREE GIFT WITH THE START OF YOUR HOME SUBSCRIPTION

Our readers tell us that these books sell out very fast in book stores and often they miss the newest titles. So Zebra has made arrangements for you to receive the four newest novels published each month.

You'll be guaranteed that you'll never miss a title, and home delivery is so convenient. And to show you just how easy it is to get Zebra Historical Romances, we'll send you your first 4 books absolutely FREE! Our gift to you just for trying our home subscription service.

BIG SAVINGS AND FREE HOME DELIVERY

Each month, you'll receive the four newest titles as soon as they are published. You'll probably receive them even before the bookstores do. What's more, you may preview these exciting novels free for 10 days. If you like them as much as we think you will, just pay the low preferred subscriber's price of just $3.75 each. *You'll save $3.00 each month off the publisher's price.* AND, your savings are even greater because there are never any shipping, handling or other hidden charges—FREE Home Delivery. Of course you can return any shipment within 10 days for full credit, no questions asked. There is no minimum number of books you must buy.

4 FREE BOOKS

TO GET YOUR 4 FREE BOOKS WORTH $18.00 — MAIL IN THE FREE BOOK CERTIFICATE TODAY

Fill in the Free Book Certificate below, and we'll send your FREE BOOKS to you as soon as we receive it.

If the certificate is missing below, write to: Zebra Home Subscription Service, Inc., P.O. Box 5214, 120 Brighton Road, Clifton, New Jersey 07015-5214.

FREE BOOK CERTIFICATE
4 FREE BOOKS
ZEBRA HOME SUBSCRIPTION SERVICE, INC.

YES! Please start my subscription to Zebra Historical Romances and send me my first 4 books absolutely FREE. I understand that each month I may preview four new Zebra Historical Romances free for 10 days. If I'm not satisfied with them, I may return the four books within 10 days and owe nothing. Otherwise, I will pay the low preferred subscriber's price of just $3.75 each; a total of $15.00, *a savings off the publisher's price of $3.00*. I may return any shipment and I may cancel this subscription at any time. There is no obligation to buy any shipment and there are no shipping, handling or other hidden charges. Regardless of what I decide, the four free books are mine to keep.

NAME _____

ADDRESS _____ APT _____

CITY _____ STATE _____ ZIP _____

TELEPHONE
( ) _____

SIGNATURE _____
(if under 18, parent or guardian must sign)

Terms, offer and prices subject to change without notice. Subscription subject to acceptance by Zebra Books. Zebra Books reserves the right to reject any order or cancel any subscription.

ZB1193

GET FOUR FREE BOOKS

(AN $18.00 VALUE)

ZEBRA HOME SUBSCRIPTION
SERVICE, INC.
120 BRIGHTON ROAD
P.O. BOX 5214
CLIFTON, NEW JERSEY 07015-5214

AFFIX STAMP HERE

investigation. He suspected that they hadn't done so before only because of the long friendship they shared with his mother. But that wasn't going to hold much longer if they kept finding dead bodies around the opera house.

"Wasn't a pretty sight, I can tell you," O'Leary commented dryly as they walked around the spot where Warring's body had landed in the alley. "It's amazin' to me that the coroner could tell he'd been strangled, the body was so smashed up."

"Coroners know what to look for," Josh answered as he bent to look closer at the pavement. "I suppose there's been traffic through here since?"

"We tried to cordon it off but the opera hands screamed bloody murder, if you'll pardon the reference. Seems they use this alley to cart sets back and forth from the warehouse."

"I thought they stacked most of them on the sidewalks. Well, there's nothing much left here to tell us anything. Let's go have a look at the roof."

A series of narrow dark stairwells led them finally out on the roof of the building, among the elevator housings and soot-covered tiles enclosed by a waist-high railing. O'Leary pointed Josh to the right spot where he peered over at the alley below.

"It wouldn't be difficult to throw a body off this building, especially if the man were already unconscious. You'd think they would have put up a higher railing."

"They probably never figured anyone would be

up here at all unless it was to work on the lifts. It's not exactly a place where you'd come to take the air." O'Leary brushed at the front of his coat with a look that said he found the place disgusting.

"They went over this carefully?"

"Every piece of lint. There were signs of a scuffle, all right. A pretty fierce one. There was some blood, too, but it was hard to tell if it was the victim's or the assailant's. By the time we found Warring he was pretty bloody."

"Yet if he had been strangled first, that would rule out a lot of blood from the victim. I think we'd better consider it as coming from the murderer. Warring probably fought back. Was there any kind of weapon?"

"None. If Warring drew blood it was probably with his fingernails. If the assailant used a weapon, he probably took it away with him."

Josh got down on his knees to look closely at the ground in front of the concrete rail. He ran his hand over the tiles, looking for anything out of place and sensing a growing disappointment at the lack of clues. Either this man was very clever, or very lucky. Either way, they would have to have more to go on than he'd been told so far.

"We did find one strange thing," O'Leary muttered. "Some of them tiles were lathered with chicken fat. It was kind of rancid by the time we found them but that's what it was all right."

"Chicken fat? What conclusions did you draw from that?"

"Only that maybe someone'd been eating his

lunch up here. It could have been left here before the murder. Even so, it wasn't much to go on."

Josh rose to his feet. For the first time since he'd been called back to New York he felt that familiar sense that things might be beginning to fall into place. "You've questioned all the stagehands, I presume?"

"Yes. At least, we questioned them early yesterday morning. Not all of them were here. We were leaving the rest until you came in today."

"Let's get at it, then."

Josh started back down the stairs, quietly sorting out the things he knew and trying not to let his expectations rise too high yet. Ten minutes later, when he reached the hall in front of the greenroom, he scanned the line of men's faces waiting there to be interrogated without seeing the one he most wished to see. They were a surly looking group, put out at having their morning interrupted. None appeared too guilty or worried, as far as he could tell. He heard a voice call his name and turned to see Cannio hurrying toward him.

"Castleton, I'm so relieved you're here. We've got to get this thing solved right away. We're going to be ruined if this keeps up! You've got to . . ."

"I know, Maestro. We want to solve it as much as you want it solved. Please calm down and just allow me to do my job."

Taking the worried manager's arm, he led him into the room and closed the door. "I'm going to talk to those fellows first because of all the employees here at the house, they would be the ones most likely to use the roof. But there are a few things you can help with first."

"I hired all those men. It's unbelievable that they would do a thing like this, and to a member of the orchestra! I tell you, Detective, this house is going to be ruined if we don't . . ."

"I know. It will be solved. I've seen them bring their supper with them to the house. Do they ever go up on the roof to eat it?"

Cannio ran his hand through his sheaf of hair. "Sometimes, I suppose. In warm weather. Though why one would go up there now, in November, is beyond knowing. Although, come to think of it, it was rather fine yesterday morning."

Yes, Josh thought, it was fine yesterday morning. He had a brief image of sequined water and billowing sails, and Caty, her beautiful face lifted to the sun. Quickly he forced the tantalizing picture from his mind. "Is there any one particular man who usually went up on the roof?"

"There were two or three. I asked them, you see."

"Good thinking. Who are they?"

"Let's see . . . Patrick Batterson, Tonio Lupi, and Boris Borinsky."

Josh allowed himself a tiny smile of satisfaction. "I recall Borinsky very well. I think I would like to start my interrogations this morning with him."

Cannio ran a hand nervously around his high starched collar. "Well, you see, I had the same thought earlier. I sent for him the moment I arrived. It was then that I learned that Boris had not come in for yesterday's performance, nor this morning."

"You mean he hasn't been seen since this happened?"

"Yes. That is correct. It rather casts suspicion on him, doesn't it?"

Josh grabbed for his hat. "There is only one thing more I need to know. Where does this Borinsky live?"

"Somewhere down on the Lower East Side, I believe. I have his address upstairs."

He was already out the door. "O'Leary, tell the rest of these men they may go back to work but not to leave the house. We'll question them later. Right now we're going to take a trip downtown."

A leaden sky hung over the city. Gusts of wind off the East River tugged at coats and sent hats reeling down the street. The farther Josh and his sergeant went into the narrow tangle of streets, the more they were accosted by flying newspapers, paper bags, and cardboard boxes suddenly transformed into missiles.

Josh knew the weather was the remnants of yesterday's storm but he tried not to let it remind him of the way he and Caty had passed the time in the small log house in Piedmont. His instinct told him that he was finally going to hang something on Boris Borinsky. Moreover, if he could connect Boris to Warring's murder, he could damn sure connect him to Magda's as well. It was an exhilarating thought.

The brick tenements rose up along both sides of the narrow streets like the walls of a canyon. Dirty awnings extended out over the walkways. The curbs were crowded with pushcarts, barrels, and makeshift stands on which all kinds of vegetables were displayed for sale. The unkempt aura of the place was heightened by rows of small iron balconies, each bearing its quota of bundled laundry, and even a mattress or two, set out for airing.

And yet for all the dirt and clutter, a vibrancy crackled in the air. The throngs of people, speaking mostly in Yiddish, all seemed to know each other. They gave the two policemen furtive, suspicious glances but were polite enough when O'Leary stopped to ask directions to Boris's address. By the time they reached the building they had collected a small crowd of children and interested onlookers, following them in a procession.

The address they sought was the worst of a row of dilapidated and filthy buildings that lined one of the dreariest of the narrow streets. Both Josh and his sergeant hesitated before moving up the low steps to the front hall. With a word to the crowd to wait below, they walked into a dark, musty hallway reeking of human excrement. Josh choked back the bile that rose in his throat and started up the stairs, being careful where he stepped.

"Gor!" O'Leary muttered. "I've seen some poor places before but this is the worst."

"It's not that they're poor. I've been in homes of the poor that were spotless. These people have either given up or they don't have the strength of character to better themselves."

He felt as though he should eat those words once they opened the door to Boris's flat. A muffled voice had told them to enter when they knocked, yet they eased in carefully, half expecting Boris to jump out at them. What they saw was a filthy, cluttered room with a bed along one wall, a square table with two chairs in the center near a dry sink, an iron-bellied stove and three greasy pallets lying around on the floor. When the gringy bundle of clothing on the bed began to move, Josh looked closer and saw an old man with a tangled beard struggling to sit up.

"What d'you want?" the old man screamed. "Come to help? It's about time. You know how long I been waitin' . . ."

"We're looking for Boris Borinsky," Josh said, taking one careful step farther inside the room.

"T'hell wi' 'im. It's me that needs help!"

"Do you know Boris Borinsky?"

"I disowned 'im, the ungrateful bastard. What d'you want wi' 'im, anyway?"

"Are you related to him?"

"No more, I ain't. Come 'ere and gi' me a hand."

Josh looked around the room. There was no place to hide unless it was under that cot and that did not seem likely. A tin plate with half a toasted piece of bread was on the table. It looked as though it had been partially eaten. "Was Boris here?" he asked the old man who was growing more frustrated by the fact that the two visitors refused to come into the room.

"Maybe. Maybe you gi' me a little help, I'll tell you more."

Sergeant O'Leary began to swell with indignation. "Now look here, old man . . ." he began, but Josh stopped him.

"We're policemen and we're looking for Boris Borinsky. If you know where he is and don't tell us, you could be arrested for complicity in a homicide case."

"What do I care? Take me to jail. It's bound to be better than this."

Josh was tempted to agree. "What's wrong with you?"

The old man's rheumy eyes glinted with pleasure. "It's me legs. Can't use 'em no more and nobody to help me. That bastard son of mine's no good. Here now, just you hand me that bottle over there and I'll tell you where he is."

The old man gestured at a half-full whiskey bottle standing on the dry sink. "O'Leary, get it for him," Josh said as his sergeant threw him a glance brimming with distaste.

"He put it over there on purpose," the old man went on while O'Leary edged his way around the pallets and picked up the bottle gingerly between two fingers. "So's I couldn't get at it. Then ran out, he did, when he saw you comin' down the street. Give it to me!"

O'Leary held it just out of reach. "Where is he?"

The old man glanced between the two men. "Give it to me and I'll tell you."

"Oh, no. You tell us and then I'll give it to you."

"How'll I know you'll keep yer word?"

Josh broke in in exasperation. "We're wasting valuable time, Mister Borinsky, if that is your name. Tell us where to find Boris and you can have your whiskey and our promise to send someone from uptown to see you get the help you need. Otherwise, we'll pour the whiskey down the sink and leave and forget we ever saw you."

"He's in the back," Borinsky said quickly. "In the crapper. He always used to hide there when I was lookin' to give 'im a whippin'. Never was no good."

O'Leary thrust the bottle toward him and he grabbed it from his hands, burying himself down in the filthy covers. By the time he had the stopper out Josh and his sergeant were already running down the stairs.

The backyard was even worse than the street. A large cistern stood near the house and a dilapidated outhouse sat in the far corner. The space in between was littered with newspapers and debris, and the smell was enough to knock them over. Ignoring it, they ran toward the outhouse, nightsticks gripped in their hands. O'Leary took a position next to the door while Josh stood in front of it.

"Boris Borinsky. You're wanted for questioning in the death of Herman Warring. Get out here."

They waited a moment, ignoring the excited chatter of people who had clustered around the back door.

Once again Josh went though his statement, at the same time motioning to O'Leary to be ready to yank the door open. Before he finished there was a loud swish as the door flew back, knocking the sergeant off his feet, and a huge torso went flying into Josh, sending him careening on the stones of the courtyard. He jumped to his feet just as O'Leary went flying by him to tackle Boris to the ground. By the time Josh got to them the sergeant was sitting on top of the man, pinning his arms behind his back and fastening steel handcuffs on him.

"Congratulations, O'Leary. I never knew you could move that fast."

"I just want to get out of here," the sergeant said, hoisting Boris to his feet. With his free hand he grabbed up one of the pieces of newsprint and began wiping at his clothes with it. "I lived in the city long enough to be used to horse dung, but this place is just about more than I can take!"

It was the middle of the week before Caty returned to the city. While Mrs. Schyler urged her to stay longer, she felt she had to return or risk having the opera house management decide that they could do without her. She spent the two days following her sailing mishap in bed, nursing a sore throat. When it did not lead to a full-fledged cold, she breathed a sigh of relief and began making plans to get back. In order to do so, she had to not only put off Frances Schyler but also Charlie Poore, who had decided that without Josh around as competition, the way was clear for his courtship. He pleaded with her to accompany her on all sorts of excursions, but only succeeded in having her company for one afternoon's ride. Caty found it pleasant enough—Charlie was shallow, but an entertaining companion—yet she longed to go back to New York and take up her duties with the chorus again.

And see Josh. There was no denying it. He had left so abruptly after they reached home that night that there had been no time to see how their intimacy affected their relationship. She wondered if she would be embarrassed when next they met—or would he? The flaming warmth that surged through her when she remembered lying in his arms only made her want him the more—she hardly cared where or when. Did he feel the same way about her? Or was that lovely experience just a casual happenstance brought on by the convenience of being cocooned in a shelter out of the storm? She longed to know yet was afraid to find out.

And then, her first day back at the Met, Josh Castleton was nearly the first person she saw as she entered the building.

She had come to work that morning almost fearful at how she would be received after her enforced absence. The first face she saw as she entered the stage door was Arthur, the elderly official whose job it was to keep out all unauthorized personnel. The smile that lit up his wrinkled face when he saw her gave her a deep sense of relief.

"Miss Caty! Welcome back. We missed you while you was gone."

"Thank you, Arthur. It's nice to be back."

He leaned out of the cubby where he kept watch on the stage door and said in a loud whisper, "Just between you and me, the chorus don't sound as good without you. That lovely voice of you'rn needs to be there."

Caty opened her mouth to thank him again but caught sight of Josh hurrying down the hall and stopped in midsentence. The surprise and delight she felt was like an electric shock going through her body. Intent on something he was saying to the policeman accompanying him, at first Caty thought he was not going to notice her. Then he looked up, paused and stepped over to her.

"Hello," he said.

"Hello." There was an awkward silence as all of Caty's delight began to be replaced by a slow, agonizing fear.

"So, you're back," he said awkwardly.

"Yes," she answered. "Back to work, back to the real world. It's going to be difficult after that pleasant interlude."

He did not seem to know what to say though

his eyes devoured her face. "I suppose you know about . . ."

"Oh yes. It's why you were called back here, remember?"

"Yes. Well, we're working on it. Should be all wrapped up soon."

Perhaps that was why he was so preoccupied. "Oh, that's good. Well, I suppose I'd better be getting to the rehearsal room."

Josh stood back. "Of course. And I was just on my way to the station."

Another awkward silence. "So . . . I'll see you soon." She tried not to make it sound like a question.

"Oh yes. Once this is all finished . . ."

"Good. Well, excuse me, then."

She hurried down the hall, attempting to keep a jaunty step though her heart drooped. Of all the scenarios she had imagined when they came face to face once more, this was the least likely. She could not tell if he was glad to see her or simply embarrassed by what had taken place between them. Certainly he had not seemed to feel any great sense of joy. And the fact that he had made no suggestion about seeing her again weighed like a lead anchor in her chest.

This was foolish. She should have known the relationship they shared in that log house would never carry over into the real world. Even the fact that he had asked her to marry him must have been the result of the moment's closeness, not a sincere offer encompassing the rest of their lives.

She would be better to forget it and try to focus on the career that had been so important to her before that rainy afternoon.

As if to emphasize her thoughts, she tightened her arm on the copy of Prosper Mérimée's novel on which the opera *Carmen* had been based, and which she had been avidly reading ever since Frances Schyler told her she would star in its new production. That was what mattered now, not Detective Josh Castleton. That was what she must keep first in her heart and her mind.

"Caty!"

Hearing her name called, Caty looked up and saw Charlotte hobbling toward her, leaning on a cane. With a rush of pleasure at seeing her friend again, she ran to gingerly embrace her.

"You can walk! What happened to the cast? Can you perform again?"

"Whoa," Charlotte said, laughing. "Yes, my leg turned out not to be actually broken, just badly sprained. They let me sing as long as I stay in the back row and don't have to move around too much. But what about you? How was your trip to the elegant Schylers?"

"Now, how did you know about that?" Caty asked, lowering her voice. "I didn't tell anyone here that I was going to Westchester. In fact, I was so annoyed that they asked me to leave, that I didn't tell them anything."

"Well, someone knew because I heard it spoken of among the chorus members. They are all green with envy."

They were going to be more envious still, Caty thought, once they heard about the new production. But she couldn't even tell Charlotte about that yet and perhaps it was just as well, considering how quickly rumors moved through the group.

"Signorina Charlotte," a voice boomed behind her. "You will-a introduce me to your friend . . ."

Caty turned to see a short man with an imposing chest and ramrod stance walking toward them. A wide grin lit up Carlo Gregorio's broad, expressive face as he reached out a chubby hand and enclosed her own, his eyes twinkling up at her.

"Oh, Signor Gregorio, this is Catherina Mandesi, one of my dearest friends. Catherina, Carlo Gregorio."

"I have not-a seen you before, signorina. You, I would-a remember. You are a singer, no?"

Caty smiled in spite of herself. The little man's ego was bigger than himself, yet you could not be put off by it. His humor was much too vivacious.

"Yes. I sing with the chorus and understudy. Someday I hope to sing the leads."

"Ah, you are-a not Italian. And I guess that your name is not-a really Catherina Mandesi. No?"

Caty laughed. "That's right. It's really Cathleen McGowan, and I'm Irish-American."

Gregorio reached for her other hand, enclosing them both in his own. "I like-a that better. We must be honest, eh, if we are going to be good friends. And I think we are going to be very good-a friends."

Caty suppressed her desire to laugh again as she

saw that he was very serious. A head shorter than she and several years older, Carlo Gregorio radiated a sensuality and *joie de vivre* that enveloped her in its intensity. She looked away, wondering if her experience with Josh somehow made her more susceptible to men like Carlo, an obvious womanizer.

Yet he was very likable and his reputation as one of the world's leading tenors was not to be ignored. She carefully removed her hands from his grasp but chatted amiably with him while a bemused Charlotte watched them both. When he bustled off down the hall, the two girls collapsed in giggles.

"You'd better watch out for that one. He's made 'overtures' to half the women in the house already, and he hasn't been here that long."

"Don't worry. I think I can hold him off."

Her laughter faded as she saw a woman approaching them from down the hall. She was tiny, graying, and dressed all in black. The severity of her white face was exactly opposite to the good-natured banter they just shared with the affable tenor. She carried a costume over her arm and had a pin cushion attached to one wrist and several safety pins fastened to the neck of her dress.

Caty searched her mind, knowing she had seen her somewhere before.

The woman glanced up at them, frowning briefly as she passed by.

"Who was that?" Caty whispered to her friend.

"That was Lulu, don't you remember? She was Magda Dubratta's maid."

"Of course. That's why I thought I had seen a ghost. But what in the world is she doing here? I'd of thought this was the last place she would want to be."

"I guess she needed the job and the management felt sorry for her. She's with the costume department. Evidently, she's good at it or they wouldn't have hired her."

Caty shrugged. "Well, I hope I don't have to see much of her. She doesn't exactly bring back pleasant memories." She slipped her arm through Charlotte's. "Come on. The maestro will be shouting for us to come inside in a moment and I want to hear all about what's been happening while I was gone."

Thirteen

Josh looked down at the water oozing up around the soles of his shoes. Even under his huge black umbrella there was no way to stay dry in a downpour like this. He shifted to slightly higher ground and tried to concentrate on the small crowd clustered around the gravesite, instead of on the cold wind seeping through his coat.

He did not like funerals anyway, and this one was particularly pathetic. From everything he had learned about Herman Warring, he was a reclusive, retiring little man with few friends. In fact, most of the people who had braved the terrible weather to show up here were musicians from the opera house orchestra. Josh recognized four members of the violin section standing across the gravesite from him, and a conductor—Josh searched his memory for the name—von Rankin, Manheim von Rankin—huddled at the end of the row. He wondered idly if the man knew that he shared with the deceased the distinction of having been one of Magda Dubratta's husbands? Perhaps that was why he was here when none of the other conductors were.

Gregory Stillman had come running up halfway through the brief service, setting Josh to wondering why a stage manager should be interested in paying his last respects to a back row violinist. A woman whose entirely black costume cried "recent European immigrant" had also aroused his curiosity, until he learned through a discreet question that she was Warring's landlady. Evidently he had been a very good tenant.

It was too bad Boris Borinsky was still languishing in the city jail. It might have been interesting to see if he attended this sad, quiet funeral, and whether his demeanor might indicate his guilt.

The priest conducting the service muttered a few closing words, shut his book and hurried away, huddling under his umbrella. Relieved that it was over, Josh joined the small group as they made their way to the row of waiting hansom cabs, and listened for any threads of conversation. Unfortunately no one had much to say so Josh lingered near von Rankin and Stillman until they were forced to speak to him. Stillman recognized him at once, but it was obvious von Rankin either did not or was too preoccupied to remember.

"So sad, Inspector," Stillman muttered. "Such a terrible thing. So unfortunate for the company."

"Did you know Warring well, then?"

"Not exactly well. I don't think anyone really knew him well. But we were neighbors when he first came to New York. He moved on two years ago but since we both were employed at the opera house we used to have a friendly drink now and then. He was a pleasant enough man."

Von Rankin's aristocratic face showed no trace of emotion, yet his voice carried warmth when he spoke. "Herman was a fine musician, too."

Josh took advantage of the opening. "I heard that he was an outstanding violinist when he was young, that he had a great career ahead of him. What happened?"

Von Rankin stared out over the cluster of headstones, barely visible in the rain. "He had some . . . disappointments."

"That is true," Stillman said. "Yet he was still quite a fine musician. One only had to hear him play to know that."

"How sad that he ended up in the back row of the violin section of an orchestra," Josh commented. "It must have left him wondering what meaning his life had."

Von Rankin seemed to swell up. He turned blazing, black eyes on Josh. "Let me tell you something, Mister Policeman," he said in a heavy Germanic accent. "Tomorrow I will begin to advertise a vacancy in my orchestra and by the end of the week I will have forty fine performers begging me to let them sit and play in the back row of my violin section. You think there is no meaning in that!"

"Excuse me, Maestro," Josh quickly said. "I meant no offense. It was a careless remark."

Stillman laid his hand on von Rankin's arm in

a conciliatory gesture. "You are right, Maestro. It is a great honor to play in a fine orchestra like the Metropolitan's. But sometimes outsiders don't realize that. Come along. I think we will all feel better if we get out of this terrible weather."

Von Rankin threw Josh a last indignant look and allowed himself to be led to a waiting cab. Josh followed and climbed into the cab that had brought him out to the cemetery, drying off some during the long ride back to town and using the time to brood about the case.

Von Rankin had had every right to be annoyed by his words. People often saw things differently, depending on where they stood. He'd never again feel sorry for those musicians in the back rows.

All the same, von Rankin's heightened response suggested that perhaps he felt more for Warring than the simple respect a conductor might have for a member of his orchestra. It might be a good idea to look into von Rankin's life a little closer, particularly as to the connection he and Warring shared with Magda Dubratta. It was all part of a puzzle, Josh felt certain. If only he could find a few missing pieces, he knew he could put the whole thing together. It was so frustrating that they stayed just out of reach, and just out of sight.

He knew Boris was guilty. The man had endured hours of questioning without admitting it, but Josh was certain it was true. Eventually he would break down and confess. There was already enough to charge him, if only it wasn't so circumstantial. That chicken fat, for example. He recognized right away that toasted bread, rubbed with garlic and lavered with rendered chicken fat served as a meal for many a family in the Lower East Side area where Boris lived. What the police had found was probably the remains of the lunch he had eaten up on the roof. He was surly and argumentative and had antagonized Magda. No doubt he antagonized Warring as well. The little musician would have been no match for a bully like Boris if the stagehand had lost his temper and attacked him. Boris probably strangled him in a fit of anger, then threw the body off the roof to hide his deed. Otherwise, why had he tried to run from the law when they went downtown to question him?

Yet proving that was the problem. If only he could find one small piece of evidence that would conclusively prove both men were up on that roof. Either that, or keep Boris under intense questioning until he finally broke down and admitted his guilt. Those were his only choices.

The bridge into Manhattan was crowded with lorries and hansoms. Josh's musings were briefly interrupted when the horse pulling his own cab shied briefly at a disturbance on the road and tried to rear. The driver, using a strong hand and a calm voice quickly regained control and set off again at a sedate pace, talking quietly and patiently to the nervous animal.

For some reason the driver's sympathetic, loving response to his horse reminded Josh of the first morning he had met Caty—perhaps because this driver was in such contrast to that one. He smiled to himself at the thought of her until he recalled their brief meeting in the hallway backstage at the opera house just a few days before.

Why had he been so withdrawn? His blood had warmed just seeing her again, looking so lovely in her fur-trimmed cloche and muff, and with her cheeks shining from the cold air outside. Yet the instant he found his concentration veering away from Boris and on to Caty, he forced himself to step back and pull away.

He knew what his fellow officers said about him—that once he was on a case he was as stubborn as a terrier following a scent. That was why he had been so successful in his profession. Because he allowed nothing to interfere with his pursuit, his dogged determination had paid off by solving nearly two-thirds of the cases assigned to him since he became a detective. As much as he felt drawn to Caty and longed to be with her again, he feared that she might become such a distraction that he would lose the promising threads of this case. It still bothered him that he had not solved Magda's murder. There was a chance now to wrap up all that had happened at the opera house and charge Boris with the crimes, and nothing was going to get in the way of that. Not even the beautiful Caty McGowan.

However, once it was solved . . .

With a start of surprise he realized the cab had stopped outside the police station. Josh hopped outside to pay the driver and quickly realized that the rain had turned to sleet and the temperature had dropped even deeper on the ride home from the graveyard. There would probably be snow tonight.

It was just as well because he did not intend to go home. He was going to get Sergeant O'Leary and they were going to go over to the jail and question Boris Borinsky again. And they were not going to stop until he broke down and confessed. It was time to get this over with.

He headed straight upstairs to find O'Leary. Halfway up he met the sergeant on his way down, carrying a box of old files.

Yet when he told the sergeant to go get his coat, that they were going over to the tombs to do anything it took to get Boris to confess, he was met with a blank stare.

"You haven't heard, Inspector?"

"Heard what?"

"Oh, no you wouldn't, would you, traipsing about to funerals and such." O'Leary set the box on the stairs. "We can't question Borinsky."

Josh felt a cold sensation deep within his chest. "And why not?"

"Because he isn't here. Some fancy lawyer came along and said we had no right to hold him, then came up with the money to make bail—and that was no small amount, neither. Our Boris is probably back at work by now."

Josh stared in disbelief. "But who . . . ? Where would Borinsky get . . . ?"

"I don't know, sir. I just know he was out of here like a jackrabbit with a fox on its tail."

Josh felt a slow, simmering anger brewing up

inside. "Give those files to someone else, Sergeant," he snapped. "Then get your coat. We're going over to the courthouse and read that order."

"That was the worst singing I ever heard!"

Caty winced as the music she had been holding was grabbed from her hand and slammed down on the piano. Her teacher, Marta Della Russo, turned her back and stalked up and down the room, her arms tightly folded across her chest and her face florid with her anger.

"Here you have the opportunity of a lifetime and you cannot seem to get your mind focused on it. Do you realize how fortunate you are?" Since Madam Della Russo talked with her hands, her arms did not stay pinned against her chest very long. With a theatrical gesture, she threw out her arm, flailing the air like a conductor wielding a baton. "I am disappointed. *Very* disappointed in you. My best pupil receives the greatest opportunity of her career and this is how she uses it. This is the reward for all my hard work!"

Caty resisted the urge to remind the madam how hard she herself had worked. "I'm sorry, Madam Russo," she said, quietly hanging her head in what she hoped appeared to be remorse. "It's just that today I've had a difficult time concentrating. So much has happened at the opera house . . ."

"That is no excuse! An artist never allows anything to break her concentration. How do you expect to be a great diva if you do not learn this basic rule? I knew it was a mistake to take all that time away from your lessons, even if it did get you your chance to sing *Carmen*. The middle voice, she is still exquisite. But the head voice, very bad. And the chest—completely lost!"

"I promise you that by tomorrow . . ."

"Bah! Tomorrow is not good enough." She stopped in midstride and took a closer look at Caty. Beneath the heavy makeup, her face softened a little.

"Yes, I see you do look pale. But that is no excuse, mind." Walking back to the piano, she took Caty's hand and led her to a settee along the wall. "We take a minute to allow your wandering thoughts to come together, then we begin again." She sat down beside Caty, folded her arms again and looked at her from under heavy, thick lashes. "Now, tell me the truth. What is the matter? Is the idea of singing the lead in *Carmen* making you too nervous to study? Does it keep you awake at night? If that is the problem, believe me, it is nothing. Every singer has gone through it. All your qualms will disappear the first time you step out on the rehearsal stage."

Caty shook her head. "No, no. It isn't that. Actually I'm looking forward to *Carmen* very much. I've read the novel twice and studied the score until I know everyone's part."

"Then I don't see what else could matter."

"It's . . . it's the opera house. Manager Cannio and the board members. Even some of the chorus members. They look at me like I'm some kind of pariah. You see, the word got around somehow that the police think I might have been involved in Magda Dubratta's death because I handled the knife she used to . . . well, to . . ."

"I know. But what nonsense is this? The police must be idiots if they think you could have done such a thing."

"Yes, but now the board believes I am so identified with her death that they don't want me to sing even a secondary role for fear it will remind people of it. Everyday when I walk in I am afraid they will call me aside and tell me I'm fired from the chorus."

"Bah! They have better sense than that. After all, it is the voice that makes an opera house and surely they have the sense to know that your voice will be for them a gold mine someday. You are a foolish girl to let these things trouble you."

"I know you are right, madam, and yet I cannot seem to shake off the fear that I feel everytime I walk into the opera house."

Madam Della Russo reached out and took Caty's hand, a gesture as surprising as it was kind. "It does not matter what other people think about you, but it does matter very much how you think about yourself. If you allow these unpleasant events to ruin your great opportunity, it will be a tragedy."

"I do not intend for that to happen. I want to sing this role as much as you want me to. And yet nothing has been said, and Mrs. Schyler has not sent me any word about the production. I'm afraid the board may have refused to allow it if I am to sing."

Marta threw up her hands. "Now that is, as you Americans say, 'borrowing trouble'. You have had no indication of such a thing, have you?"

"No. Only the coldness of the manager and the board members."

"Then cease thinking of it. Tell yourself you are going to sing Carmen and you are going to be a great success. The greatest Carmen that ever was. Let nothing divert you from that conviction!"

Caty caught some of her teacher's fire for a moment and made a vow to herself that she would do just that. And yet . . .

"Now, it is time for my medicine. Stay here and set your mind in the proper mode until I return, and then we will work on the "Habanera" like you have never thought of it before."

She watched her teacher sweep from the room, then smiling, walked back to sit at the piano, letting her fingers roam lightly over the keys. Along with all the madam's other pupils, Caty knew her teacher had left the room to take a quick swallow from the brandy bottle. The fiction of her "medicine" was something all her pupils went along with simply to study with her. She had been only a mildly successful singer in her youth but she was a superlative teacher, the best in the city. It took most of Caty's earnings plus all the money her mother could scrape together to pay for her daily lessons. And, of course, Madam Della Russo was right about her taking the time off to go to the country, as well as about letting the unreasonable attitudes of the board members bother her so much.

And yet, that time in Westchester had been worth all the scolding. Her smile widened and her body warmed just to think about it. But that was the trouble, wasn't it?

Like a candle flaring to life, she realized that her depression began, not when she returned to a dubious welcome at the opera house, but when Josh Castleton passed her in the hall with barely a civil greeting. And that it had been exacerbated in the time since she returned, by the fact that he had not tried to see her, or written her a note, or dropped by the opera house, or anything else. And after all they had shared!

It was mortifying. It was infuriating. And she was not going to let it get in the way of her career. She slammed her hand down on the keys with a discordant slap.

Who needed him anyway? Though he had denied it, he probably had been the one who told the management she was a suspect and got them thinking she was a liability. Why should she spend one second regretting that he didn't want her, much less allow him to get in the way of her career. Madam Della Russo was right. The only thing that mattered was becoming a great diva!

Angrily she reached for the score to *Carmen* and began searching the first act for the music to the "Habanera." By the time her teacher came sweeping back into the room, her face slightly more florid than before, Caty had already begun to accompany herself to its tune.

The rest of the lesson went better and by the time Caty pulled on her coat to leave, she felt more like her old self. She was almost out the door of the studio when her teacher called her back.

"Catherina, you told me, did you not, that Signor Gregorio showed you some interest?"

"Yes. He's gone out of his way to be friendly. Too friendly."

"Meaning . . . ?"

Caty felt a sudden sense of embarrassment. "He's sent me flowers, he's asked me to have dinner with him after the opera twice, and when I'm around him his hands seem to be everywhere. I wish he would just let me alone."

"Why? He is personable enough, is he not?"

"Oh yes. He's quite good fun, actually. I'm just not . . . well, not interested."

The madam clucked her tongue. "There you go again, letting your feelings interfere with your judgment. I suggest you encourage this fellow. Oh, not as he would like, for we both know what he wants from you. But just enough to keep him interested. He is becoming the 'star' performer at the opera house, and he can be a great help to your career."

Caty's jaw dropped. "Encourage him, just so he could help me sing! I never shall!"

The madam threw up her hands once again. "Bah! you want to be a great singer, you must forget to be a good Irish girl. I tell you, Catherina, you keep him on your string and you will not have to worry about managers and board members again."

Caty slammed her hat on her head and drove the long hat pin through the topknot of her hair. "Thank you for your advice, madam," she said through tight lips. "I'll think about it."

Yet as she closed the front door and started down the steps, she realized that once, before she met Josh Castleton, she would have simply laughed at the madam's suggestion, and might have even seriously considered it. Her reaction now was just another miserable example of the havoc she had allowed that wretched policeman to make of her life!

Her enthusiasm carried over until she walked into the opera house. Not even the cheery welcome Arthur gave her at the stage door entrance helped to offset the feeling of dread that crept slowly over her as she hurried down the hall.

She paused in the wings to watch the stage where rehearsals for *Tosca* were underway. It amused her to see Carlo Gregorio walk through his paces, delighting everyone with his good-natured banter, and frustrating Gregory Stillman who was desperately trying to familiarize the cast with the stage directions. When Carlo looked up and saw Caty standing in the wings, he casually walked over to her, leaving the rest of the principals and the stage director to fume.

"Catherina! My lovely little-a diva," he said, taking both her hands and kissing them with two loud smacks.

Embarrassed, Caty tried to pull away. "Please, Signor Gregorio. Shouldn't you get back to the rehearsal?" She was painfully aware of the black glances Stillman was throwing her way, even if the tenor was not.

"Bah! Let-a them wait. Gregorio does-a not grovel for any stage-a director."

"But . . ."

"I look for you all day, Catherina. You take-a supper with me tonight, after the opera, *si?*"

Caty could see Stillman swelling downstage even as she felt the flame in her own cheeks. "No, I'm sorry, but I can't tonight. I'm . . . that is, I have another engagement."

"Ah, always I ask and always you-a refuse me. But I don't give up. I ask you again-a and again-a . . ."

"*Signor Gregorio!*" Stillman shouted from the stage.

"Please, signor, you'll get me in trouble," Caty pleaded.

With a painful squeeze of her hands he relented and turned back to the stage. The baritone, Pierre Dupleux, who was singing Scarpia, saw a chance to needle the tenor. "That's all right, Carlo," he quipped. "We wouldn't want anything as trivial as the opera to come between you and your girlfriends."

Carlo walked back to his position on stage. "You-a had better watch out, Scarpia, or else I-a nail Tosca's fan to the floor-a and when you have to pick it up, you in big-a trouble."

Pierre had heard about Carlo's antics onstage, and he knew this was no idle threat. He laughed and replied, "You do, and I'll put real bullets in the guns of the firing squad when they execute you at the end of the third act."

"Gentlemen!" Stillman snapped. "Can we please get back to work? We have a lot to cover."

A voice behind Caty spoke close to her ear, "It's a wonder they ever get any serious work done, much less put on anything as complicated as grand opera."

She turned quickly and saw Josh standing close behind her. A mild shock coursed its way through her body, a mixture of both delight and consternation. The delight quickly faded as she remembered the last time they met and she took a quick step away from him.

"I didn't know Gregorio was going to come over here," she said. "I just wanted to watch him rehearse. He's such a fine artist."

"That was obvious," Josh answered, smiling. "He seems to have quite a crush on you."

"It's just his way. He's like that with all the women."

He looked exceptionally handsome in his tweed overcoat and felt hat that was much too fine for a policeman's salary. But then, he had a private income, she reminded herself. All the same, she had to tear her eyes away from his lean face, the long lashes that framed his enigmatic gray eyes, the strong chin with the tiny cleft. She felt the hairs on her neck come alive as she remembered his naked body lying over hers. If he hadn't been blocking her way, she would have hurried away from him.

But Josh was not going to let her by. He could not take his eyes from her face, the beautiful lines of her cheeks, her lusciously shaped lips, still pink from the cold, the tiny tendrils of her red hair that peeked from under the brim of her hat. And he recognized the hurt in her large, emerald eyes. With a sudden remorse, he realized that he had done that to her by avoiding her since their return from Westchester. Even the good reasons for it did not excuse the fact that he had hurt her deeply. All at once he didn't care if she got in the way of his investigation. It was going very badly anyway. Besides, he had heard that little Italian's invitation and seen the way he squeezed Caty's hands. He'd be damned if he was going to lose her to a tenor!

"Do you really have a previous engagement tonight?" he asked, closing the space between them.

"Yes," Caty said emphatically. Then thought better of it. "Well . . . He's been pestering me, you see, and . . ."

"Then spend it with me. We'll have supper together at Maison Doreé."

"But my brother is meeting me."

"Tell him I'll take you home." He reached out and took both her hands as Gregorio had done, only without squeezing them so painfully. His fingers were like hot flames on her skin.

"Please, Caty. I . . . well, I've missed you."

She looked deeply into his eyes and saw only sincerity and longing. All her hurt and anger melted away. "I've missed you, too," she whispered.

"Good. That's settled, then. I'll meet you at the stage door after the opera. With flowers, like any respectable Stage-Door Johnny."

Caty laughed. "Now you sound like Charlie. He's been pestering me, too."

For the first time Josh gave her a broad smile. "I see I shall have to be more attentive if I want to get ahead of the competition. If I haven't been before, it's because I've been trying to track down a murderer and didn't want to let anything get in the way of that. I hope you won't hold it against me."

She felt a great sense of relief. "It's true you haven't been at the opera house much lately."

"I only came today to get some information on why the man I arrested was released." He looked around. "I'm glad I did, though I suppose I ought to get back to the business at hand."

"I'm glad, too," Caty said. He was still holding her hands and both were reluctant to pull away. In the silence that came between them Stillman's voice could be heard shouting directions on the stage.

"No, no, no, Signor Gregorio. You really must do as I say or you will throw everyone off. We are accustomed to things being done in a methodical way here at the Met. We cannot have everyone wandering about a stage this vast, following their own whims."

Gregorio drew himself up, his massive chest expanding a few more inches. "I know-a what Cavaradorsi would do, and he would-a not stand there. He must-a follow his-a heart."

Stillman forced his voice down a few conciliatory notches. "All the same, the effect I want depends on you standing right here." With a strong hand on Gregorio's shoulder, he maneuvered him back from the center-front of the stage.

"And-a nobody hears the voice from here!" Gregorio exclaimed defiantly. "I go to the front and face out at-a the audience. Then they hear-a me as God-a meant them to."

Caty and Josh glanced at the stage and smiled. The great tenor might be one of the world's best singers, but his ego made it difficult to blend him into the story.

"I'm glad I'm not Stillman," Josh said. "It's easier to catch criminals than . . ."

A horrendous crack cut off his words. It came from above the stage, so loud that it drew all eyes upward. Something came hurling downward in a gray streak, crashing to the stage with a loud roar that sent the dust flying.

It happened so fast that Caty did not realize what it was until she saw the hundred-pound counterweight lying in a heap on the stage floor, inches from where Gregorio stood, his face as white as the settling dust.

Fourteen

Before she realized what was happening, Josh grabbed her and threw her to the floor, shielding her with his body. The shock of the crash immobilized everyone for several seconds, then pandemonium broke loose. Caty could not see what was happening, but she heard the screams and yells of the people onstage, prominent among them, Gregorio's dulcet tones, soaring over everyone, shrieking his outrage.

Gradually Josh loosened his tight hold on her arms. "You're all right?" he asked, as he helped her back to her feet.

"Of course. But I'm not so certain Carlo is."

"Get away from here. Go back to the chorus room, anywhere away from this stage."

Before she could argue with him, he ran out on to the stage to look over the huge weight that lay smashed on the floor. She really could not see why she should leave when it was obvious she had not been the target of this latest catastrophe, so she followed him at a distance. Stillman desperately tried to calm the tenor while at the same time, making sure he was not injured. The weight had missed him by inches.

Carlo issued a string of Italian invectives, among them the accusation that Stillman had deliberately led him back to the spot where the weight fell. The stage director drew himself up in indignation.

"That is preposterous! Why would I do such a thing?"

"How-a the hell do I know?" Carlo shouted. "This house, she try to destroy all who sing here. I quit!"

Josh stepped in to try to restore calm and assure them both that he would find out why the weight fell. Once Carlo learned he was a member of the New York City Police force, he let himself be soothed enough to leave the stage, though his step was still unsteady as he was led away.

"Do you think it was deliberate?" Caty whispered behind Josh as she looked up at the forest of curtains, ropes, weights, and counterweights above the stage.

Josh, too, peered upward. "I don't think so. It looks to me like another accident, as unlikely as that sounds. Some of those ropes look frayed, but we won't know for certain until we get up there."

He turned suddenly. "I told you to get away from here. We still don't know what caused this or if something else might happen."

"But if anyone was trying to get Carlo, they wouldn't be interested in me."

He took her elbow and propelled her off the

stage. "All the same, I'll feel more confident if you are not around here."

"Why? Surely you don't suspect me of this."

"Caty . . . just go. I can get to the bottom of this thing much quicker if you aren't around."

"Oh, all right. But will I see you tonight?"

"Yes. Whether there is an opera or not, we'll have supper."

The chorus rehearsal room was almost as chaotic as the stage had been. Word of the accident had spread quickly and more and more the talk centered on the misfortunes of the house and whether or not it was becoming unlucky. Caty argued it wasn't, but the growing momentum for some kind of curse hanging over the opera house overshadowed her reasoned remarks.

Even Maestro Walters in his most tyrannical pose could barely bring order to the rehearsal until Cannio appeared to reassure the group that the opera would go on as usual that evening and every evening afterward.

"I have been assured by the police that this was simply an unfortunate accident," he said in his clipped tones to the chorus. "Following as it does, on the heels of the bridge accident, it does appear that things are not so . . . 'orderly' as they should be. However, I assure you all that every effort will be made to see that nothing of this kind happens again. We already have a crew checking every rope and weight.

"Unfortunately, Signor Gregorio is still so shaken by this accident that he has had to cancel his next few performances. Rodrigo Estes will be taking his place until Gregorio feels he is ready to perform again."

There was a scattering of applause. Rodrigo had been a standby replacement for several years and the chorus knew and liked him.

"Now, I expect you all to go back to work with the same enthusiasm you have always shown."

He left quickly to go make the same speech to the crews working in the costume and wig departments, leaving behind a much calmer group of people than he had found. The opera scheduled for that evening, *Aida*, was glorious enough to wipe away most of the day's unpleasant events, though Caty noticed during the crowded scene in the second act that everyone at one time or another glanced nervously over their heads at the warren of ropes above. However, it all went smoothly and by the time the curtain fell on the tomb scene, she was dressed in her street clothes again and excitedly looking forward to meeting Josh.

He was waiting for her with a large nosegay of flowers in his hand. Caty smiled with pleasure at them and buried her nose in their fragrant blossoms. He had obviously bought them off the street and they were already half wilted, but it was the thought that counted, after all.

"I don't suppose they measure up to Charlie's bouquets," Josh said, taking her arm, "but then I have been considerably busier today than Charlie has ever been in his entire life."

"I love them," she said, tucking her hand in his

arm. "Besides, I've never accepted Charlie's. He probably gave them to some other girl."

She deliberately forced herself not to talk about the accident while they were in the cab, quietly clopping down the darkened streets. She was too busy anyway, enjoying the lovely feel of his body alongside her own. It was dark and close inside, and rather cold. Josh laid a lap robe over her knees, put his arm around her shoulder and drew her close. She lifted her face to him as he bent to kiss her warm lips. The fire that surged through her body was so strong that Caty was taken aback and deliberately pulled away a little.

Josh had felt his own surge of fire and understood. He allowed the small space between them, removing his arm but capturing her hand in his own.

They said little until they arrived at the restaurant. Inside all was light and glitter and noise, the glass chandeliers, red velvet walls and gold and white appointments made a luxurious setting for a glittering jewel of socialites. Caty was pleased when Josh had the waiter lead them to a private table in a corner, away from the noisiest part of the room.

"So, do you know what really happened?" Caty asked, once their order was taken and they were left in comparative quiet.

Josh leaned back in his chair, as though distancing himself from her inquiry. "Everything points to the fact that it was an accident. A lucky one, too. A few inches to the right and Signor Carlo Gregorio would no longer be among the living."

"But, if the collapse of the bridge in *Butterfly* was an accident, and this is an accident . . . Isn't that rather incredible?"

"Exactly. That is the most disturbing aspect of this whole thing. My minds tells me one thing and my instinct tells me something else. The trouble is, I can find nothing that proves my instincts are correct."

Caty leaned across the table toward him. "So do you think all these 'accidents' are related?"

"Yes. I cannot find a single thread to link them together, but I do."

"What about Magda? Could she be the thread?"

He smiled at her. "I'm convinced that she is."

Caty stared down at her hands. "Poor Carlo. They say he is still shaking."

"I'm surprised they found someone to take his place so quickly. I would have second thoughts about stepping out on that stage."

"That's because you don't know anything about the ambition that burns beneath the breast of a secondary role singer. I know Rodrigo Estes. He is so glad to have a chance to step into a leading role that he wouldn't care if the building burned down around him. He's rather good, too, though certainly he's no Carlo Gregorio. But he'll make a worthy substitute."

Josh reached over the table and took her hands. "Like a member of the chorus stepping into *Carmen?*"

She looked up at him, her green eyes twinkling in the light. "Of course."

"And is Estes also a member of the chorus getting his big break?"

She found it difficult to keep her mind on the conversation with the warmth of his fingers on her hands. "No. He had a career in Europe before coming to the Met. But he's only sung the secondary roles here. This will be a great opportunity for him."

Josh could not tear his eyes from her face. Though he had managed to put her from his mind while he was away from her, now that he was so close to her, touching her, all the longing he had suppressed came surging back. "My dear," he said breathily, "I'm finding it very hard not to kiss you right here in public."

Caty felt her lips drawn toward his. Then, suddenly conscious of the people around her, she drew back, her cheeks flaming. "I'm finding it hard not to let you," she whispered.

"How long do you have before your mother begins to worry that you are not home?"

"As a matter of fact," she said, unable to look directly into his eyes, "I sent word with my brother that I might spend the night with Charlotte, and not to worry about me coming home."

"Oh? And did Charlotte agree?"

Caty looked up at him, her emerald eyes brilliant with mischief. "I didn't ask her."

He could hold back no longer. He pulled her to

him and lightly kissed her silken lips. "I have a place in the city. You could always stay there."

With an effort Caty pulled away, smiling with delight. "How nice of you to offer. I'd love to."

A cough announced the waiter coming to bring them the first course. They drew back and launched into light conversation while they unsuccessfully tried to concentrate on the excellent meal. The waves of longing drawing them together settled around them like a tent, isolating them from all but each other. When they were only halfway through the meal, they both realized they were no longer hungry, at least not for food.

"Come on," Josh said, reaching for her hand. He paid the bill without a qualm for all they had not eaten and helped her into her coat. Outside, he quickly found a hansom, gave the driver his address and climbed in after Caty. As the cab pulled away he had her in his arms, kissing her hungrily, reveling in the feel of her lips, her smooth skin, her body against his. Her hat fell awry and he laced his fingers in her flaming hair and went back to drinking from her lips.

When at last he released her, Caty gasped for breath and forced herself to remember where they were. "Josh," she whispered, "I don't want to look too disheveled when we get there."

He laughed and pulled her back against him on the seat, burying his lips in the hollow of her throat. "There's only the driver to see and who cares what he thinks."

She pushed him away a little. "I do. Oh, Josh

". . . you do have a way of . . . making me forget . . ."

His hand slipped inside her coat and fondled her breast through the silk of her dress. Caty felt herself going limp in his arms.

She was relieved when the cab came to a stop. Pulling herself together, she stepped from the cab and found herself looking up at a handsome brownstone, narrow and neat, with a small crescent of an iron balcony framing the tall window on the top floor. It was very expensive and very fancy for a policeman but then, of course, Josh was not your ordinary policeman, she reminded herself. He took her arm and led her up the low stone steps.

"Is this all yours?"

"Yes. But I rent out the two lower floors." Taking out a large key, he opened the outer door, and then an inner one that gave onto a marble foyer. Caty saw a narrow hall dominated by a stairway which he drew her toward. At the third landing he stepped to a door, pulled out another key and led her inside.

She stood in the hall while he turned up the gas on the wall lamp. It was an elegant little foyer with English hunting paintings on the wall above a half-moon end table with a silver tray. Josh gave her little time to appreciate it, however, taking her coat and hat and leading her through a set of double doors to an exquisite little parlor whose long windows looked out on to the street.

"Let me show you the upper floor," he said, breathing against her bare neck. Taking her hand, he led her up a stairway carpeted in a plush burgundy rug. There were two doors on either side of the hall. He opened the first one and entered a room dominated by a very large bed at one end and by French windows at the other. Through the lacy curtains Caty could see the outline of the iron balcony she had noticed on the street.

Josh stepped away to turn up the gas on a Tiffany lamp near the bed, then moved to the window and closed the drapes. He came back to her and laid his hands on her shoulders.

"I hope you don't mind the light. I want to see you. Ever since that day in Piedmont I've pictured your lovely body, imagined you here in my rooms, in my arms again. I want to know it is true."

She slipped her arms around his waist. "I've thought about it, too. I can hardly believe I'm really here."

"Then I must prove it to you," he whispered, smiling down at her.

"Yes," she said, lifting her lips. "Please do . . ."

He took her face between his palms and kissed her lips, drawing from them as though he was eating a precious fruit. Reaching up, he loosened her hair from its chignon, letting it cascade around her shoulders like tendrils of fire. His hands slid down to her throat and across her shoulders, pushing down the narrow sleeves of her dress until the edges of her bodice barely covered their fullness. He placed one hand on either side and pushed them together into a full, ripe, swelling caress, dropping his lips to taste them, licking them with his tongue.

The sweet flare of her need built as he fondled her. Smoothly he stepped behind her, lifting her hair to unfasten the buttons of her bodice, the tapes of her skirt, working at the intricate garments with a sureness of intimacy which she barely recognized. The flame consumed her. As he worked, he tasted her skin, her smooth shoulders, her long back. Working away her voluminous skirts, he had her standing there before him, her skin shining with the sheen of good health, statuesque and tall, her hair flaming to her waist. She stretched, lifting her hair with her arms high, her rich, full breasts jutting outward. His arms went around her and he lifted them higher, caressing them, lightly stroking the nipples with his thumbs until she gasped for breath. Lifting her in his arms, he carried her to the bed and laid her there while he pulled off his clothes.

She was ready for him and he could wait no longer. He fell on her, driving apart her legs and thrusting into her with a desperate need. Her nails dug into his back as her hips rose to meet him. He maneuvered his body so that his long, hard shaft could slide against the pleasure of her womanhood while he thrust again and again. Her frenzy rose with his, on waves of delight in an aggression that consumed them both until with a cry, they both soared into that brief, exquisite madness that is the culmination of love.

She lay exhausted in his arms as her pounding

heart slowly eased and her breathing returned to normal. Beside her, she could feel Josh, too, settle, satisfied and surfeited. He rolled over on his back and pulled her against him.

"Oh, Caty. My dear girl. You get better every time."

Caty giggled and kissed the damp hollow of his neck. "I have a good teacher."

"I think you have natural talent."

Caty sighed, contented, and snuggled against him. She hadn't realized how much she wanted this again until now, with her arm across his chest and her head nestled against his throat. All the emptiness of the recent days, the terror of the accident with the counterweight, faded away against the pleasure of being one with this man, of melding with him into one whole person.

After a long silence in which she began to realize that Josh's thoughts were wandering, she said, "What are you thinking?"

Absently, he stroked her forehead. "The same thing I've been thinking ever since I learned that Boris was released. Who was behind the lawyer who got him off?"

"Don't you know?"

"No. Whoever it is, he obviously has money because the bail was paid in cash and that lawyer doesn't come cheap. Why would anyone with that kind of wealth care about a stagehand from the Lower East Side who can barely speak an articulate sentence?"

Caty casually stroked his chest with her finger. "Because he, too, has something to hide?"

"Exactly. He's afraid that Boris will connect him somehow to all that has happened. So afraid that he went to great expense to make certain Boris can't do that."

"Perhaps you had better keep an eye on Boris. If he is that dangerous to this person, he might be the next victim."

Josh laughed and kissed the top of her head. "You would make a good policeman. We've thought of that and we are keeping a watch on Boris day and night. At the least, we hope he might lead us to this influential mystery man."

Caty sat up and caught her arms around her knees. "Josh, do you realize what this means? That all the things that have happened at the house might point to someone very high up. Could that be possible?"

He ran his fingers along her back, reveling in the long, smooth feel of it. "Anything is possible. All I need is one good connection . . ."

Caty hugged her knees, thinking of all the wealthy men who ran the opera house, Morgan, Vanderbilt, Belmont, Stevens—moguls of industry and giants of finance. But that was crazy! Why would any of them need to be involved in the kind of dirty little crimes and ineffectual accidents which had occurred at the house in the last two months? If they wanted Magda murdered, or Gregorio out of the way, they could afford to do it quietly and simply. And why would they even bother with someone as mundane as Herman Warring? It made no sense.

Josh heard her sigh. "Now it's your turn to tell me what you're thinking," he said, sitting up to lightly kiss the back of her neck.

"Mmmm," Caty sighed again, this time with pleasure. "Nothing as important as this," she said, lifting her hair to allow his lips to explore the sensitive hollows behind her ears.

He sat up behind her, his arms closing around her waist to cup her breasts. "Do you know you have a beautiful body?" he murmured, catching her earlobe lightly in his teeth.

"I'm too tall," she murmured back. "And too heavy."

"You are perfect. I love your long legs, your small waist, your wonderful, full breasts, your neck, your smooth shoulders . . ."

"Stop!" she said, laughing. "This sounds like an anatomy lesson."

". . . I love to kiss the little hollow behind your ear." His lips coursed downward to the small of her back. "Your exquisite navel."

"You are facing the wrong way for that," she said breathlessly.

"Your splendidly round hips . . ."

"Oh, Josh . . ."

He stood up on his knees, one on each side of her, and began exploring her breasts in earnest. Caty arched her back to him as a warm thrill went trembling through her body. He bent over her, one hand stroking her breast while the other slipped downward between her legs, tantalizing her with his touch. She grew helpless against him as he fondled and stroked her, raising a flood of desire with his insistent fingers. When she moaned with pleasure, he turned her in his arms, still clasping her below, but maneuvering her breast to allow his lips to enclose the erect, taut nipple. His lips were cool on her flesh until the waves of hot desire drove away all other sensation. His fingers against her hot womanhood grew stronger, more insistent, caressing, tantalizing until she was weak and helpless. The need for him, for his fulfillment, drove her to a frenzy.

"Oh . . ." she heard herself cry, then lost all knowledge of her pleas. He only teased her more, drawing on her breast with his mouth, rubbing against her, probing his finger into the moist cavity that longed for him. She hovered on the edge of an exquisite plateau, unable to go over, unable to go back, unable to move. Her pleas grew stronger, her cries more unreasoned and only then, when she thought she could bear it no longer, did he move to stand on his knees before her, thrusting into her, lifting her with his own hard, driving need. She sat back, cradled in his arms as together their passion carried them over the edge into the void of fulfillment and they fell back on the bed.

For a long time they lay there with his body stretched on top of hers. She did not want to feel the sadness of him pulling away and she clasped him to her, wishing this wholeness could last forever.

Of course it could not. When Caty finally got her breath again she sighed and whispered, "I didn't know you could do this sitting up!"

Josh laughed and turned over on his back. "There are lots of ways to do this and it is going to be my pleasure to show you several of them. If I can last that long."

She nestled against him once more in a companionable silence. It had not escaped her notice that twice now he had worked her up to a frenzy of need where she practically begged for him to take her. What had happened to her determination to make *him* beg for *her*? She certainly had not put it into effect.

Ah well, she thought. The night was still young. And she still had the prospect of sharing these hours with Josh in the exquisite privacy of his bedroom. There was still time.

Caty did not leave Josh's house until late the following morning. Her good intentions of the night before had given way before an exhausted sleep that overcame them both. Once, just before dawn, he had roused her from her dreams again with his fondling and teasing, working her up to another frenzy of need that culminated in the heavenly pleasure of their joining. When she woke a second time, he was gone, leaving a note for her that he had to be at work and hoped he would have any strength left after the night they had just shared. Beside the note was a key to his house.

She bathed and dressed, all the while enjoying the pleasure of using and moving about among his things. Her heart sang with happiness like none she had known before. It was wonderful to feel so much a part of another person, to thrill with the sense that she belonged with this man. She was a singer who would soon be starring in her very own leading role, and she had a lover whom she adored. The world was a very fine place!

Her euphoria lasted until she walked backstage at the opera house and nearly careened into Lulu, the little maid who now worked in the costume department. The withered little woman was dressed in her eternal black that made the sallowness of her face even more pronounced. Her graying hair was pulled back into a bun, so tight that her skin seemed stretched over the sharp planes of her skull. The edges of her mouth, as withered as a prune, scowled downward as she glared at Caty.

"Oh, I'm so sorry!" Caty cried. "I didn't see you."

Unsmiling, the woman stooped to gather up the folds of a brightly colored costume that had fallen from her arms. Without a word, she clasped it to her thin chest and moved to step around Caty.

"I said I'm sorry," Caty added. The woman threw her a black glance of sheer hostility and hurried off down the hall, muttering to herself. Catching the words, "second-rate soprano," Caty looked after her in mystification.

She knew Lulu was a strange creature but this was really too much. The least she might have done was to accept her apology. Instead, the woman's bad nature brought back all the unpleasantness that had occurred in the house, and with it, all the fear and trepidation. It also took the edge of delight off the happiness Caty had felt so strongly when she came into the building. That was the most unforgivable thing of all.

Fifteen

"Caty!"

She looked up to see Gregory Stillman hurrying toward her. Though every hair in his sheaf of white was in place, his chubby face reflected the anxiety that had been there since the accident with the counterweight.

"I've been waiting to catch you the moment you arrived. Manager Cannio wants to see you in his office immediately."

Caty felt her chest constrict. "Oh? Why?"

"Never mind why. How should I know?" He laid a strong hand on her shoulder and propelled her back toward the elevator. "Go up there and find out. He does not like to be kept waiting."

Though she tried to put a good face on it, inside Caty felt as anxious as Stillman looked. The old gnawing fear that a summons from Cannio meant she was going to be fired returned in full force. Why else would he want to see her the moment she arrived? Unless . . .

Perhaps he knew that she had spent the night

in Detective Castleton's house and wanted her out for "bad character." Yet that was absurd, she told herself. How could he know? Even if he did, affairs were so common in the opera house that managers usually turned a blind eye to them. No, it probably has more to do with that old, miserable business of being identified with Magda's death. Sometimes she wished she had never been given the opportunity to sing that night!

She stepped off the elevator and walked down a carpeted hall to the thick, paneled door of the manager's office. Inside she found Cannio's pale-faced secretary leafing through some papers on her desk.

"Oh, Miss Mandesi. The manager is expecting you. You can go right in."

"Thank you, Miss Frierson." She laid a hand on the brass knob and hesitated, taking a deep breath and drawing herself up to her full height. He might fire her but she would never let him know how much it hurt.

She walked into a group of several people clustered around Cannio's desk. The one woman in the group looked around and rose to her feet. Caty felt the tightness in her chest ease as she recognized Frances Schyler.

"Caty, my dear. Come in. We've been waiting for you."

Frances looked as elegant as ever in a mauve walking suit with a smoky gray blouse that rose in tiers of exquisite lace up her throat. A diamond pin twinkled on her bodice, holding in place a single strand of creamy pearls. She took Caty's arm and led her to a chair which one of the men rose to pull forward. Caty remembered him vaguely as one the set designers. She smiled and thanked him, feeling considerably better until she saw Cannio's frowning visage across the desk.

"My dear, it is so exciting," Frances gushed beside her. "Mister Stockton here, has brought in the final designs for the new production and it appears we are finally ready to begin work on it. That was why we called you in today."

A thrill of joy went through her body, starting at her toes and exploding upward. "Oh . . . how exciting," she said, deliberately restraining herself from dancing around the room.

Stockton pulled some large drawings toward her. "This production is going to be different from the familiar, classic look of *Carmen*. You'll have to learn some new moves, but they shouldn't be too difficult."

Caty took the plans and looked down at a drawing of a Spanish courtyard, rather stark compared to the usual sets and full of clever rises and steps on many different levels. Though there was a minimum of clutter, what was there suggested not only the beige, stucco forms of Spain, but the hot, glaring sun as well.

"Oh, I like them," she breathed. "They're beautiful."

Stockton lifted the top drawing to reveal the interior of a cafe and its courtyard, as stuffed full of Spanish regalia as the former one had been sparse.

"And this is the mountain retreat," he went on, pulling out another drawing, "and, the *pièce de résistance*, the last scene outside the bullfight arena. What do you think?" he asked, sitting back and puffing out his chest.

Caty knew that even though she was singing the lead, her thoughts on the set design carried little weight. Yet the enthusiasm she felt for the new sets was genuine. She praised them, asked a few logistical questions and then looked up to see that Cannio's scowl had grown darker than when she had entered the room. She tried to ignore him.

"You've saved the most colorful set for the final act," she said. "That's unusual. Most of the time it is the first act that earns the applause."

Stockton beamed. "I did that on purpose, you see. More than most operas, *Carmen* builds toward that inevitable, tragic final conflict. I want to emphasize the drama of it by making the world Carmen wanted to be a part of as colorful and inviting as possible, thus emphasizing the starkness and poverty of a life with Don José. It's effective, don't you think?"

Frances Schyler leaned forward to take the drawings out of Caty's hands. "It is very effective, Mister Stockton, and exactly what I wanted. This production must offer a new look as well as a new voice. I'm very pleased."

Caty decided she might as well bite the bullet.

Looking directly at Cannio, she said, "Do you like them, Maestro?"

Cannio chewed his lower lip for a moment. Then he leaned across the desk, folding his hands in front of him, and spoke directly to Caty.

"You might as well know, Miss McGowan, that I am very much opposed to having you sing the lead in this new production. I have tried to convince Mrs. Schyler that a singer whose name is already famous and whose interpretation is well known, would add stature to her new production. I also think it is unfortunate that you carry the stigma of having been involved in that unhappy production of *Madama Butterfly*. However . . ."

Frances rolled up the drawings and glared over them at the manager. "However, you have been overruled, Mister Cannio, and I will thank you to say nothing more about it. This is my production and I insist I have the final say about how it is presented."

Cannio stared down at his hands a moment, regaining his control. "I understand, Mrs. Schyler, and I shall say no more. However, Miss McGowan should know how I feel."

"How you feel has nothing to do with it. Caty will be a sensation, I am sure. Launching her career with a new *Carmen* will be a triumph." She turned to Caty. "Are you ready to begin rehearsals, my dear?"

"Oh, yes. I've been studying the score, the novel, and the stage notes until I know them by heart. I've also worked with my teacher on the music and the movements. She sang the role herself years ago and she's been quite helpful."

"No, no. You must forget all the old ways of acting Carmen. We are going to try to make her look entirely new. Mister Stillman will help you with that."

"Have you decided who will sing Don José?"

"Well, I wanted Gregorio, of course, but he may not be available. It could be Lars Svenson or Rodrigo Estes. I haven't decided yet."

Cannio broke in, anxious to reassert some of his authority. "We will let you know about that as soon as the decision is made. Can you begin rehearsals next week?"

Anytime you say, she thought. "Why, yes."

"Good. We will start first thing Monday morning. Now, let's finish this up. Where are those contracts . . ."

He opened a drawer and began leafing through a stack of papers while Caty gripped her hands in her lap. Contracts! She was about to sign a contract to sing the leading role in *Carmen*! Her heart threatened to burst within her.

"Here they are." Cannio handed two papers clipped together to Caty and she looked them over, stifling a gasp when she saw what they were going to pay her to sing this role. If they had only known, she would have paid *them* to sing it.

"I believe this is all acceptable," she said, amazed at the level quality of her voice.

"Good," Frances answered. "Give us your pen, Maestro, and we will have this done." She thrust the pen at Caty, who scratched her name in the two places designed for it. Frances then added her name and gave them back to Cannio for his signature.

"There! That's done. Congratulations, my dear," Mrs. Schyler said, getting to her feet. "I know you are going to be a great success. And now, I really must be going. I have to be at a meeting of the Lady's Suffragette's in half an hour."

Stockton jumped to open the door for her. "When can I expect to see the first sets, Mister Stockton?" she asked, pausing a moment.

"Very soon. We've already done some preliminary work."

"Good. That's what I like. Dispatch! Good day, all."

She swept out, leaving Caty to follow, a little unsteady on her feet. At the door she paused and looked back at Cannio, who had risen to his feet but not moved from behind his desk.

"I thank you for being honest with me, Maestro," she said, taking a deep breath. "I know you don't want me as Carmen, but I will tell you now, I am going to sing it as well as or better than anyone has in this house before. I intend to be as great a success as Mrs. Schyler expects me to be!"

Cannio glared at her, drawing his thin lips tighter. "I hope you are, Miss McGowan. After all, the well-being of this house is what matters most. To all of us."

Caty glared back at him. It was probably as close to a gracious statement as she was going to get. "Yes, it is," she answered. She swept through the outer office with the grand assurance of a genuine diva.

"So, you are no longer in the chorus?"

There was a note of approval in Josh's question. Caty smiled and dug her hands deep inside her fur muff.

"Once we start rehearsals, no. Until then, I will continue to sing. Retirement is not good for the voice."

They were walking along the sidewalks under the trees of Gramarcy Park, ambling toward a restaurant which was one of Josh's favorites. Though the day had warmed a little the wind was picking up with the coming of evening, sending the dried leaves left from fall scudding in their path. There was no one in the park. The last of the nannies with their prams had hurried inside, the children who had pushed hoops earlier were having their supper, the ladies who met to gossip and sew had long since gone to prepare for their husbands' return. In the houses that bordered the square, lights twinkled behind lace curtains, and the gas street lamps glinted on silver windowpanes.

The cold wind teased her cheeks and she shivered in spite of her warm coat. Seeing it, Josh took her arm and drew it through his, enclosing her hand in his own gloved fingers.

"It's not much farther. What do your friends in the chorus think of your sudden good fortune?"

Caty pulled the warm muffler that was wrapped several times around her throat a little tighter. "That's the most difficult part of this whole thing. They all try to be happy for me and yet there is not one of them who would not give all they had for the same opportunity. I can see it especially in Charlotte's eyes. She tries hard to rejoice for me yet the envy is always there. It's rather embarrassing."

"I can see how it would be, but it's one of those aspects of winning that cannot be helped. I've seen it in the police department, too. An advancement for one man usually means some other man was passed over. It can be very painful."

"Is that what you want someday? Advancement?"

He smiled. "Oh, I suppose I wouldn't object if they offered to make me the new Chief of Police. However, that isn't likely to happen anytime soon. Especially since I haven't been able to solve these problems at the opera house. In fact, if I don't get some answers soon, a demotion might be more likely."

"Oh, surely not . . ."

Her comments were cut short when Josh stopped before an alcove where a paneled door was lit by an overhead gas lamp. Pushing open the door, he led her inside the room, dimly lit, but beautifully warm and cozy. A waiter greeted them both and led them to a table near the window where a fat candle in a glass lamp cast a bronze nimbus on a checkered cloth.

Once they were settled and their meal ordered, Caty sat back and studied the man opposite her. The lamp cast the planes of his face in shadows which emphasized the severity of his expression. In the soft light his gray eyes appeared almost black, with none of the usual amused humor she was used to seeing there. Yet she knew it was not the light that made them so severe.

"You really are worried, aren't you?"

"Don't you think I should be?"

She ran a finger lightly across the knuckles of his hand. "But sooner or later you will solve everything. I'm sure of it."

Josh gave her a wry smile. "I'll tell that to my chief."

"Well, he hasn't taken you off the case, has he? He must believe that you're doing a good job."

"No, he hasn't, though I'm not sure why. I think he either wants to see me fail and is giving me enough time to do it, or he simply likes to see me suffer."

"Nonsense. He knows you will get to the truth, so he allowed you to keep at it. And you've done everything you can. The only mistake you might have made . . ."

She stopped abruptly as Josh's glance focused firmly on her face.

"Yes, go on," he said quietly.

"Now don't get angry at me for saying this, but I think perhaps you are too convinced that Boris What's-his-name is the criminal here. Isn't there just a slight possibility that it could be someone else?"

"Now, Caty, do I try to tell you how to sing?"

"Of course not."

"Then allow me the same consideration. I think I know more about what has been going on at the Met than anyone, and everything points to Boris Borinsky. If I had been able to keep him in custody I would have got a confession from him somehow. As it is, I don't even know how he was able to get bail."

"Oh, I can solve that for you," Caty said as the waiter stepped up to fill their wineglasses. She paused until he moved away, lifted her glass and took a sip which warmed her all the way down. "In fact, I thought you must have learned by now that it was von Rankin."

Josh stared at her. "Von Rankin? The conductor?"

"Yes. Maestro Manheim, we call him. He hired the lawyer and paid the bail money."

It was a moment before he found his voice. "Now how did you learn that!"

"I heard him talking to Gregory Stillman. I was watching Rodrigo rehearse his *Tosca* when Stillman and the maestro stepped up alongside the curtain not ten feet away. They were arguing, and though they were speaking softly, I couldn't help but hear what they were saying."

The expression on Josh's face hovered between pleasure at learning something he had wanted very much to know, and irritation at being told it in such a cavalier way. "And what were they saying?"

Caty set her glass down and stroked a finger along the stem. "Von Rankin was complaining that it had cost him so much money. He told Stillman he should have found a lawyer who wasn't so expensive and Gregory answered that the man had 'got the lout off, hadn't he'. Then Gregory said that Manheim had better watch his step or there would be such a scandal as would make all the other things that had happened look like a tea party. At that point I realized I wasn't supposed to be listening to this and slipped away."

"Well, I'll be damned!" Josh exploded. "Here I've been quietly asking questions all over the house of anyone I can find without learning anything, and all the time all I had to do was ask you. I don't know whether to be pleased or just chagrined!"

"I should hope you're pleased," Caty quipped, smiling at him over the rim of her glass. "You needn't be embarrassed. Lots of people in the house knew von Rankin had got Boris out of jail, but they would never say anything to you or any other policeman about it."

"But why on earth not?"

She leaned across the table and whispered: "Because there is a conspiracy of silence. You see, in any artistic profession there are bound to be a few . . . well, people who live differently from most of us. They are often fine artists, but their private lives are . . . well . . . what some people would call perverted."

"I think I know what you are trying to say. And there is a group of these people at the opera house?"

"At any opera house, anywhere. And in any theater. They are writers, painters—talented, artistic people with different preferences."

"I'm only interested in one opera house. Is von Rankin one of these people? Stillman?"

"No, not Stillman nor von Rankin. But Herman Warring was. That is why Manheim is protecting Boris. He doesn't want any scandal associated with his precious orchestra."

Josh rubbed a finger along his chin. "I still don't see why they wouldn't tell me. Why go to all these lengths to protect a stagehand?"

"Because according to law, you have the right to put them all in jail. Boris was involved in that group with Warring. If he is accused of 'unnatural practices', he might point a finger at several other singers, instrumentalists, designers, and even other stagehands. You could arrest all of them for being perverts and once you did, the newspapers would tell the world. As long as it remains quiet, no one cares."

Josh shook his head. "I'm only concerned about solving a murder. What these people do in private is none of my business."

"That's how the rest of us feel. We are all too busy with our own careers to care what anyone else does at home behind closed doors."

"But I've been involved with the opera house for years. You would think they might trust me more."

"Oh, Josh. You sit among the swells in the boxes, you drink with the patrons and the board, and you've been attending the opera since you were a boy. But you are still a policeman and that is how they see you. You're a terrible threat."

Josh shook his head. "I never expected to get into anything like this when I set out to get to the bottom of these incidents. What a mess! I almost wish I had never attended the opera that night."

She lifted her glass and gave him a mischievous grin. "But some good has come of it. After all, otherwise we might never have got to know each other."

"That reminds me," he said, reaching into his coat pocket. "I brought you a Christmas present."

Caty smiled with surprised pleasure as she took a small black box from his hand. Opening it, she gave a quick gasp. Resting on a velvet cloth was a round, engraved gold pendant attached to a delicate thin chain. She took it from the box and held it up in the light from the lamp to examine it. The face of a lion was carved into the gold, with amber eyes and detail that made it throb with life.

"It's beautiful," she cried. "It's so lifelike I feel it will break into a roar at any moment."

Josh sat back, obviously pleased at her delight in the necklace. "I saw it in a jeweler's window and liked it."

"How kind of you. Thank you, Josh. I shall treasure it always."

Handing it to him, she bent her head to allow him to clasp it around her neck. Her fingers lightly touched the cool surface. She was almost as pleased at the fact that he gave her a gift as she was with the gift itself. "Does it have some significance?" she asked. "It's so unusual."

Josh resumed his seat. "Yes. It's designed after a Scythian relic found several years ago by an archeologist. The original is much larger and in a museum, of course. The Scythians made some glorious carvings of animals from gold. They believed that carrying a living spirit in model form helped to sustain life."

Caty looked up sharply. "A kind of 'good luck talisman'?"

"You might say that."

She laughed. "I think you are giving me the ancient version of a Saint Christopher's medal. Well, that's very nice. I shall wear it for protection, just as I would a Saint Christopher's."

He leaned forward, taking her hand. "It becomes you. You should wear gold more often. And pearls and fine jewels."

"Oh, I intend to." She laughed. "Once I become a famous diva, I intend to be dripping in gold and jewels!"

She wore the gold talisman all through the rest of the week and though she knew it had no magical powers, somehow it made her feel safer. She thought it fitting that her last performance as a member of the chorus should be in two of her favorite operas, the duo, *Cavalleria Rusticana* and *Pagliacci*, where the chorus plays an important role. It was a long evening and by the time the curtain fell on the tragic close of *Pagliacci*, Caty was exhausted.

It was only after she was dressed and ready to meet her brother at the stage door that she remembered she had forgotten the colorful shawl she wore in the last act of *Pagliacci*.

"Darn!" she exclaimed to Charlotte who was about to leave the dressing room. "That shawl is my mother's and I intend to wear it in *Carmen*. I must have left it on the stage."

"They must have struck the sets by now. Perhaps they threw it in the box of props."

"Then it should still be there."

"Look for it on Monday."

"No, I don't want to lose it. I'll just run back and get it. Kyle won't mind waiting."

She was off running toward the backstage area before Charlotte could talk her out of it. Only one small gaslight burned backstage, casting an eerie glow in a puddled gold arch and leaving thick darkness in the vastness beyond. Caty was so familiar with the stage that the darkness caused her no more than a momentary hesitation. Most of the benches used in the last act had been stacked toward the rear of the empty stage and she decided to look there first. Finding no shawl, she turned to go back to the wings and look for the box where odds and ends were thrown by the stagehands striking the sets.

Then she heard the sound.

The weird silence of the stage was almost a noise in itself. It throbbed and pulsed with a life of its own. Caty caught her breath, standing frozen, listening, straining to hear again the sound that should not have been there. A step, quiet but unmistakable.

"Is anyone there?"

The silence seemed even louder, more deathly still.

"Who's there?" she called again.

In an instant the euphoria she had felt on completing the opera and looking forward to new rehearsals was transformed into sheer, utter terror. There was no reason for it, she told herself, as a wave of panic swelled up within her. There was no reason to be afraid.

She stood silent and still, fighting the demons of fear and telling herself she was being foolish. Yet, there was something out there in the darkness. She could feel it. Her skin crawled with it, the hairs on the back of her neck were alive with it.

Then she heard it again, the quiet creak of a floorboard, the sense of a threatening presence nearby.

If a friend was there, surely they would answer. She glanced over at the darkened wings and caught the glitter of a white fringe hanging over the edge of the prop box. In order to reach it she would have to cross the nimbus of light, fully revealing herself to whoever was there. She felt rooted to the floor and yet she knew she had to get away from this stage.

She took a hesitant step, and then another. Her throat felt tight with fear, constricting her breath. Gathering her strength, she ran across the circle of light and into the darkness. Something brushed against her, she couldn't see what. She reached out, clawing the air as her whole body was consumed with fear. She fell to the floor and heard herself scream.

"Caty . . ."

Kyle's voice. Scrambling forward on her knees, she struggled to call out.

"Caty, where are you?"

The tightness eased as her numbing fear receded. Her knees went watery and she sat back on the stage, gasping in long ragged breaths for air.

"Kyle . . ." she said in a whimpering voice.

He came running to her. "Caty, what happened? Are you all right?"

She clutched at his strong arm, leaning all her weight on him. "Yes, I'm all right."

"For heaven's sake, you're trembling. Are you hurt?"

All at once she felt foolish for allowing her fear of the dark to overcome her common sense. Yet someone had been there, she was certain. Still, nothing had happened, and she had not really been able to see anyone.

"I guess I fell," she said, clutching at him. "Must have stumbled over something."

He took her arm and helped her to her feet. "It's a good thing I came looking for you."

A very good thing, she thought. She was still so shaky she could barely walk. "I came back for my shawl," she said, leaning on him. He helped her to the box where she grabbed the shawl and clutched it to her breast. "Let's go. Let's get out of here."

Once they reached the lighted hallway she began to feel stronger. "How did you know where I was?"

"Charlotte told me. She told me I should go after you. You shouldn't go into dark places like that by yourself, especially now with all that has happened here. Are you sure you are all right?"

"Yes. I'm fine."

Once outside the building she took a deep breath of the cold air, filling her lungs with it. Nothing had ever felt so good. Kyle hailed a hansom cab for the trip to the ferry and helped her inside where she sank back on the leather seat, resting her head against the cushion, and trying to allow her anxious body to calm.

What had happened? She still could not be sure. Had her fear and concern led her into believing there was someone waiting to attack her when actually it was fear itself that had caused her panic?

No. Someone *was* there—she was absolutely certain of it. Yet why? Why would anyone want to bother her? Was there a maniac loose in the opera house? Was it the same person who had been behind the two deaths and the accidents onstage, and now lurked in the shadows waiting for another victim?

She had no answer and yet she knew one had to be found. She reached up to touch her throat—still tight with the residue of her fear—and realized with a sinking heart that her good-luck talisman was gone.

Sixteen

"That finishes it. You are not going back in that building again!"

Caty stared open-mouthed at Josh, wondering if she had heard him correctly. Across the room Sian McGowan nodded gravely.

"Listen to Mister Castleton, Caty, dear. He knows what is best."

Caty looked from one to the other. "Have you both lost your senses? I have a debut to perform. If you think I am going to give up the chance to appear as the lead in a new production, you are very much mistaken."

Her mother's dark brows melded into a straight line across her face. "And much good it will do you to sing the lead in any opera if it costs you y'er life. Y'er a stubborn girl but it's time you listened to reason."

"Your mother is right, Caty," Josh added. "Postpone the debut until I've had a chance to find out what is going on down there. I won't have you taking unnecessary chances."

"*You* won't? And what gives you the right . . ."

"Listen to the gentleman, Caty," her mother broke in. "He only has your best interest in mind, as we all do."

She forced herself to calm down, gripping her hands in her lap until she had her emotions under control. A log in the fireplace collapsed, sending a brief shower of sparks onto the hearth. The sitting room of her mother's house was warm and comfortable, yet outside, a strong wind off the harbor fluttered noisily at the windowpanes. If only Josh hadn't come out this Sunday afternoon to visit her, and if only she hadn't weakened enough to tell him about the incident onstage the night before. Worst of all, if only her mother hadn't walked in and overheard. Once Sian learned about that incident she wanted to know everything. Now she was going to be as difficult to handle as Josh.

And yet, she thought grimly, why should either one of them have any say about her career? She glared at Josh sitting across from her in a chair of flowered chintz.

"And when did I move from being a suspect to becoming a victim?"

"A suspect!" Sian cried. "Surely not? How ridiculous!"

It gave Caty some satisfaction to see Josh look uncomfortable. "It's not that your daughter was a suspect, Mrs. McGowan, as that she happened to be close to several of the incidents that have happened. I had to consider this thing from all angles."

"Sure and that's what policemen are supposed to do, now isn't it? But I know you would never think of Caty as a criminal. Why she couldn't . . ."

"Mama, please!" Caty flounced from her chair and stood staring down at the fire, one hand resting lightly on the mantel. When she turned back to her mother it was with a calm voice. "Detective Castleton did not come out here today to talk about these unpleasant things. Can't we just have a simple conversation and not think about the opera house at all?"

Sian stood, smoothing down her apron. "Well, if that's what you want, all right. I'll go and make us some tea. And I've some fresh soda cake, Mister Castleton. You'll have some now, won't you?"

Josh gave Mrs. McGowan a wink. "I'd love it."

Caty silently watched her mother leave but once the door was closed she turned on her companion. "You two! I don't know which of you is the most meddlesome. And now you're such good friends, I haven't a chance of finding any peace."

"I like your mother very much," Josh said. "I like her humor, her friendliness, and her common sense." He rose easily from the chair and stood before her, slipping his arms around her waist. Smiling down into her upturned face, he bent and kissed her lips, lightly and sensuously.

"And I like her daughter even more," he whispered.

Caty felt her body meld into his. Her arms eased around his shoulders to clasp him, her lips opened to his. The warmth he so magically evoked within her shuddered to life and flamed into the familiar need.

Suddenly she pulled away. "Oh, no you don't, Detective Castleton. You think that if you start kissing me I'll forget all about your overbearing ways. Well, I won't."

Josh's strong arms tightened around her. He could feel the points of her breasts against his chest, stimulating the desire for her that was like an obsession once she was in his arms. "What overbearing ways?" he murmured, nuzzling her throat.

Caty put her hands on his shoulders and shoved him away. "Now behave yourself. Mama could come back in any moment. Besides, I won't let you cajole me into agreeing with you. I'm not going to give up my debut. Rehearsals start Monday morning and I plan to be there with bells on!"

Josh shook his head at the set stubbornness on her face. She was so damned beautiful, so damnably captivating and so stubbornly infuriating. He jerked down the tabs of his vest, looking for all the world like a stern schoolmaster. "If I go to the board with this latest incident they are sure to close the theater. Then you'll *have* to stay away from there."

Caty's chin went up. "If you do that I'll deny it ever happened. I've told no one about it but you so there's no one to verify it."

"Your brother saw you on the floor."

"I'll say I tripped over something in the dark."

"Do you realize how foolish you are being? You could get hurt!"

"You are just annoyed because I won't do what you want me to."

He realized there was some truth in that. He had the experience and knowledge about these matters and she refused to listen to him. "That's not it at all," he answered rather lamely. "I'm not asking you to give up your debut, just to postpone it for a while until I can find some proof strong enough to arrest Boris. Is that asking so much?"

Caty folded her arms across her chest. "Yes, it is. I've been waiting all my life for this and nothing is going to prevent me from having it."

There were two scarlet spots on her cheeks, contrasting with the pale creaminess of her skin. Josh struggled for a moment, hating to give in and yet realizing that it was hopeless to argue with her. "I could go to Frances Schyler, you know. She would listen to reason."

That gave Caty a momentary pause. "If you do that I'll never forgive you."

And she wouldn't. He knew that. He turned away and pulled the round watch from his fob pocket, glancing absently at the time. "No, I won't do that. I just hope I won't regret not doing it."

Caty breathed a silent sigh of relief. "Then that's settled. Let's not speak of it again."

They both resumed their chairs, sitting opposite each other as an invisible chasm opened between them. Nothing was heard in the ensuing silence but the flame of a log in the fireplace and the ticking of the old-fashioned clock on the mantel. Caty stared at the fire, hating the gulf that separated her from this man with whom she had known such joy and shared such passion. Though she was not going to stay safely away from the opera house even for Josh, yet the thought that disagreement should fray the edges of their happy relationship made her terribly sad. She looked over at him and saw that he, too, was staring at the fire. His hands lay folded across his vest, his long legs stretched out before him, and his chin was resting on his shirt collar. He looked as miserable as she felt.

She reached out her hand. "I'm glad you came today," she whispered.

He looked up, his eyes reflecting irritation for an instant. Then he reached out and clasped her fingers in his own.

Josh was at the opera house early the following morning. He fully intended to drop in on Caty's rehearsal later but he had actually come there to see the conductor, von Rankin. After three fruitless attempts to arrange an interview with the distinguished maestro, he had been assured that the man would be at the house and available by nine o'clock that day.

The meeting had been arranged to take place in Cannio's office and Josh found that both men were there waiting for him, looking very unhappy. Von

Rankin did not bother to deny that he had been the person behind Boris's release.

"Though I don't know how you found about it," he said testily, running his long fingers through a shock of white hair. "We took every measure to keep the thing secret."

Josh did not think it was necessary to tell him that he had learned the truth from Caty. "I'd like you to tell me why."

Von Rankin's eyes flew to Cannio for help. "I suppose if someone talked about this, they told you the rest of it as well."

"They did," Josh said simply. "Knowing what he was, why did you hire Herman Warring?"

Von Rankin laughed, a short, bitter, humorless laugh. "Because he was a superb musician. That is all I cared about. His private life was his own concern."

"Did you know he had once been married to Magda Dubratta?"

Again the maestro and the manager exchanged glances. "Yes. But it was a long time ago. And after all, quite a few of us were married to Magda at one time or another. It's difficult to keep track of all her husbands." His voice softened. "Poor Herman. They were both very young and I think he only married her to convince himself and the world that he was 'normal'. It did not take him long to realize it had been a mistake."

"I don't suppose it was too easy for Madam Dubratta, either," Josh commented dryly.

Von Rankin's sculptured lips rose in a ghost of

a smile. "No, I don't suppose it was. She was very bitter about it at first—at least that's what she told me. Later I don't think she remembered him much. However, years later, when he tried to approach her once or twice, she cut him dead. Magda was not the forgiving type."

"And did she forgive you?"

For the first time von Rankin appeared more irritated than worried. "Our careers kept us apart. After a year of this we realized it was futile to continue."

Cannio interrupted with a cough. "Really, Detective. Isn't all this water under the bridge? What possible bearing can it have on Warring's death?"

Josh ignored him. Boring into von Rankin with his steely eyes, he went on. "Tell me about Boris Borinsky."

The maestro squirmed in his chair. "I have little to tell. I hardly know the man."

"And yet you went to a great deal of trouble and expense to get him out of jail."

"You know why I did that, Mister Castleton. I . . . we . . . cannot afford a hint of scandal on top of all the accidents and . . . other things . . . that have taken place in this house recently. It would undo us completely. I'm sure you can understand that."

"Did Boris murder Herman Warring?"

"How should I know? He . . . well, he might have been friends with Warring. I suppose you might say they were friends. Good friends."

"You mean that the two men were involved?"

"I suppose you could say that. At least, that was the rumor."

"And if Borinsky did indeed murder Herman Warring, what possible good did you think it would do for this house to set him free to murder again?"

Von Rankin pulled at his collar. "I didn't think about that. I only wished to avoid a trial which would mean a lot of newspaper coverage."

Josh stood up. "Well, the only way to do that, Maestro, is to have the man confess and be done with it. A grand jury hearing is already scheduled, assuming our friend Borinsky doesn't use the opportunity you've given him to leave New York." He looked over to the manager. "Both of you might as well face the fact that this man is going to be tried and, I fully expect him to be convicted. I hope we can keep the more unsavory aspects of this thing out of the papers but I won't guarantee that we can. You'd both better start thinking about how you're going to deal with the scandal."

He was at the door when von Rankin rose and spoke. "Detective Castleton, does this mean that you do not intend to make any arrests for illicit behavior?"

Josh threw him one last glance. "I consider that among the things that have recently taken place in this opera house, private behavior among consenting adults is the least of my worries."

It took only the first morning for Caty to realize

she had a difficult job ahead. Unlike most established singers who could appear a few days before the performance and attend rehearsals mostly to become familiar with the stage, she had to learn every nuance of the role. She wanted to *be* Carmen, not simply act her or sing her. She came to the first rehearsal having studied the part and the score until she felt she knew it thoroughly, and yet, within half an hour she realized that knowing and actually doing were two quite different things.

Nor was she accustomed to having to act a part that required so much movement and emotion while she was also singing it. It was difficult to keep her mind and her voice both focused, yet she was determined to be a complete success at both. By the time Stillman called their first break, depression was beginning to set in and her previously unshakable faith in herself was fraying at the edges.

"Don't be discouraged, signorina. It is always like this when one learns a new role."

Caty looked up from her coffee cup to see Rodrigo Estes sitting down beside her. Rodrigo had sung Don José many times and during the long morning he had mostly waited around while Gregory Stillman ranted at her.

"Was it that bad?"

"I've seen worse. Remember, this is your first leading part. You don't have the reservoir of confidence that more established singers bring to the role. But you will do well. You have talent, *mia piccola amica*."

He patted her hand in a fatherly gesture. Caty had been a little disappointed when she learned Rodrigo was to sing opposite her instead of Gregorio, and yet, watching the tenor's homely but kindly round face, she began to think it was probably better that way. He would be far more tolerant of her inexperience, and he would not dominate the opera as a tenor of Carlo's standing might.

"I'm grateful for your patience, signor. But have you really seen a singer more unsure of herself than I feel at this moment?"

Estes leaned back against the set and sipped at his coffee. "Well, of course, I usually sing with divas with whom I am fortunate if I am noticed at all. But once or twice I have assisted in the debut of promising young singers. I like it because they focus more on merging their role with mine than they do on enticing applause from their private claques. It is a refreshing change."

Caty laughed. "You certainly know how to raise a girl's flagging spirits, signor. I wonder if I shall someday be one of those self-assured divas."

"But of course. Although I suspect you might retain a little more of your softer personality than some I have known. Naturally, such overbearing tendencies are not limited to sopranos. I have known quite a few tenors almost as bad, not to mention a baritone or two. But the very worst are usually sopranos."

"Don't tell me. Magda Dubratta."

Rodrigo laughed. "Yes. How did you know?"

"I caught the lash of her tongue, too, remember? I'm sure she never suffered from lack of confidence."

"Not once she was established, no. However . . ."

Estes hesitated, as though wondering whether to go on or not. As Caty's curiosity rose, he appeared to think better of continuing and Caty said quickly, "You knew her before she was a famous diva?"

He shrugged. "In Europe, a few years ago. When she was just beginning the downward slide that became so obvious when she was here."

"I've heard that in her prime there was no one better," Caty said in an effort to urge him to continue.

Rodrigo sipped from his coffee cup. "That is true. She had an uncanny blend of acting ability and beauty of voice that, at its best, lifted one's soul. Sometimes I wondered if it wasn't that very depth of emotion that finally drove her to the excesses of behavior she became famous for later. Eventually it was those excesses that took over and something of the true feeling was lost. And, of course, the voice suffered terribly as well. But in the beginning, to hear and watch her at her best . . ."

He hesitated, unable to find the words to describe the experience.

"Then you were friends?" Caty asked.

Estes gave a short, bitter laugh. "Friends? No, I would hardly call us that. In fact, I accidentally ran into her the morning of the day she died and she cut me dead. We nearly collided with each other on Fifth Avenue. I was going into a building and she was coming out. We were nose to nose, as the saying goes. I smiled and spoke and she looked daggers at me and walked on as though I wasn't there. Madam Dubratta was not known for her social graces."

Caty sighed. "A great diva does not need social graces. I only hope I, too, am capable of creating Carmen as a complicated woman while singing the role at the same time. It's not easy."

Rodrigo patted her hand again. "No, but you are already on the path toward doing that. I could sense it the moment we began rehearsal. Many of the great singers I have known could only stand and gesture while performing their role. Several thought that was all that was required. If you can bring the fire to this part, which I believe you can, you will be a great success, signorina."

Her smile lit up her face. "Thank you, Rodrigo. I shall remember your encouraging words when I begin to feel overwhelmed by all these challenging directions."

Gregory Stillman's voice boomed. "Let's go, everyone. We've a lot to do and have only just begun."

"Back to work," Caty said, setting down her cup. Her heart was immeasurably lighter as she walked back on to the rehearsal stage.

On Sunday Caty took time off to travel up to Westchester and visit with Josh at his family home. He met her at the train driving his own buggy, a beautiful chestnut gelding between the traces. Caty paused long enough to stroke the horse's velvet nose before climbing up into the carriage.

"Is he new?" she asked. "What happened to the mare you drove last time?"

"Oh, she's still around. But I saw this lovely creature at a sale in the city and thought he would make a perfect addition to our stable. I knew you would be impressed."

"He's lovely. Can I drive him while I am here?"

He smiled down at her. "I'm counting on it. I bought him for you."

He seemed so pleased that Caty caught back her dismay over the thought that he would go to so much expense for her sake. Nothing about this gift made her comfortable. In the first place she was not going to have the time to be up here very often. And in the second, her life was too full right now to allow any pleasurable pursuits to divert her from her real purpose—to learn her role in *Carmen* as thoroughly as possible. There was also the nagging thought that Josh was taking a lot for granted by thinking of her in terms of anything related to his household.

Yet she did not want to talk of these things. Instead she told him about her conversation with Rodrigo Estes and how encouraging it had been.

"I know what he means about singers standing in one place and letting their voices do all the work. I call it the 'stretch and lurch' style of acting."

Caty laughed. "What does that mean?"

"You must have seen it many times from the chorus. The singer stretches one arm full-length, lurches one step forward, and bellows forth."

Innumerable images rose in Caty's mind at his description. "Oh, I have, now that you mention it," she said, giggling. "Though it doesn't look quite so obvious from the rear of the stage."

Mrs. Castleton was standing in front of the parlor window when they entered the room. She looked more fragile than ever in a high-necked, robin's egg blue silk blouse with a watered silk skirt that trailed behind her for a good three feet. She gave Caty a politely mannered welcome.

"I've arranged another of my 'high teas'," she said, leading her to the sofa. "I hope you are hungry."

"Starving," Caty answered, as Mrs. Castleton settled beside her. This rather surprised her, since, by her manner, she assumed Josh's mother was not all that happy to see her. She learned the reason a little later when Josh was called out to the stables to deal with one of the work horses who had suddenly gone lame. The parlor door had barely closed behind him before Lavinia Castleton set down her cup, folded her manicured hands in her lap and gave Caty a tight smile.

"You know, my dear, it isn't very often that my son brings one of his lady friends to visit me, much less returns her for a second visit."

Caty took a sip from her cup to hide her embarrassment. "Really?"

"Oh yes. Of course, I confess I have often despaired of seeing him involved with anyone at all. He's always been popular, but he seems to put so much of himself into his work that he never has any energy left for his personal life. Like most women my age, I long for grandchildren."

Caty coughed, not knowing how to answer. Lavinia Castleton went on, blissfully unaware of her discomfort.

"And such work! I don't need to tell you that from the very beginning I was distraught over his choice of such a demeaning profession."

"It means a great deal to him."

"I know, and I shall never understand why. He could have taken the bar, practiced law, gone into business—anything except crime where he has to deal every day with danger. I so want to see him get out of it, and I've always hoped that the love of a good woman might be able to persuade him."

Caty set her cup on the table. "A good woman?"

"Yes." Lavinia Castleton fastened her gaze on the teapot. "One of his own set. There are so many lovely girls Josh has known since childhood. I always hoped that one of them might someday become the daughter I never had."

Caty suppressed a smile. This conversation was obviously causing Mrs. Castleton some distress. Well, it served her right for assuming "the wicked opera singer" wanted nothing so much as to marry her son.

"Of course," Lavinia went on, "I've attended the

opera all my life and I have a great appreciation for its artistry."

"But you'd prefer not to have that daughter be a professional singer?"

Mrs. Castleton gave her a hard look. "Thank you. That is exactly what I would prefer, but I found it difficult to say."

"I understand. What is it you want of me, Mrs. Castleton? To refuse to see your son again?"

"Oh, no, nothing that drastic. I just thought perhaps you might encourage him to . . . well, think more about his future."

"My thoughts are almost wholly concerned with my future, Mrs. Castleton, and that involves an operatic career, not marrying a policeman. Besides, if you think I have any influence over Josh, you are very wrong."

"Perhaps so now. But . . ." Her voice trailed off as the door opened and Josh came back into the room.

"It looks like a bog spavin. I've told Teddy to call for the veterinarian if it's not better by tomorrow."

Caty barely listened as he went on explaining the problem to his mother. She felt a growing turbulence in her chest. Clearly Lavinia suspected she and Josh felt more for each other than friendship, and she could hardly wait to enlist Caty's aid in luring Josh away from his profession. Mrs. Castleton's confidence in her only made the vague uneasiness she had felt when Josh told her about the new gelding swell into a genuine discomfort. She did not want to be involved with this family at all, and certainly not now, when her own life was so full.

On the other hand, it amused her to see Mrs. Castleton struggling between her efforts to squash her son's budding romance with an opera singer, and, at the same time, enlist that singer's efforts to persuade her son to change careers. It had been difficult for Josh's mother to talk so privately with her, and yet she had done so. This once, at least, Lavinia Castleton's concern had obviously outweighed her good manners.

Caty decided to shrug it off and try to enjoy the rest of the meal.

It was too cool for driving out after the high tea so instead Josh took the time to show her around his home. Built in 1805, the century-old house was full of interesting nooks and crannies, most of which were no longer used now that the family was so diminished. At the top level was a room under the eaves which had served as a schoolroom for the young Josh. Carrying a lamp that fell dimly on dusty desks and chairs, boxes of games and stacks of old books, Josh led her inside. Outside the circle of lamplight long shadows stretched darkly back under the eaves. It was the most private place they had visited and Josh lost little time setting the lamp on a table and drawing Caty into his arms.

His kiss was long and lingering, lightly tasting of her lips, and tracing the outline of her mouth with his tongue. His fingers lightly searched her back and circled her waist, then traveled upward to tease her breast beneath the lace of her blouse.

"Your mother will wonder what has become of us," Caty murmured when she could talk.

He nuzzled her throat. "No, she won't. She thinks I am too much of a gentleman to take advantage of you."

She slipped her arms around his neck, lightly coursing his cheek with her lips. "You know, she asked me to lure you away from the police force, don't you?"

He lifted his head. "I trust you discouraged her. She has a fixation about my work."

Caty pulled back a little. "Whatever gave her the idea that anyone could influence a man as stubborn as you? Much less me."

"It's wishful thinking. She'd like to see me honorably wed and working at some boring, respectable profession."

Caty smiled up at him. "Honorably wed, but to one of your own kind. She wants grandchildren, too."

She expected him to react angrily at his mother's foolishness. Instead he ran a finger down her cheek, along her throat, and down her blouse to lightly stroke a nipple that sprang erect at his touch. "Being wed might not be so bad if it included a certain opera singer I know."

Caty felt herself losing control and she stepped away. "Be serious, Josh. You know I can't think about such things right now."

"Oh, yes," he said wearily. "Your career."

He felt a sudden irritation, both at the way she had pulled away from him as well as at hearing the same old tune about how important her career was when he was practically offering her his life and his future children.

"Or is it your career?" he heard himself saying. "Maybe it's something more prosaic, like Charlie Poore. Oh, I know how he's been badgering you," he added at the look of astonishment on her face. "Perhaps you should encourage him. After all, he can give you marvelous gifts of diamonds and other expensive baubles, which an ordinary policeman could never afford. He's done it for plenty of other lovely young artists."

Caty fought down the anger his words sent surging through her. "That's not fair, Josh. I know what Charlie is. I've only had supper with him once or twice and that's only because he drove me crazy to go out with him."

Josh perched on the edge of a desk and folded his arms across his chest, studying her. "And is that all?"

"No. Once I let him accompany me to an after-the-opera party because there was no one else to go with. You were not around and Kyle could not meet me." She looked up sharply. "But you knew that, didn't you? You were trying to see if I would tell you."

He did not deny it.

"I've had no gifts from Charlie, diamonds or otherwise. I wouldn't accept them if they were offered."

"Oh, they will be in time. Men like Charlie count on that."

Her fury surged past her control. "How dare you! That is an insulting remark."

Josh rose and reached for the lamp. "All right. I take it back." His hand fell away and instead he moved back to her, slipping his arms around her. "I'm letting my jealousy get the better of my judgment. I cannot bear the thought of you in any other man's arms, especially a professional roué like Charlie Poore. Men like him prey on young women like you, and they have only one thing in mind."

Caty felt consumed with conflicting emotions. It was infuriating that Josh did not realize she could see right through the shallowness of a man like Charlie Poore. She resented his accusations. And she resented even more the fact that he thought he had any right to keep her out of another man's arms if she wanted to be there. She was still uneasy over the way he and his mother both assumed she was waiting around for the ring on her finger when marriage—even to a man like Josh, whose touch could turn her bones to water—was out of the question right now. When nothing else mattered but the priceless opportunity to use her voice as the gift God had given her.

She felt herself wavering under the swelling warmth that he had such power to evoke within her. Deliberately she put her hands on his shoulders and pushed him away.

"We'd better go back downstairs. It's getting late

and I don't want to miss my train. I'm due at the opera house by eight tomorrow morning."

Josh waited a moment, studying her face, before reaching for the lamp. "Of course. We wouldn't want anything to interfere with that, would we?"

Seventeen

By the time she got back to New York, Caty made up her mind to accept the customary invitation from Charlie Poore for supper the following evening. She didn't really want to be with Charlie but, with Josh's accusations still ringing in her ears, she would go with him out of pure spite.

The rehearsal the next day had been long, and hard, and frustrating. Something was not going right about *Carmen* and she could not put her finger on what it was. She had studied, concentrated, worked hard and with enthusiasm and yet her part seemed stagnant and unexciting. At this point it appeared that her debut was going to be just another *Carmen*, enlivened by the new sets and little else. Her voice was at its peak and yet she felt it was not going to be striking enough to make her debut the stunner she wanted it to be.

She remained rather silent throughout the elegant meal and the hansom ride home to Charlotte's apartment where she was spending the night. For once she was thankful that Charlie was such a babbler that he barely noticed how unresponsive she was. At least she thought he hadn't noticed until, on the ride home, he captured her hand, laid an arm around her shoulder and began nuzzling her ear.

Caty pulled quickly out of his embrace. "Now, stop that, Charlie. You know I'm not interested."

"So you've said. However, I'm counting on my charm to break through that wall of ice someday and I thought perhaps tonight might be the night."

"Well, it isn't."

"I have this stunning little . . ." He started to reach into his pocket but Caty gripped his hand.

"How many times have I told you that I do not want your presents! Can't we just enjoy each other's company without all these complications?"

He laughed, sat back on the seat, and ran a finger down her arm. "These 'complications' are the spice of life, m'dear. Surely you'll come to see that someday. Only, let it be soon! A man can only stand so much."

Caty bit her lip to keep from telling him that he should stay away from her if he didn't wish to be frustrated.

"But I'm convinced that someday you'll give in," he went prattling on. "Yet perhaps tonight is not the right time. You've been unusually self-absorbed this evening. I've run through all the gossip I know, and used up every line in my repertoire to entice you out of your introspection, and all to no avail. What is it, love? Fixed on another man?

Suffering a broken heart? Charlie's just the one to take your mind off troubles of that sort."

"No, nothing like that. I suppose it's the opera I'm rehearsing. It's hard work and I'm a little tired."

He lifted her hand to nibble at her fingertips before she could withdraw it. "Of course, the opera. *Carmen*, isn't it? Oh, one of my favorites. So many operatic heroines are straightlaced little virgins, but Carmen, now she is my kind of woman."

Caty was not surprised to hear that. "Why?" she asked absently.

"Why, she's a Gypsy, of course." He leaned closer, his breath warm on her neck. "She's wild and womanly. She likes men and . . . well, making love to men. No straight-laced hesitations for our Carmen. When she likes what she sees she goes after it, enjoys it completely, and when she tires, looks elsewhere."

"Like some men I know."

"Well, yes. Now that you mention it."

Caty extricated herself once again from his creeping hands, nestled into the corner and began thinking. An intriguing idea was taking shape in her mind.

"Come now," he said, following her. "Just a little kiss. It was an expensive supper, after all."

She put a hand on his shoulder and pushed him away, thankful to feel the carriage drawing to a stop.

"You'll get a good-night kiss at the door."

And that was all he did get, a brief, chaste kiss

which Caty broke off before he could make it into something more.

"Good night, Charlie," she said, slipping out of his arms and dashing inside. "And thank you for the supper."

She closed the door and turned to lean against it, smiling to herself. "Thank you for everything, Charlie Poore. You've helped me more than you'll ever know!"

Caty spent the following morning working in Charlotte's small apartment. She closed the door of the second bedroom for privacy and for the next three hours concentrated on her role, adding, changing, practicing. By the time she joined the rehearsal that afternoon, she could barely contain her excitement.

They had only rehearsed the first half of the first act before she had the director, the conductor, and the other lead singers staring at her with gaping mouths, as though she had lost her mind.

"What do you think you're doing!" Gregory Stillman sputtered, breaking into the action. "You've disregarded every move we agreed on. You're throwing Rodrigo completely off, not to mention Maestro von Rankin."

Caty glared at the conductor. "Am I throwing you off, Maestro?"

"Well, not really. But I confess . . ."

"What about you, Rodrigo?"

The affable tenor laughed. "You had me confused there for a while but I was more astounded than thrown off."

Caty glared back at Stillman. "I don't see that there is any problem. I've simply made a few changes."

"A few changes! Madam, you're making a spectacle of yourself. May I remind you that this is a respectable house."

She walked to the edge of the stage, fixing him with a stubborn intense stare. "And may I remind you that this is my debut and I intend to do it my way. I've tried all the usual stiff acting which you like so much and it doesn't work. Carmen is a real woman. She's alive, wild, and . . . and . . . sexy!"

There was a collective gasp among the men.

"Madam . . . please!" Stillman exclaimed, his face growing beet red.

"No, it's true. And that is how I am going to play her. If Mary Garden can make Salome sexy, then I can certainly make Carmen just as much so."

Stillman's cheeks began to swell. "Please do not use that word in my presence," he said between pursed lips. "And remember, madam, that Mary Garden does not sing *Salome* in this opera house. Once was enough."

That was true, Caty thought. She had no desire, like Mary Garden, to create such an uproar that she would never be allowed to sing again.

"Carmen is not Salome, Mister Stillman. There is nothing repugnant about her story. It is tragic because she loves life so much and makes such wrong choices."

Stillman, sensing he was winning, opened his mouth to tell her to forget all this nonsense but he was interrupted by von Rankin tapping his baton on the music stand.

"I believe Miss McGowan has a good point. I admit I was a little astounded at first but the more I think about it, the more I feel her version will be accepted. It will cause a stir—after all, opera usually focuses more on the voice than on the acting—but this is a new production and she is making her debut. A stir is not without its compensations."

"I agree," Rodrigo joined in. "In fact, I may rethink a few things about Don José. It should be refreshing to allow him more room for histrionics."

"But I don't want histrionics!" Stillman interjected.

"I don't want histrionics, either," Caty said in a level voice. "I only want to convey what this woman was and the sense of drama in her life."

"Opera is singing," Stillman said stubbornly. "The music must be paramount. The story is incidental."

"I disagree," von Rankin said. "Certainly the music is first but I think more latitude in conveying the drama of the story will only enhance the music."

Stillman glared at him knowing he was outranked. He might force Caty to follow the rules but the conductor had the last word.

"I'm against it," he said lamely.

"You've made your position plain," von Rankin said. He smiled up at Caty. "Go ahead, Miss McGowan. Throw yourself into the role. I'll let you know when it is too much."

Delighted, Caty blew him a kiss. She went back to her position more excited than she had been since the first day of rehearsal.

Josh returned to the precinct on Monday morning in a black mood. Caty's visit, which he had looked forward to with such pleasure, had turned out to be unsettling and vaguely unpleasant. The last thing he had planned to do was to quarrel with her and yet a quarrel had sprung up out of nowhere, leaving him disappointed and discouraged. When she was away from him all he wanted was to hold her in his arms. When she was there, it seemed all he could do was raise issues that divided them. And now he was carrying his disappointment over into his daily work and letting it affect his mood—something he had sworn to himself he would never do. Sometimes he wished they had never met.

A brisk knock at the door jarred him out of his thoughts. He looked up to see O'Leary standing there with some papers in his hand.

"Excuse me, sir, but I've just come across something rather interesting."

"Come in, Sergeant, and have a seat. What kind of 'interesting'?"

"Well, sir," O'Leary said, laying the paper on

Josh's desk, "I was going through Warring's things and I came across this. It's an insurance policy on his violin. Worth a lot of money that little fiddle."

Josh scanned the paper, whistling under his breath. "Quite a lot. It was a Guarneri, del Gesu. Rare and expensive."

"Yes, sir, but where is it?"

Josh looked up. "There were three violins among Warring's things. Wasn't this one of them?"

O'Leary sat ponderously on the chair opposite Josh. "There were two there and one at his flat. I went back and looked all of them over carefully and frankly, I couldn't see that any of them looked like they were worth so much. But then, all fiddles look alike to me. We ought to check it out, though, sir, don't you think?"

"Surely a Guarneri would have some distinguishing mark. They're too valuable not to. No violin case was found on the roof or in the alley."

"Precisely," O'Leary beamed.

Josh studied the paper thoughtfully. "There's a certificate that describes the color and texture of the wood grain. It also says there is a maker's label under the F hole." He broke into a smile. "That should pin it down. By God, O'Leary, we find that violin and we find our killer!"

He stopped, frowning. "Of course, there might be some other reason why it wasn't with the body. It could have been stolen from the roof before we got there. Or Warring might have put it somewhere in the opera house that we don't know about, someplace he thought it would be safe."

"That's true. But if he didn't . . ."

Josh felt a small stir of excitement. "And if the murderer took it with him . . ."

"Just what I was thinking, sir."

"It's worth pursuing," Josh said, getting to his feet and reaching for his hat. "Let's go, Sergeant."

O'Leary was right behind him. "To ask for a warrant?"

"Not yet," Josh threw back over his shoulder. "First we'll find out if Warring stored his 'fiddle' somewhere else."

The rehearsals had been ordered closed by Maestro von Rankin, who wanted to create a surprise when the new production was unveiled. Caty was grateful for his order for as she worked through her role, adding new moves and discarding others, she appreciated the privacy the closed set gave her. Thus when the door opened while she and Rodrigo were deeply into the love scene of the second act, it was a few moments before she was jarred out of her role. The fact that Josh and his sergeant entered the back of the room was even more disconcerting. They waited there patiently, watching the rehearsal until Stillman came up and whispered to the conductor who then stopped the action and called a break.

It was obvious that Josh had come to speak to the maestro so Caty slipped out of the rehearsal room and down the hall. She had no wish to make idle chat with the other cast members and instead found herself outside one of the dressing rooms. The door was open so she walked inside and looked around.

This was the room set aside for the soprano who was to sing *Aida* that evening. Caty smiled to herself, thinking how she, too, would have a dressing room all to herself once *Carmen* was underway. She ran her fingers along the table, took in the huge bouquet of flowers that had been delivered only shortly before, examined the cubicle for clothes and the long mirror with its bright lights. Then she sat at the dressing table, admiring the pots of makeup, the big powder puffs, the towels and creams.

A step behind her brought her around. She recognized the slight, black-robed figure with the bright-figured costume over her arm immediately.

"Oh, Lulu. You startled me."

The tight face drew itself together. "Excuse me, madam. I'm just delivering the costume for tonight. I'll hang it over here."

"Yes. I was about to leave."

Yet she did not rise. Instead she watched as the woman crossed the room, carrying her tent-like shroud of self-containment with her. What a funny, pathetic, ugly little creature she was. Caty all at once was consumed with pity for her.

"Do you miss Madam Dubratta very much?" she said on a sudden impulse.

Lulu was already on her way out but at Caty's question she paused, her back to the room, her head slightly to the side and speaking over her shoulder.

"There will never be anyone like my lady. She was . . . a genius. Such a voice! Such ability! No one will ever come close to matching her."

Well, Caty thought, I suppose that answers my question.

"You really loved her, didn't you?"

To her surprise Lulu turned suddenly, facing her. She half-expected to see tears, crumpling features, pitiful emotion. Instead the woman's dried, withered face flamed with passion.

"I adored her. She took me from nothing and let me share her life. I would have done anything for her!"

As though she realized she had revealed something of herself, she drew in again just as quickly. "What does it matter now?" she mumbled, slumping again into her shuffling pace. She turned her back to Caty again and headed for the door.

"Don't go yet . . . please," Caty called, feeling that this rare opportunity to learn more about Magda should not be lost. "Tell me about her. Were you with her from the beginning?"

Lulu assumed her reluctant pose once again, speaking over her shoulder. "Yes. From the very first."

"Did she ever teach?"

"No, madam. She thought she might someday but she loved performing." Her voice broke momentarily. "She gave everything of herself to the role she was playing. For three days before a performance she would draw the shades, rest and concentrate on the role. On the day itself she would lie in bed until it was time to leave for the theater. It was my privilege to protect my lady from any intrusion. My privilege and my joy!"

Caty noticed that when the woman spoke of caring for Magda her whole posture changed. Her shoulders went back and she drew herself up. Once she finished, she went back to the dejected pose of before. Her whole purpose in living had been wrapped up in this singer. What a sad life!

"I really must get back," Lulu said, hurrying toward the door.

Caty knew Lulu would not be called back this time. It was just as well. She had a rehearsal to get back to herself. She glanced around the room one last time, thanking heaven that she was a singer and not a singer's maid!

That evening she stayed backstage to watch the opera. She wanted especially to study the soprano singing Aida because she was an experienced singer who had sung in many of the opera houses of Europe. Caty watched how she moved, especially the little nuances which conveyed emotion and drama, as well as how she concentrated on using her voice. She felt she learned a few helpful things though in a general way the performance was too stiff and too concentrated on the voice for her taste. It only helped to convince her even more that she must cut loose from the operatic stereotype if she really wanted to make her Carmen a sensation.

She left the dressing rooms to walk to the stage door, wondering what excuse she could give Charlie this evening. To her surprise, instead of the tall, lean Stage-Door Johnny, she looked up into the gray, steely eyes of Josh Castleton. He was wearing his coat and twirling the band of his hat in his long fingers impatiently.

"I thought you were never going to leave," he muttered, taking her arm.

"I didn't expect to see you. It's been awhile since you were free after the opera."

He pushed open the door. "I suppose you expected good old Charlie. Well, I sent him away. I told him you were already promised to me this evening."

"This is the first I heard of it," Caty quipped, a little annoyed at his overbearing manner. "It's customary to ask."

"I want to talk to you. Your brother wasn't at the theater. Does that mean you're staying in town?"

"Yes. At Charlotte's. It makes it easier to get to early rehearsals and late lessons."

Josh thought a moment. He had seen Charlotte leave with a crowd of laughing men and women just before Caty showed up. With any luck she would not come home for several hours.

"Can you make me a cup of coffee at Charlotte's?"

"Of course," Caty said, a little surprised that he

did not want to go to supper. "It's not far. We can walk."

As it turned out, once they reached the apartment, Caty brought out a bottle of Portuguese sherry which seemed more attractive than coffee. She poured a glass for them both but Josh was too busy walking the narrow room to pick his up. She settled on the sofa and watched him for a few moments before setting down her glass, folding her arms and getting to the point.

"All right, what is bothering you? You accost me at the door, take it for granted I'm going with you, then act cross as a bear all the way here. What is the matter?"

He turned to face her, fixing her with an angry stare. "I stopped into the rehearsal today."

"I saw you."

"You saw me once. I went back just to verify that I had really seen what I thought I saw."

"What are you talking about?"

He came to bend over her. "I'm talking about your behavior. Throwing yourself around like some kind of wanton. Making suggestive gestures with your body. What are you trying to do? Make a scandal of your debut?"

She stared open-mouthed, unable to speak for a moment. Then she laughed. "You mean my Carmen! Good heavens, Josh. It's just a role, for God's sake."

"It may be just a role but it's too graphic and too obscene. I won't have it! I won't allow you to make such a spectacle of yourself."

"You what!"

"You heard me. Half the people I know will be scandalized. My mother would die of embarrassment . . ."

"That's enough!" Caty jumped up from the sofa, squaring off in front of him. "How dare you try to tell me how I should play this part! Carmen is a wanton and if I want to play her that way, I will!"

His eyes took on the gray of flint. "No, you won't! You won't ruin your career and mine, too, by turning the operatic world on its ear."

"This has nothing to do with *your* career. It's *mine* and *mine* only! And if Maestro von Rankin allows me to play it as *I* want, *you* have nothing to say about it!"

"I won't have the girl I intend to marry disgrace . . ."

"And that's another thing," she shouted back. "I never said I would marry you but you and your mother both think it's a settled thing. Well, it isn't! That's all I need, a husband who will be ordering me around, and telling me how to run my life."

"You need someone to tell you how to run your life. Taking up with Charlie Poore. Getting involved with murders. Flirting with scandal . . ."

Caty flounced to the door, trying to open it. "Get out! Go home and leave me alone. I don't want to see you ever again."

She pulled furiously at the door which stuck fast in its frame. In an instant Josh was across the room, grabbing her arm, twisting her around, his fingers digging into her shoulders.

"You are the most infuriating, stubborn little fool I've ever known."

She tried to twist out of his grasp and when she couldn't, began pounding his chest with her fists.

"You're the most pigheaded, overbearing, bossy . . ."

His grip on her wrists was like iron, his face only inches away from hers. In a sudden instant their fury was transformed to a flaming, all-consuming desire. He pulled her into his arms, crushing her mouth, forcing her lips to receive his tongue, thrust deeply within. She gasped and clutched at his shoulders, digging her nails into his jacket. His hands searched her back as her fingers slipped beneath the fabric to work at the buttons of his shirt until she could thrust them against his flesh. Her touch was like a firebrand. He worked at her bodice, pulling away the buttons and tearing it from her shoulders, until he could reach within the low chemise and lift out her breast which he began sucking greedily.

She moaned, arching against him, her senses soaring. She never knew how they got out of their clothes, only that his arms were encircling her naked body, and he was sliding down to kiss her all over, enticing her to levels of ecstasy she had never known. And when she felt she could no longer bear it, he drew her down hungrily on the carpet, kissing her wildly, crushing her beneath him to thrust inside her, again and again, aggressively, long and hard and eternally pushing until they both went crashing over the edge of complete satiation.

When her breathing eased Caty looked around to see they were both lying on the rug. Giggling, she reached for her petticoat and drew it around her. Josh pushed it away.

"I like seeing you this way. You're so beautiful."

She moved sensuously against him, reveling in the feel of his body against hers. How lovely it was to be in his arms, knowing he thought she was beautiful.

Josh smoothed her hair away from her face. It had come undone in their frantic gyrations and lay in long red-gold strands that framed her face and spilled over on to his chest. "And so desirable," he said, kissing her lightly on the lips.

Caty nestled her head in the hollow of his neck. "Oh, Josh, you make me forget everything when I'm with you. Nothing else in the world matters but being in your arms this way."

He smiled down at her. "Dare I call that 'love'?"

Caty hesitated a moment, then abruptly sat up, drawing up her knees and circling them with her arms. Her long hair fell around her like a cloud.

"It's true. I do love you. But . . ."

Josh leaned on his elbow, waiting. Somewhere deep inside an emptiness began to form.

"For that very reason," Caty went on, "I don't think we should see each other anymore."

The emptiness swelled to a sickening depression. "Well," he tried to say lightly, "that is certainly a new way of expressing one's love."

Caty rose and pulled a long fringed paisley shawl that decorated the sofa around her shoulders. She walked to the window where she stood for a moment, trying to find the right words and fighting the sick feeling within her.

Josh watched her, the long shawl around her tall frame, her hair falling over it down her back. He remained silent, refusing to help her.

"It's just that we are so different," Caty said, forcing the words. "We come from very different backgrounds . . ."

He wanted to remind her how easily she moved in both worlds but he didn't interrupt.

". . . but, even more, we live in such different worlds. The things I want and the things you want are so entirely opposite. You want a traditional wife and home, I want a career that will take me out across the world. I must be free to pursue that. It means more to me than anything else."

"Even me?"

The words were spoken so softly that she almost did not hear them. She turned and walked back to him. "Yes," she whispered, forcing herself to answer. Dropping to her knees, she clasped the ends of the shawl tightly in her fingers, her large eyes glistening with unshed tears. "Please try to understand, Josh. If I could give up my ambition for anyone, it would be you. But if I did, I would spend the rest of my life regretting it and wondering if I made the right decision. I must know if I can succeed or not."

"But I'm not stopping you, Caty. Good God, I was the one who introduced you to Frances Schyler in the first place, remember?"

"I know. And you say you won't stand in my way, but you do! You try to censor my acting, you complain about other men, you try to hold me up to a standard that is of your world, not mine."

He reached for her hands, clasping them in his own while the shawl fell open over her shoulders. "Because I love you."

"But don't you understand? You make claims on me that I don't want right now," she cried in a voice urgent with feeling. Her eyes grew luminous with unshed tears.

He tore his eyes from her beautiful body so near him. Drawing her to him, he circled her with his arms, pressing her head to his bare chest. He could feel the wetness of her tears against his skin.

The words seemed to lodge in his throat. "All right. I can see that this distresses you. It distresses me, as well. But what you say is true. Perhaps we should each go our own way for awhile, if only to see whether or not what we feel for each other is genuine."

Caty slumped against him, relieved and yet utterly dejected at the same time. He caught her hair in his fingers, turning her head to lift her lips to his.

"But we still have tonight. Let's make it one we'll always remember."

She caught his face between her palms and smiled up at him. "Yes." she said simply. "One we'll always remember."

He did not leave until dawn was just beginning to tinge the windows a slate gray. Caty was thankful that Charlotte had not returned and they had shared this one last night of blissful privacy. She stood with him at the door holding him one last time, not wanting to let him go.

"I refuse to say goodbye," Josh said, clinging to her. He had put his clothes back on but she was still wrapped in the paisley shawl. He took the ends of it and draped them over her shoulders, creamy and pale in the growing light.

Bending, he kissed her throat, then, remembering, raised his head. "I just realized you are not wearing the talisman I gave you," he said, more to avoid leaving than out of a real curiosity.

Caty's hand went to her bare throat. "It fell off that night on the empty stage."

Josh's face hardened. "Or was pulled off. Oh, Caty, how am I going to take care of you if I can't be with you?"

"I'll be all right. I won't do anything foolish like going on to an empty stage alone again, I promise. You must let me look after myself, Josh."

"That's going to be the most difficult thing about this separation," he said, shaking his head. "But if that's what you want . . ."

She reached up and kissed him. "Goodbye, Josh."

"Good night," he whispered.

He left quickly, pulling the door closed behind him. Caty turned and leaned against it for a whole moment before bursting into tears.

Eighteen

Early the next morning, Josh set off with Sergeant O'Leary in tow to search Boris Borinsky's squalid apartment, resolutely trying to ignore the feeling that something was broken inside him. Determined not to allow his private grief to interfere with his work, he forced down the images of Caty's oval face, her large eyes as lively and green as the summer mountains across the Hudson, her enticingly shaped lips . . .

It wouldn't do. Instead he concentrated on finally enjoying the satisfaction of putting Boris behind bars. He knew in his heart they were going to find Herman Warring's Guarneri in that shabby apartment on the Lower East Side.

Yet once they reached there, he was surprised to see that the room was not as shabby as before. In fact, it was surprisingly clean and neat. The old man, still lying in bed, was covered with freshly washed sheets while he himself was shaved, his hair combed and his mottled face cleaner than Josh remembered. The change, however, had not affected his disposition. And they had barely entered before he was snarling at them.

"I see the lady's aid is working out," Josh commented, which led to a string of complaints about how bossy and irritating she was. Josh and the sergeant ignored him while they set about searching the room. For a small place there were an amazing number of cubicles where something could be hidden. Yet it only took them a few minutes to find the violin case, tucked far behind the general clutter in a cabinet high above the dry sink. Josh smiled at O'Leary.

"Touché."

O'Leary tucked the case under his arm as if it were made of glass. Josh turned back to the old man as they started to leave, asking where his son was.

"How should I know. He don't tell me nothin'."

"Probably at the opera house," O'Leary commented.

Josh nodded, feeling pretty sure that they would find Boris there. As they left to return uptown, closing the door on the old man's loud, imperious demands, Josh found himself wondering why he did not feel more elation having the proof he had sought for so long.

Caty had arrived at the Metropolitan that morning even before Josh and O'Leary had left for the Lower East Side. Rodrigo's *Tosca* was to debut in two nights and she wanted to wish him well since he would not be rehearsing with her for the next two days. She found, however, that she arrived before any of the other cast members. The rehearsal room was still locked and dark, though she expected the others to arrive at any moment.

She debated going back outside to a coffee shop but decided it was too cold and damp for that. Instead she sought out a coffee urn which was usually placed in an alcove at the end of the hall below the rehearsal room. There were two threadbare chairs flanking a table which usually held a tray containing a coffeepot and cups and saucers. Here again she found she was too early. There was no coffeepot and barely any light. She settled in one of the chairs, pulled out her score to study and tried to read it in the dim nimbus from the one gas lamp above the table.

Any moment now she expected one of the serving girls to arrive with the coffeepot, and when she heard a step down the hall, she looked up expectantly.

Boris Borinsky stepped from the shadows of the hall holding the tray. He appeared as surprised to see her as she was to recognize him. He frowned, laid the tray on the table and stepped back. Caty's "good morning" died on her lips at the glower on his face. She waited for him to leave and when he did not, she began to grow uncomfortable. To mask her discomfort, she concentrated on filling one of the cups from the steaming coffeepot.

He took a step toward her and instinctively, she moved back. Caty was tall, but he towered over her, more muscular than she remembered. From a distance one might think him flabby but Caty could see that he wasn't. His arms, bare below the rolled-up sleeves of his shirt, were hard, and swelled with muscle. She had the uncomfortable feeling that he could reach out and twist her neck without even exerting himself. Automatically her hand went protectively to her throat and she took another step back. Why didn't he leave?

"Did you want some coffee?" she asked, knowing a stagehand would never drink with a singer. He shook his head.

She lifted her chin. "You're not supposed to be here. Don't you have some kind of work to do?"

"I go where I want," he muttered in his usual sullen tone.

"Then go. You're making me uncomfortable."

"You're just like her."

"You said that to me once before. Who are you talking about?"

"Like her."

All of a sudden she felt very angry with Boris, who seemed to take a perverse delight in threatening her. "Look, I don't know what you want here but whatever it is, get it done and leave."

He reached out and touched her hair. "You're pretty, too."

She shrank away in horror. "Get away from me!"

"You don't like me to touch you, do you? Too good for the likes of me."

Something rang false to Caty in his strange

words, even to the stupid, lascivious grin on his face. It was commonly known around the opera house that he had been involved with Herman Warring, and that he belonged to the group von Rankin had been trying to protect. She felt certain that he had no real interest in women. He was probably just trying to scare her.

She looked around and saw there was nowhere to run. Drawing herself up, she glared at him. "I've had enough of you. Go away."

"You can't tell me what to do. You ain't nothin' but a singer. You got no authority 'round here."

Caty tried to peer over his shoulder. Where was Rodrigo or Stillman, or someone from the chorus. How was she going to be able to keep this oaf at bay until one of them showed up? She could only hope to keep him talking until one of them came down the hall.

"You didn't like Magda Dubratta, did you?" she asked.

His beefy face became transformed with ugly rage. "I hated her! I hate all you people. You think you're so much better than everybody else 'cause you can play a fiddle or sing a song. Think you can use people, then just throw 'em away when you've had all you want."

He took a step closer and Caty felt the hard surface of the wall behind her.

"Did Magda do that to you?"

He leaned toward her as she pressed back against the wall. She could barely breathe for the heavy garlic on his breath.

"Is that why you killed her?" she asked, turning her face aside.

He raised his hand briefly, then let it drop. A thin, menacing smile touched his lips.

"No one is trying to use you," she said hurriedly.

"Don't tell me. I know better."

She reached out and shoved him in the chest, pushing him back just enough to slip by him. But he caught her arm in an iron vise and pushed her back against the wall.

"You're a dangerous man!" she cried. "You shouldn't be working here at all. I don't know why they keep you on."

The smile grew more wicked. "You don't know anything."

She yanked at her arm. "Leave me alone!"

He reached out with his other hand and grabbed a strand of her hair, pulling it through his fingers. Her bluster was rapidly turning to sheer terror.

"Don't you dare touch me!" she cried. "Get away from me!"

"Boris!"

The voice came from the other end of the hall. Boris dropped his hands and moved away from her, leaving her to slump against the wall. At the far end she saw one of the stagehands watching them.

"What are you doing, Borinsky? You're wasting time. Come on, we've got work to do."

Still he did not move, glaring back at her.

"Let's go, Boris."

He knew he had frightened her and from the satisfied smile on his face, it was obvious that was all he meant to do. Even so, Caty's breath came more easily as she saw him start back down the hall. She groped for a chair and sat down, waiting for her pounding heart to calm. By the time Stillman arrived five minutes later she had recovered and could feel only a searing anger that this horrible man was allowed to be in the house at all.

In the early afternoon Charlotte came running up to tell Caty that Boris Borinsky had just been arrested for the murder of Herman Warring. After finding Warring's violin in Boris's apartment, the police finally had the tangible evidence needed to link Boris to the murder. Detective Castleton himself had made the arrest.

The relief Caty felt at this news seemed to be reflected throughout the entire house. The pall that had lain for so long over the opera had finally been lifted. Everyone felt the lessening of tension, from the members of the board to the members of the chorus. And Caty felt it most of all, especially after the peculiar way Boris had treated her that morning.

Caty had expected to watch Rodrigo's performance in *Tosca* from the wings backstage, but when Charlie unexpectedly asked her to join a party of his friends in his family box that night, she accepted at once, for several reasons. For the first time she felt able to purchase the kind of dress and jewelry which would be acceptable in such surroundings. She and her mother put together a beautiful wine colored satin dress decorated with glass beads and ecru lace. It was the prettiest dress she had ever owned. With it she wore her mother's topaz necklace and newly purchased tiger eyes and pearl earrings. Long satin gloves reaching high up her arms and a gold bracelet set it off perfectly.

She was pleased at the way Charlie's eyes widened with admiration when he called for her, even though it was harder than ever to keep him at a distance in the cab to the opera house. Once they entered the box he behaved himself, introducing Caty politely to the other couple who were already seated and helping her to a chair directly behind the white and gold rail. Caty looked out over the house, buzzing with people finding their seats and glowing with the elegant dresses and twinkling jewels of those patrons who had deigned to arrive before the first curtain. A discordant accompaniment of orchestra instruments warming up served as an obligato to the noisy chatter in the house.

Caty laid her arm along the rail and smiled to herself with excitement and anticipation. Though she loved *Tosca* she had never seen it from the audience before. It was going to be a wonderful evening.

"Don't know why we had to come so early," Charlie grumbled beside her. "Not the thing you know. Anyone who's anyone never arrives before the second act when they can make an entrance and draw all eyes in the house to themselves."

"That's all right for society ladies, but I want to see the opera. Besides, one of Rodrigo's great arias comes right after the curtain and I wouldn't miss it for the world!"

"The things I do for you," Charlie said with a good-natured sigh. One of the other women spoke to him and he turned away from her, leaving her to look out over the house. Almost at once she spied Josh entering a box directly opposite, following his mother. Lavinia, recognizing Caty, gave her a polite wave while Josh stared, frowning as he recognized Charlie behind her. Caty smiled back at him, trying not to think how wonderful it would have been to be over there with Josh and his mother.

Not even the pleasure of watching *Tosca* unfold could drive away her nagging awareness of Josh across the way, or the disappointment she felt when he did not come to speak to her during the intermissions. She tried to tell herself it was what they both agreed they would do, what they both wanted. But she wished that tonight, of all nights, he had not chosen to attend the opera.

The tragedy on stage mirrored her growing sense of depression. Rodrigo sang beautifully and she could see that this performance was going to raise his reputation several notches, which could only be to her benefit when they appeared together in *Carmen*. Charlie had planned an after-the-opera supper party at Delmonico's and, of course, she was expected to attend. When the last act began she spent the first few moments wondering how she could get out of it, knowing that her determined escort was not going to accept any excuse she might make. On the other hand, perhaps it might be best to attend and hope that company, and good food, would drive thoughts of Josh Castleton from her mind.

But she soon forgot all that as she became lost in the music of the last act. It was unbearably beautiful. Rodrigo, sitting alone on the dark ramparts of the Fort St. Angelo in Rome as represented on the stage, sang his second great aria, "E lucevan le stelle," with passion and beauty of tone. The lovely words and gorgeous music as Cavaradossi sang his despair to the night stars brought tears stinging behind her eyes, it so closely echoed her own loss. She leaned forward over the rail, caught up in the beauty of the music as Tosca and Cavaradossi recalled happier times together. She watched enthralled as Tosca warned her lover to pretend to be dead while the mock execution was carried out, then restlessly prowled the stage encouraging him as the small group of soldiers with their rifles formed their place in front of him. To the echoes of the drums the guns fired and Tosca's lover fell. The guards trooped off while Tosca excitedly called to Cavaradossi to get up, gradually realizing that the execution had been all too real. As her despairing cry rose with the orchestra, and the soldiers rushed back to arrest her for murdering the villain, Scarpia, she dashed to the parapet and with one last thrilling line, "Scarpia, avanti a Dio!" threw herself over.

The last crashing chords left Caty limp. The drama of the music reached deep down within her, touching some universal depth of feeling beyond the scope of ordinary life. She turned away to regain her composure as the applause in the house rose in a noisy crescendo.

"Oh, well done," Charlie cried with enthusiasm, loudly applauding. "Did you like it, Caty?"

"Very much," she murmured as the golden curtain parted to allow for the singer's bows. Caty reached for a small bouquet of flowers she had brought for this moment. She intended to throw it to Rodrigo onstage, hoping he would notice it came from her. The applause grew in intensity as the crowd waited for the principals to appear.

It was a full minute before Caty felt the first dread tinge of fear. Though the applause continued, the stage remained bare. This was unheard of, except once before, when the crowd had clamored for Magda Dubratta to acknowledge the adoration of her public.

Caty gripped the rail as her small bouquet fell to the floor.

Charlie glanced over at her and noticed how the blood had drained suddenly from her stricken face. "What's the matter?"

"I don't know." Even as she spoke, she looked across the house and saw Gregory Stillman enter the box where Josh was sitting with his mother.

Josh looked around, rose hurriedly and slipped out the door.

"Something is wrong," Caty answered, jumping to her feet.

"Where are you going?" Charlie cried as she dashed to the rear of the box. "What about supper . . ."

Caty did not bother to answer. She went racing down halls and stairs to the door that led backstage, urged on by a growing sense of alarm. She tried to tell herself she was being foolish, that it was probably only some ordinary delay which had held up those last bows, yet her swelling panic refused to be appeased. She climbed the steps backstage and dashed into the wings where she was able to see several people in a group on the stage behind the heavy closed curtain. The soprano who had sung Tosca was standing near the back of the set, sobbing in the arms of the conductor. Gregory Stillman, his white face a mask of horror, stood bending over the backs of two of the soldiers, still in their uniforms. As Caty watched, Josh Castleton rose to his feet above the huddled group, looking down at the crumpled form lying on the stage.

"Oh, no!" Caty cried. She ran out onto the stage and tried to push through the small group. Josh, seeing her, moved to grab her arm and tried to pull her away.

"What are you doing here? Go back outside."

She looked up at him, her eyes huge and frightened. "What's happened?"

He shifted in front of her to put his body between her and the people grouped on the stage. "Believe me, Caty. It would be better for you to wait down the hall. I'll come to you in a few minutes and explain everything."

How could he believe she would calmly walk away when she knew in her heart that it was her friend who was in trouble? Once again, she thought angrily, he was trying to hide her from reality, to shield and protect her from the truth. Her face went rigid. "No. I want to see . . ."

Yanking her arm away, she forced her way through the people bending over the crumpled form lying on the stage, and fell to her knees beside Rodrigo Estes, sprawled on the floor, blood oozing from a small, neat hole in his chest.

Nineteen

"The opera house will be closed and that is final."

Caty studied the steely determination etched on John P. Morgan's round face and her heart plummeted. All her dreams began to evaporate, like dew on a warming summer morning.

Cannio drummed his fingers on the desk, his face a mask of anxiety and pain. "You realize that the loss will be catastrophic to the proceeds for the season?"

Morgan, who had been pacing the room, turned on him with all the deadly intensity of a warship about to fire its heaviest batteries.

"Proceeds! Of course, I realize we will lose money. A lot of money. But if we do not halt all operations until this mess is cleared up, we risk the failure of the house itself. Who will want to come near a place where murder occurs with impunity?"

"It brought in the public once before," Belmont offered in a tentative voice. "Though, naturally, we do not want to let that influence our decision."

Caty gripped the arms of her chair. Naturally they would not want to be influenced by anything so crass as profit. She looked from Morgan's continued pacing to Belmont's timid, anxious long face, to Cannio, like a death's head hovering over his wide, mahogany desk. Across from her Josh sat observing them as closely, his face masking whatever thoughts he had on the matter.

"Don't you agree, Inspector?" Morgan boomed, turning on Josh. "I think the police should order this house closed."

Josh rubbed a finger along his underlip, hesitating before replying. "Yes, the house should close, at least temporarily."

"I should think so. Soon we'll have patrons coming to the opera not to hear the music but in order to see who will be killed that evening! It is an untenable situation and it must be brought to a close. Immediately!"

Josh resisted the urge to rise to the defense of his department. "It will be."

Belmont turned to him, his level voice a pleasing contrast to Morgan's pomposity. "Was there nothing to indicate who did this terrible thing? Surely someone must have seen something."

"The only person we can't account for is a woman who was glimpsed sometime during the second act—a buxom woman with long, black hair, wearing a dark opera cloak. Of course, she could have been one of the chorus."

"Not in *Tosca*. They're finished after the first act."

"The shot came from about twelve feet above the stage floor so the person firing it must have stood on one of the platforms that give access to the ropes and weights controlling the curtains."

Morgan came to a stop at last beside the high arched window where he turned to face Josh. "But surely the flame when the gun was fired would have attracted some notice."

"Not if it was hidden by one of the upper curtains. And if this person wore one of those dark cloaks, he would easily blend with the shadows above the stage. The shot was perfectly timed to coincide with the music and the blanks from the soldiers' rifles."

"So this person was familiar with *Tosca*."

Josh drummed his fingers on his knee. "Yes. Obviously."

"And an expert shot since he killed Estes so cleanly with one bullet."

Josh nodded and waited for the expected next question.

"And you're certain it was not that fellow you arrested—Boris somebody-or-other?"

"That's not possible," he said grimly. "The man was safely behind bars during last night's performance."

Of all the eyes focused on him in that room, only Caty, who knew how his inner emotions were mirrored in the cold barrier of his gray eyes, realized the turmoil and shame he was feeling. It must be galling to have these things happening while he was helpless to prevent them. He would not let himself dwell on the word "failure," yet she knew he was blaming himself.

"But why Rodrigo?" Belmont cried. "I've asked myself that question over and over and I cannot see how anyone could have nurtured a grudge against such a pleasant, talented artist."

Josh spoke evenly. "There might have been something going back to his days in Europe. On the other hand, it is possible that someone is simply trying to ruin the opera house and Estes was a random victim."

"Surely not our rival . . ."

"No, no," Josh spoke quickly. "I don't think even a rival house would go to these lengths to put a competitor out of business. This has more the feel of a grudge, a long, seething vendetta which some unbalanced mind has finally acted upon."

Morgan plopped down heavily into one of the wide leather chairs. "Well, if their motive is to bring down the curtain permanently, they have very nearly succeeded. I don't see how we can continue, not knowing when another singer is going to die on stage."

"We shall cancel the rest of the performances," Cannio said sadly. "It will mean the loss of all the revenues but it cannot be helped."

Morgan's shoulders slumped slightly as it dawned on him just how much the house was going to lose. "No, there is nothing else we can do," he said sadly. "We cannot risk another death."

"Might I suggest . . ."

The eyes of every man in the room turned to Caty. She hesitated under the blast of all that worldly power focused on her, then took a deep breath and continued.

"That is, I think we should go ahead with *Carmen*."

Cannio gave a thin smile. "Naturally, you are disappointed to lose your debut, Miss McGowan, and yet, I am sure you can see how impossible it would be to continue with any productions. We can schedule it next season."

Caty's cheeks flared under his naive assumption that all she cared about was her own career. "It is not the debut I am thinking of," she stated emphatically. "I believe the production might help solve the problem once and for all."

"And how do you see that happening," Belmont commented dryly.

Caty sat forward in her chair. "You see, I think this person, whomever he or she is, might also want to harm me. If I appear in a new production which could lead to enhancing my career, he might try to kill me at the end of *Carmen*, as he has the other singers. If we are ready, we just might be able to catch him before that happens."

"Absolutely out of the question!" Josh exclaimed.

"A shocking risk!" Cannio echoed.

"Think what it would mean if it fails," Belmont added.

But Morgan sat quietly, thinking over her comments. Caty turned to him, hoping he would not be as negative as the others.

"What makes you think this person might want to harm you?" Morgan asked.

Caty exchanged a brief glance with Josh. "Oh, just little things. The inspector knows about them. They did not amount to much but they were suggestive."

Morgan turned to Josh who threw Caty an angry glance before answering. "Yes, there have been one or two small incidents. We have had people watching Miss McGowan for some time, both to protect her and in the hope this maniac might reveal himself."

Caty had a brief image of the stagehand calling to Boris that morning in the hall. "Was that . . . ?"

"Yes," Josh said quietly. "He was one of our men."

"Well then," she said quickly to the others. "That just proves it. If I am a target, what better way to draw this killer out than to present myself in another opera?"

"It's too dangerous," Josh spat out the words.

"I agree," Cannio added. "You could be murdered, Caty, and then where would we be? The opera house could never survive another such killing."

Caty caught back a bitter laugh. "I'm willing to take the risk. In fact, I insist I be allowed to do it. I know the inspector will find a way to protect me. And think about it a moment. Unlike Butterfly and Cavaradossi in *Tosca*, Carmen is stabbed on stage in front of the audience and the company. If this person is going to murder in the same vogue as he has done in the past, he is going to have to be out there. It would be the perfect opportunity to catch him."

She could see Belmont weakening. "That is true. It might work. What do you think, Castleton?"

Josh's face settled into stubborn lines. "I am against it. It's foolish, foolhardy, and unnecessarily risky. I won't have it."

Morgan turned to face him. "Do you have a better plan?"

"Not at the moment but I'll find one."

"Nevertheless, I think Miss McGowan's idea has merit. We can close the house for two weeks, then reopen with the new production." He turned to Cannio. "Can it be ready by then?"

"Well, it will be difficult but I think we can do it. Especially if the house is closed during that time."

Josh sat and fumed as he listened to these businessmen making decisions which were better left to the police. It was a moment before he admitted to himself that, had another singer been doing *Carmen*, he would not be so against taking this chance. It was Caty he feared for. Caty, with her flaming hair and emerald eyes that glinted with excitement now at the thought that she was going to have her debut and in the face of great danger. She reveled in this. But what would he do if something went wrong and he lost her? He would never be able to live with that.

He realized he was grinding his teeth with inner turmoil. He had been so sure that Boris was behind all the trouble. But Boris was safely in jail when Rodrigo Estes was shot during the last scene of *Tosca*, and could not have possibly been involved. Now this nameless, faceless maniac was still out there, waiting for another victim to come forward. And this time it would be Caty who might die!

He realized that Morgan was speaking to him and shook off his anxious thoughts.

"Then it's decided, Inspector?"

"What? No, it isn't."

"Perhaps I'll just have a little talk with the Police Commissioner this afternoon. I'm sure he will see the value of this plan even if you do not. However, we will be counting on you to make certain that stage is crawling with officers. We do not want to risk Miss McGowan's life any more than necessary."

Josh looked over to see Caty settle back in her chair, glowing with triumph. His answer was choked back by his anger and his fear for her.

He was not too choked to speak, however, once he was alone with Caty. She had barely left the manager's office before he gripped her arm and pulled her toward the small lift which would take them back downstairs.

"I'd like a word with you," he said grimly.

She pulled at the tight, painful grasp he had on her arm. "You are not going to talk me out of this. And you don't need to yank my arm off!"

Josh poked at the lift button and the doors opened. He shoved her inside before anyone else could catch up with them. Once the doors closed and the lift began descending jerkily, he relaxed his grip and she pulled away, facing him across the small interior.

"Of all the crazy, foolish, insane stunts . . ."

"You made it clear how you felt back there in Cannio's office. Do you intend to yell at me all the way down, because if you do, I'll get off right here."

She made an effort to push one of the lift's floor buttons but he caught her hand.

"I don't want to see you get killed!"

The angry sparks in her eyes subsided as she realized his opposition came from his concern for her. "But I'm willing to take the risk. No one is making me do it."

He gripped her hand tightly in his fingers. "There are other ways to draw this maniac out, ways which are not so risky. I simply won't allow you to put yourself in such a dangerous position."

Her chin went up and she glared at him. "You don't have any choice, Josh. I won't give up my debut, not even if Jack the Ripper stalks me across the stage! Can't you understand that?"

The lift came to a stop with a loud thump. Slowly the mesh doors slid apart while the two of them stood, stubbornly staring each other down.

"I beg your pardon," said a voice from the hall. Caty turned and saw three of the members of the chorus waiting for them to step off the elevator.

"Oh. Sorry," she murmured and, throwing the long fur-trimmed stole of her jacket over her shoulder, stepped off. She had walked only a few steps when Josh was beside her, taking her arm again.

"Where can we talk?"

"Josh, it's no use. You're not going to change my mind." She paused, looking up at him, remembering something that had occurred to her that morning. "There is one thing about this case that I would like to discuss with you. Something I recalled while I was walking here today. We can use the lounge if you promise not to try to convince me to postpone *Carmen*."

The stubborn set of Josh's jaw convinced her he was not going to go along. To her surprise, he dropped her arm and fell into an easy step beside her. "Is it something important?"

"I don't know. Perhaps not. I'd like to know what you think."

There was no one in the singers' lounge when they entered. They sat on a couch across the room near a tall, clouded window, both of them careful to leave a space between. Caty knew that she was too conscious of his nearness, of the warmth his firm, strong body evoked within her at the least provocation, to get too near him. All her resolve to make their relationship into a simple friendship was beginning to slip away. And yet, it might be that she had remembered something worth pursuing. At least she needed to have his opinion.

Josh crossed his legs and drummed his fingers on his knee. He was fighting his own demons, the futility of this miserable case and the longing to take her in his arms, unpin her hair and cover her porcelain face with his kisses . . .

"So, what did you remember?" he said, matter-of-factly.

"Well, it might not mean anything, of course. But I had a conversation with Magda's maid the other day and she told me that before a performance Magda would stay in her bedroom, resting on her bed, and allowing no one to bother her. It was the maid's duty to keep people away—one she seemed to have taken very seriously."

"Is that unusual behavior for a singer?"

"No, not at all. Some disappear for days before a performance. Some speak only in a whisper. Each artist does what is most helpful for them in order to sing well once they get on stage. Only . . ."

Josh waited, trying to force his eyes from the crescent of darkened lashes that lay on her creamy cheeks as she studied her hands in her lap.

"Only, before he was killed, Rodrigo told me that he met Magda on the street the morning of the day she was killed. She was coming out of a building as he was going in."

Forcing his thoughts back to what she was saying, Josh sat up, leaning forward and resting his elbows on his knees. "And you think that might be significant?"

"Well, I don't know. It might not be. Perhaps she went out that one time and Lulu just didn't mention it."

"Or didn't know."

"Possibly. The woman idolized Magda but she was also very possessive about her responsibilities for taking care of her. I suppose it's silly to make anything of it."

"I wonder where Magda went."

He does think it's significant. Caty felt a small sense of excitement beginning to build. "Rodrigo did not identify the building except to say that it was on Fifth Avenue."

"That doesn't exactly narrow it down."

Caty sighed. "I know. I wish I could help you more."

Josh thought for a moment, then smiled over at her. "Perhaps you can. Let's examine it from a policeman's point of view. Did Estes live on Fifth Avenue?"

Caty frowned. "I don't think so. No, I remember once he mentioned how he had to travel uptown from Fourteenth Street everyday and what a nuisance it was."

"Then what reason would he have for going into a building on Fifth Avenue?"

"There could be a hundred reasons."

"True. But let's think of one that might occur

often. Like, visiting his mother, or his tailor, or his doctor."

Caty sat up quickly. "Or his voice coach. That's it! He studied with Lorenzo Givens and he has a studio at Fifth and Twenty-eighth."

Josh's face fell. "Then Magda could have gone there for a lesson?"

"Perhaps. But I should think it unlikely. Magda could have been a voice coach herself. I doubt that she would have gone to one for advice."

"There is only one way to find out," Josh said, rising to his feet and reaching for her hand to pull her up. "I think I'll take a little ride down Fifth Avenue. Do you want to come?"

Caty was already throwing the end of her stole over her shoulder. "Just try to go without me!"

All four corners of the intersection contained stone buildings several stories high. Caty had no idea which one contained Lorenzo Given's voice studio, so they began by entering each one to examine the names listed on either mailboxes or a wall directory. The first two were entirely made up of apartments, none of them registered to Givens. The third was more promising since it also included two doctors' offices and one lawyer's office. At the fourth, they found Given's listed on the sixth floor.

"Wouldn't you know it would be in the last place we look?" Caty commented as Josh ran his finger up and down the two columns of names.

Actually, she was so encouraged by the fact that Josh had said nothing more about canceling *Carmen* that she hoped the search would go on for a long while. At least they weren't arguing while they were looking.

"Didn't you say Magda would not have come here to meet with Givens?"

"It's unlikely, but we should ask him, just in case."

Josh's finger held poised over one of the names. "On the other hand, she might have been seeing someone else in the building. Someone like J. Johnson, Diseases of the Throat."

Caty leaned to look more closely at the board. "Why, I'll wager that's it. It was just a coincidence that Rodrigo was coming here to see Lorenzo Givens as she left."

Josh frowned. "It's certainly possible. Let's go and ask."

"Will they tell us?" Caty asked as they started toward the stairs.

"A police officer? Oh, I think so."

They began by climbing to the sixth floor to knock on Given's door and ask if Magda had ever sought out his help. Givens was a flamboyant, opinionated figure with long, shoulder-length hair and a face so pale it might have been carved from marble.

"Magda Dubratta? That has-been? Certainly not. Had she asked me I would not have taught her. She was far too over the hill to be helped by anyone, even a teacher of my caliber. Besides, from what I know of the 'great Dubratta,' she would not seek out any coach. She'd never admit she needed one."

"I thought as much," Caty murmured.

Givens focused his long-lashed eyes on Caty. "On the other hand, I've heard of you, Miss Mandesi. I'm convinced I could make you a great singer. And I just happen to have an opening . . ."

"One that used to belong to Rodrigo Estes, no doubt," Caty said in a chilling voice. "No, thank you. I'm quite satisfied with my voice teacher."

They thanked him and closed the door before he could begin listing everything that was wrong with Madam Della Russo. "Arrogant beast," Caty grumbled as her shoes clicked on the marble steps. "I wouldn't study with him if he was the last voice teacher left in New York."

"He certainly seemed all broken up over Estes's death, didn't he?" Josh said sarcastically.

"Imagine. Poor Rodrigo. To think he wanted me to take his place . . ."

The throat doctor's office was one floor down and they were standing in front of the door before Caty could finish her grumbling. A small, neat bronze plaque announced the offices of J. Johnson, M.D. Josh knocked once and opened the door.

It was a lavish office. An exquisite Oriental carpet covered the entire room. Two overstuffed armchairs on either side of a table with a jeweled-tone Tiffany lamp sat near the window. Across the room was a Louis XIV desk, clear except for a large ledger and a silver inkstand. A woman behind the desk looked up as they entered. She was the picture of stylish proficiency with her high shirtwaist and long black skirt, hair neatly pulled back into a chignon at her neck, round glasses perched halfway down her small nose, and a watch and chain clipped to the front of her blouse.

"Can I help you?" she asked in a voice that suggested they were intruding on her privacy.

Josh explained that he was from the Metropolitan Police, seeking information about a singer who had possibly come to the doctor for treatment. As he was speaking the woman casually closed the ledger in front of her and laid her hands on the top possessively.

"Our clients expect privacy when they see Doctor Johnson. I'm sure you will understand, Inspector."

Caty took a step back, expecting Josh to leave. She quickly realized she had never been with a policeman on the trail of a lead.

"I have no intention of invading anyone's privacy," Josh said, politely but determined. "I simply wish to know if Magda Dubratta was a patient of Doctor Johnson's and whether she happened to consult him on the morning of October twentieth, last."

"I'm afraid that information . . ."

"I can always ask for a warrant, miss, but that would involve unnecessary time. And I suspect Doctor Johnson might find it more embarrassing and inconvenient."

The woman's already tight face fastened inward,

as though someone had pulled it on a string. "I really don't think I can help you, Inspector, at least, not without the doctor's permission." Meeting Josh's cold gray eyes, she hesitated. "I think it would be fair to say that no one named Magda Dubratta has ever been to this office."

"Oh? And have you been here long enough to know everyone who comes in to see Doctor Johnson, Miss . . . ?"

Her thin chest swelled. "I'm Miss Allen and I've been Doctor Johnson's personal secretary for twelve years. I'm sure I would know if such a person consulted him."

"Then perhaps, Miss Allen, you won't object to allowing me to see your schedule for the twentieth of October?"

Miss Allen glanced toward the inner door. She knew the doctor was with a patient and hated to be interrupted. It suddenly seemed the lesser of two evils to show this stubborn policeman the book and be rid of him.

"Oh, very well," she said, leafing through the pages. When she found the correct one she turned the book around so Josh and Caty could both bend over it.

"No Dubratta here, I'm afraid," he muttered. "What about these names? Are you familiar with these ladies, Miss Allen?"

The secretary pushed up the glasses on her nose and peered at the page. "Mrs. Fountain, Miss Jones, and Mrs. Calswell and her young son. Yes,

I know them all. None of them are professional singers, I assure you."

Josh and Caty exchanged disappointed glances. "Very well. Thank you for your cooperation, Miss Allen. We will try not to bother you again."

The door barely closed behind them before Caty vented her frustration.

"Well, if Magda didn't come here to see Givens or Doctor Johnson, who did she come to see?"

Josh pulled down the brim of his hat. "It could have been anyone. We cannot go through the whole building knocking on doors."

"But we have nothing else."

They started together down the stairs. "Perhaps we could find out from some of the other musicians whether she had a paramour who lived in this building. That would narrow it a little."

Caty pulled her stole more closely around her neck as they prepared to go back out onto the street. "Yes, I suppose we could ask."

"Meantime, how about a cup of coffee to take off the chill?"

She looked up at him, conscious of the old glow spreading inside. "Do you think we should, Josh?"

He smiled down at her. "I promise not to seduce you over a cup of coffee. After all, we did say we'd remain friends."

She could not refuse. "Yes, we did, didn't we? And I know the coziest little place just around the corner."

He drew her hand through his arm. "Then, *andiamo*. Let's go."

Twenty

The cold breeze off the waters of the bay ruffled the fur that framed Caty's face and pricked a vivid flame in her cheeks. Josh admired the beauty of the effect even as his better judgment told him they should probably be returning to the house.

"Your mother is probably waiting on us," he said in a halfhearted attempt to assuage his guilt. Though it was cold on this ledge overlooking New York Harbor, there was also something refreshing about being there. The wind blew away the cobwebs that accumulated from being inside drafty buildings with stuffy stoves for far too long. He loved visiting Caty's home on Staten Island. There was a coziness about the old, comfortable farmhouse, and Siam McGowan's twinkling smile always cheered his heart. He wondered why he never felt that way about his own, far more elegant home, near the Hudson River.

"Oh, Charlotte will keep her occupied. They are both such talkers that we'll never get a word in edgewise when we do go back."

She pulled her coat closer around her throat and turned her face to the invigorating wind. "I love winter, don't you? There is something so elemental about it. It forces you to concentrate on survival, it makes getting around work. It makes you reach down to your deepest levels of strength."

Josh smiled down at her. "It certainly separates the weak from the strong. Yet, on the whole, I think I prefer the more comfortable seasons."

Caty took his arm and they started at a leisurely pace back toward the house. She was still not sure that she had done the right thing by allowing Josh to accompany Charlotte and her on this Sunday visit. He wanted to be there to keep watch over her, of course, and he was fond of her mother. Yet, for two people who had said they would not see each other anymore, they seemed to always end up spending a lot of time together. It was making it more and more difficult to forget the times she had spent wrapped in his arms, lost in the passion of his embrace, as well as to force down the desire to be there again.

"Speaking of the strong and the weak, what has happened with Boris? Have you been able to learn anything that might lead to Rodrigo's killer?"

"He has finally confessed to the murder of Herman Warring, but he still insists he had nothing to do with Magda's death or those two incidents with the bridge and the counterweight. And, of course, he was in jail when Estes was shot and could not have been involved."

"Unless he was part of a conspiracy," Caty murmured. "Did he give a reason for Warring's death?"

"Yes, but I don't think you want to hear it."

"Nonsense. I promise not to swoon from shock."

He laughed. "No, you're not the type for that, are you? Well, it seems Warring and Borinsky had a 'liaison' with each other, to put it in the nicest terms possible. Warring wanted out. They went up to the roof to talk about it privately, Borinsky lost his temper in a fit of rage and heartbreak, and strangled Warring. He might not have been dead but Boris thought he was and threw him over the side so it would look like an accident. He meant to throw the violin into the river but couldn't do it. Evidently, he had some deep feelings for the man.

"As for a 'conspiracy', I thought of that. People like Boris and Warring band together to hide their secrets. Yet there is no one else who would be involved."

"Unless they, too, are keeping it secret. After all, we don't know everything about everyone, do we?"

"No, and we never will. But I just can't find the common thread in it. Warring is connected to Magda and to Boris, but he's dead. Von Rankin is connected to Magda but not to Boris, that I can tell. Cannio also had his problems with Magda, as did Rodrigo. Nothing links them to her death and now that Rodrigo is dead, too . . ."

"There is always Lulu. But she would never

have hurt Magda, would she? And I can't see her involved in any way with the kind of life Boris and Warring led."

"She's also too frail to have arranged for that bridge to break, not to mention dropping that counterweight."

"There must be someone we're leaving out."

They were approaching the kitchen door to the farmhouse. Josh stopped before they walked up the low steps to the back porch and took Caty's gloved hands in his. "Is there no way I can talk you out of going ahead with this dangerous production of *Carmen?*"

"No, Josh. Everything we've just said makes it more obvious that this is our best chance of drawing out this maniac. I'm not afraid. I know you will be there to take care of me."

He squeezed her hands. "I'll try, but there are so many things that could happen that I can't foresee. I . . . I don't want to lose you, Caty. I know we said we'd stay apart, but I find I can't give you up. I want you back in my arms, back in my bed . . ."

A surge of warmth coursed through her. "Oh, Josh. I want you just as much. But we would only be letting ourselves in for more arguments and more unhappiness."

He drew her toward him. "I don't care. Come home with me tonight, Caty. Be mine once more, just for a while."

He leaned forward and kissed her cold lips, warming them with the ardor in his own. Caty felt herself falling toward him, sinking into his arms. Her body began to sing with the delicious desire he evoked and she melted toward him.

"Are you two ever coming inside?" said Charlotte's voice from the porch. "Supper is on the table and I'm starving!"

They broke apart quickly. Embarrassed, Caty pulled her hood around her face. "We're coming right now."

Charlotte threw open the door while they hurried inside. "It's freezing out there," she cried. "I don't know why anyone in their right mind would want to go walking in that cold air. Especially when the parlor fire is so cozy. Not to mention risking the chance of catching a cold! Just think what that would mean, Caty, right before your big production."

Caty pulled off her coat and hood, smiling over at Josh. "I told you we wouldn't get a word in edgewise."

"That's all right," Josh said. "I'm too hungry to talk anyway."

His wicked wink told her it was not food he hungered for.

By the end of the meal Caty has made up her mind to be strong and resist temptation and not return with Josh to his apartment. Although she had to be at the opera house for rehearsal early the following morning, Charlotte had time on her hands since the house was closed until the *Carmen* debut. When Sian McGowan invited Charlotte to stay for a few days in "the country," she accepted at once, and Caty felt her resolution beginning to waver.

By the time Caty and Josh left for the return trip to Manhattan, Caty's resolve had considerably weakened. Once they left the ferry for the small, enclosed cab of a hansom, it melted away altogether.

Josh gave the driver his address and settled back in the darkness, taking her in his arms.

She made one last effort. "You are very sure of yourself, Josh Castleton."

"It's a characteristic of my profession," he murmured and drew her lips to his. She gave up fighting what she wanted so desperately and simply enjoyed the feel of his moist, warm mouth on hers, as soft as petals on her skin. She nestled in his arms against the cushion, sliding easily down against his body. His lips moved sensuously against her own, his tongue flicked them lightly, working his way into her mouth, darting and tasting the warmth of her, filling the emptiness of her.

Caty moaned under his insistence. She knew he wanted her, needed her badly. And she wanted him. Her hand slipped inside his coat, down his chest to the swelling hardness of him. Everything in her burned to have him within her.

The cab slowed and she realized they had arrived. Reluctantly, Josh pulled away and helped her out of the cab, handing the fare up to the driver. A single gas street lamp cast an eerie glow around them as he sought his key, opened the door, and hurried her inside and up the stairs to the third-floor landing. Once inside his apartment, he closed the door, turned swiftly and pressed her against it, covering her face with his kisses.

"Caty . . ." he whispered. "I've never wanted you so badly."

Her coat slipped off her shoulders and fell in a dark heap at her feet. He lifted her in his arms and carried her up the stairs and down the hall, setting her down just inside the bedroom where he kissed her hungrily.

She managed to get her hands on his shoulders, forcing him away. "No," she said. "Not so quickly. We have all night. Help me with these buttons."

She stepped away from him, standing in the center of the room and lifting her hair free of her neck, waiting.

Josh caught his underlip in his teeth. Everything in him rebelled against waiting anytime at all. He wanted to throw her on the bed and ravish her, to pour himself into her with all the desire that was in him. And yet . . .

There was delight, too, in going slowly, in enjoying each enticing moment. He let his coat and jacket fall to the floor and moved behind her, his fingers clumsy with haste as he unfastened the back of her shirtwaist blouse. It was halfway open when he pushed it down her arms, pinning them to her sides. Burying his face in the hollow of her neck, he slid around her to clasp her breasts, one in each hand, tenderly teasing the nipples with his thumbs. Caty leaned back against him, fighting the moan that rose to her throat. Josh moved against her back and she could feel the swelling hardness of him against her buttocks. Her hands moved back to clasp his hips tightly against her and she heard him give a sharp cry.

"Not yet . . ." she breathed. He nuzzled her neck, then pushed the blouse down, freeing her arms. His hands cupped her breasts beneath her chemise, lifting them free. The ripe fullness of them in his fingers was like a hot brand.

Josh quickly untied her petticoats and let them slip to the floor. With practiced speed he got rid of the chemise so that she was standing still in front of him, pristine and naked, her lovely body prone against his. Still he did not move to stand in front of her as she expected. Instead, he slid to his knees, his hands roaming the slim lines of her waist and her hips. One hand slipped between her legs until he was cupping her body with his arm while his lips coursed her back and her buttocks.

Caty felt herself go weak. She meant to tease him, lead him along until, for once, he begged for her, but her resolve was fast melting under his insistent fingers and lips. In a fluid motion that she barely recognized until it happened, he drew her down to the floor and bent her forward. Spreading her thighs, he bent over her, reaching around her to cradle her breasts in his hands and teasing the hard, erect nipples with his thumbs until she began to feel her body was awash with sensation. He reached underneath and rubbed the flaming nub of her passion, sending her soaring. It was easy to enter her, she was so ready for him. Clasping her beneath him, he thrust again and again until she was choking back screams of ecstasy, crying for release. When, at last, it came, their cries mingled in an explosion of glorious delight.

Caty sank beneath him. Still clasping her he pulled away, turning her over to lie in his arms on the carpet, their deep gasping breaths the only sound in the dark, silent room.

"I . . . didn't know . . . it could be . . . done like that . . ." she stammered.

Josh waited for his pounding heart to ease. "There are quite a few innovative ways you probably have never heard of."

She nestled close to him. "Will you teach me all of them?"

He laughed. "Well, I can't pretend that I know them all but I'll teach you the ones I'm familiar with. After all, you're such a willing pupil."

Caty stretched against him. "Yes, I am, aren't I?"

He reached down to lift her breast to his lips, lightly circling that taut protuberance. "And I'm such a good teacher."

"Yes, you are." She shifted her body to sit up beside him. "But a good teacher has to at least be as naked as his pupil. You don't quite make it."

Josh lay back, exhausted for the moment. "I was in too much of a hurry. Why don't you finish the job?"

"That is just what I was thinking," she said, and bending over him, began slipping off his clothes. The shirt was easy and the trousers, already open, were not difficult, either. She took her time, letting her fingers play against his skin when she removed a garment, bending to lightly lick his chest, then course downward to the flat stomach. When he lay naked beside her, she ran her hands along his body, reveling in the feel of his strong, muscular torso.

He lay limp, delighting in the feel of her hands on his body, surprised at the obvious enjoyment she was getting out of exploring and teasing him.

"Mmmm," Caty whispered. "You do taste delicious."

She could see that he was so lost in delight he could not answer. Spreading his legs, she took him between her fingers, stroking him to wake the length of him back to life. She bent and licked the round tip with her tongue, pleased to see that her actions sprang it to immediate hardness. When he moaned with pleasure, she pulled away and, in a sudden motion, moved astride him, lifting her body to allow her breasts to hang just above his lips.

He reached for one, pulling the nipple between his lips to suckle it. Her body arched, thrusting her breasts closer as his need for her grew. She felt his fingers against the wetness of her thigh, slipping deeply within while with his thumb, he massaged her until the flame of her need flared again to life.

She moved against him, back and forth, as together again they sought that consummation of fulfilling love. She felt his long shaft enter her and she sat up, impaled upon him, their movement carrying them to the heights once more. When he could bear it no longer, he grasped her, turning her over upon her back and thrusting deeply within, again and again until he emptied himself to her precious depths.

Josh fell over her, so weak he could not move. Caty clasped him until she found his weight was making it difficult to breathe and shifted so that they were lying beside each other once more, still joined together.

"Oh, Josh," she murmured. "And I thought I could live without you!"

He smoothed the long strands of her hair back from her face. "I love you, Caty. You've become a part of me forever. I could no more cut you out of my life than I could cut off part of my body. I love you with all my heart, with more love than I've ever felt for anyone in my life."

She was moved by his words. "I love you, Josh," she answered, tracing the length of his cheek with her finger. "God help me. I don't see how we can live apart or how we can live together. I only know I don't ever want to be without you."

He bent and kissed her, not with the crushing need of desire this time, but as a pledge of the love he felt for her. Caty wrapped her arms around him and hugged him against her, a part of herself completed, come home. Tears burned behind her eyes, but she smiled to herself as she realized they were tears of joy.

"We won't think about anything else but tonight," she murmured against his cheek.

"Just tonight," he agreed. "Only . . ."

Caty rubbed against his chest, reveling in the feel of the soft, dark hairs against her skin. "Only what . . . ?"

Josh gave a soft chuckle. "Only I do hope that sometime tonight we manage to make it to the bed!"

The afterglow from the glorious night Caty and Josh spent together warmed within her until the pressures of the approaching opening night began to affect everyone's nerves. Between the stage director and the conductor, no one could do anything right. Stillman, with his customary venting of emotion, loudly complained that all his work up to this point had been in vain and lost on a group of musicians whose like for density had never been matched. Von Rankin, on the other hand, managed to convey with the tapping of his baton on his music stand and the cold glare of his Teutonic eye a complete disgust with all that had been done up to that point.

For Caty, the only encouraging thing to happen was the return of Carlo Gregorio who, on hearing of Rodrigo's death, found his reluctance to have anything to do with such an unlucky opera house overcome by an even stronger conviction that Caty deserved a worthy replacement for her debut.

"Aren't you afraid?" she asked him when he kissed her hand and expressed his determination to help her through her first-night jitters.

Carlo bent to kiss each of her fingertips in turn. "Afraid? Oh, *mia cara,* Carlo Gregorio does not-a know the meaning of the word. Besides, Don José is-a not the victim in *Carmen,* only Carmen herself. I will-a protect you."

Caty did not remind him that he had been the one who walked out after the close call when the counterweight fell. After all, it was a feather in her cap to have him singing opposite her. She only hoped that his natural talent and exciting voice would not eclipse her own debut.

Because all other performances had been canceled until the *Carmen* debut, she was given a dressing room of her own two days before the performance. It proved to be a great comfort for not only was she able to rest there between stage calls, but she also felt safer than any other place in the building. Although the police were everywhere, she only saw Josh once and then from across the stage. He waved and smiled at her with that secret intimacy lovers share across a distance, but they were both too involved with their work to stop and talk. Still, Caty felt sure he was the one responsible for the presence of the policeman who always seemed to hover close behind her wherever she went, even to standing outside the door of the dressing room when she sought its sanctuary.

With only two days to go, the air of nervous mania seemed to be affecting everyone. The paint was not yet dry on some of the last-minute changes to the sets and her last-act costume was not yet completed. That, added to the nervousness of both the conductor and the stage director made the morning particularly unpleasant and left Caty with a dull, throbbing headache. She tried not to remember that lack of sleep the night before probably had something to do with it as well, and, once Stillman directed his latest outrage of the morning at her, she fled to her dressing room fighting tears. She sank on the stool at her dressing table and stared at her reflection in the mirror.

"Caty McGowan," she said aloud to the image in the glass, "this is your opera and no one is going to ruin it for you! Sing your heart out and be damned to conductors and stage directors and all their ilk!"

"Talking to yourself?" said a cheery voice from the doorway. Caty turned swiftly to see Charlotte poking her head around the jamb, and smiled sheepishly. Charlotte must have just arrived in the building for she still wore her heavy wool coat and wide-brimmed hat.

"That's the first sign of senility, you know," Charlotte went on as she closed the door behind her and pulled off her coat. "May I join you, or would you rather be alone with your demons?"

"Come in, please," Caty said. "I can certainly use a friendly face. There aren't very many around here this morning."

Charlotte sank onto the plush sofa against the wall opposite the dressing table. "Don't let it get to you. It's probably just that everyone is jittery. You look smashing. Is that the first-act costume?"

"Yes. It turned out rather nicely, didn't it?"

"Stand up and let me see."

Caty obliged by pirouetting around in the off-the-shoulder blouse, colorful skirt, and the fringed shawl pinned at her waist.

"It's beautiful," Charlotte said. "And your mother's shawl goes with it perfectly."

"It's my good-luck piece. You look rested, by the way. Mama must not have worked you too hard."

Charlotte laughed. "She was very understanding about my reluctance to milk cows and feed chickens. Actually, I had a wonderful, restful time out there. I can see why it is such a refreshing refuge for you. However, now it's back to work. We've just been given the word that after *Carmen* the regular schedule will resume and that means all of next week on stage. Oh well, it was pleasant to be on vacation but the rent must be paid, after all."

Caty gave a sigh. "Right now, I almost wish I was going back to work in the chorus. At least there, the success of the whole opera doesn't rest on your shoulders."

"Nonsense," Charlotte scoffed. "You wouldn't trade this opportunity for anything in the world and you know it. Besides, you're going to be a great success. Monday morning you probably won't even bother to speak to a lowly member of the chorus like me."

"You know better than that."

"Look at the advantages you've already gained. This room all to yourself, flowers, gifts from admirers . . ."

"A policeman just outside the door."

"That's probably a good thing considering all that's happened around here. Who are the flowers from, anyway?"

Caty gestured to the large vase of chrysanthemums on the table. "The bouquet is from Mama and Kyle and the single yellow rose is from . . . a friend." Somehow she could not reveal that it came from Josh early that morning, a touching memento of the night they spent together. A single, exquisite rose was so like him—eloquent, beautiful, understated. It meant more to her than any huge spray of flowers could ever mean.

"I think the candy is from Charlie, though I can't think why he thought I would want it now when I don't dare touch the wrong kind of food."

Charlotte picked up the pink and white box. "Sugar gives one energy," she said, pulling away the tissue paper. "Oh, marzipan. I love almonds. May I try one? After all, it doesn't really matter if I have to miss Friday's performance."

"Please do. Perhaps I ought to pass them around. It might sweeten a few sour dispositions around here."

Charlotte bit into a sugary orange concoction. "Are things really that bad?"

"Everyone is on edge. I couldn't do anything to please Stillman or von Rankin this morning. And the worse part is that it undermines my confidence. Right now, I must not allow that to happen or I'll never be able to walk out on that stage Friday night."

Charlotte licked her fingers. "You needn't worry. Once that curtain goes up you'll be raring to get out there and sing. And you'll have a wonderful time doing it. I bet you'll be the best Carmen ever."

"Charlotte, you are such a comfort. Keep telling me that, at least until Friday night."

A brisk knock on the door was followed by its opening just wide enough for one of the young gaffers to stick his head around it. "The maestro is asking for you, Miss McGowan," he said.

"Oh, so soon? Very well. I'll be right there." Caty turned to peer into the mirror and give her hair a pat. "Darn. I was hoping he'd take out his bad temper on someone else for a while."

She turned to rise but stopped when she caught Charlotte's reflection from across the room in the mirror. Turning swiftly she stared at her friend, whose hands trembled at her throat, her eyes growing large and round.

"Charlotte, what's the matter?" she cried, rushing to the sofa. Charlotte clutched at her throat and gave a strangled, choking cry. Her eyes began to bulge in a face, swiftly draining of all color. Even as Caty gripped her, calling loudly for help, she saw Charlotte's body stiffen as though her spine had turned to a board. Then she fell backward in Caty's arms.

"Help! Help, someone!" she cried again as the policeman came rushing into the room. He shoved her aside and bent over Charlotte who slumped over on the sofa. "Do something," Caty screamed. "She's choking . . ."

"Hold her a moment, miss," the policeman said and took off at a run. He was back almost at once with several other men, Josh close behind them. Caty cradled the comatose Charlotte in her arms. Her face had gone almost pasty white. One of the men took her from Caty and pushed her back out of the way.

"What's wrong with her?" she said to Josh, who pushed in front to peer over the man's shoulder. Caty fought back a chilling stab of fear as she heard Charlotte's rasping breathing growing more strident.

"Vincent, take Miss McGowan out of here," Josh ordered.

"No. I won't go . . ."

"Go on, Caty. There's nothing you can do here. I'll let you know how she is as soon as possible."

There was something in Caty's throat, a fist-sized lump that prevented her from swallowing. She felt her body begin to tremble. Reluctantly, she allowed the policeman to guide her gently out of the room.

Twenty-one

It was twenty minutes before Josh returned. He caught sight of Caty sitting dejected and worried on a straight-back chair in the hall near the stage entrance. He hurried to her and laid a hand on her shoulder. He could feel the trembling of her body through the thin linen of her blouse, but when she looked up at him, her eyes were more questioning than apprehensive.

"How is she?" Caty whispered as though afraid to hear the answer.

"She'll be all right. The doctor induced vomiting and that quick action seemed to make the difference."

"It was the marzipan, wasn't it?"

"It appears so," he answered simply. "The sugared candy was apparently laced with some form of cyanide. We won't be sure what it is until we test it." He pulled up another chair and sat opposite her, his elbows resting on his knees and his fingers laced. His heavy brows creased over deep-set eyes as he searched for the right words, words that would not set her off and yet might bring home to her the urgency he felt.

"I know what you're thinking," Caty said, sparing him the need to express it himself.

Josh plunged ahead. "That box of sweets was meant for you. If you had sampled it alone in your dressing room while you waited to be called back onstage, there might have been no one nearby whose quick action could save you."

"But, Josh, why? Why me? I don't have any enemies. As for the box of candy—I don't even know how it got in my dressing room. It had no card of any kind and I simply assumed it was from Charlie or, at the very least, was one of the pleasantries that came with the room."

He reached out and gripped her fingers in his own. "Obviously someone does not want this opera to go on, or doesn't want to see you sing it. Caty . . ."

Caty pulled away, stood up and folded her arms across her chest. "Don't say it! You cannot tell me anything I haven't already thought about while I was waiting here wondering if Charlotte was dead or alive. I can't let this stop me. Don't you see? Going through with this performance may be our last opportunity to catch this maniac, whoever he is."

"If you survive it."

There was such misery on his face that she took pity on him. Resuming her seat, she reached out and pulled his hands to her face, kissing the palms.

"I'll be careful. More careful now than ever!"

And she was. Throughout the rest of that day and all of the next she went through her paces, always on the alert for anything suspicious. Once the rehearsals were over she went straight back to Charlotte's apartment and barricaded herself inside, resting, going over last-minute details, vocalizing. When the doorbell rang, she pretended no one was home, except for the one time when Josh stopped by the evening before the performance. He only stayed long enough to share a cold supper and sit with his arm around her shoulders on the sofa while they talked briefly of all that had happened. They both had so much on their minds that even that shared closeness failed to heat the deep reservoir of passion that usually awoke at one another's touch.

Caty nestled her head in the hollow of his neck, staring at the fire that burned listlessly in the grate before them.

"If only we had been able to learn something from that throat doctor. I can't get it out of my mind that if we only knew Magda's state of mind the night she died, we might be able to figure out the truth."

"We do know something of her state of mind. Her estranged husband conducted the opera, the manager was a man she had done out of a job years before, and the first husband, whom she loathed, was playing in the orchestra. She sang very well until fatigue began to take its toll, and even then, her dramatic abilities carried the performance. I don't see how a throat doctor could add anything to that. A better bet would have been that coach, but he still swears he never saw her that day."

"He might be lying."

"Yes, well, if he is, I haven't found anything that suggests he has a motive to lie. And God knows, I've looked."

Caty reached up to lightly kiss his cheek. "I know you have. Were you able to trace the box of candy?"

"No. Charlie swears it did not come from him, but other than that, anyone could have slipped into your room and left it on the table."

He stroked her hair away from her forehead. The light from the fire cast golden sparks on its reddish strands, and created tiny flecks of gold in the green of her eyes. If he hadn't been so worried about the next day's events, he would have longed to slip his arm around her and bend over her, tasting her lips . . .

Deliberately he pulled away. "I'd better go. Going over these things yet another time gets us nowhere, and you need your rest."

Caty reluctantly sat up. "That's true. I don't think I've really realized that I'm actually singing the lead in tomorrow's opera, but I expect to at about three o'clock this morning. Then I'll wish you were there beside me to hold me and shoo away the jitters."

"Mmm," he murmured, kissing her neck. "I'd like that myself."

"No," she said, laughing and pushing him away. "It's better that you go. When I'm in your arms I can't seem to focus on anything else."

As it turned out, she did wake early that morning and for a long time she lay in bed, her mind in a whirl, trying unsuccessfully to go back to sleep. Eventually sleep returned until dawn when she woke for a second time. She knew then it would be useless to lie there, so she rose, threw on a robe, and brewed a pot of coffee.

Her common sense told her she ought to be resting, or at least, concentrating on her role that evening. Yet the nagging thought that had come to her early that morning as she struggled to go back to sleep would not go away.

They had missed something, she felt certain. And the answer did not lie in the opera house but somewhere in that office building which she and Josh had examined so eagerly, and with such disappointing results. It was just a feeling, but such a strong one that the more she thought about it, the more certain she became that something was there and they had overlooked it.

Leaving her coffee on the table, she dressed warmly, wrapped a long woolen scarf around her throat, and slipped from the house to make her way back to the elaborate marble facade of the corner structure at 28th and Fifth just as the offices were opening for the day. Inside the building, she stood before the directory, studying it, taking more time than she had with Josh to examine every name, hoping something would jog a memory or dredge up a forgotten association.

Nothing did. Increasingly it appeared just a long list of names, none of whom meant anything. She gazed at it over several minutes before finally giving up the effort as hopeless.

As Caty turned to go back outside, her eye briefly fell on the name of the throat doctor on the fifth floor whom they had questioned on their first trip here. *If only he had turned out to be important,* she thought ruefully. After fastening her scarf in place over her throat, she had her hand on the brass knob to open the door when she stopped, remembering there were two doctors listed in the directory.

Caty walked back and ran her finger down the glass to the second name—William Merton, M.D.

Just that. Nothing to indicate he was any kind of specialist, much less one who would matter to a great singer like Magda Dubratta. Yet there was nothing else, no one else. She took the lift to the fourth floor.

It was an even more sumptuous office than the one belonging to the throat specialist. Paneled oak walls with landscapes in gilt frames and blue satin drapes highlighting the tall windows. As with the previous office, a lone receptionist sat at a long, polished desk so free of clutter Caty wondered if she ever did any work.

The small brass nameplate informed patients that Miss Treadwell was on duty. As Caty slipped into the room, Miss Treadwell looked up from the one book on the desk, a large ledger, and glanced over the tops of gold-rimmed glasses.

"May I help you?" she said in a cultured, frigid voice.

Caty almost mumbled that she had made a mistake and slipped out, for Miss Treadwell appeared even more intimidating that Dr. Johnson's receptionist. Dressed in the height of elegance, her hair neatly and professionally waved, Caty would have sworn that the large brooch on her silk shirtwaist held a real amethyst. The slightly affronted look she focused on Caty, suggested she was more annoyed than pleased to have a new patient appear.

Yet it would be foolish to let a professional watch-dog frighten her away now. She marched straight to the desk, drew herself up and announced that she wished to see Dr. Merton at once.

Miss Treadwell's chin lifted, in a gesture that allowed her to look down her nose even though she was sitting and Caty standing.

"Do you have an appointment, madam?"

With the ledger in front of her, she knew very well that Caty did not. "No. But I hoped I might be worked in."

"I'm afraid the doctor only sees patients by appointment."

"But this is an emergency. I can't wait another

day or I shall be too sick to . . . to go on. Possibly even beyond help."

Miss Treadwell casually turned one of the pages in the appointment book. "I can perhaps fit you in on Monday next."

"No! That won't do." Caty leaned both hands on the desk and bent toward the woman, trying to convey a sense of frantic need. "I really must see him this morning. It's of the greatest urgency."

"You have been ill? What are your symptoms?"

Caty hesitated only a moment. "Oh, they are of the most severe nature—spells of coughing, difficulty in breathing, headaches, back pain . . ."

She stopped, hoping she had mentioned enough areas to cover Dr. Merton's field of interest.

"Mmmm," the receptionist's narrow lips drew even tighter. "Headaches. That could be neurological. Have you experienced any blurred vision, or dizziness?"

"Oh yes," she cried, raising a hand languidly to her brow. "Such pounding pain, and such dizziness that at times I almost lose my ability to walk. And you see . . ."

She bent forward, whispering in a conspiratorial way: ". . . I am a professional singer and I must perform tonight. So I simply must see the doctor this morning."

She was taking a risk to tell Miss Treadwell of her profession, for it could be possible that this proud paragon would hold her in contempt once she knew she was a professional entertainer. But to Caty's relief, the woman seemed intrigued rather than put off. Her manner softened imperceptibly.

"Dear me. I see. Well, as it happens Doctor Merton is in his office preparing for his first patient. You may have just enough time to tell him your symptoms and set up an examination, and he might be able to prescribe something to help you get through this evening. Would that be to your satisfaction?"

"Oh yes, thank you, it would indeed," Caty cried with such sincere conviction that she even wrung the ghost of a smile from Miss Treadwell.

"Very well. Have a seat please, Mrs. . . . ?"

"Castleton," Caty said without hesitation. "Catherine Castleton."

"Very well, Mrs. Castleton. I'll just ask if the doctor will see you."

Wavering on her feet, Caty groped her way to the plush velvet settee against the wall and waited until Miss Treadwell disappeared into the inner office. At once she scrambled over to the ledger lying open on the desk and began turning the thick parchment pages back to October twentieth. They crackled noisily as she ran her finger down the long list of names entered in a beautiful hand on each page. Once she found the correct date she bent, hoping to see a Madam Dubratta listed. If Magda had come to this office she would probably have been one of the first patients of the day, for Rodrigo said he saw her leaving as he entered that morning.

Yet Caty's heart sank as she saw no Dubratta

on the list. She skimmed through the names again as she heard Miss Treadwell's heels on the tiled floor returning to the reception room. She was about to flip the pages back to today's date when her eye went back to the name at the top of the list.

Mrs. H. Warring.

The door was opening as Caty flipped the pages back and darted to the sofa, her heart pounding. By the time the efficient Miss Treadwell came back into the room, she was half-lying on the couch, one hand over her eyes.

Mrs. H. Warring. It might just be a coincidence, and yet . . .

"Doctor Merton will give you a few moments, Mrs. Castleton, and then he would like to set up an appointment for a more extensive examination. Please come this way."

The interior office looked like a small study in Frances Schyler's country house. One wall was lined with books bearing verbose medical titles. Before it lay a carpet at least two inches thick, two comfortable chairs placed strategically before a wide mahogany desk, and framed hunting pictures on the wall.

Caty took one of the upholstered chairs before the desk just as Dr. Merton entered the room. He was a short, paunchy man with a monocle covering one very blue eye and a brisk, no-nonsense manner. He greeted her formally, sat behind the desk and folded his hands, looking at her as though he could see right through her skull to the mind beneath.

"Miss Treadwell tells me you are a professional singer, Mrs. Castleton. I don't often see professionals. How can I help you?"

Caty leaned forward. "You've not treated singers before?"

"No. I can't say that I have."

"Oh. Well, thank you for taking the time to see me, Doctor Merton. I've had these . . . problems, you see, and . . . well, you were recommended to me as being the very best."

Dr. Merton allowed himself a tiny smile. "A doctor is always pleased to hear that one of his patients thought enough of him to recommend him to others. May I ask which patient of mine spoke to you?"

"Mrs. Warring. Mrs. Herman Warring."

For a moment he looked at her blankly. "Oh, yes. Now I recall. I am somewhat surprised to hear that since I only saw Mrs. Warring twice and only for diagnosis. I presumed she decided to seek treatment elsewhere. How is she doing, by the way?"

Caty hesitated, knowing that doctors could not discuss their patients with other people. She decided to take the risk. "Unfortunately, she is dead. She went very quickly," she added, holding her breath.

Dr. Merton drummed his fingers on the desk. "I'm sorry to hear it. A terrible thing, that. It pained me to tell her. Sometimes I wonder if people don't associate bad news with the messenger and that is why they immediately turn to another doctor, hoping the first one was wrong."

Caty sat forward in her chair. "That's why I came to you. I started having these symptoms, you see, and I was so afraid they might be the same thing that Ma . . . Mrs. Warring had. That disease . . . what do you call it?"

"Amyotrophic lateral sclerosis."

"Yes. That's it. That's the name. Of course, I know very little about it . . ."

"Unfortunately, we doctors know little more. It is a very cruel disease due to its slow, crippling effect."

"Does . . . does one lose one's voice, by chance?"

"Along with everything else. The last thing to go is the ability to breathe. Tragically, as the body fails, the mind remains intact. As I say, a very cruel disease."

Caty gripped the arms of her chair. "And Mrs. Warring had this awful sickness?"

"Yes. She came to me with symptoms that suggested the disease was already well established. I made some tests and had to inform her that they were unfortunately positive."

Caty stared at the doctor, her mind racing as everything began to fall into place. She recalled an image of Magda dropping the fan Lulu had just put into her hand. She remembered other times when props had seemed to slip through the woman's fingers, the awkward gestures, the frequent stumbles, the way Magda leaned so heavily on Stillman leaving the stage.

The great diva hadn't been addicted to drink. She had been ill and desperately trying to conceal it!

"Doctor Merton, did you by any chance happen to tell Mrs. Warring this on the morning of October twentieth?"

"I can't be sure of the date but it was the last time I saw her."

Caty leaned back against the soft cushion. "Thank you, Doctor Merton. You have helped me more than you'll ever know."

He worked the glass of the monocle in place against his eye. "I can't see how. We've not discussed your symptoms at all. I must warn you, that without a proper examination I can make no proper diagnosis."

Caty swiftly got to her feet. "As a matter of fact, I feel suddenly so much improved. No blurring of vision, no dizziness, and the headache has quite disappeared. Just talking to you has made everything better."

Dr. Merton got to his feet as she collected her purse and threw the end of the scarf over her shoulder. Reaching across the desk, she took his hand as he looked wonderingly up at her.

"I'll just let myself out. Thank you, again, Doctor."

"Really, Mrs. . . ."

She hurried through the outer door and past the

startled receptionist who looked up from her ledger.

"Mrs. Castleton, your appointment . . ." Miss Treadwell called as Caty threw open the door.

"I'll come back another time. Please send me the bill," Caty called over her shoulder as she ran swiftly for the stairs, not bothering with the lift. She took them several at a time all the way down. At the last one she burst through the heavy glass doors and out onto the street just as a limp shaft of sunshine broke through the overhanging winter clouds.

Caty looked up into it and smiled. She knew all the answers now. Everything had fallen into place back there in Dr. Merton's elegant office. And now she also knew who it was that they must unmask that evening during her performance of *Carmen*.

Twenty-two

Once she entered the opera house Caty looked in vain for Josh before going to her dressing room to prepare for her performance that night. Told he was not in the building yet, she left word for him to see her the moment he arrived. By the time she finally closeted herself behind her dressing room door, first-night jitters had begun to set in so strongly that she almost forgot about all she wanted to tell him.

He had not forgotten her, however. One single exquisite yellow rose accompanied by a note wishing her luck, stood on her dressing table next to a huge, floor-sized spread of mixed flowers from Charlie. There were several other bouquets from family and friends, as well as one large vase from the chorus, glad to see one of their own make it to the top.

She had the help of a hair dresser and a maid, both of whom had been assigned to her. The maid, a tiny French woman, had a brisk, rather curt attitude which suggested she was more accustomed to assisting better-known singers than to waiting on this novice. Caty ignored her and concentrated on looking her best. Once in her costume for the first act, she took time to vocalize, all the while fighting down the tremors of excitement that sent an occasional shiver through her body.

Only a few people stopped by to interrupt her concentration. Her mother, Sian, was there, along with her brother, to wish her well and put some last-minute pats to her costume. Sian, dressed in her finest gown, had been given a choice seat in the orchestra section from which to enjoy her daughter's long-awaited debut. She fingered the fringed shawl which Caty had wrapped around her waist and fought back tears.

"Your papa brought that to me from Spain before you were born," she said quietly. "He would have been so proud this night. It's a dream come true, isn't it?"

Caty bent to kiss her mother's cheek. "I'll never forget all that you both did to make this possible."

She embraced her mother and sent her off to take her seat with a whispered warning to Kyle that no matter what happened, she was not to be allowed backstage. He understood all too well what she meant and nodded gravely as he led their mother away.

Only a few minutes later Gregory Stillman poked his head around the door to wish her well. His short, portly frame radiated anxiety but his smile, though nervous, seemed genuine. "We haven't agreed on much these last weeks, Caty, but this is your night. I hope it turns out to be everything you want it to be."

Caty's teacher, Marta Della Russo, pushed past him to offer her a little last-minute instruction and encouragement. Caty murmured her gratitude to them both but felt only relief when they left. As the time for the opening chords of the opera drew closer she forced her concentration on her exercises and tried to forget her nerves. More than anything she longed for Josh to come and take her in his comforting arms.

And then the call came.

She moved backstage waiting for the *"Carmencita"* from the chorus to summon her onstage. From the wings, she could see the women cavorting around the sets, dressed in their colorful costumes—low-necked blouses, flounced skirts, long hair, some of them caught in scarves. As she watched she caught a brief glimpse of a familiar face and stared, startled.

Charlotte? But she was supposed to be still in her hospital bed. Surely she could not have recovered this quickly!

"Go on!" Stillman whispered frantically beside her. He gave her a push as she recognized her entrance music. A door in her mind closed on all else and when she stepped onto the stage she was no longer Caty McGowan, who used to be also known as Catherina Mandesi, the Irish lass from Staten Island with the beautiful voice who aspired to be a great singer. She was Carmen, the Gypsy girl, whose unbridled passion for love and for freedom would bring her to a tragic end.

Her first aria, the familiar "Habanera," began right away. Caty felt only a slight falter at the beginning when, blinded by the lights that masked the high tiers of the auditorium, she fought down the realization that there were several thousand people out there listening to her. That was soon overcome, however, by launching into the long practiced and ingrained positions onstage she knew so well, and by the sudden thrilling realization that she was out there amid all the lights and color, singing to a vast audience. The joy she began to feel resonated through her voice and gave an added dimension to her singing. Her voice warmed almost at once and she had to deliberately hold back, knowing she had a long evening ahead.

Yet she knew she had never sounded better. The applause at the end of her aria encouraged her as did the wink Carlo Gregorio gave her before losing himself in the role of Don José, the timid, shy soldier who is tragically drawn to Carmen while, at the same time, he is repelled by her.

Carlo was in fine voice and between the two of them, they had the audience mesmerized by the end of the first act. They took their curtain calls to thundering applause, after which Caty found herself surrounded by cast and crew congratulating her. She searched the crowd for Josh, but did not see him before being whisked away to change her costume for the second act. She felt more nervous about this act than any other because it required her to dance while playing the castanets, and was the scene which Gregory Stillman had criticized the most.

The exciting Gypsy Dance that came early in the act worked up the passions of everyone onstage. Her solo did not go too badly, though she felt the castanets could have been better. Afterward, Carlo sang his familiar "Flower Song" so beautifully that no one would remember them anyway.

At one quiet moment she remembered Charlotte and searched for her among the women without finding her. Then the action of the opera drove everything else from her mind. After the curtain calls she was once again hurried away to make her third-act costume change. Act three was a dark, moody set in which the joy and vitality of all that had gone before became transformed into a brooding darkness reflective of Don José's growing despair over Carmen's indifference to him. Caty had by now so thoroughly thrown herself into her role that she felt she *was* the Gypsy girl, not simply acting a part. The restlessness, the hot temper, the impatience over a now boring love affair, the fatalistic acceptance of an impending death, were all emotions she felt as deeply as though they were happening to her.

She was weak when the curtain swept down to close the act, but she had little time to rest since her most important costume change came now, with the fourth act when Carmen—who has run off with the bullfighter, Escamilo—appears with him outside the bullring in Seville. She is dressed in all the finery she can muster—a scarlet dress with long ruffled flounces trailing behind her, brilliant jewelry, black hair piled high and topped with a tall comb which holds in place a long lace mantilla. Caty stared at herself in the long mirror and knew she had never looked more beautiful. Her own well-rounded figure enhanced the dress while the makeup emphasized her large eyes, classic cheekbones, and sculptured mouth. All the natural beauty and sexual appeal of the Gypsy girl, Carmen, was perfectly realized in the image that looked back at her.

The nervous flutter in her stomach reminded her that if anything was going to happen in this opera, it would be now in the last act. Everything had gone so well up to this point. She knew from the increasing enthusiasm of the audience that she had been a huge success up to now, and she could hardly bear the thought that she might lose all that triumph and promise. And yet, if she were right about what she learned this morning, the twisted mind behind all the misery that had occurred in this house, would be sure to see this final act as a last, golden opportunity.

She heard the call and walked down the hall to the wings where she stood listening as the music for the final act began, knowing there was nothing left to do but move ahead to Carmen's fate. And her own.

* * *

It had been one of the worst evenings Josh had ever lived through. And it wasn't over yet.

In fact, if a climax was coming, it was sure to be now, with Carmen's death at the end of the last act. He had tried to prepare for every possibility. Because of his familiarity with the opera he knew that when Carmen is stabbed at the end of the act, she and Don José are the only two people on the stage. There might be a threat to Caty from someone backstage or in the labyrinth of ropes and platforms above, but it was difficult to imagine how that someone could actually make it work. It would be damned difficult do to, especially since he had men everywhere searching the wings and the heights above the stage for any unusual movement.

He had even deliberately stayed away from Caty in order to allow her to concentrate completely on her singing. Her role tonight was to become a star. His was to keep her safe while catching a killer. Neither of them needed any distractions.

After the third act, he moved restlessly behind the great curtain, watching while the scene shifters transformed the set from a dark mountain hideaway to a glittering street in front of a festive bullring. He had men working among the stagehands but they were too busy right now to acknowledge him. It all seemed very normal, and yet . . . something bothered him. Something he felt he had overlooked.

"Inspector . . ."

Josh turned to see O'Leary come hurrying out on to the stage from the wings.

"How is it going?" the sergeant asked.

Josh knew what he was referring to. "She's superb. If tonight doesn't make her the new rage of the opera world, I'll be very surprised."

O'Leary beamed. "I knew she'd come through. She's got a good Irish spirit, that lass."

Josh frowned at his sergeant. "Why are you here? You're supposed to be at the hospital."

"Oh, Miss Charlotte checked herself out. She's gone home."

Something pricked at the back of Josh's neck and he felt a sudden coldness.

"What?"

"She told me she had your approval for it. She said she felt ever so much better and wanted to be home. I asked her to wait until I could check it out with you, but she went and did it while I was getting ready to send a man over."

"Good God, O'Leary. I told you to make sure she stayed in the hospital where we could keep an eye on her." He looked around the stage where everything seemed to be going normally, mentally checking off all the things that could possibly go wrong. "Well, it can't be helped, I suppose. As long as Caty is alone with Don José on the stage when she's stabbed, I suppose it will be all right."

They had moved over to the wings where one of the men who worked the lights was sitting on a stool eating a sandwich. Josh barely noticed him until he spoke up.

"That's not the way it's going to happen, sir?"

Josh looked around. "What do you mean?"

"Why, Mister Stillman decided he wanted something more dramatic. He's got the chorus streaming out of the bullring to gawk at Carmen's body at the finish. Two or three of them are supposed to bend over her, in fact."

The coldness on his neck deepened. "What?"

"Yes. It's different from any *Carmen* I've ever seen, but there you are. Mister Stillman wanted this to be a 'first' in every way."

"Where is Stillman now?"

"I don't know, sir. Haven't seen him since the beginning of act three."

Pushing past O'Leary, Josh darted down the steps toward the hall behind the wings that led to the dressing rooms.

"Inspector," O'Leary called after him.

"Stay there and watch while the rest of the set is put up," Josh called back over his shoulder. "And don't move until I tell you to."

"But where are you going?"

"Never mind. Just do as I say!"

The glittering spectacle and festive music that begins the last act of *Carmen* only presages its tragic conclusion. Caty's role involved little difficult singing, but dramatically, it was the high point of the opera. She moved out on the stage on the arm of the baritone singing the dashing Escamillo, looking she knew as gorgeous as any Carmen ever, and determined to act her heart out. Any nagging worries over the climax were quickly subdued once she got into her role.

Carlo, as the distraught Don José who detains Carmen outside the bullring while the bullfighter and the chorus move offstage, was so marvelously convincing that Caty could not help but be drawn into Carmen's broad range of emotions: sympathy, restlessness as she hears the people inside reacting to Escamillo's prowess in the ring, and, finally, searing anger as she tries to convince José once and for all that their love affair is finished.

Gregorio managed to convey pleading, despair, and, then, fury over being scorned after giving up everything in his life for this woman, and doing it all while he sang gloriously. Caty matched him every step of the way.

She had rehearsed the scene so often that she could do it in her sleep. It was just as well for when she threw off José's arm and turned her back to him to enter the arena, she was all at once filled with a sense of pure terror.

She felt the driving shaft of the stage knife between her shoulder blades, arched her back, and, with a choking cry, turned to grasp Gregorio's arm, looking up at him with sudden, astonished acceptance as she slid to her knees and fell on her side to the floor. The crowd came streaming in from the ring entrance, fanning across the stage in horror as José knelt beside her.

Caty knew she had to lie deathly still. Under other circumstances she would have closed her eyes as well but this time, she raised her lids just enough to see the three or four chorus members who came surging forward to bend over her.

A man's face—swarthy with makeup, a striped bandanna half covering his forehead and holding the straggly black wig in place. His face was obscured by his arm, half concealed in a wide-sleeved shirt, raised . . .

She forced herself not to move. A woman's face suddenly thrust between the man's arm and her limited vision. She caught a brief glimpse of rouged cheeks, black-lined eyes and brows, a red mouth, long, flowing black hair that cascaded around the face as she bent toward her.

Charlotte?

Then a silver flash of metal reflecting the footlights . . .

Caty tried not to gasp. Surely not Charlotte . . .

The point of the knife thrust into her chest with a searing, stab of pain. The music crashed around her, she heard the long swish of the great curtain as it closed off the stage. She gave a cry as her body went crashing over and she was shoved on to her back. She forced herself to roll over again, scrambling to her knees, scarcely conscious of the roar of applause on the other side of the curtain. Another noise went wailing over it—an animal howling that came from the gargoyle shape of the red mouth screaming into her face. She stared in horror at a woman with long black hair, who was held tight in the grip of the man in the Spanish bandanna. He had one arm locked around her waist while the other protruded stiffly out gripping the wrist of a clawlike hand holding the knife that still glinted in the stage lights.

The knife clattered to the floor as the vicious howling intensified.

Caty scrambled farther away, still on her knees, staring at the woman.

"Charlotte?" she breathed, her voice tight in her throat. "Why?"

Her only answer was a long, incomprehensible string of oaths. The woman struggled to jump at her, clawing the air with her long fingers, straining against the iron grip on her waist and arm.

Caty looked up at the man and recognized Josh's triumphant eyes behind the dark makeup. Her body began to tremble uncontrollably.

"It's all right, love," Josh said. "Everything is all right now."

She could only stare at him, her eyes full of questions, still not believing. The lights caught a glint of gold at the woman's throat, highlighting the shape of a lion's head carved on a pendant that hung from a chain around her neck.

"My talisman," Caty cried.

Reaching out, Josh grabbed a handful of the long black hair and pulled. It came off in his hand and Caty found herself staring up into Lulu's black, flashing, hate-filled eyes.

Twenty-three

Caty was never sure afterward how she ended up in her dressing room. It was all a blur—Gregorio pushing her out through the curtain to take her bows to thundering applause; that one, long, delicious solo curtain call where she stood alone onstage with flowers raining down on her while the bravas of the house rang sweetly in her eyes and tears stung behind her eyes; that headlong shove through a crushing crowd toward the sanctuary of her dressing room where Stillman, fussing over her like a mother hen, implored her to hurry and dress so she could greet the mob that awaited her in the greenroom.

It was almost too much. She sank down on the stool before her mirror, still wearing the high black wig and lace mantilla and waited for her senses to sort themselves out. Her eyes scanned the laughing, talking, crowd in her dressing room searching for Josh and not finding him.

"Oh, my love," her mother cried, pushing through the group of people around her to embrace her daughter. "You were wonderful! And all that applause. If you're not the next great star of opera, I'll never believe anything again."

"Madam must remove her costume," Caty's French dresser said, quietly removing Sian's arms from around her daughter's neck. The woman's former coldness was considerably thawed by the acclaim being given her, Caty noticed. Since Caty found herself in her dressing room the little maid was showing her more interest than at any time since the evening began.

"I'll be ready in a moment, Cecile," Caty said emphatically. "Don't go, Mama. Wait while I change."

"Caty . . . Caty!"

She looked around at the familiar voice just as Charlotte shoved her way through the crowd to throw her arms around Caty's neck.

"It was grand! You were grand!"

Caty returned the embrace with fervor, but was shocked when she pulled away and her eyes scanned Charlotte's drawn, white face.

"What are you doing here, Charlotte? You're supposed to be in a hospital bed."

Charlotte laughed. "You don't think a little thing like prussiate acid was going to keep me away from your debut, do you? I sneaked out—right under that odious policeman's nose. I told him I wanted to go home but I came straight here instead. I would have crawled all the way on all fours before I would have missed your performance."

Caty, remembering that awful moment when she almost believed Charlotte was trying to kill her, grasped her friend's hands tightly in her own. "Thank you, Charlotte. You're such a good friend."

"Then don't forget me when you're famous and I'm still in the chorus."

"Never!"

A commotion at the door drew both their eyes around. With a lift of her heart Caty recognized the swarthy man in the striped bandanna who was forcibly shoving everyone out of the room, to the accompaniment of their loud protests. Friends, family, eager-to-be-hangers-on—all were shoved through the doorway until he was the only one left except a pleased Caty and her outraged dresser.

"You, too," Josh said, firmly propelling the little French maid toward the door.

"But madam must change. How dare you! Take your hands off me, sir. I protest . . ."

"You can protest all you want later," Josh said, pushing her into the hall. "This is police business."

Slamming the door shut, he turned to face Caty, holding out his arms. In an instant she was across the room, melting into them.

"You don't mind being alone with me, do you?" he said, covering her face with kisses that left streaks of dark makeup across her cheeks.

"Mind? I couldn't wait another minute." She kissed him back warmly, her arms winding sinuously around his neck, her body pressed into his. He clasped her tightly, pressing her hips close against him. For the first time that evening, Caty felt really safe.

"Oh Josh," she breathed, nestling her face in the hollow of his neck. "I'm so happy. I really was good, wasn't I?"

"You were stupendous. And somehow I have the feeling you'll never ask that question of me again. From now on, you'll know."

Caty giggled. "Yes. I know I was good tonight. It all felt so right, especially the voice." She pushed away slightly to look up into his eyes. "And everything worked out well, didn't it? For a moment there I wondered, but it all turned out for the best."

His arms tightened around her and he kissed her again, his lips lingering as though he was loathe to let her go. "I had a few bad seconds, too," he said when he could get his breath, "but it turned out all right."

She took his hands and drew him down beside her on the settee. "What is going to happen to Lulu?"

Josh settled back with his arm protectively around her shoulder. "She's still raving, but a lot of information is coming out along with all the hate. Her vitriolic obsession toward anyone who ever harmed her beloved Magda is beyond belief."

"And that's why Rodrigo died?"

"Yes. Long ago, in Europe, Magda tried to have him sacked, believing he was not worthy to perform with her. What she didn't know was he had relatives who ran the house and instead, they managed to send her packing. She went on to greater things and Rodrigo assumed it was all forgotten.

"But Magda never forgave an injustice. She fed on them and, evidently, she used Lulu as a sounding board. Once she was dead, her maid looked around and saw several of her adored mistress's former enemies and decided to even the score for her."

"Rodrigo. Herman Warring, Maestro Manheim, Manager Cannio . . ."

Josh leaned his cheek against her forehead, reveling in the feel of her safe in his arms. "Actually, she never got to von Rankin and Cannio. And Warring was one she intended to go after but Boris beat her to it. That is one of the things that threw me off."

Caty looked up at him, her green eyes flecked with light from the gas jets over the couch. "But why me? I never did the woman any harm."

"In her twisted mind she saw you as responsible for Magda's death. Your sudden opportunity to sing that night and the notoriety that accompanied it— she determined that you had engineered it all in order to boost your career. That fact that you were seen handling the knife before the third act convinced her that you were probably responsible for killing Magda as well.

"So it was Lulu who poisoned the marzipan? And I suppose she was also the one who brushed by me that night onstage."

"Yes, in both instances. If your brother had not called out to you when he did, she might have tried something then. She had a lot more talent and agility that was ever apparent under that mousy exterior. Using a wig and padding she disguised herself as a long-haired, buxom woman in a cloak, climbed the lower catwalks, and shot Rodrigo dead just at the moment he was supposed to die in the opera, and, incidentally, just as Magda had died. Of course, she knew the music well from long years of watching Dubratta's performances."

"Then she was responsible for the bridge and the counterweight falling."

Josh sighed. "No. And that's another of the things that threw me off. They were accidents, pure and simple. Unfortunately, they came on the heels of the two murders and so added to my belief that the person responsible had to be a strong male. Like Boris."

Caty ignored a knock at the door, nestling closer in Josh's arms, her hand lightly stroking the soft hairs of his chest beneath the wide opening of his shirt. "What was the other thing that threw you off?"

"Lack of a motive. Lulu obviously adored Magda and wouldn't hurt her. She still insists on that. It was the first thing—and still the one thing—that I can't resolve."

Caty sat up, her eyes sparkling. "But Josh, I can solve it for you. I found out just this morning that Magda was seriously ill. I followed a hunch and went back to see that other doctor in the building we visited and he told me that he had diagnosed a Mrs. H. Warring on the morning of October twentieth, with 'amyotro . . . later . . . sclerosis', or some such name. It's a horrible disease that destroys the body but leaves the mind intact. And one of the first things to go is the voice."

Josh stared at her, his eyes white against the dark makeup. "Are you telling me that . . ."

"Yes. Magda killed herself behind that screen. She was the consummate dramatic egotist and I think she deliberately committed suicide just as Butterfly did, when her world fell apart. And if her death cast suspicion on everyone around her, so much the better. It probably gave her some sort of twisted satisfaction to take her secret to the grave with her."

"And all the time I wore myself out searching for some way to prove she was murdered." He drew Caty back into his arms. "By God, Caty, you should have been the detective!"

Caty laughed. "Well, I cannot return the compliment. You will never look comfortable as a member of the chorus, even though I was never so glad to see anyone as I was to recognize you on that stage tonight."

He kissed her again, his lips warm and insistent against hers, his tongue eagerly seeking the enticing spaces beyond. The flame flared between them but was rudely quenched when the banging on the door grew to thundering proportions before it was jerked open.

"Caty!" Gregory Stillman yelled, poking his

head around. "Get dressed and get out here at once or you will lose your public just at the moment you've found them!"

"Oh dear," Caty said, pulling away. "I must go. Here, help me with these laces."

"I'll take care of that, sir," Cecile, the French maid declared, taking advantage of the opened door to push her way inside.

Josh suppressed a sudden jealous twinge over the demands these people were making on Caty. Yet it was no more than he had expected. "It's just as well," he said calmly. "I need to divest myself of these ridiculous clothes before someone on the force notices me. I'll see you later."

She blew him a kiss as Cecile ushered her behind the screen.

Yet, as it turned out, she barely saw him at all. From the moment she walked down the hall dressed in her blue silk gown to greet the crowd waiting for her in the greenroom, until she finally fell into bed at dawn there was so much going on around her that her head seemed in a permanent swirl. It was an almost eerie feeling to have people shoving programs at her for her autograph. Caty started out trying to write the recipient's name as well as her own but soon gave that up and began scrawling a pen scratch that only faintly resembled "Cathleen McGowan." Sometime before the last scratch, Frances Schyler pushed her way through the fawning crowd, with Charlie Poore close on her heels. Between the two of them, they bundled Caty into a fur-lined cloak and ushered her into a coach for the ride to the Waldorf and an exuberant celebration. She caught sight of Josh as she was being helped into the cab and called for him to join them. However, when she arrived at the party, she found the crowd so large and so boisterous that once again, she only glimpsed him on its fringes. When he slipped away an hour later, Caty was engrossed in a conversation with her agent and failed to notice him leaving.

Remarkably, she found she had many friends now whom she never remembered having as plain Caty McGowan. Some of them were influential people in the world of opera and several were already making plans for her. Caty felt as though she had been sprinkled with some magical fairy dust which had transformed her life, and she had to force herself to remember that she was the same Irish girl from Staten Island she had always been.

Still, she could not deny that all the attention and admiration were intoxicating. When Charlie finally escorted her home to Charlotte's flat, she fell into bed as weary and happy as she had ever been in her short life.

Not until she went drifting off to sleep did she begin to wonder what had happened to Josh.

Josh spent the night fighting his own demons. He rejoiced in Caty's success, and was not surprised at the tumultuous reception she was getting.

He had deliberately slipped away because he could see that she was increasingly immersed in a world he could not share. Still, he wished she spared a little more thought for him in her hour of triumph. Of course, he could understand why she hadn't. Anyone's head would be turned by that kind of sudden adulation. And when one worked as hard for it as Caty had, well, that would only make it all the more precious. Small wonder she hadn't thought of him.

So he decided to go on home to bed. Tomorrow, when everything had quieted down, he would stop by the flat and give her the kind of special congratulatory kiss that could come from him alone.

He could hear the chattering of loud voices inside even as he approached the door. Though he feared Caty might not be up yet, he found her sitting on the couch, attired in a pale yellow satin robe with her long hair flowing down her back. A cup of coffee, barely touched, sat on the table in front of the couch but had been pushed aside to allow for a pile of papers that covered the tabletop. Josh could see that most of them were telegrams.

She looked up as he entered the room and rose to throw her arms around his neck and kiss him quickly.

"Where did you go last night? I missed you."

He smiled down at her. "Oh I could see you were very involved. I thought I'd wait until this morning to . . ."

Caty took his arm and pulled him toward the couch. "Josh, have you met Gordon Eley? He's my agent—as of last night. Detective Castleton, Gordon."

A thin, long-faced man looked up from a stack of letters and nodded blankly to Josh. "The policeman who caught dear old Lulu. Pleased to meet you, Detective."

"And this," Caty went on, "is Richard Islip. He's some kind of publicity man. Gordon thought I should meet him right away. And this lady . . . what was your name again?"

A small woman dressed in severe black but with a round face and blue twinkling eyes nodded at Josh. "Edith, ma'am. Edith Starling."

Caty drew her arm through Josh's. "Miss Starling is a 'lady's maid'. I absolutely refused to ever have the horrible Cecile come near me again so Gordon sent Edith over for my approval. What do you think? She's nothing like, Lulu, is she?"

"Nothing. Look here, Caty, I was hoping we might have a moment alone."

"Oh, I know. And I want one, too. Only, look at all these wires. I'm getting offers from everywhere, Josh. Can you believe it?" She rifled through the papers and lifted one. "From Milan. Already! Gordon thinks it might be wiser to turn it down and establish myself here at home first. I've already agreed to do four more Carmens in New York, but I have a little time in between and Gordon thinks I should accept an offer from Chicago."

"Well, of course, Gordon knows best."

Caty drew him down beside her on the sofa. "Just think, Josh. Chicago. They are very insistent. They want me to do *Cavalleria* but I think I'd like to do something not so well known. Rossini, perhaps."

"Shouldn't spell yourself a little? You don't want to overdo things all at once."

"Oh no, there's no danger of that. And, of course, I don't want to lose this initiative. I can take the train to Chicago Thursday, sing two performances and be back in New York in time for the next *Carmen*."

"Caty . . ."

"Caty, dear," Gordon Eley interrupted. "Have you thought about this one yet? It's from San Francisco. It's the devil of a long way off, but it might be a good move for you."

Caty took the wire as Richard Islip slid down next to her. "Miss McGowan, we must finish this interview if you want it to be in tomorrow's Sunday edition. Even then, that will be cutting it pretty close . . ."

"Oh dear, yes . . . well, we ought to finish it then."

Josh was forced to the other end of the couch as Islip slid down between him and Caty. He looked up to see Charlotte standing at the kitchen door smiling at him.

"Would you like a cup of coffee?" she mouthed.

He fled to the kitchen and gladly took the cup

Charlotte offered him. "Has it been like this all morning?"

She nodded. "Since nine o'clock. That Gordon person was on the doorstep as the clock struck, with a fistful of wires. Caty hasn't come down to earth yet."

They all seemed to be talking at once in the next room. Josh shook his head, smiling ruefully to himself. "Somehow I never thought I'd be jilted for fame. Charlie Poore maybe, but not this!"

Charlotte cocked her head, studying him. "Dear old Charlie never had a chance. But she really does care for you, even though it may not seem so now. Don't let all this discourage you too much. Fame can be fleeting and fickle, you know. When the smoke clears away she's going to need you more than ever."

Josh looked through the doorway where Caty was bent over the table, her flaming hair spilling over her shoulders and down her back.

"I wonder," he murmured.

Though Caty became increasingly involved in all the myriad decisions that had to be made concerning her career, Josh had been wrong to think she was unaware of him. She felt more than a little hurt when he slipped away once again without speaking to her, but she assumed he would be back, perhaps even later that day. When two days passed and he still hadn't stopped by, she began to wonder if her preoccupation with business had offended him. Yet surely, he of all people, must understand the need to attend to such matters now. She longed for him to be there, to take her in his arms, to make love to her in the wonderfully passionate way they had shared. Having him with her now would be the final perfect ingredient to her happiness.

At the end of three long days she began to suspect that he was not going to come, that he had assumed she did not need him any longer. Well, she thought, he could not be more wrong. Perhaps it was time for Mohammed to go to the mountain!

Accordingly, she made her way to the ugly police headquarters building one cold, sunny afternoon, bundled in a new wraparound cloak fringed with sable fur a foot wide. Her hat trailed a single long egret feather and her elegance was out of place in those drab halls as a diamond would be in a paste setting.

Yet Caty did not care. She received a warm welcome from several of the patrolmen who recognized her and O'Leary himself ushered her up to Inspector Castleton's tiny, cramped office.

Josh looked up from the desk where he was sitting in his shirtsleeves. The stunned expression on his face almost made her lose her courage but she quickly overcame it.

"This is an unexpected pleasure," Josh said, quickly reaching for his coat.

"You don't need to be so formal with me, you know," Caty answered, sweeping forward to plant a kiss on his cheek. It seemed to embarrass him so she moved quickly away, taking a chair in front of the desk.

Over her head Josh could see a whole range of interested faces in the adjoining office. He moved quickly to shut the door against them. "You look stunning," he said, perching on the edge of the desk near her and fighting the sudden urge to take her in his arms.

"Thank you. I know I've surprised you by coming here but . . . well, you didn't come to me . . ."

"But you've been so busy. I figured you needed time to get your life in order."

"Yes, well, I've done that. Gordon . . ."

"Oh yes, Gordon."

"Gordon has laid out my schedule for the next two months. I'm to go to Chicago tomorrow, but I'll be back in New York in two weeks."

"You should like Chicago though I'm told the weather there in winter is even worse than it is here."

"I won't see much beside the inside of the opera house. Did you read the write-up in the paper?"

"Last Sunday? Yes. It was very nice considering it was done in such a hurry."

"Wasn't it?"

He tore his eyes from her face. "I suppose they've retired *Madama Butterfly* from the repertoire?"

Caty fussed with slipping her cloak down over her shoulders. "No, as a matter of fact, they are going to present it again with Geraldine Farrar in the title role. The composer, Puccini, is coming over from Italy to supervise the production. That should do away with all the bad memories."

Josh rested his hands on his knee. "And how is Miss Starling working out?"

"Edith? Oh fine. She's terribly independent. I can't see her ever becoming as devoted to me as Lulu was to Magda. But then, that's a good thing, isn't it? What's happened to Lulu, by the way?"

"She's going to be institutionalized. She's quite insane, you know. Not fit to stand trial at all."

Caty hesitated, feeling all kinds of cool currents between them. It left her confused and a little sick inside. "I wonder sometimes if the opera world doesn't do that to people."

He looked at her in surprise. "What a strange thing to say. Don't tell me the golden edge has worn thin already?"

"Oh no. Only there is so much to handle. I like Gordon and I trust him, yet I wish I had someone I knew better helping me make these decisions. Right now he is doing everything and I don't think that's very healthy."

"But, Caty, you can afford to hire anyone you need."

"I know. And eventually I'll sort it out." She studied him, longing to reach out and grasp his fingers in her own. "Oh, Josh, I've missed you. What's wrong? Why haven't you come to me?"

"I wanted to, Caty. You can't know how much."

"But . . . ?"

"But when I saw all those people around you and all the excitement you had in plotting your career, it came home to me again that we live in two different worlds." He gestured around the drab little room. "Can anything be more different from your glittering operatic world than this? This is grim reality, while you'll be making your life among the lights and music of fantasy. We . . . well, we just don't go together, do we?"

Caty felt a huge lump that was suspended in her throat, making it difficult to swallow. "But we are so good together in some ways."

He looked away, forcing himself to focus on the patterns of light reflected in the glass of a framed certificate hanging on the wall.

"I would only drag you down. You have the world at your beck and call while I'm stuck here, dealing with my dirty little crimes day after day. It just wouldn't work."

She tried to smile. "You've been talking to your mother."

"No," he said, laughing. "She's going to be disappointed, in fact. You were such a success last week that it went a long way toward helping her adjust to the idea of a singer for a daughter-in-law."

Tears stung behind her eyes and she got quickly to her feet, pulling her cloak up around her shoulders. "Too bad, isn't it?" She turned away from him toward the door. "Well, as I said, I'll be gone for two weeks, but then, I'll be back in New York. Perhaps . . ."

Josh moved to her side and took her hand in his. "Perhaps we can have a supper together, assuming you can work it in."

She looked up at him through a blur of tears, her green eyes as lustrous as the sea. They stood locked together, neither wanting to move. He fought back the words that he longed to speak: *Don't go away. Stay here with me. Nothing else matters but to have you here in my arms.*

Caty could almost hear him and her whole being reached out, begging him to ask her not to leave. She fought hard against speaking the words herself, wishing with all her heart that he would beg her to stay.

The moment passed and with a sinking heart she turned toward the door. "I'll work it in, I promise."

"Good. Let me know when you get back."

"Goodbye, then."

He lifted her hand to his lips and lightly brushed her fingers. They burned in his hand like a hot brand.

"Goodbye, Caty . . . my love."

Twenty-four

It was just as well that she was leaving New York the following day, Caty thought, for it kept her so busy she had no time to think about her conversation with Josh. At those unguarded moments, when the memory came thrusting back, she found herself wrapping her arms around her waist to stiffen herself from the sharp pain they brought with it.

She would not give in! There was too much excitement, too many new triumphs to think about to dwell on what she was losing. Everything Josh had said was true—in fact, hadn't she made the same arguments to herself once before. Why then should it sear like it did? Why should she feel this terrible sense of loss, this cutting away of part of herself? She was being foolish to let it hurt her so badly just when she had been given so much.

The arguments went on until finally, weary of fighting, she gave way to an overwhelming sense of loss and wept bitter tears. That behind her, she threw herself into packing for her trip, even to venturing out for some last-minute shopping. By the time she was ready to take a cab to the train station, she was able to hold her sadness at bay with a weary resignation.

"You look marvelous," Charlotte said, kissing her on the cheek as she left the apartment.

Caty caught a last-minute glimpse of herself in the mirror. "Thank you," she answered, feeling that she did look very well indeed. She wore a new traveling dress of striped silk bordered with a Greek pattern in black velvet, a huge hat dripping black feathers, and a new sealskin coat whose tight tufts of jet fur kept her snug against the winter blasts.

"Thank you for all you've done. I could never have managed to work everything out if I had gone back to Staten Island."

"I enjoyed being part of all the excitement. I only wish I could go to Chicago with you, but duty requires me here in New York. I suppose you'll be staying at the Plaza when you return?"

"Not if you'll take me in once more."

Charlotte gave her an enthusiastic hug. "Dear Caty, I think no matter how famous you become, you'll still be my old friend, Caty McGowan."

"Well, I should hope so," Caty answered, returning the embrace. "Although I won't promise not to develop a few traits peculiar to divas. I've already learned that a tantrum thrown in the proper place goes a long way toward getting one's way in things."

"Then I shall look forward to seeing you throw a few when you get back to the Met."

Caty hesitated. It was on the tip of her tongue to ask Charlotte to keep tabs on Josh for her, but she decided not to. What was the use when everything was over between them?

The day was bitterly cold with frigid winds blowing off the Hudson to creep up beneath her long coat and raise the color in her cheeks. The cab was uncomfortably cold and the vast, open station even more so. Gordon met her at the door to tell her she had a pullman compartment on the train, which she could take possession of now.

Caty gave her hand luggage to the efficient Edith and sent her bustling ahead to ready the room. Then, wrapping her fur stole around her throat, she leisurely dawdled across the cavernous hall, scanning the faces of the people milling about. She was about to start down the narrow, drafty corridor that led to the train platform when her eye was drawn to a commotion about twenty feet away. An old woman, shrouded in a ragged shawl and threadbare shoes, had a boy by the arm. She began screeching at him while, at the same time, swatting at him with an umbrella. The child, who looked to be about nine years old, struggled vainly against the woman's grip and jumped around trying to avoid the blows on his shoulders. He wore a ragged jacket and an oversized cap, his stockings were full of patches and the soles of his boots were parting company with the tops. Caty stood frozen, staring at the two of them, knowing she ought to move on, yet filled with a swelling sense of injustice.

"Lousy, no-good brat!" the woman screeched. "I teached you better. You don't never learn!"

Swat went the umbrella, thudding across the boy's head.

"Lemme go!" the child yelled. "Ow! Lemme go!"

Caty could stand it no longer. Sweeping down on the two of them, she grasped the umbrella in midswing, wrenching it out of the woman's hands.

"What do you think you're doing?" she exclaimed to the startled woman. "Striking a child like that?"

"Who the devil are you?" the woman said, taking in all the richness of Caty's dress. "Mind y'er own business."

"It is my business when I see a defenseless child being beaten."

"He's my grandson. I can beat 'im if I likes."

The boy, whose eyes were quite free of tears in spite of his noisy cries, took advantage of the momentary lull in the beating to wrench himself free of the woman's grip and dart around Caty, peering from behind her skirts. The old woman's rheumy eyes focused on Caty's face, though her arm shot out, trying to grab the child.

"Surely there must be a better way . . ." Caty started to say before finding herself caught between the two of them, one trying to grab and the other attempting to keep out of reach.

"He et my biscuit. I was savin' that for the trip

and he et it, dirty little bugger. Never was no good."

"I was hungry," the boy said defiantly. He looked up at Caty with a deliberately fashioned pitiful expression. "An't had nothin' all day."

"That's a lie!" the old woman yelled. "Makin' out I don't feed you to get sympathy. He's a liar, he is. I takes care of 'im."

"Yeah, when it don't interfere with your own stomach."

Darting her arm out, the old woman managed to grab a clutch of the boy's lanky hair. She pulled him around Caty's skirts, slipping her fingers to his ear which she twisted savagely.

"Ow!" he cried squirming. Caty reached for the woman's arm, tugging at it.

"Let the boy go! For heaven's sake there's no need to be so abusive."

"I told you to mind y'er own business," the woman screamed, reclaiming her umbrella and lifting it as if to strike Caty.

"All right now, what's the trouble here?"

They both turned to see a barrel-chested policeman in a long blue overcoat bearing down on them. He reached out and took the umbrella from the woman's hand while Caty and the old woman both began talking at once.

"That woman is beating this child. This is clearly a case of abuse."

"Tell this fancy swell to mind her own business. I can do what I like with my own."

"Just a minute, one at a time, if you please. Now then, miss you first."

"She was beating this child."

"He's my grandson and et my biscuit. I can do as I please."

"There are laws on the books about abuse."

"Not if it's y'er own."

"There are laws against abusing animals and children. I'm very familiar with them."

"Just a moment," the policeman broke in as both women's voices began to rise. "You're both right. There are laws against abusing children but if this lad's her own . . ."

"Me grandson, that's right."

"If he's her grandson, there is nothing we can do."

"What do you mean you can't do anything? Look at him, he's nothing but skin and bones. This old woman isn't taking proper care of him. Why, she beat him for eating her lunch. What kind of lunch was he supposed to have?"

"None a'tall," the boy said from behind Caty's skirts. "That's the usual way of it."

"You lie!" the old woman screamed. "He's always lyin', sir," she said, turning to the policeman. "Never could tell the truth even though I tried to beat it into 'im."

"Officer!" Caty cried in indignation. "You heard it from her own lips. Are you going to give this child back to a woman who beats the truth into him?"

"I'm afraid there is nothing I can do, miss."

Caty's sense of justice began to swell to a bubbling boil, like an angry sea in the first throes of a storm.

"Well, I can do something!"

Gordon Eley pulled at Caty's sleeve. "You're going to miss your train. For God's sake, let it go."

"He's right," the officer said. "There's hundreds of poor kids like this in this city. If we tried to interfere in every case, we'd do nothing else."

The old woman laughed, showing several missing teeth. "Hear that. Buttin' y'er nose where it don't belong."

"You miserable old hag. You don't deserve to have a grandchild!"

"You hear that," the old woman said, hopping up and down. "I don't have to take insults from some fancy swell . . ."

"Now, miss, there's no need to get abusive."

"There's every need!"

"Having a little trouble, officer?"

Caty spun around. Beyond the patrolman's burly form Josh stood watching them, his eyes twinkling as he took in the scene. He was trying to keep his lips from smiling and not quite managing it.

"Oh, Inspector," the patrolman said, relief in his voice. "It's nothing, really. Just a little difference of opinion."

Josh stepped up beside Caty. "Is this woman making a nuisance of herself?"

"Yes," the old woman said quickly.

"Well, I wouldn't say that."

Josh looked sternly at Caty. "She's done that before. In fact, she has a reputation for doing it."

"Arrest 'er then," the old woman cried. "Buttin' in where she's got no right."

The patrolman eased the old woman away with a firm hand on her shoulder. "Now, now. There's no need for that. Just take the boy and go along on your way and we'll just forget about this."

Reaching out, the woman grabbed the boy's thin shoulder and pulled him to her. "Come on then, Jamie. Let's leave this place. There ain't nothin' for us here."

"Wait a moment," Caty said, at last finding her voice. She reached into her purse and pulled out a coin, handing it to the boy. He opened his palm, gasping.

"Wow! A dollar. Look at that, Mam."

The woman's grasping claw went to his hand but Caty pushed it away. "Here. This is for you," she said, handing another silver dollar to the old woman. Out of the corner of her eye she saw that the boy's money had already disappeared somewhere in his jacket while the woman gaped at the coin in her hand. She watched as the two of them shuffled quickly off as though afraid she would change her mind and reclaim her money.

"I'll take care of this lady, officer," Josh said, taking Caty's elbow and propelling her toward the platform.

"Thank you, sir," the policeman answered gratefully.

They hurried off, Gordon scrambling ahead to find the compartment.

"Why did you give anything to that old hag?"

"Because if I hadn't she would have taken the money from the boy." She stopped, oblivious to the people moving around them as the call came for the train to board. "Oh, Josh. I didn't think . . . I mean, I hoped you would come to say goodbye, but I'd given up . . ."

He put his hands upon her shoulders, looking deeply into her eyes. "I would have been here sooner, but there was a line for the luggage."

"I don't understand," she said as her arms slipped up around his neck.

He laid his palms on either side of her face and bent to kiss her welcoming lips. "Well, someone has to keep you from getting into trouble with the law every time you see an injustice. It might as well as be me."

Her heart began to flutter with hope. "But your work?"

"I've resigned. You did say you needed a business manager, didn't you? It so happens I'm looking for a job. I can make myself available if you want."

"If I want?" She tightened her arms around him and kissed his wide, warm mouth. "Oh, Josh, I want it more than anything in the world. Everything I have means nothing without you to share it with me."

His sparkling eyes scanned her face, drinking in every lovely line. "I know. It finally dawned on me that I feel the same way." Laughing, he nuzzled her neck beneath the fur stole. "Besides, Mother will be ecstatic."

"Even though you're marrying an opera singer?"

He tipped up her chin and lightly kissed the end of her nose. "A *famous* opera singer."

Caty heard the far-off conductor's call of "All aboard" down the train platform. At the end of the gray walkway she could see Gordon standing beside an open door, gesturing frantically. A bell began a sharp clanging, setting a discordant obligato to the blare of the train whistle.

"Come on, then," she smiled up at him, her heart overflowing with happiness. "We've got a performance to make in Chicago."

"Then why are we dawdling, Madam Caty?" he said, chuckling. "Let's go!"

One hand tightly held in Josh's grasp, the other clutching her hat, she laughed with delight as they took off running down the platform toward the waiting train.

Author's Note

One of the things I enjoy most about writing an historical novel is doing research on the period. In the case of SO WILD MY HEART, not only did I enjoy learning about the young days of the Metropolitan Opera House, but I also came across one of those coincidences which always gives an author pause. In 1905, while Heinrich Conried was General Manager of the house, a bridge accidentally collapsed during a performance of CARMEN, injuring several members of the chorus. A month later, during ROMEO ET JULIETTE, a counterweight weighing several hundred pounds fell to the floor, narrowly missing the tenor, Albert Saleza.

Seldom do actual events fit so neatly into the plot of a romantic suspense novel set at the same time and in the same place. Was I going to pass them up? Not on your life!

Which is to say, at least two of the 'red herrings' in my story actually did occur and are not the product of a wicked imagination. I hope they add to the enjoyment of the rest, which is all entirely fictitious.

I enjoy hearing from my readers. Please send my letters to PO Box 8496, Tampa, FL 33674-8496. Please include a self-addressed stamped envelope if you wish a response.

Ashley Snow

EVERY DAY WILL FEEL LIKE FEBRUARY 14TH!

Zebra Historical Romances
by Terri Valentine

LOUISIANA CARESS	(4126-8, $4.50/$5.50)
MASTER OF HER HEART	(3056-8, $4.25/$5.50)
OUTLAW'S KISS	(3367-2, $4.50/$5.50)
SEA DREAMS	(2200-X, $3.75/$4.95)
SWEET PARADISE	(3659-0, $4.50/$5.50)
TRAITOR'S KISS	(2569-6, $3.75/$4.95)

Available wherever paperbacks are sold, or order direct from the Publisher. Send cover price plus 50¢ per copy for mailing and handling to Zebra Books, Dept. 4363, 475 Park Avenue South, New York, N.Y. 10016. Residents of New York and Tennessee must include sales tax. DO NOT SEND CASH. For a free Zebra/Pinnacle catalog please write to the above address.